Travel Page

Every publication from Rippple Books has this special page to document where the book travels, who has it and when.

Balaclava

Campbell Jefferys

Rippple
Books

The right of Campbell Jefferys to be identified as the Author of the
Work has been asserted in accordance with the Copyright, Designs
and Patents Act 1988.

First published in 2023 by
Rippple Books

Cover design: Claudia Bode
Editor: Jeff Kavanagh

Rippple Books
Rippple Media
Postfach 304263
20325 Hamburg
Germany
www.rippplemedia.com

A CIP catalogue record for this book is available from the British
Library.

ISBN: 978-3-9816249-8-4

Prologue

The yellow envelope slides through the slot in the door and lands on the floor with a soft thud. The noise makes him turn from the desk, moving the left wheel slightly backwards to swivel the wheelchair and look towards the door, at this fresh gift on the floor. After wasting the first hour of the day, staring at the blank page on his laptop's screen and questioning where to start, Russell Wex is grateful for the distraction. He's mid-30s and prematurely grey, but has a youthful face. He backs away from the desk and rolls over to the door. There's space enough to veer to the right, spin around and scoop up the envelope with his left hand. With the door at his back and the envelope in his lap, he stops, turns his head, and looks into Mara's room. The bed is still a slept-in mess, a crumpled fort of blankets and pillows. The room is untouched since she left, and he has kept the door open all this time as a reminder that she's still out there, fighting her fight. The police uniform remains a cast-off bundle on the floor, shed like old skin.

A couple of firm pushes gets him back to the desk. The bulky envelope is addressed to him, with no sender and no postage. As he opens it, he wonders who passed it through the door. Inside is a stiff folder that photos come in when developed. It makes him smile a little, envisioning analogue Mara at protests and demonstrations with her disposable cameras. The desk is already covered with such photos, as well as strange-angled headshots of the important members of Circus; every photo something he can hold in his hands and scan for details. Every photo telling a story. That's the problem; there are so many stories, he doesn't know where to start.

He digs into the envelope and extracts a single-page letter, folded into a small, tight square.

Hey Russ,

Greetings from Stuttgart. I guess I could be clever and say Greetings from Baghdad, given everything that happened this morning, but that would be a stretch. I'm not sure what to call this, but despite all the big talk, I'm not calling it war. I was at the protest, right in the middle of it, but I got out just as things started to go bad. That was hours ago. I write this from Zina's apartment. Truth is, I'm scared to go outside.

This could be the last letter for a while, and the last batch of photos.

1

I'm thinking I better go off-grid, just to be safe. I've given you more than enough material. Time to publish your article, Russ. Don't think too hard about it. Just start writing. We have to get the story down, get everything in print and on the record, to make it clear you had the story first. Because something big is coming. I don't know what exactly, but something's coming.

I drove down here yesterday with JJ and we spent much of that time talking. It was like conversational chess, with us moving pieces around each other. I started to get through her walls. Among the amazing things she said is that groups are being mobilised all over Europe, for some kind of coordinated coup, I think. They're doing that without tech, so it can't be tracked or followed. I described this to you before: the messengers taking trains from place to place to spread the word, deliver information and give orders. Like it's the freaking olden days with guys on horseback carrying scrolls with wax seals. They know the police are monitoring phones, emails and social media, so they stay well off that. It means when the attacks come, or this whatever coup, no one will be ready for it. Maybe your article can somehow sound the warning, or at least act as proof that there was a warning.

There has to be a date for this. I don't know it, and I don't think JJ knows it either. Maybe it's coded, or something significant, like an important holiday or solstice. If I find this out, I'll let you know, somehow. I'll send you a scroll. It can be I'm overthinking this, because all the group leaders I've met so far aren't nearly as clever as they think they are. Still, asking anyone outright could blow my cover. I can't risk that.

But know this: something's coming. The word they've all been using is revolution. Yes, really. There won't be anything peaceful about it. People are angry, Russ, and this anger has been building up for a long time. So many people out there feel like they don't have a voice. You can see it in the photos I took this morning. Look at the passion, the determination, the anger. When you're in the middle of it, you can't help but get swept up into it. They want blood. It's a ticking fucking bomb. This isn't about protest anymore, or politics, or police brutality, or looting. This is about change.

I'm scared, Russ. I thought I had a handle on right and wrong. Things used to be clear. I joined the police to be on the side of good, to make a difference. But everything is just ambiguous right now. There are bad elements everywhere. The police are no better than the protesters. Who's right? Who's wrong? Who's good? Who's bad? I don't know.

JJ put it to me yesterday in plain terms: "Do you want to make the world a better place?" A loaded question, I know, but I swear I couldn't answer her honestly. The question really is: what does that better place look like? This is a key part of the rhetoric, changing the world for the better. Leave no one behind. Everyone getting a fair share. Everyone having the chance at happiness. People all over Germany are gearing up to fight for this. The expectation is that once this fight begins, others will join in. That's Vilem Kollar talking, possibly as a conduit for Milan. It's hard to say who's at the top of this tree. Maybe you know. Maybe that's where the story begins: from the top down, instead of from the bottom up.

Take care of yourself. Stay safe. And get to work. That was a great article on Spitz. Don't stop there. Your next piece has to go out before this revolution begins.

Love, Mara

He reads the letter twice, then adds it to the file of letters, concluding Mara wrote it without the knowledge of what happened later in the day. He wonders where she is now, and how she is.

The candid shots have a striking intimacy and reality; this moment in time captured without posturing. The angles are haphazard, with Mara perhaps cupping the camera in her hand so others wouldn't see it. While there's limited posing, the photos still have that interchangeable look of protests: people gathered close together, eyebrows knitted, eyes fierce. Some have their fists raised, some hold makeshift weapons, and others have their hands loose at their sides, spoiling for a fistfight. He sees it, the determination and anger, but what is more apparent is the impatience. They want change and they want it now. A generation reared on instant gratification isn't prepared to wait.

He likes that take, but that's the bottom-up story. The oppressed masses, with an overwhelming number of stories. There are too many to tell, because every person in these photos, and in all the photos scattered on his desk, believes their story deserves to be told. He realises this is why the page has remained blank for so long, even if he has written the article in his head a thousand different ways already. He was wrong in trying to tell the protester story, trying to

3

capture this world at street level. Mara nailed it: the right approach is top-down.

He types: "Prince Vilem and the New Revolution". From there, the words flow.

The twin-bell alarm clock trills at 1745. She reaches back, blindly, missing on the first try. On the second, she locates the clock and slides its little lever across to stop the hammer from hitting the bells. She rolls onto her back. She doesn't want to get up; doesn't want to start another shift. No uniform, no boots.

Everything hurts. New pain added onto old. It seems wrong to be awake at this time, on a Sunday; wrong to be living to this routine and facing these responsibilities. But she has to move.

She pushes the blankets off. Getting upright requires a strategic, slow shift onto her side. She brings her knees to her chest, then swivels so her cracked heels brush the bottom sheet and her feet reach the floor. She levers herself up to be sitting on the edge of the bed, in shorts and a singlet. There are bruises on her shoulders, arms and legs, with each bruise at a different stage of purpling and healing.

The room is neat and organised. A dark-green single-speed bike leans against a wall. A punching bag hangs in the corner, its middle area slightly concave from excessive hitting.

She pushes up from the bed, feeling a general relief that everything still works. She's sore, but not damaged, yet should still be moving better for someone 26 years old. A few steps towards the punching bag, plus a ginger one-two into the bag's dented middle. A couple of yoga stretches, with groans that sound more "Ow" than "Om". The blood starts to flow. Berlin's streets are calling.

She takes underwear, socks, bra and a singlet, all white – like they came together in a single packet – from the dresser and drops the clothing on the bed, then heads for the bathroom.

A hot shower helps remove the fog of afternoon sleep and the stiffness from her joints and muscles. She takes a little too long washing her shoulder-length blonde hair. It's tempting to stay in there, sit on Russell's fold-down chair, under the glorious cascade that steams up the shower's glass, but she can't be late.

Wrapped in a towel and dripping, because she's too lazy to completely dry off, she pads through the apartment. The almost-empty fridge yields nothing appealing beyond the last mouthful of orange juice. She should have shopped on the way home this morning, as a good housemate would have. But she couldn't face people; couldn't push a cart, jostle for things, make decisions and stand in lines. Most of all, she wanted to avoid all the judgements that result from moving around in public in uniform; avoid being subjected to insults whispered and shouted, and avoid being held accountable for any perceived injustices suffered at the hands of the police.

Back in her room, the uniform comes on, piece by piece, and the aches start to feel good. They morph into small bodily badges of honour. In her mind, the pain turns from grey to gold. She certainly didn't sign up for any of the violence that happened last night, but there's still the sense that putting on this uniform feels a little like slipping into the role of a small-time superhero. Someone fighting the good fight, even if some members of the public don't think so.

Set, she ties her hair into a ponytail, grabs the bike and wheels it towards the front door. When she opens it, Russell is there, his lap full of shopping bags.

"She's alive," he says with a boyish smile.

"Barely. Let me take all that."

She leans the bike against the wall and picks up the bags.

"Thanks. All that weight made me lose feeling in my legs."

"Not funny."

"Come on. A little bit."

She leads the way through to the kitchen, Russell following in his chair. The three-room apartment they share has a combined kitchen and living area, divided by a low counter they use as a dining table.

"You shouldn't have done this," she says, putting the bags on that counter.

"What? Have a sense of humour?"

"Shopped, on a Sunday even. It was my turn."

"It's always your turn. Don't worry. You'll catch up, at some point. I fully appreciate nightshifts throw you out of whack."

"It does."

"Leave it all," Russell says. "I can put it away. You don't want to be late."

"Then I'll be on nightshifts for the rest of the year."

Russell gives her a searching, caring look. "All right?"

"Yeah. No. A bit sore."

"That looked like a serious battle last night. I saw some of the footage. On the news."

"You know they never show the real stuff."

"It reminded me of the organised fights hardcore football fans have before a game. Or after."

"These guys were a level up from hooligans," she says. "Right-wingers, ex-army, I think. Tough and trained."

"Everyone was in black. Hard to tell who was who."

"You can tell who the bad guys are because they have weapons. We're not allowed to use ours. We're out there fighting mercenaries with freaking pepper spray and our fists."

"Is that why they're winning?"

"Is that what it looks like? If you ask me, nobody's winning. There are just ..."

She looks at Russell, amazed that two people who have known each other a short time can have so much shared history; amazed that it was barely a year ago that she beat back half a dozen vandals who were pummelling him for photographing their looting. She got him to safety, dragging his broken body with one arm. His photos helped with making the arrests of a dozen looters, who served pathetically short prison terms. Her broken arm eventually healed, but Russell ended up in a wheelchair. No one took the heat for that.

"Victims," he says.

"Yeah. That. I was going to say there are no consequences."

"Good save."

"Except for us. There are consequences for us. If any of those right-wingers get hurt, or any protesters for that matter, it becomes a legal and media circus."

Russell starts putting the groceries away. "A fine line."

"Speaking of lines, the city's being divided up. Did you know that? Local crime families and gangs are taking over some places. We can't go there anymore."

"Sounds like a good story. Berlin divided again. Great headline. Give me an example. An area that's off-limits."

"Pick any dead-end street in Neukölln or Kreuzberg. Anywhere that has only one way in and one way out, with guards at the entry. That's the modus. Cave mentality, basically."

"Interesting."

"Please don't go looking, Russ."

"What? In my condition?"

"Stop that. I don't want you getting caught in the middle of a territorial battle."

7

"But then we'd have so much to talk about, because you do that just about every day."

"You want to be able to compare notes with me?"

"I want to tell these stories. Remember, criminals care just as much about their public image as politicians and the police."

"True. But be careful."

She starts to leave the kitchen.

"Stay safe," Russell says.

"I'd much rather stay home."

"No, no. Get out there and make a difference. You know you want to."

She nods, then goes to the door, wondering what that difference is and if her efforts have any impact. She grabs the bike and heads outside.

Berlin, with its broad avenues and flat layout, is good for cycling, even though the automobile still dominates. While the German capital has always been a place in flux, car dependence is something the city can't seem to shake. She uses the bike path whenever there is one and stops at every red light, as it's safer that way and she sets a good example. Russell, a native Berliner born in the eastern part of the city just before the Wall fell, believes vehicles are a remnant of the East-West divide, both on the streets and in the mentalities of locals: before the Wall fell, for the Americanised West Berliners, four wheels meant the freedom to traverse and escape their "island", while for the Trabant-driving East Berliners, just having a car was a show of status. But Mara thinks this is changing, as more people ride bikes and more years pass from unification.

On the ride from the apartment in Tiergarten through Mitte to Kollwitzkiez, early evening Berlin shows itself as a city both thriving and in decay; some people live on the street, others drive fancy cars, and plenty just try to get by, one day at a time. In this place where so much generation-defining history happened, it now seems that just going forward through the gridlock is an achievement: to drive to work and get somewhere to park, to find a spot on the bus and make the next appointment on time, and to ride to the police station without missing the evening briefing. But somehow, she loves it, this city that remains a canvas for people to paint their lives on. She could do without all the roadside political advertising, the parties identifiable by their colour schemes and their specific

8

interpretations of blame and solution. But the posters rarely stay untouched for longer than a week: they get covered in graffiti and with advertisements for bands, events and protests, as the locals show just how much they care about politics.

She really likes the huge murals that decorate whole sides of buildings.

At the Kollwitzkiez station, her colleagues arrive for the evening shift with purpose, despite many of them being banged up from the night before. One has a large bandage over his forehead and the dark outline of stitches underneath. Even those who limp do so energetically.

Everyone looks tired. They smile through it and nod at each other, sharing the camaraderie of exhaustion and experience.

She locks her bike and heads inside, where it's crowded, stifling and noisy. People jostle at the counter, like strugglers competing for handouts, each person convinced their own concern is the most pressing. The attending officers try to maintain order, but don't try very hard, with eyes on the clock and the changeover imminent.

She pushes through the throng and gets behind the counter, hoping like hell for patrol duty with a tolerable partner. The first stop for everyone is the assignment board, which has its own jostling crowd. Among the many things she doesn't like about *Hauptmeister* Spitz is his approach to shifts and assignments, especially that disgusting reward system of his. Rub him the right way, and all will be well; rub him the wrong way, or not at all, and a shift can turn into an unbearable eight hours with someone detestable. Kollwitzkiez, like other stations she has worked at, has its share of discreet right-wingers who are awful to work with and best avoided.

It's everything she can do to keep from groaning audibly when seeing she's in vehicle 4, with Lauter. They've clashed in the past, their problems having as much to do with gender as with politics. Lauter is that unfortunate kind of guy living in the wrong time; a product of an era when men felt they had the right to dominate women, who lives today like the world is the same one he grew up in. Lauter expects that women will answer any phone that's ringing, write all the reports, do any filing and make the coffee. To make it worse, he constantly claims to be a feminist, saying he's all for equal rights.

Mara turns and sees Lauter standing next to her. He's a head taller, effortlessly good-looking and the uniform fits him perfectly. He's potentially an ideal match, despite him being six years older, until he opens his mouth.

"I'm driving," he says, holding up the keys. "Are you ready? Or do you need ten minutes to do your hair?"

She thinks she could land a one-two cheek-chin combo before he blinked and have him unconscious on the floor for everyone to see.

"I'm ready. Let's hope it's a quiet one."

There are murmurs of agreement from other officers.

Lauter walks through the station with the confidence of someone who inherited this place, or will one day. Mara follows. They weave between officers, criminals and lawyers. Lauter slaps a high-five with his buddy Brennhof on the way.

"Heard it got heavy last night in Pankow," Lauter says over his shoulder.

"Where were you?"

"I had a meeting at Jan's school. Spitz let me switch shifts."

"On a Saturday? Good timing."

Outside, they head to vehicle 4 as the other vehicles start pulling out of the lot.

"Believe me, I'd much rather be breaking heads in Pankow than have some student-teacher lecture me like I'm six years old."

"I'm guessing the teacher's a woman."

Lauter opens the driver-side door. "What does that mean?"

"Nothing."

Mara gets in the car. Lauter takes his time, nodding and waving to a few other officers getting into cars, then lowers himself behind the wheel.

"She was out of line," he says. "Kept blaming me for Jan behaving badly at school."

"Teachers blame the parents, and the parents blame the teachers. Isn't that how it goes?"

"I'm doing a great job with Jan. But this teacher, she wouldn't let me get a word in. She just put it all on me. Totally unfair. You know me, Steinbach, I'm all for equality, but that teacher didn't give me a chance."

"Sounds like you didn't give her a chance either."

"Whose side are you on? Forget it. All you women just support each other, no matter what the situation. I don't want her teaching my son."

"Another girl who would be prettier if she smiled more?"

He shoots her a glance. "What the fuck is wrong with you today?"

"Sorry. I'm just ... tired. And sore. It was brutal last night, and it's all still fresh."

"Well, don't dump your crap on me." Lauter reverses aggressively, then lurches the car out onto the road, pushing into the traffic. "But yeah, that teacher could definitely do herself a favour by being friendlier and smiling more."

Mara's response is ready. She just has to open her mouth and let him have it. But she knows it's a waste of time. Lauter's a wall. There's no getting through. He doesn't listen and he doesn't get it, and there is no way she can ever change him. She doesn't want to. Lauter isn't her problem to fix.

So, she stays quiet and lets him drive. Engaging with him will just make the night that much longer.

All she has to do is get through the shift. She wonders if Lauter feels the same way: that he would much rather be partnered with someone else and now he's trying to finish the shift as best he can. Or did he ask Spitz for this pairing? The idea that Lauter might want to have sex with her sends a wave of disgust through her body, causing her almost to throw up the orange juice she drank earlier.

"You all right, Steinbach?" Lauter asks. "You look a bit green."

"Yeah. Fine. How old's Jan?"

"He's eight. Dominating his football team. A star in the making."

Lauter continues talking, but she's not listening. She despises him, not because he's a right-winger and a chauvinist, but because he has a confidence and superiority that feels bestowed rather than earned. Through his whole life, he didn't have to fight for anything. Never struggled. Never had to prove himself. While the loathing is strong, she also feels a degree of sympathy, primarily for the people in his orbit. His ex-wife, whatever her name is, and whoever else is forced to spend time with him. She feels especially sad for his son, who would already be wrestling with conflicting ideas about what it means to be a man.

It's almost 1900. Berlin is beginning its transition from a bustling city that will chew a person up and shit them out to a place of decadence, adventure and leisure. A place where there's something on offer for all tastes and lifestyles, if you know where to look, and a

11

place of danger if you head down the wrong street. Nine-to-fivers swap suits for clubbing attire. Graffitied roller doors open onto boutique bars that will later spill out onto the streets and have pyjama-clad neighbours yelling from their balconies for everyone to shut up. There are people everywhere: walking quickly, bounding up the steps from U-Bahn stations, sitting in groups and drinking. The city has seamlessly switched gears and it now seems most of the locals are nocturnal. They bring with them a sense of abandon and aggression. And they bring their money. Berlin's not a cheap city anymore. It's decades since poor was sexy here. The *Silikontal* tech boom was the final nail driven into Berlin's affordability coffin. Every second person under 30 works for a start-up. As a richer city, it has attracted urchins and weasels from far and wide. Don't leave a bag unattended in Berlin, nor purchase "genuine" pieces of the Berlin Wall, nor believe you can beat the guy on the corner at three-card Monte.

This all means that as evening turns to night and all these elements start to mix, along with thousands of tourists, things are bound to go wrong. The police radio becomes an unending monologue of minor disturbances, the duties assigned based on officer proximity. For the first few hours, they get lucky, never being the nearest vehicle to a call. Until they're asked to assist at a sports hall in Friedrichshain.

When they arrive, there is another police car out front, plus a handful of other vehicles hastily parked near the entry. They gear up and head inside.

The shouting can be heard from down the hallway. Mara jogs to the court, running towards the noise. The scene she finds is a stand-off: men, some in basketball uniforms and the rest in street clothes, shouting, finger-pointing and posturing. Each team and their supporters are occupying a side of the court, with two police officers in the middle working hard to keep the groups apart. Mara joins these officers at the centre line and pushes a few guys back, thinking a lot of this is just show, the kind she's seen before. None of these guys wants to fight, but they all want to show that they are ready for it.

Lauter goes to the referees at the bench. One, a skinny teenager who reminds Mara of her brother, is holding a white towel splotched with blood to his head. The other, slightly older, is on his phone and points at a player standing at the back of the team wearing blue, red and white uniforms. Lauter nods. Mara watches all this, thinking the player is far too stocky and short for basketball. She wonders if he took out his limitations on the referee.

The arrival of a pair of EMTs brings a strange calm to the hall, as if the presence of medics is grounds for a temporary truce, far more than the presence of police. The shouting dies down. The EMTs tend to the injured referee. Mara and the two other officers take this chance to separate the groups further. The contingent in red is guided to the far exit. The other team isn't interested in leaving and gather around their bench. They have a crate of beer and start drinking.

The EMTs prepare to take the injured referee to the ambulance. But Mara goes over to them.

"Can you wait a few minutes?" she asks.

The EMTs, seeming to sense the situation and their role within it, look at each other and nod.

The other referee puts the game ball in a bag and packs up the scorers' table. This includes turning off the electronic scoreboard. The score was 2-6, the game having barely begun.

Lauter saunters over to the remaining team.

Mara grabs his arm. "Leave it. The ref knows who it was. They can make the report. An arrest can be made later, away from here and without escalating this situation."

Lauter shakes her off and keeps going. "I'm arresting him now."

Mara is impelled to support her partner. The other two officers stay with the EMTs.

Lauter points between the players, at the culprit, gesturing for him to come forward. No one moves.

"I guess that means we have to arrest of all you," Lauter says.

"We didn't do anything," one says.

"They paid off the refs," says another.

"Did they? This was clear in the first two minutes of the game?"

"They got all the calls."

"Maybe. The Turks cheat any way they can. Everyone knows that." Lauter smiles. "They'll bribe and bully refs at any level. You should see them at my son's football games."

"It always happens with us," the culprit says. "The refs are always against us."

"Maybe you should stop hitting them." Lauter moves closer. "Maybe you should respect the rules."

The players step forward as well. Mara gets in between and starts moving Lauter backwards.

"Okay," she says, not wanting to take on two dozen burly guys. "They got the point. They'll respect the rules from now on."

"The refs are the authority on the court," Lauter says. "Respect that. If you don't like it, go back to your own country. What is it? Serbia?"

The players bristle at this comment, but Lauter finds it all amusing. He turns his back to them, like they mean nothing to him, and walks to the scorers' table. The players go back to their beers. Some sit on the bench, others on the floor. The culprit stays standing, at about the same height as the tall guys sitting on the bench.

"We'll get him later," Lauter says to Mara.

"What are you doing talking like that?" asks the officer with HEBEL on his shirt.

Lauter is unapologetic. He's even a little shocked that his actions are being questioned.

"It's that kind of talk that makes people hate us," Hebel adds.

"I didn't say anything wrong. I simply told them to respect the refs."

One of the EMTs shoulders his medical bag and says, "I'm from Greece. Should I go back to my own country as well?"

"No. That's not it. You're missing the point."

"Can we go now?" asks the other EMT.

Mara nods. "The situation's secure. We'll go with you."

The police officers escort the EMTs and referees out of the hall. On the way, they pass the players who are drinking and toasting the culprit as the hero of the night. There's something routine about their behaviour that makes Mara think this is just a regular night of basketball for them.

Outside, the hastily parked cars are gone. Mara offers a supportive wave to Hebel and his partner, who are taking details from the other referee. Then she gets in the car.

Lauter gets in as well and says, "What a waste of time. Fucking foreigners."

Mara doesn't reply. She shakes her head slightly.

Lauter interprets this as agreement. "I know, I know. It's always the same groups making trouble."

"That's not what I was thinking."

"Doesn't mean it's not the truth." Lauter starts the car and moves it forward. "I think we've earned a coffee. That'll perk you up and put a much-needed smile on your pretty face."

Lauter drives them to nearby Ostbahnhof, stopping in a no-parking zone in front of the kiosk at the station's north entrance. He gets out and joins two security guards standing at a circular table. He looks at Mara, still in the car, and flicks his head in the direction of the kiosk, signalling for her to get the coffees.

Mara doesn't move. She looks at the guards, at how their triceps and biceps bulge in their tight shirts.

Fake muscles, she thinks. The result of chemistry, not work.

Lauter, clearly annoyed, goes to the counter and gets a coffee for himself, which he takes back to the guards' table. It's at that point that Mara climbs out of the car and goes to the counter.

"A bottle of water, please," she says. "Did he pay for his coffee?"

The attendant, who's in his 20s and wearing a Turkey football jersey, shakes his head.

"Sorry for that. I got it."

Lauter makes room for her at the table, but she walks away from him. She leans against the police car and sips her drink, watching the steady stream of people flowing in and out of Ostbahnhof, scanning for potential troublemakers. It all looks tame, the station mainly a meeting point. There's plenty of drinking going on, but the alcohol is amplifying the fun of the night out. There's no sense of trouble.

Mara remembers when she used to have that kind of fun.

A few lone guys wandering around, feigning to be checking things on their phones, have the shifty moves of drug sellers; the police presence has held up business for the moment.

She finishes the water and takes the bottle back to the kiosk. She puts the refund in the attendant's tip jar.

"Thanks," he says with a smile. "That gets me 25 cents closer to my dream car."

"What is it?"

"Not saying. It's my dream and mine alone."

She digs in her pocket and pulls out a two-euro coin. "Dream big," she says, dropping the coin in the jar.

"Always. Have a good one."

15

She backs away from the counter as a dozen softcore left-wingers jostle forward to buy drinks. They're young, most likely students, or dropouts, all dressed in slightly varying combinations of black jeans and hoodies that have *Antifa* slogans on them. She gets a few nasty looks, which she shrugs off. This projection of hostility is far more preferable to being actually attacked. While these anti-fascists are at the opposite end of the political spectrum, they still remind her of the street battle in Pankow last night. The police had been sent there to provide a secure space for the right-wingers to hold their protest, or meeting, or whatever it was. She can't remember what it was about. Lack of jobs? Anti-immigration? But then it turned ugly, and with such groups, once it starts, it becomes difficult to stop. It was only the belated arrival of a water cannon that sent them scurrying for safety down the side streets. The police made arrests, which is always required, to keep the stats up, but all of those guys probably walked free today.

Lauter leaves his coffee cup on the table and comes back to the car. The wind blows the empty cup to the ground.

"Why do you have to be so anti-social?" he asks.

She doesn't reply. Back in the car and on the road, Mara becomes aware that she has reached that point in a nightshift where she's half awake and on autopilot. The rest of the night is a blur, as they go from one mild disturbance to another, but fortunately without encountering anything threatening enough to snap her fully awake. It's the kind of nightshift that results in a lot of paperwork, which Lauter will no doubt expect her to do.

Things get quiet around dawn, as Berlin settles down and prepares for the transition back to a working city. The radio stops crackling and there's silence in the car as Lauter, who gave up hours ago trying to make conversation with Mara, drives them back to the police station in Kollwitzkiez. She struggles to keep her eyes open. Back-to-back all-nighters leave a very specific type of exhaustion; a deep fatigue she feels in her bones and a weird kind of nausea that could be an oncoming sickness or the result of not having eaten enough. All she wants is to sleep.

But the city seems hopeful in the morning, cleaned up, in fresh underwear, ready for a new day. People up early are exercising and trying to get things done before work. There are children to get ready for school, trash bags to take out and refrigerators to restock.

She's incredibly grateful to have Russell in her life.

At the station, it's good to be out of the car and away from Lauter, but the shift isn't over yet. There's still the morning briefing, followed by a round of paperwork, which she will divide with Lauter, 50-50. Because as he says, he's all about equality.

In the meeting room, those coming on for the day shift sit at the tables in ironed uniforms while those who worked through the night stand in a haggard line, shoulder-to-shoulder, along the back wall.

Hauptmeister Hans Spitz enters at bang on 0700. The room falls silent.

He's in his early 60s, tall and lean. His grey hair is closely cropped, army-style, which makes it harder to discern that it's receding. It also lends him an authoritarian edge; important, given he's a control freak and puts his stamp on every inch of his domain. Spitz is equally loved and loathed, the division closely mirroring the gender split. While he positions himself as the station's wise, fatherly figure, the only possible familial thing about him is the nasty air of wicked uncle he gives off. Anyone with a good arsehole radar, like Mara, can pick him out from miles away.

"Morning," he says. "Good to see we all got through the night unscathed."

In recognition of this, fists knock against tables and walls.

"I'm especially proud of those of you who assisted in Pankow on Saturday night," Spitz continues, "and showed up again last night and today. That shows a lot of character and dedication, but I would expect nothing less from this group. We made 28 arrests at that protest, and that's a really good number. But we still need to hold our lines, stick together, do our jobs and make as many arrests as we can. There's no such thing as a peaceful protest anymore. We have to remember that, going forward."

Spitz pauses to let these words sink in, then nods at the tech guy who turns on the screen and dims the lights.

"Of course," Spitz says, trying to lighten his tone, "it meant I had 28 lawyers to deal with yesterday who all claimed their clients were innocent."

A few officers laugh; it sounds forced, to Mara. Ingratiating.

"But that was my problem, not yours." Spitz turns to the screen. "Now, I'm sure most of you are aware of what happened in Hamburg last night. An utterly vile act. It's imperative the perpetrator is

17

caught. Run the footage, Julian."

The screen shows a protest, lit by streetlights, flares and burning cars. An aerial view, from a drone. Mara recognises the triangular intersection of Neuer Pferdemarkt in the Schanzenviertel. A huge number of protesters, dressed in black, wearing balaclavas and brandishing flares, clash with police. It's violent and messy. A mobile water cannon comes in from the side and blasts the protesters, driving them back. The police move in, with shields and batons, but there's little coordination among them.

"As you can see," Spitz says, pointing at the screen, "our colleagues in Hamburg had real trouble keeping these rioters under control. They were outnumbered against a ruthless opposition. But, and this is important, look at their lack of organisation and teamwork. They get isolated and end up on their own against two, three or four protesters. You can't let that happen. Stick to the strategy and work together."

The footage cuts to a bodycam perspective, at street level.

"Because when you end up alone, something unfortunate like this can happen."

Two protesters, in balaclavas, with the angularity of young men yet to fill out, confront the officer wearing the bodycam. There's a tussle, bodies close together, two against one, and it's hard to see what happens. Then the camera is pointing upwards, not moving. The two protesters bend over the officer. One appears to be concerned with the condition of the officer, before being pulled back by the other and they move out of view.

"Go back a few frames, Julian," Spitz says.

The video rewinds.

"Stop. Hold that."

The paused image is the protester in front of the bodycam. His balaclava makes it impossible to identify him. Except for Mara; she would know those grey eyes anywhere.

The room is silent.

"You fucking idiot," she says softly.

"Language, Steinbach. But yes, this fucking idiot is the most wanted man in Germany right now. Him and his friend. It's one thing to smash windows and loot shops, or even torch cars, but taking the life of one of our own demands an immediate response. This is absolutely not on."

"Finding him is going to be tough," Lauter says.

"Yes, thank you for pointing out the obvious, Lauter." Spitz points at the screen again. "There are facial recognition experts working on this as we speak. There's also phone tracking, to place people at this point and time. We will find him. I'll let you know when we have a name to go on."

Spitz nods to Julian. The lights come on.

"That's it. Stay safe out there, and stick together. The assignments are on the board."

The officers coming off the nightshift are the first to move, keen to get their reports done and go home.

Mara stays where she is.

"Better get moving, Steinbach," Spitz says. "You don't want Lauter doing all the paperwork. He's terrible at it."

"Yeah."

"Come on. Get it done and go home. We'll need you tomorrow. Word is there'll be an impromptu *Antifa* rally in front of the Chancellery."

"May I have a moment, sir?"

"Walk with me."

Spitz leaves the room and heads down the hallway. Mara follows, noticing his slight limp. He's favouring his left leg, but clearly trying not to. In the crowded hallway, the officers part to let Spitz through.

"What is it?" Spitz asks over his shoulder.

"You think these guys might end up here?"

"That's been a strategy in the past of hooligans and extremists." Spitz enters his office. "You'd think they'd go to ground in a forest or some far-off village, but it's much easier to get lost in a big city and lean on any support networks here. We both know Berlin has groups for every possible movement, political or otherwise."

"They've probably gone underground in Hamburg, hiding out somewhere until it blows over."

"This isn't going to blow over. This is a nationwide manhunt."

Spitz's office is small and cramped, with a large glass desk flanked by an armchair on one side and a spinning bike on the other. There's no paper in the office. Spitz is very proud of winning "Most Sustainable Station" in Berlin three years running, the awards displayed on the shelf behind him. The only thing remotely like paper is the box of tissues on the corner of the desk nearest the

19

armchair.

Spitz shimmies awkwardly between the desk and bike, and lowers himself onto his blue inflatable ball. He bounces a little, his back ramrod straight.

Mara stays in the doorway.

"Come in, Steinbach. Close the door."

Mara takes a few steps inside, but leaves the door ajar. As there's no chair in front of the desk, she stands, two metres from the desk, hands behind her back. She's certainly not going to sit in the armchair that Spitz now gestures towards.

"I don't want to take up any more of your time than necessary, sir."

"Yes, good, good. What makes you think they haven't left Hamburg? Our sources say they're already here. But that could be misinformation to throw us off. Get us looking in the wrong places. Wouldn't be the first time that's happened."

"They look like students. Or even high school kids. They might even be already back at school."

"Right," Spitz says, eyes on his computer screen. "Hiding in plain sight."

"They're young. Teenagers, I'd say."

"Agreed. These rioters get younger every year. As if Fridays for Future was their training ground. Or is."

"You don't sound like you trust the sources. Don't we have reliable people in place?"

"It's not people we have to trust," Spitz says. "We monitor certain phones. Social media. We trust the data. We're supposed to. If you ask me, it'd be better to have people on the ground."

"I could do that. I'm from Hamburg."

Spitz gives her a leery look. "Go inside? Are you volunteering?"

"Anything to help. Sir."

Spitz bounces on the ball. "Not everyone's cut out for undercover work. It can get rough, inside."

Mara fights fatigue and her impatience. It feels like there's no air in the office to breathe.

"What makes you think you can handle it?" Spitz asks.

"I think my background ..."

"I know all about your background. You had quite a life before pulling on the uniform. Junior boxing champ. A few stints in juvenile

20

detention. Arrested half a dozen times before you even finished school."

"I ran with a bad crowd for a while."

"Your father got you out each time. Must've been great growing up with a lawyer for a dad."

"Please leave Richard out of this, sir. We're not in contact."

"So, what are you proposing?"

"My background can be useful," Mara says. "I know a lot of people in Hamburg. I know the scene. I could go back there, get involved again. Find these guys."

"Slow down, Steinbach. You're mine, remember. Though I do admire your enthusiasm. The question is, what do we do about it? How do we channel it?"

Spitz's eyes flick towards the armchair. Mara stays right where she is.

A few moments pass.

Spitz lets out an annoyed sigh. "I guess I could make some calls, to Hamburg. I also know a lot of people there, significantly more important than your contacts, I'd bet."

These words hang in the air between them. Mara and Spitz look at each other. Mara assumes he's expecting something in return for his generosity; she wants to stuff his mouth with tissues until the box is empty.

"I'll bring them back here. When I find them."

"Your confidence is inspiring," Spitz says with a thin smile. "I'll see what I can do."

"Thank you, sir."

"Go home, Steinbach. Get some rest. You look like hell. I expect my officers to look their best."

Mara leaves the office and closes the door. Lauter is in the hallway, chatting with Brennhof. He gestures towards a sign on the wall – "Please remember to wash your hands" – and gives her a knowing look.

"Finished all the reports already?" she asks.

"Your job."

"Not this time. I just got ordered home, by Spitz himself."

"Then I guess you need to wash more than your hands," Lauter says.

Mara is tempted to deck him, but Lauter's not worth the bruises

21

on her knuckles. She heads out of the station, deciding right there that even if Spitz doesn't set up an undercover operation, she will take time off and go to Hamburg anyway. Because it's Anthony. It's fucking Ant. She wonders what the hell he's got himself into.

Outside, she takes out her phone, opens her contacts and calls ANTMAN. It rings and rings. She pockets the phone, unlocks her bike and starts the long ride back to Tiergarten.

The exchange with Spitz leaves her wanting a shower, even more so than the long night in the car with Lauter.

She's passing through Brandenburg Gate when her phone rings. It's a number she doesn't recognise.

"Ant?"

"Ah no. This isn't … Ant. This is Christoph Perceval. I received your number from Hans Spitz."

"Hey, hi. That was fast. Are you in Hamburg?"

"I'm part of the extended group investigating last night's incident, yes."

"Count me in."

"Excellent. I need you to travel to Hamburg immediately. Don't delay. Don't talk to anyone."

"What? Today?"

"Immediately doesn't mean tomorrow."

"I'd need to get someone to cover my shifts."

"If you want to take on this assignment, your life as you currently know it is over. Do you understand?"

"Yeah. Sure. But what do I tell people?"

"As I stated, you don't tell anyone anything. I will send you my location in due course."

Perceval hangs up.

"What the fuck?" Mara says to herself.

Back riding, fast, thoughts compete for prime consideration. How did Anthony get mixed up in this? Can I handle going undercover? Can I lie to Russell? Will Spitz expect me to sleep with him for this? How does he get away with being such a sleazebag? Have I done my last nightshift in this city? Are my police days over? Is Anthony a killer?

It's everything she can do just to concentrate on riding and get back to the apartment in one piece. She arrives jittery and drained. As she wheels the bike inside, Russell turns from his gym mat in the living room, where he's doing his morning physio routine.

"Mara?"

In her room, she leans the bike against the wall and peels the uniform off, layer by layer, leaving it piled on the floor. Then she's into the shower. It feels good, but she knows the traces of guys like Lauter and Spitz don't wash off so easily; they linger.

Russell appears in the doorway. "Hey. What's going on?"

"Come on in, why don't you."

"You always talk to me when I'm in the shower. This bathroom is where we've had some of our best conversations."

"No time for that. Sorry."

"You look in a serious hurry. What's up?"

Mara turns the water off. "Can't say. Towel, please."

"You have to," Russell says, passing a towel into the shower. "No secrets between us. Remember? We agreed to that on day one."

"I know. The Sambuca pact."

"We never lie to each other."

"There's an exception for every rule. I'm withholding this time."

"Why?"

She comes out of the shower, the towel wrapped around her. At the sink, she starts putting a toiletry bag together.

"Where are you going?" Russell asks.

"Home."

"To Hamburg?"

"Yeah. Let's go with that. A little bit of truth, just for you."

Russell watches her. "This has something to do with what happened last night. The cop that was killed."

"You know about that?"

"It's all over the news."

"Any excuse to keep showing the footage, as you'd say."

"Do you know him?"

Mara zips the bag closed. "I thought I did."

"What does that mean?"

"Oh, you mean the police officer. No, I don't know him."

"Who did you think I meant?"

Mara moves to leave the bathroom. Russell blocks the doorway.

"Don't make me get physical with you, Russ."

"You need to tell me what's going on," he says.

"Look, I appreciate your concern, but all I can say is that it involves Anthony. I have to pack a bag and go now."

"I thought he was in the States, on that basketball scholarship."

"Richard told me he rejected it, last time we spoke."

"When was that?"

"Months ago. Please, Russ. Let me pack."

Russell rolls back from the doorway, allowing Mara to pass, still wrapped in a towel, toiletry bag in hand. He follows her into her room.

"You don't need to tell me everything," he says. "Just correct me where I'm wrong. Yes or no."

Mara takes a battered backpack from her closet and starts stuffing it with clothes.

"Is Anthony in trouble?"

"Yes."

"Big trouble?"

"Yes."

The old alarm clock goes into the backpack, along with a pair of boxing gloves.

"That's not him in the footage, is it? In the balaclava."

"My God. Yes. But nobody knows that. Yet."

"The eyes, right? You recognised his eyes."

"Yes."

"Fuck."

"Yes."

Mara takes off the towel and drapes it over Russell's head.

"After everything we've been through together, you're still shy?"

"Yes."

Mara puts on underwear and a bra. Russell removes the towel to watch her shimmy into an old t-shirt and an even older pair of jeans.

"Are you going to pretend to be a homeless person in Hamburg?"

"Pretty much. You're amazing, Russ. You're piecing all of this together just by looking at me. You should've been a detective."

"I'm a journalist. It's kind of the same thing. Articles are like cases that need to be solved."

"Think you can solve this one?" Mara asks.

"A cop dies at a protest. Your brother was caught on the bodycam. You're wearing clothes you haven't worn for years, like you're getting into character. You can't tell me anything about it. I'd say you're going to Hamburg to find your brother and get him

24

somewhere safe."

Mara, tightening the straps of the backpack, stops in mid-action and stares at Russell. "Fuck me. Yes."

Russell looks at the uniform on the floor. "You quit the police?"

"No. Maybe. I don't know."

"So, this is sanctioned? You're going undercover for the police?"

"Stop getting everything right."

"Maybe we should take a moment to think about this," Russell says. "You have no idea what you're getting yourself into."

"It's Ant. I have to go. You can't tell anyone, Russ. They told me not to say a word."

"Well, you haven't really said anything yet. Not outright. Who's they?"

"You're too clever for your own good."

"So you keep saying. Look, Mara. You need to be careful. I've done this. I've been there. It's no fun."

This takes Mara by surprise. She sits down on the bed, getting at Russell's eye level.

"Don't be shocked. I'd done a lot by the time we met. About ten years ago, I was asked to get in with the Union Berlin Ultras, after that Syrian stadium guard died. It turned out I'd gone to school with a couple of them. It was for *Der Spiegel* and I knew it was the kind of big story that would establish me at the magazine. Serious money, too, eventually. I worked in a bar in Marzahn while I was undercover. Lived in one of those soulless concrete high-rises. God awful. The whole thing took a year, then another year to get me safely out of there."

"That's why you have those tattoos."

"I got the more hardcore ones removed."

"What about the story?"

"My name wasn't on it. But it was huge. When it ran, I had to pretend to be just as angry as all the Ultras were. I even participated in their vicious little internal traitor hunt. I was the one who convinced them it had to be someone from a rival club, trying to undermine them, which is why there were all those fights with the hooligans from Hertha Berlin around that time. It was war, almost. A very modern, very pathetic, battle for Berlin. Which I guess I started."

"I had no idea. You sound like the one with all the secrets."

"That's the biggest one. You need to keep it to yourself."

25

"I will." Mara leans forward, elbows on her knees. "How was it? Being undercover?"

"Hard. You start out playing a role, a character created for the situation. Then the character becomes you, and you're never the same person again, even when it's over."

"I'm going back to who I was. They want to use my background to my advantage."

"That makes things easier," Russell says. "You can be a version of yourself, rather than an entirely new person."

"I'm scared, Russ. But I'm also really motivated. You know what I mean?"

"I know. I know. You need to keep your emotions in check. But not too much. Don't go all stony and poker-faced and giving nothing away. That'll make people suspicious. If you think a situation requires a certain reaction, go with it. Don't hold back."

"That's good. What else?"

"Are you asking me for tips about going undercover?"

"Yes."

Russell smiles a little. "This is one conversation I never thought we'd have."

"You want to move it to the bathroom?"

"Hah. No. In my opinion, it's not that complicated, and it applies to just about everything in life."

"Hit me."

"Please excuse the corporate speak, but the key is to manage your stakeholders."

Mara laughs.

"I'm serious. You don't need to convince everyone or win over every single person. You need to identify the key people and get them in your corner. Radical groups and hooligans, even offices and boardrooms, they're ridiculously tribal. Having one important person vouch for you can make the difference to whether you get accepted into the tribe or not. Once you have that person on your side, manage that relationship, and also try not to piss off anyone dangerous."

"The same applies to working at the Kollwitzkiez station."

"So much in life is about managing people," Russell says. "Managing relationships. It requires being genuine. So, here's another important point. Don't lie. Stick to the truth as much as you can. It can be hard to keep track of lies, because lying normally leads to more lying. If you get caught in a lie, that will most likely blow your cover."

"Sounds like there's a book in this."

"That time in my life, that's really something I want to forget. I did things then I never thought I was capable of."

"We'll have to save that for another time. I need to get going."

"Be careful. I'll miss you, Mara."

They hug.

"There might be no turning back from this." Russell spins the left wheel, pivoting the chair and manoeuvring out of the room. "But maybe there's a good story in it. From your inside work. I'd keep your name out of it, of course."

"There could be two, if I burn my bridges to the police and there really is no going back."

"Spitz?"

Mara nods. "He's a creep. He has to go down."

"You go to Hamburg, save Anthony and get all that material. I'll start researching into Spitz."

"Deal."

They share a smile.

"We should secure this with Sambuca shots," Russell says, "but it's too early in the morning for that."

"And no time." Mara shoulders the backpack.

"Send me everything you can. Photos, documents, notes. Do it by post. Nothing digital, because that's too easy to track and monitor these days."

"I'll try. It might take some time to get established. Don't give my room away."

"I would never do that."

Russell opens the door. Mara squeezes his right shoulder as she passes.

"Stay safe out there, angel."

"Take care of yourself, Russ."

He holds the door open for her. When she gets to the building's front door, she turns to see him just outside the apartment. He gives her a confident, reassuring nod, then she exits the building.

Day 1

The train is half full and speeds west. The passengers are mostly businessmen, in shirtsleeves, their suit jackets looped over the little hooks near the windows. They work on laptops and talk on phones, with a self-importance that Mara thinks belongs to another era. She slouches in her seat, not wanting to be seen by these guys; not wanting, even indirectly, to be part of their lives. She puts her knees against the back of the seat in front.

The display at the end of the wagon shows the train is travelling at 190 km/h, but it sure doesn't feel like that.

She thinks of Anthony, of where he might be right now; what he might be feeling. Who does he have in his corner? Who's helping him? Richard?

Anthony, eight years younger, who came into the world just as her parents' marriage disintegrated. The baby she looked after and cared for. Restless Ant, who could never sit still, never stick to things. Until he found basketball, and that became the only thing. Ant the loyal follower, always in search of someone to look up to and admire and copy; always needing guidance, but selective about who he would listen to. Superstar Ant, untouchable on the court and with the kind of dominance, even before he was a teenager, that resulted in coaches being replaced if he didn't like them.

Now, it was protester Anthony; police murderer Anthony.

She can't believe it. He's no killer. She has to find him before the police figure out it's him in the footage.

The train starts to slow, lurching everyone forward. Those on tight schedules groan with annoyance at this delay. The train stops at a station without a name. The platform is overgrown with grass and weeds. Some of the businessmen stand up and go to the windows on the platform side. Mara looks as well and sees a young couple, both barely 20 and both dressed in anti-establishment clothes getting kicked off the train, presumably for not having tickets. The conductor tosses their backpacks off as well, which land on the platform and roll forward a little.

"Serves them right," some guy says.

The two are left on the platform as the train jerks forward again. The girl picks up something and throws it at the train.

Mara's phone buzzes, a message from Perceval. The address in

28

Hamburg is in City Nord, where numerous police buildings are clustered on and around Hindenburgstraße. She searches online for Christoph Perceval. When only links to amateur table tennis competitions come up, she wonders if she has the spelling right. The Perceval she sees in the photos – small, slight and bookish in tracksuits or table tennis outfits – looks nothing like a man who investigates the crimes of radicals, anti-fascists and protesters; nothing like a man running undercover agents. The Perceval she envisions is big, tough and worldly. Older too, a drinker maybe, someone straddling the pre-digital and post-millennium police eras. Because that's how he sounded on the phone; old-school educated.

She pockets the phone and closes her eyes. In her mind, all she sees is Anthony, in a balaclava, his grey eyes looking straight at her; wanting her to come find him and also to stay the fuck out of it.

When she opens her eyes again, the train is edging into Hamburg's main station. The businessmen form a line down the middle of the wagon, suit jackets on, standing close together. Once fully stopped, the train disgorges its passengers. They flood onto a platform crowded with people waiting to catch this train back to Berlin.

Mara's the last to exit her wagon, forcing her way past passengers already trying to get on. On the platform, she weaves between all the people and their luggage. There are also many just hanging around the station, taking advantage of its coverage and relative warmth: homeless, addicts, refugees, transients, bored-looking youths, beggars. But there's no threat or sense of danger, unlike Berlin. She doesn't think someone will run off with her backpack if she leaves it on the ground and turns her back on it.

Two drunks are asleep on the stairs leading down to the U-Bahn station, throwing the usual keep-to-the-right system into disarray. Someone knocks over the battered cup that's in front of them, spilling a handful of copper coins onto the stair's edge.

The U-Bahn train is modern and sort of clean, save for the scattered detritus left by those who just got off: takeaway coffee cups, newspapers, food wrappers and even the odd tissue. Mara finds a rubbish-free seat and sits down, plonking her backpack on the seat opposite to hopefully deter anyone from sitting there. The stations come and go as the train makes a long underground arc before heading north, emerging into daylight after Klosterstern.

Looking out the window, she gets a sense of being home. Leafy, swanky Eppendorf isn't her area, having grown up near the river in Othmarschen until her father took a bazooka to their comfortable life, left the law firm and moved them out to that barn in Moorfleet in Hamburg's southeast. But this is her city and she knows it well, having boxed in gyms and taken Anthony to basketball games in just about every one of its suburbs. It appears safer and more settled than Berlin; a place with its identity intact and not metamorphosising every twelve hours. She accepts this could be the result of doing too many late shifts, during which she often experienced Berlin's night-time Mr Hyde.

Alsterdorf station is her exit. The backpack bounces on her back as she descends the stairs. Now close to the start, she feels nervous. Entering unknown territory, with no experience, and with an objective she needs to keep to herself.

But this is it: a briefing, instructions, Perceval imposing himself as her boss. She wonders how much he will be involved, and how much she will be allowed to improvise.

Fuck, she thinks. Undercover. No. Anthony. Focus on Anthony. Find him.

She passes the Polizeipräsidium, then follows Hindenburgstraße to Sydneystraße, which reminds her that she would like to visit Australia, one day. Maybe that's where she and Anthony could escape to. Board a freighter and disappear down under.

The address Perceval provided leads her to a bland office building. The signs on the front wall look hastily attached, the companies dubious: XYZ Import/Export, Smith Tradings, Jensen & Sohn.

Fronts, she decides.

The bells are labelled, but she doesn't know which one to press. She looks up at the camera, positioned just above the door. The lock suddenly buzzes, and she pushes the door open. In the cramped entrance, she's unsure where to go. There's a wrought-iron elevator going straight through the centre of the building, a spiral staircase wrapped around it.

The man who comes up from the basement is the Christoph Perceval from the table tennis photos, but he's taller in person.

"Follow me," he says, heading back down the stairs.

The basement office is windowless and bare. There's one desk, with a laptop on it, and one chair. The office feels recently cleaned, or cleaned out, and is lit by fluorescent tubes, giving the feel of an underground operating theatre.

"Thank you for undertaking this journey on short notice," Perceval says.

Mara is taken aback by his formal way of speaking. "Yeah. Sure."

"May I add further that your timing, I believe, is ideal."

"What does that mean? Are you just starting?"

"Correct."

Mara looks around. "Where is everyone?"

"How do you mean?"

"A protester kills a police officer, and this is the task force set up to find the killer?"

Perceval goes to the desk and pulls the chair out to sit down. Instead, he stays standing and grips the back of the chair.

"This section ..."

"Where are we anyway? You seem like a decent guy, but this office is throwing up a lot of red flags for me."

"Please, do not interrupt. You can be certain Hamburg's finest detectives are working to locate the suspect caught on video."

"Which means you're not one of them. You know, down here, in this cave on your own."

"My task is to research into the various radical groups in Hamburg. Specifically, the financial side of things. The flow of money and the paperwork behind it all."

"Really? You're a bookkeeper?"

"You say that with disdain, but some of the worst criminals in history have been brought to justice by investigators like myself."

"Looks like you've accomplished a lot so far," Mara says.

"Indeed. You are here. You will assist me in solving this case far sooner."

"Faster than Hamburg's finest detectives? I'll try, but I don't understand why a group of radical protesters would leave a paper trail. Not exactly ticking the sustainability box."

"An excellent point. However, there is always paper behind the scenes. These groups are not completely digital reliant. Do not think they do everything by smartphone and cash, nor utilise digital networks and make strategic use of social media."

"They don't?"

"It is what my overlords believe. Their approach to investigating radical groups is to monitor phones and computers. Across the street, there's an entire floor dedicated to this. It is an utter waste of time and resources."

"Yeah? How so?"

"Because," Perceval says, leaning over the desk to wake his laptop, "the protesters know they are being watched."

"Well, you got me now. A person on the ground."

"Yes. You are here. A stunning development, wholly unexpected. We must get you started. I assume you have participated in your share of protests recently."

"On the police side. I'm still recovering from the last one."

"Let me ask you this. Whenever you arrested a protester or radical, did they have a phone on their person?"

"On their person?"

"Were they carrying a phone?"

"Why not just say that? No, not lately. Used to be like that. I guess they started leaving them at home, so they wouldn't get damaged. Those things break so easily."

"No, no, no. This is a clear change of strategy." Perceval plays a video on his laptop. "This was the climate change congress in Munich two years ago. Look at all the protesters holding up phones. Filming the event for them was just as important as attending. They wanted to show that they were there. This has changed, and it's true of protests all over Germany, regardless of their political extremes. No phones. It's almost as if someone gave the order for this."

"That implies there's someone high up, on top of all these groups, left-wing and right-wing, who's giving such orders, and that people are following them."

"Yes. Fascinating, isn't it?"

"It also implies," Mara continues, "that all the disparate groups are unified and organised, with a common leader and common goals. I find that hard to believe."

"Or there is someone posing as the leader, pandering to all sides of the political spectrum, in clandestine fashion, so the other groups don't know about it."

"Possible. Still hard to believe though."

Perceval gives her a curious, searching look. "May I be candid with you?"

"You're about to send me in undercover, with no support. If you're the only one I can trust, then yeah, we better be honest with each other."

"Agreed. Your superior, this Spitz fellow. He was, how shall I say this? He didn't speak very highly of your intellect, when I conversed with him on the phone. Not the smartest bullet in the clip, quote-unquote."

"Really?"

"I'm not getting that impression from you at all. I have the sense now he was trying to get rid of you. To palm you off onto me."

Mara laughs. "That's the right way of saying it. He's an expert at palming."

"Ah, he's one of them."

This takes Mara by surprise, especially Perceval's tone when saying it, and she feels for the first time that he could be an ally; that her initial read on him may have been wrong. She's glad to be away from Spitz and Lauter and all those other creeps.

"Look, can we forget about Spitz? I'm guessing this paper trail will be a key part of the investigation, because the groups aren't as digitally connected as the big boys think, and that the paper will lead to this mysterious figure up the top."

Perceval gives her a conspiratorial smile, which makes him look strangely handsome. "Exactly. Organisation and hierarchy require paper. Documents people sign and copy. Agreements in triplicate. But there are also financial records and legal cases."

"Nothing catches a killer quite like paper."

"Your sarcasm is unwarranted and unappreciated. I understand you're nervous, maybe even scared, but this is not the way to compensate for that. Focus on the task at hand."

"Yes, sir."

"You must not call me sir."

"Okay." She's tempted to call him Percy, but holds back. "Where do we start?"

Perceval hands her an old flip phone and a set of keys.

"Very modern," she says, taking both.

"The phone is just for us. Keep it safe. Do not contact anyone else with it."

"And the keys?"

"Your apartment. It's imperative your life appears normal. That

33

you have made all the decisions regarding your return to Hamburg. Your lodgings shall reflect that."

"Lodgings?"

"You are a person cast out of the police and looking to rebuild."

"Is that the story?"

"You quit, technically. But you could say you were forced out for reasons you won't disclose."

"I was getting close to that point anyway."

"Good. Expand on that. It will help with authenticity. Your first task is to infiltrate Circus. Do you know who they are?"

"I've heard of it. But I don't remember the groups ever having names. You know, a brand."

"They set up after your time," Perceval says. "That is, they only recently gave themselves this name. You are right to use the word brand. Giving groups names and designating people as leaders helps with obtaining followers, making organisational charts, establishing chains of commands and so on."

"Sounds very corporate."

"That's one way to approach it. More accurate, in this context, is that it's militaristic. Think of Circus as a division or unit belonging to a larger army. I especially want to know who the general of this army is."

This analogy, and the seriousness with which Perceval delivers it, shakes Mara to her core. She'd never thought about it that way. Her brief foray into the radical left scene as a teenager, dragged along by friends, consisted mainly of going to concerts and clubs, supporting the left-wing football club FC St Pauli, and marching in protests. It was rarely violent and never felt like it made any difference. If anything, it seemed to her like a lifestyle choice. This was where these people chose to hang out. It was their community. To now consider these people as soldiers in a burgeoning army changed everything.

"An army? To do what?"

"I know it sounds extreme," Perceval says. "It is just a theory at this stage. My theory. We need proof. I'm confident your investigations will help prove the theory correct, because I think you are the smartest bullet in the clip."

Mara wonders if this is Perceval's version of a pep talk. "Uh, thanks."

"Circus is a threat. Be aware you are entering enemy territory."

"A threat? To what, national security?"

"One police officer is already dead."

"Do you think they'll try to overthrow the government? Come on."

Perceval's face is blank, but Mara thinks his eyes give away something; that others have questioned his army theory and maybe even mocked him for it, sending him down to this lonely basement.

"Does anyone know you're here? In Hamburg?"

"Just Spitz."

"That's all? Remember, we need honesty if we're going to trust each other."

She thinks of her last conversation with Russell. "Just the palm-off king."

"Keep it that way. You're starting a new narrative now."

Perceval snaps his laptop shut and picks it up.

"I'm ready," Mara says.

"Then let's go."

He holds the door open for Mara, then turns the lights off and locks the door.

Outside, Mara squints at the light. Perceval, more experienced with the switch from harsh fluorescent to raw daylight, already has sunglasses on. He unlocks a white, mid-90s Mercedes SL convertible that has the top down.

"Now that's a police car," Mara says, putting her backpack on the narrow back seat and getting in.

"Thank you."

"I'm pretty sure you still see pimps driving cars like this. Around St Pauli."

"That's where we are headed."

Perceval puts the key in the ignition. The keyring is a small, red table tennis bat.

"We'll blend right in then."

"Do not speak badly of this car," Perceval says. "It was my mother's."

As they head down Hindenburgstraße, Mara wonders what kind of upbringing Perceval had. He drives quickly, weaving between the traffic; not with aggression, but with the purposefulness of someone trying to make good time. With the top and windows down, it's too loud for conversation. They skirt the north side of the Stadtpark and pass the modernised villas of Rothenbaum.

Waiting at a traffic light, the car stands out among the grey and black vehicles, which are mostly SUVs. Perceval rests his left arm on the door, visibly proud.

"What can you tell me about Circus?" Mara asks.

"To begin with, it's far more than a mere protest group. They have their own fashion label. An upcycling project involving refugees. I need you to delve into that."

"How is that helpful?"

"It's likely the label is a front for moving money. To handle outside financing, maybe launder money gained through nefarious means."

Mara smiles, enjoying the way Perceval talks.

The lights turn green. Perceval is efficient and crafty in getting the Merc ahead. This results in making a succession of green lights and they are soon on the Reeperbahn. Mara observes that a few things have changed. Some of the grimier restaurants are gone. A few clubs have been rebranded. But the general usage of this street remains the same. It's not her favourite part of the city, but she concedes being based here will suit the purpose.

Perceval turns down Hamburger Berg. The bars, open in the late morning, are the same as Mara remembers. Even the clumps of street people are somehow familiar, like they haven't moved in the last decade. There's a lot of garbage on the ground and the street smells. Urine stains mark the walls of just about every building and trickle across the footpath towards the gutters.

The car slides in diagonally between a pair of blue vans in front of a dilapidated apartment building. It's painted, Mara thinks, bordello red, and the paint looks reasonably fresh.

Perceval turns the engine off and gives the building a wistful look.

"Top floor," he says.

"The penthouse suite? Lucky me. What do I charge per hour? Or is payment, uh, you know, on a sliding scale?"

Perceval shakes his head a little. "This is no time for humour." He takes money from his wallet. "Here. That's €200, to get you started and set up. There's not much in the apartment, last time I looked."

"I need one of those bum-bags the girls wear. For this money, a box of condoms and that ancient phone you gave me."

"Listen to me," Perceval says. "Put all your attention on what you

36

are doing right now. Everything you do, every word you say, every plan you make, it is all for a singular purpose. I understand you're nervous. Anyone would be in this situation, and you're attempting to compensate with wit. It's not working. It's juvenile and counterproductive."

"Sorry."

Perceval leans closer and lowers his voice: "Get into it. We can be the ones who blow this thing wide open."

Mara nods, stopping herself from making a joke using the word blow.

"You are a local," Perceval continues, "back in your old hunting ground. These are choices you have made."

"Right."

"Because you are doing that, you should get in contact with old friends. Visit the Schanzenviertel. Have a drink. You're out of the police. Let loose."

"Good idea." Mara starts to get out of the car, but Perceval stops her.

"One definite thing. Make contact with Lersner."

"Nicola? Why would I do that? I haven't seen her in years."

"Her law firm represents Circus."

"She's a lawyer? So, she turned out just like her mother after all."

"In the end we all become our parents."

"Fuck, I hope not," Mara says.

"Lersner is a lawyer, but she has political aspirations."

"No surprise. She always considered herself a leader. Can I get out now?"

"One last thing." Perceval looks around a little, then back at Mara. "We have three weeks. To make an arrest."

"Why three?"

"For the record, that deadline isn't coming from me."

"I get the feeling none of this is on the record. You gave me money from your own wallet. You look at this building with the watery eyes of someone who grew up here."

"In less than three weeks is the G8 meeting in Stuttgart," Perceval says. "It has been made very clear that we can't have protesters who murder police officers running around on the streets when all those leaders start arriving. We have to make a statement before then."

"You make it sound like it doesn't matter if we get the right person or not."

Perceval offers a thin, sly smile. "Anyone in handcuffs on the front page will most certainly be helpful."

"Uh-huh. Getting the perpetrator will just be a bonus. But why bother? Why not just arrest anyone?" Mara gestures towards the street people. "You could quite easily make one of them your scapegoat."

"That is unfair. I'm confident it won't come to that. Now, get settled. I will check in with you tomorrow morning. On that ancient phone, which still works perfectly well. It will be like a normal conversation and we simply know each other. Just in case anyone might be listening."

"Who would be listening?"

"Well, I have a theory …"

"Another theory."

"Please, do not interrupt. It could be from our side. But my theory is that Circus has their own floor of people monitoring phones and social media."

"Radical hackers?"

"Or tech-savvy teenagers. There are plenty of them around. Hopefully, you will soon find this out."

Perceval gestures for Mara to get out of the car. She does so, lifting the backpack from the rear seat.

The car reverses, then drives down Hamburger Berg.

Mara heads towards her new home. A scrum of men is huddled outside one of the bars, close to her front door and partially blocking it. They have the half-closed eyes and sweaty faces of people who have been drinking all night.

"Hey, babe," one says. "I got a hundred for you. Let's party."

"Move," she says.

"I'll buy you a drink for hand-job," says another. Their drunken laughter rings out as she goes through the door of the building.

"Fucking men," she says. "Like they're evolving backwards. But not you, Russ."

The entrance is cluttered with trash and old flyers. Half the metal mailboxes are hanging open, the top sections bent and twisted. Further down the hall, there's a pram missing three of its wheels. The stack of greasy pizza boxes is waist high. The garbage in bags, tied up, has flies buzzing around the tops, like it's been there for weeks.

She counted four floors from the outside. The stairs creak underfoot and start to feel less sturdy with each floor she ascends. The handrail is rickety, sticky and unsafe. She half expects to see some addict shooting up, or maybe a couple of scrawny kids huddled on a stair while their parents fight inside one of the apartments.

Based on the collections of shoes in front of each door, all the apartments appear occupied.

At the top floor, the ceiling is lower and the landing is void of shoes. There are two doors. None of the keys work on the first door, so she crosses the landing to the other. Inside, the apartment has two rooms, a small kitchen and a cramped bathroom. The only furnishings are a mattress on the carpeted floor and a cheap-looking closet that leans to the left.

While it all looks awful, she has lived in worse places. She sees potential. It just needs some more stuff inside; stuff she can call hers.

"Won't get much with €200," she says to herself.

The closet has sheets, blankets and pillows, all of them well-used and musty smelling. She's too tired to care. Her fatigue crashes down on her now she has the time to rest. Her last action is to dig the alarm clock out of her backpack and set it for three hours ahead. Then she's out.

***

It's drizzling as Mara walks down the hill to the city centre. Without an umbrella, she keeps close to buildings, for the cover they afford.

The workday is over. People ride bikes home and hustle towards the stairs leading down to S-Bahns and U-Bahns. There's surprisingly little traffic in downtown Hamburg. Those that work here choose to leave their cars at home, unlike Berlin, which is all cars all the time.

The buses that rumble past are full, the passengers with heads bowed over phones.

She doesn't quite feel like she's here yet. I need to get earthed, she thinks, recalling something Zina used to say. Stick my feet in the sand at Övelgönne and let the Elbe wash over them. Or swim in a lake. Get grounded. Get attached.

Reminded, she sends a quick message to Zina, saved as Z in her contacts, to ask how she's doing. She also asks if Stuttgart is already preparing for the G8 conference.

On Alter Wall, she breaks one of Perceval's crisp notes to buy a coffee from a bakery. She stands outside, drinking it, under an awning that's cradling water. One of the bakery staff comes outside with a broom and pushes the awning up with its handle, so all the water sloshes off to the sides and into the gutters. Some of the water splashes the shoes of a pedestrian, and an argument ensues that Mara tries to ignore.

Across the street are the offices of Lersner-Löwe. They used to be at Gänsemarkt, back when her father and grandfather worked there, before the Lersner and Löwe families teamed up, in an old art deco building that somehow survived the war. But that building has long been torn down.

The firm's logo, two overlapping L's in a circle, is on the wall out the front.

The bakery worker and pedestrian continue to argue. It reminds Mara how the rain in Hamburg often annoys the locals.

"Hey," she says to the pedestrian. "It's just a little water."

The man, who's in his early 30s and wearing a suit a size too small, comes towards her. "These shoes cost €150. All leather."

"Wrong choice for this city," she says, getting a laugh from the bakery worker. "Get yourself some designer rubber boots instead."

"Ah, fuck off," the man says, and he continues on his way.

"You could also spend that money on politeness classes."

The worker gives her a smile and takes his broom inside.

Mara sips coffee and considers her options. Going into the office to find Nicola would be too suspicious; just to show up out of nowhere with so much time in between, Nicola will surely see through that. Calling the office could be interpreted as premeditated, so also suspicious. Lurking outside like this, where Nicola might see her from a window above, is seriously suspicious.

The realisation that she has absolutely no idea what she's doing is both funny and frightening. She wishes the pedestrian with the wet shoes was still there; she could channel her fears into humour at his expense. But he has clumped to the end of Alter Wall. He darts across the road, looking at the puddles to avoid them, and is narrowly missed by a bus.

She wonders if she should call Perceval for advice, but it doesn't seem he quite knows what he's doing either. Anyway, she left the flip phone in the apartment.

The drizzle has stopped. She moves away from the bakery and around the next corner, out of view of the Lersner-Löwe windows, but still with her eyes on the entrance.

She asks herself: what would Russ do?

She's tempted to call him and flat out ask, but concedes that would be a dumb-arse rookie move. First day on the case and already needing help. She checks her phone anyway. No reply from Zina, who's probably on a shift. There are other messages and updates, but she ignores them.

She realises the only way this could be convincing is if it happens by accident. A chance meeting that surprises them both and provides the opportunity for reconciliation between two friends who were once inseparable.

But how to manufacture that?

She looks down Alter Wall, in both directions. There are cars parked here, the usual sedans, wagons and SUVs. Nothing ostentatious, which is what she thinks Nicola would drive. Because she would drive. Mara can't see Nicola taking the train or bus, or riding a bicycle. Or has she changed?

No, Mara thinks. Nicola was a child of privilege, and that sense of entitlement rarely fades in adulthood. She drives, something with flair. A head-turner, which is how Nicola always saw herself.

It's then she sees her, coming out of the building with a flourish. Big heels. A knee-length charcoal coat over a white skirt and black blouse, the coat open and billowing behind her. No attaché case. No laptop. Not even a handbag. Just a set of keys in one hand and a stack of what looks like three phones in the other as she strides, arms swinging, in Mara's direction.

Mara backs behind the corner of a building, out of view. She waits, then walks with her head down, timing her approach so she and Nicola just about collide.

"Sorry," Mara says, keeping her head down. She walks on, like she's got somewhere to be.

"Mara? Is that you?"

Feigning annoyance, Mara stops and turns.

"Oh, my God, it is you." Nicola comes towards her, arms out.

"Nicola, hey."

41

Despite everything, Mara thinks it's good to see her.

They hug.

"Colour me stunned." Nicola, pulls back, then puts her left leg slightly forward and leans back on her right, to give Mara a full appraisal. "You have totally changed. I almost didn't recognise you."

"Look at you. Very professional."

"It was your voice. That's what I recognised. You look so different."

"What are you doing these days?"

"What else could I be doing," Nicola says, breathing out the words.

Mara tries not to let it show that Nicola's snobbish, superior way of speaking, as if she wants to end every sentence with a pedantic "darling", is already getting on her nerves.

"You didn't become a lawyer, did you? Because you kind of look like one."

"Oh, please. I couldn't possibly have done anything else. It's all so easy. You just need to have good assistants and show up on time with the right documents."

Nicola starts walking, expecting Mara to walk with her, which she does, but giving Nicola a bit of width to avoid the billowing coat.

"My car's down here," Nicola says.

"I'm not going this way."

"It's just a few metres. Walk with me."

Mara attempts to muster the enthusiasm she thinks would fit such a coincidental meeting. "You look great. Nice outfit."

"Oh, this? Well, you know, legal life is 90 per cent fashion and ten per cent work, which I don't really do anyway. You'd be amazed how many judges are actually dirty old men in disguise. They can't resist a low-cut blouse and are so easily swayed. Opposing lawyers too."

Nicola stops at a silver Maserati, low-slung, with two massive doors. "What are you doing in Hamburg?" she asks, clicking the key fob in blasé fashion. "I heard you ran away and joined the police. In Bonn, or somewhere."

"Berlin. But I quit. Couldn't take it anymore."

"I don't blame you. The police are so unappreciated these days. Still, not exactly the right side for you anyway."

"Yeah. Something like that."

Nicola opens the broad car door and stands in the opening, one heel inside.

"Are you in contact with anyone from the old group?" Mara asks.

"Why would I be? I left that world behind ages ago. I'm sure you'll find them all in the same old places bitching about the same old things."

The open door extends a fair way across the road and blocks traffic. Nicola ignores the horn that sounds, or perhaps thinks it's not meant for her.

"Nice car," Mara says.

"This is Flavio's. His second car. I hate it. It's got rich footballer written all over it."

Mara wonders if Nicola loves the car more than she loves Flavio.

"Wonderful to see you, Mara. This has absolutely made my day. Let's catch up properly soon."

"Sure."

"We'll do lunch. Stop by the office one day. Or call my assistant. Ciao."

Nicola gets in, but keeps the door wide open. More horns, with traffic now backed up to the corner. The car is ridiculously loud when it starts up; a high-pitched feline growl. Nicola closes the door and pulls straight out, as if all those drivers are patiently waiting for her. The car roars down the street and darts through the intersection as the traffic lights turn red.

She feels a strange sense of pride in accomplishing her first task undercover, as haphazard and improvised as it was. She made contact with Nicola, which is what Perceval wanted. This renews her energy as she walks up the hill to Großneumarkt, past the square's cafés and bars, and back to St Pauli. She passes a supermarket on the way and buys some basic supplies. She also gets a notepad, a packet of pens, five padded envelopes and a pile of disposable cameras. She takes it all home and lugs it up the rickety stairs to her apartment.

Inside, she flicks the fridge on, then puts everything away. The addition of food and other necessary household items help make the place feel more like home. But what she really needs is more furniture. With just the mattress on the floor, the leaning closet and the empty rooms, she feels like a drug addict shut off from the world, trying to get clean.

She takes a butter knife from a kitchen drawer and goes across the landing. The keys didn't fit on this door earlier, and she thinks she might be able to jimmy it open with the knife. It doesn't look like anyone lives there, and the handle makes her think this is potentially a storeroom or attic, with stuff inside she could make use of.

She tries the handle. It moves stiffly, but it's unlocked and the door opens. The last of the daylight is sneaking through a pair of narrow skylights blotched with dirt.

The contents of the storeroom confirm her suspicion this place was once a brothel. The furniture stored here is all in gaudy shades of red, gold, green and black. She finds an emerald chaise longue in reasonable condition and drags this into the apartment's living room. Next is a blood-red armchair, which is surprisingly heavy and also requires dragging. None of the gold-tasselled standing lamps have light bulbs, but she takes two of them, anyway. Under a sheet is an antique black table and matching chair. The ornate nooks and small shelves suggest this table was once a dresser, but the mirror is no longer attached. She takes the table and chair into the apartment.

The added furniture brings life and colour to the living room. She thinks it's best not to ponder how the myriad of stains and marks on the furniture got there, nor wonder who sat in the chair and did their make-up at the now mirror-less dresser. It's all here now and time will make it her own. She puts the notepad, pens, envelopes and cameras on the table. It's tempting to start collating things on one of the bare walls; put Circus in the middle and map around that with photos, evidence and string. But that wouldn't be the best thing for any guests to see, should they come up here. She decides to leave the gathering to Perceval, and go hunting instead.

In the bedroom, she pulls on an old St Pauli hoodie, then heads downstairs.

The day drinkers are gone from Hamburger Berg, replaced by a less desperate crowd. The bars are busy, with people spilling beyond the footpath and parking areas onto the street. Tight groups, a lot of young people, but also some who have the wide-eyed curiousness of tourists, slumming it on this famous side street to brag about it when they're back home. Different music thumps from each of the bars, resulting in an annoying cacophony.

She puts the hood up over her head and strikes a course for the Schanze.

A bottle of beer bought from a corner store makes for a useful prop. She drinks from it as she walks, blending in with the inordinate number of hoodie-wearers who are drinking and walking, beating paths from St Pauli to the Schanze, or the other way.

Her phone buzzes. A message from Z: "All fine. S a zoo and it's gonna get worse. Animals on both sides of the barricades."

Mara resolves to get to Stuttgart somehow, before the G8. It's been too long since she and Zina last saw each other.

The old haunts in the Schanze – Grüner Jäger, Knust, Dschungel – are disappointing. The first now has a relaxed beer garden vibe, the second is closed for a private event, and the third has moved from the middle of the Schanze to Sternstraße and looks more like a place old ladies have coffee and cake.

She wanders around, unsure what to do. The rampant gentrification of the area feels wrong. Worse than the typical urban evolution that sees the middle-class move into poor, cool neighbourhoods. This is a takeover. An occupation.

The Schanze has lost its edge. Its once anti-establishment sneer is now a middle-class smile of self-satisfaction.

The main drag of Schulterblatt sparks memories for her of wild May Day protests, street festivals where there was barely space enough to move, and flash concerts with local bands playing on the back of flatbed trucks. Dropping ecstasy, partying all night and sleeping rough. But all that seems long gone. Now, there are vintage clothing stores, boutique florists, pet shops, fancy cafés, and all those specialist shops for daily needs that a good area provides its community-minded residents who want to buy local. Parents push prams. There's a tangle of bicycles around every pole, plus those big three-wheelers used for zero-emission ferrying of small children to kindergartens. Bulky blocks for charging electric vehicles. Every second person with a dog. Graffiti scrubbed clean from walls, or diligently painted over. The few homeless people camped out in front of the old Rote Flora cultural centre appear half-packed and ready to move on when told to. Their little cups and dishes don't have a single coin in them. As Mara passes, she sees one battered coffee cup, set out for donations, is full of small stones.

She walks behind the Rote Flora, through a small park where a few children are playing, watched over by parents who stand together but don't talk to each other. She remembers a time when it was dangerous to walk through this park at any time of day.

The old bunker there has been turned into a climbing wall, with all those colourful ridges bolted on. No one's climbing today. A group of young people, dressed like they're part of the radical scene, or trying to convince others they are, comes out of the bunker's main door. A few of them carry big backpacks, with sleeping mats rolled up under the straps.

She follows them, down Lippmannstraße. While they're wearing the uniform of a leftist group like Circus, this could just be the local trend. They head towards St Pauli, so at the very least she will be close to the apartment and can give up for the night if they lead her nowhere.

The group turns onto Lerchenstraße, walking with purpose. At busy Stresemannstraße, they don't wait at the red light. They venture out onto the street, causing trouble, weaving between cars that are forced to brake. Horns blare. Abuse is shouted, from both sides. A truck just misses one young guy, and this is deemed funny by him and the group. All this happens right in front of a police station. The guy who avoided the accident stops to piss against the police station wall, while others film him.

Oh, yeah, Mara thinks, you guys are really dangerous. She can't imagine Anthony running with such a crowd, but it makes her wonder if her foray into teenage rebellion looked this pathetic.

She waits in the shadows, watching them, then follows as they head further down Lerchenstraße. This takes her past the old Schilleroper theatre, where she and Nicola, tripping out of their minds on something Nicola had procured, once got up on the roof during a New Year's Eve concert and nearly fell off. The building is now shelled out and skeletal, awaiting middle-class refurbishment.

At Otzenstraße, the group skirts around the red church on the hill and goes down a narrow alley. Mara lets them get ahead, then follows. The alley leads to another bunker, solid and windowless. It's a concrete cube that looks like it was dropped there by a crane. When the door opens and the youths go inside, muffled punk music comes out.

Mara looks around. The bunker is hidden behind a handsome apartment block. This area of St Pauli, away from the Reeperbahn, is quiet and residential, the rents high. She finds it difficult to believe the bunker would be a meeting point for radicals, but with nothing to lose, she heads inside.

It's loud, dark, hot and crowded. She has to push through clumps of people. Many hang in the hallway, perhaps to make fast escapes if

46

the police arrive. But the congestion thins beyond the hallway. The area in front of the band, who are really flailing at their instruments, is embarrassingly bare. It seems few are interested in the angry punk being sort of played, and the venue isn't helping the music's quality, as this place was built for defence rather than acoustics.

The darkness makes it hard to tell, but Mara thinks the people she sees have the shifty self-consciousness of teenagers. That's the vibe she's picking up on too; a certain excitement and awkwardness, plus a determination not to do anything stupid that might become the talk of the schoolyard tomorrow. Like it's a school dance moved off-site to a secret location. However they've ended up here, she doesn't think this is a Circus thing, nor anything relevant to her investigation. And she's certain Anthony's not here, as this music is nowhere near the hip-hip beats he's solely marched to since he was eight. Still, she finds herself searching the faces for him, as the light allows.

She feels like the cool kids are judging her.

There's no bar, but people are clutching bottles of beer. Mara circles the room and finds a couple of bathtubs filled with ice and bottles. The ice is melting fast, making it look like all these bottles are being washed in the bath. A lot of labels float in the water. A chalkboard shows the beers are €2. Mara has to get up close to it and squint to make that out, and to see the arrow pointing downwards to a large piggy bank on the floor. This has "*Kapitalisten Schwein*" written on the side in glowing yellow. She takes a beer, wipes the water from it and drops a €2 coin in the slot on the pig's back. She jimmies the cap off by levering her apartment key over the knuckle of her index finger wrapped around the top of the bottle's neck.

She drinks and listens to the band, who continue to give everything on the stage, as if their main goal is to convince everyone they're playing their instruments. It's more noise than music, and it makes her grimace.

If this is what Hamburg's radical scene now is, she thinks – high schoolers, bad punk and bathtub beer in a sweaty bunker – then maybe those causing the most trouble at protests come from out of town.

The beer goes down in gulps, because she sees no point in staying here. She starts to leave, but then a short girl with close-cropped blonde hair digs a bottle out of the tub, but doesn't feed the capitalist pig.

They look at each other in the near darkness. It's Susie, and she still looks like a teenager. Put in boxing shorts and a singlet, and with a padded helmet jammed on her head, Mara thinks Susie would be interchangeable with that version from ten years ago.

"Mara?" Susie shouts. "What the fuck?"

"Hey!"

They hug. It feels even less meaningful, Mara thinks, than the hug with Nicola earlier.

It's far too loud to talk. Susie motions for Mara to follow her. They go out of the main area, down another narrow hallway and into the bowels of the bunker. This gets Mara blessedly away from the angry punk noise. In a back room, also crowded, another party is happening, one that feels separate from the concert in the main area. This party has a broader cross-section of ages and a more communal atmosphere. The room hums with conversation and is stuffy. It strikes Mara as the aftermath of a meeting. Some discussions look intense, perhaps with agenda points being further debated. People lean close to hear every word, brows knitted, already formulating responses. Others joke and laugh, trying to lighten the mood.

As she looks around, she has the sense there are some people in here she needs to get to know. Potentially a stakeholder or two, and maybe even a few dangerous people to keep on the radar. It means she's highly attentive, while trying to fit in and look relaxed. Some look at her, seeming to wonder who she is.

Susie keeps motioning for Mara to follow her. They end up at two sofas in a corner, positioned together to make an L. Susie sits between two guys, both early 20s. Mara sits on the other sofa, just at the arm, as there are already three other people sitting on it and they make just enough space for her to squeeze in.

"This is Rab," Susie says, pointing with her stolen beer. "And this is Matze."

"Hey," Rab says, without any indication of committing to making small talk.

Matze nods once.

They have the bland, forgettable look of players who warm benches on low-level sports teams.

Susie leans forward. "Where have you been all this time? You just disappeared."

I didn't disappear, Mara thinks. I left you all behind to do something with my life.

"Went to Berlin," she says. "A few other places in between."

"There was this crazy rumour going around that you joined the police. I said there was no fucking chance of that. Not psycho Mara. No way. She'd more likely be beating up the police."

Mara quickly runs through her options. The mention of police has Rab and Matze listening. Lying would mean having to keep the lie going. But it wouldn't be hard to get caught in that lie, because she's in various photos on the Kollwitzkiez station's social media pages.

"Not a rumour," she says. "It's true. It was."

"What happened?" Susie asks.

"I quit, a few days ago."

"Why?" Rab asks.

"Couldn't follow orders." Mara thinks the truth sounds good, and it's a relief to talk about it. "There are some real arseholes in the police. I don't necessarily mean right-wingers, though they're also around."

"Fucking fascists beat us up every week," Matze says.

"They come looking for us," Rab adds. "At uni."

"They're not all hardcore," Mara says, trying not to sound defensive. "What I hated were the guys exploiting their positions. Like it's 50 years ago."

"To get between your legs?" Susie asks.

Mara nods. Susie looks shocked, but the vagueness of the two guys makes them hard to read.

"That's wrong," Rab says.

Susie is about to say something when a fight breaking out in the middle of the room draws everyone's attention. People nearby move back from the fight to avoid wearing a stray punch. A man in his 40s, in a St Pauli hoodie like Mara's, is grappling with a skinny guy half his age. Everyone watches as the two wrestle, but no one steps forward to stop it. The older man gets an arm free to swing a solid punch to the younger's head. As he reels back with the punch, he produces a knife. He slashes this twice through the air, making the older guy jump back, before being grabbed from behind, his arms pinned. Another man shakes the knife from the young guy's hand and it clatters to the floor. A beautiful woman, whose smooth brown skin makes it hard to tell her age, steps between the combatants.

"You can fight all you want, but no weapons," she says. "You know

49

the rules, Gomez. Now get out."

She points towards the door. Gomez is released. He holds his hands up innocently, a grin on his weaselly face, blood trickling from his left eyebrow.

"Fuck your rules," he says. "This group has too many fucking rules."

As Gomez leaves, he takes a dozen people with him. Mara thinks a few of them were in the group she followed from the first bunker.

"What was that all about?" Mara asks.

She gets no reply. Susie pushes herself up, using a knee each from Rab and Matze, and goes after Gomez.

"Who is that guy?"

Again, no reply. Mara doesn't want to sit with Rab and Matze, who are staring at her, but not talking with her. She stands up and goes to a makeshift table, which is a stack of pallets with an old wooden door precariously balanced on top. There's food, chips and nibbles in torn-open bags.

She gets a handful of nachos. A tall, lean man, about 30 and good-looking, comes up to her. His Scandinavian hair, cut short like Susie's, is so blonde it's almost white.

"Hey," he says. "You look lost."

"I found the food. That's something."

"If you can call this food. I'm Jesper."

"Mara."

"Haven't seen you before. How did you end up back here?"

"Are you the welcoming committee? I know Susie. From way, way back." When Jesper gives her a curious look, she adds, "Susie's the one who went after Gomez."

"I know who Susie is."

"Are they a couple? I haven't seen Susie in ages. We haven't caught up on everything yet."

"They're not." Jesper looks at the food on offer and decides not to have any of it. "How do you know Susie?"

"From juvie. Where all great friendships are made."

Jesper laughs. "No, really. Where? From school?"

"Believe what you want. She got beaten up by everyone. I saved her from that, then taught her how to box, so she could defend herself. When we were both back in the world, she started training at my gym."

"You box?"

"Used to." Mara finishes her last nacho, wipes her hands on her jeans and squares up to Jesper, fists raised. "Try me."

He steps back and smiles. "That was enough fighting for one night. You look like you want to hit me. Just need an excuse."

"Calling me a liar is an excuse enough."

"Woah. Slow down. I believe you now, even if you don't look like the juvie type."

"Speak for yourself. You don't look like a radical. You look like you got lost on your way home from an office job."

"Harsh."

Susie comes back in and sits down on the sofa between Rab and Matze. She folds her little arms and pouts.

"What was the fight about?" Mara asks Jesper.

"Who knows? One wrong word can set a lot of these people off. Just one big happy circus."

"Where are the animals?"

"Ha-ha. Oh, they're in here too. Can't have a circus without animals. They're what everyone wants to see."

Mara finds Jesper talkative; someone who likes the sound of his own voice and thinks himself smarter than he is. But she's not getting the sense he holds any position of importance in this group.

"I guess this circus has lots of different players. Groups within the group."

"You could say that."

"Well, as you said, I'm new. Break it down for me."

"Sure," Jesper says, moving closer. "It's no secret. Gomez has plenty of followers, and they just left with him. St Pauli fans, hardcore. Hooligans, basically, but they'd never call themselves that and you didn't hear it from me." Jesper gestures towards the woman who stopped the fight and the people surrounding her. "That's JJ, plus a few others who consider themselves the leadership group. They kind of hold this all together, but don't do a great job of it. Things would probably fall apart without JJ. She's American. Been here for years. Like, when there was the Wall."

"She stopped the fight. Is she giving all the orders?"

"She tries. But look around you. Do you think these people are good at following orders? I'm pretty sure I can't tell you what to do. You'd probably knock a few of my teeth out."

51

"Just a few."

Jesper laughs again. He points to the sofas and says, "Over there, Susie and her boys, they're, like, eco-warriors. Vegan soldiers. I don't know. They're always protesting at farms and meat factories and whatnot. Useless stuff, but very meaningful for them."

"Good to hear Susie's no longer just looking out for herself. Any protests coming up?"

"I think they're going out to some pig farm tomorrow."

"Save the pigs! Sounds like just my thing."

"Ha-ha. Yeah. I like you. What's your name again?"

"Mara. Steinbach."

"Mara Steinbach," Jesper echoes, committing the name to memory.

Mara sees that Susie is leaving with Rab and Matze, holding hands with both of them as they walk single file through the crowd, the way small children do when crossing a road.

"That's my ride. I gotta go."

"Nice to meet you," Jesper says.

Mara heads out of the stuffy room and down the hallway. In the main area, the music has stopped. The band is packing up and all the teenagers have left. Some of those she followed earlier are spreading their mats on the floor, getting ready to sleep here.

Bunkers as squats, she thinks.

Outside, she jogs to catch up with Susie.

"Oh, Mara," Susie says. "Sorry. I didn't forget about you. It's just, the party was dead, you know?"

"I was talking to Jesper. He said you're protesting at a farm tomorrow."

"Yeah. So?"

"I want in."

Susie looks at Rab and Matze, who are unmoved and expressionless.

"Sure," Susie says. "Why not? We can catch up in the van."

"Flakturm," Rab says. "On Feldstraße. 6am."

"Okay."

"If you're not there, we're not waiting," Matze adds.

"And no phone, Mara," Susie says.

"Right. Got it."

The three of them walk in the direction of the Schanze, with little

Susie flanked by Rab and Matze.

Mara heads down the short hill of Otzenstraße and back to Hamburger Berg. She has the feeling she's followed. She checks behind her a few times, but sees no one.

The bars on her street are even more crowded than earlier. She has to push past drinkers to get to her building. A couple of guys block the door, supposedly in good fun, but she's in no mood for this. She waits for them to move, and they do it, with put-on manners, sweeping hands in front of them like they're gentlemen. But as she passes, one of them grabs her left arm and tries to pull her towards him. She swings around with the momentum and absolutely decks him, knocking him out. This stuns those watching. She looks at them, to see who else might want to grab her arm. One guy takes out his phone.

"Do it," she says. "Call the cops. We can also all go together to Davidwache and I'll report your glass-jawed buddy for assault."

The guy pockets his phone.

"Yeah, I thought so."

She heads inside, shaking the sting out of her right hand.

Upstairs, there's no ice in the fridge. She runs cold water over her hand in the kitchen sink and waits for the adrenalin to subside.

Good contact, she thinks. Right on the sweet spot.

She dries her hand. It's sore, but doesn't look damaged. Just a stinger. The pain makes it hard to grip the pen as she makes notes on the pad: names of all the people she met tonight, plus the bunker's location. She puts a circle around "JJ" and three question marks behind "Jesper". The bunker being used as a meeting point and squat also feels important, worthy of further investigation.

It's late, but she tries calling ANTMAN again. No answer.

"Where the hell are you, Ant?"

She has a quick shower and falls into bed. The alarm clock gets set for 0515.

She stands in the cold shadows of the huge concrete Flakturm, recalling how Nicola had her 16th birthday party on its top floor. Mara missed it, as she was doing her first stint in juvie; caught trying to steal a car. It had been Nicola's idea to hotwire the yellow Ferrari parked just off the Reeperbahn, and she tried to do it by watching a how-to video on YouTube, played on Mara's phone. The police arrived and they both fled. But in her panic, Mara left her phone in the Ferrari and was arrested later that day.

At the time, she thought it was seriously callous of Nicola to go ahead with the party while she suffered in detention, and it marked the beginning of the end of their friendship. Because Mara met Susie and started running with her crowd once out, while Nicola pivoted towards finishing high school and the law degree that was always in front of her.

Richard always considered Nicola a bad influence, and tried to stop Mara from seeing her, which had the initial effect of pushing the girls closer together. Until the Ferrari incident.

She looks up at the big bunker, wondering how things might have been different if she'd been at Nicola's party. If she hadn't dropped her phone, her life could have gone in a whole other direction.

Zina always said that hypotheticals were poisonous, not just with boxing, but with everything in life. Sweating over all the what-ifs meant not being present. Be where your feet are, Zina said, and point them in the right direction.

It's just starting to get light, but there are still stars in the sky.

Mara tries to feel her feet on the ground, at this spot, waiting for whatever vehicle will arrive. She has no idea what to expect from the morning. It's too early to be thinking logically; to be theorising.

The knuckles of her right hand hurt as she makes a fist and opens it again. Nothing feels broken. She'd found the guy she clocked last night passed out on the ground this morning, right outside her door. All his drinking pals were gone. Someone had turned the pockets of his pants and jacket inside out. It was a pitiful scene, as the guy had also wet himself. The bar's cleaner worked around him and the few others asleep on the ground with the practised movements and blank detachment of someone going through just another morning in St Pauli.

The people on Feldstraße move with purpose; early-starters hustle to the U-Bahn station, hands in the pockets of jackets zipped up to their necks.

She's nervous. Tracking back to when they were teenagers, she can't recall Susie ever leading her down a good path. It would be easy, she thinks, to slink back into the shadows and refocus the day towards looking for Anthony. But her feet are on this ground, this curb, pointing at where a vehicle will stop for her.

When it comes, it's an old van, sporting the white and green of a decommissioned police wagon from decades ago. Rust is bubbling around the wheel arches. The side door is opened before the van stops completely. Susie is there, in the doorway, beckoning energetically for Mara to get in. The van starts moving again before the door is closed. The noise of it slamming shut echoes in the shelled-out van. In the near darkness, Mara counts ten sets of eyes, with the people sitting shoulder to shoulder, on the floor, backs against the walls of the van. Mara sits down next to Susie, against the sliding door. The handle juts into her side. The metal floor is cold.

"You owe me €10, Rab," Susie says loudly to the other end of the van.

Mara looks in that direction, trying to make out Rab in the far corner. "You thought I wouldn't show?"

"It's very early," Rab says. "I didn't think you had this in you."

"What? To wake up early?"

"To protest."

"Relax, Rab," Susie says. "Mara's the one you want in your corner. Trust me."

Mara turns to Susie and lowers her voice. "Where are we going?"

"A farm outside of Hamburg. You won't believe it when you see it. A fucking horror show."

They drive for a while in silence. Mara can feel every bump in the road through the metal floor. The van accelerates and slows down, but never gains significant speed, meaning they haven't ventured onto the Autobahn.

A bit more light starts to enter the back of the van, allowing Mara to get a better look at the faces. She sees Matze sitting with Rab, but no one else is recognisable.

"Where are your signs?" Mara asks Susie.

A few people in the van laugh. The bearded guy sitting next to

55

Susie puts on a balaclava, folding the front part up onto his forehead. This is a cue, as all the others don balaclavas and fold them up so their faces are still seen.

"Are we protesting a farm or robbing a bank?" Mara asks.

Susie puts on a balaclava as well. "You don't have one?"

"Why would I? We're picketing, aren't we? Not invading."

"You need to stay covered, because of the cameras." Susie gives Mara her blue scarf. "Here. When we get there, wrap it around your face and neck, then put your hoodie up."

"What cameras?"

"Just do what I said."

Mara takes the scarf and looks around the van. She can't decide if they all look like criminals before a heist or like riot police before a preventative action. There's something about the balaclavas that presupposes violence, and she can already feel a collective anticipation and edginess in the van. They all know what's coming, she thinks.

"There are cameras everywhere these days," Matze says.

To loop the scarf around her neck, Mara sits up and leans forward. This gives her a vantage point to see over the middle seat and through the windscreen. They are in the countryside, closely following another van. She's sure she recognises the road.

The scarf in place, she sits back against the sliding door.

"How's your dad?" Susie asks.

"I don't think this is the right time for catching up on family, Suz."

"Still teaching?" When Mara doesn't reply, Susie says to the far corner, "Her father is Richard Steinbach."

"Mad Professor Steinbach?" Rab asks. "I had a class with him last semester. It was wild. Like an introduction to conspiracy theories. Stuff I'd never even thought of."

"A long way from anything like the law though," Mara says. "Plenty of it just made up."

"I don't know about that. He showed us how cameras are hidden in everyday places, to ensure we're all being watched, even when we think there's no chance of it."

"Did he also tell you how all the cameras are pointing at him and the government is tracking his every move?"

Before anyone can reply, the driver says, "We're here. Get ready."

Everyone pulls their balaclavas down. Mara thinks they really look like criminals now. She notices that Susie's balaclava, and a few others, have a plastic cover to protect the wearer's eyes from tear gas, pepper spray and smoke. Something made in the Circus fashion factory, wherever that is?

There's no time to think about that because the van comes to a quick halt. Mara gets the scarf up over her nose and raises her pullover's hood. The door is slid open and she almost falls out. Her eyes need a few moments to adjust to the light, as the sun has come fully up during the journey. She counts 21 people, from the two vans.

Then they're moving towards the farm's main gate. A tight mob. No one has anything in their hands, and Mara recalls what JJ said at that gathering last night: no weapons. Does that also count for protests? Or for whatever the hell is about to happen?

The wooden gate is waist high and locked. They jump it. Susie gets a leg up from Matze. It looks like the workday hasn't begun yet. Smoke is curling out of the chimney of the house to the right. A handful of dirty vehicles are parked out front, including a pair of multi-level animal trailers with horizontal wooden slats.

Mara wonders if everyone in the house is still asleep.

The group goes straight ahead, towards the two large barns, which are separated by a penned-in and well-trodden paddock that's currently empty.

The guy at the front, who had cued the donning of balaclavas in the van, signals for the group to split, with eleven going to the first barn and Mara joining Susie, Rab, Matze and six others moving towards the second.

"What are we doing?" Mara asks, as she jogs next to Susie.

"We're setting the pigs free."

"Seriously? Why?"

"Because they're jammed in there. It's inhumane. We're taking action against it."

As they hustle towards the barn, Mara sees that the farm is surrounded by fencing, meaning even if the pigs get out of the barn, they certainly aren't leaving the property.

The leader's group is already at the first barn. They work together to slide the big door open. Mara's group reaches the second barn and does the same.

Once open, the stench comes out at them in an almost visible wave. It causes some to reel back from the doorway. Rab bends over

57

to throw up in the dirt.

The barn is packed with pigs. It's so tight, it's not possible to tell each animal apart. Mara uses a hand to press the scarf closer to her mouth and nose, but it doesn't make much difference.

Susie tries to open the gate, but she can't reach over the top to move the latch. Matze tries to help her. The pigs somehow sense their impending freedom and jostle towards the front. Their excited grunts sound almost human, and pornographic. The wooden slats of the pens creak and groan under this collective weight, like an old sailing ship yawing in high seas.

Mara sees that if the gate is opened, or the pens give way, those in the group would get trampled standing where they are, including Susie and Matze.

"Move!" she shouts.

The sound of a gunshot shocks them all. It scares the pigs as well. The animals try to turn and get away from where the noise came from, but they have nowhere to go and no room to move. They end up half-climbing over each other, as if engaged in panicked mating.

Those in Mara's group look towards the other barn, where the members of the other group are sprinting for the front gate, pursued by three rifle-carrying farmers, who are all wearing pyjamas and rubber boots. No further shots are fired, and Mara thinks the farmers are trying to drive them away, with that first blast being a warning shot. The eleven protesters are swiftly over the gate and into the first van, which tears off.

The three farmers turn and start towards the second barn.

Susie climbs up onto the pen gate, intent on getting it open. Some of the group run for it, including Matze, arcing left or right to get around the farmers. Susie is left on the gate, and she clings to it with her legs as it swings open. The pigs stream out. Mara climbs up onto the wall, gripping hangers that hold shit-covered shovels. The flood of pigs fills every space between the gate and the barn door.

As the pigs run out of the barn, they follow the protesters. One of the slower protesters gets trampled.

Mara can hear Susie cheering, urging the pigs out of the barn.

The farmers let the protesters go and focus on herding the pigs together, which isn't hard. After the initial burst to escape the barn, the over-fed pigs don't last long. A few fall over, exhausted.

Rab and Matze help the fallen protester, whose feet drag in the dirt as they get him towards the gate.

Mara jumps down from the wall. The last of the pigs are struggling to get out of the barn, hardly able to cover the distance from the pen to the barn door. She gets ready to run an arc around the pigs outside to the gate.

"Mara!" Susie shouts. "Help me. I'm stuck."

Susie is still on the gate, pulling at her jeans. Mara goes to her and rips the jeans free. Susie jumps down and starts running, but is confronted at the door by one of the farmers, his rifle raised.

Mara ducks down behind a pig, her hands going into what she hopes is mud.

The farmer towers over Susie, almost twice her size.

"Don't move," he shouts.

Mara, on all fours, uses the pig for cover to get to the wall. She grabs a rake and swings this down on the farmer's rifle, knocking it from his hands. She's too close to him, though, and he elbows her in the side of the head. Dazed, she sees Susie taking her chance to run for it, and she's fast. A blur between the pigs. The big farmer comes at Mara, who leans back and pivots, avoiding his attack, and punching him in the jaw on his way through. She runs for the door only to be stopped by the two others, who look to be the farmer's teenage sons, with their rifles raised. Behind them, Mara sees Rab and Matze practically throw the injured protester over the gate, then help Susie over as well. They pile into the van which takes off, the side door still open and Susie standing in its frame.

Mara edges backwards, her hands up. The last thing she sees is the big farmer picking up his rifle and its butt coming straight towards her head.

**

Zina tightens the gloves around her wrists. She can't move her fingers because of the tape around them. She can't even feel the tips of her fingers because the tape is so tight. With the gloves secured in place, her hands feel like two enormous round bricks. She wonders how she can lift these high enough to protect her face, or gather the strength to swing a glove. She imagines trying to punch and falling forward with the weight of the glove, face-first into the canvas, down for the count without even being hit.

59

She is nine years old and not yet taller than the ring's top rope.

Her mother is sitting in the stands; managing to both approve of this activity and seem bored by it. Two days later, her mother would be gone, without a goodbye, leaving just about all her stuff behind, but no note.

"How's that feel?" Zina asks.

The baggy trunks go almost to her ankles. The padded helmet narrows her entire view of the world down to a small slit. Zina is kneeling in front of her. She looks at the intricate weaving of her coach's cornrows, counting the beads.

"Hey! How's that feel?"

"Heavy."

"Raise them up. Thumbs at your temples."

She does so, but it's not easy. She holds them up as long as she can, wanting to please Zina.

"That's it. You look fine. Fightin' fine."

The zebra-shirted referee says, "One minute, girls."

Lowering the gloves to her sides is a massive relief. They nearly reach the canvas. She feels their heft pulling her shoulders forward.

She's suddenly afraid; bathroom emergency scared.

"Zina, I need to go."

"There's no time for that. Stand up straight and listen to me. Hey! Listen to me. You see that girl over there?" Zina gestures with a slight move of her head to the red corner, to the girl who's taller than the top rope and shifting her weight keenly from one leg to the other, tapping her gloves together. "She's you. Right? She's your reflection. Like, a mirror. You don't need to be scared. Because you're fighting yourself. You understand? Boxing is all about overcoming your fears and managing your fears, and all that fear is inside you. You're scared to get hit. I know. It's going to hurt. You could get hit so hard, you'll lose the fight and you won't even remember it. And you're scared you might hit your opponent so hard, she doesn't remember it. Fear. It's good. It'll help you. Use it to your advantage."

"Yes, Zina."

"Good, good. I'm proud of you, Mara. You're brave just to step into the ring. You'll learn so much in here. Don't run away from it. Embrace it. You ready?"

She isn't, but she nods, the headgear moving on her head.

Zina jams in the yellow mouthguard that makes her feel she has

60

a wedge of lemon in her mouth. She can't even get her top lip over it.

"Go on," Zina says, standing up. "Have fun, kid."

She goes to the centre of the ring. The zebra rapidly says a whole lot of stuff, like he's reading off a list he memorised, but she doesn't hear it. She's looking up at her opponent, right in the eyes. Her knees feel weak.

They tap gloves and the bell rings.

It starts out with them circling each other, settling in. She copies her opponent, mirroring her movements. Shouts come from the red corner and the stands. It all gets lost, becomes noise.

The other girl attempts a few cautious jab-and-retreats. She manages to get out of the way of these, just, with two of the jabs brushing the side of her headgear.

Then, something happens inside her. The gloves feel suddenly light, her legs strong.

She sees the fourth jab-and-retreat coming and moves aside at the last moment, getting slightly to the left of her opponent and driving a right into her exposed side. The resulting "ooof" is brilliantly loud. The red mouthguard comes out with it and the opponent is doubled over, gloves clutching at the point of contact, helmeted head exposed.

She looks to the blue corner and sees Zina mimic hitting herself in the head.

She pulls back her right hand to wind up the punch, but her opponent falls to her knees. The zebra steps between them and begins a count. She's sent back to her corner. There, Zina is both happy and disappointed.

In the stands, her mother is talking to a man who sits one row down. Neither is watching the fight.

After a count to six, her opponent is ready to go again. The zebra calls them back to the middle.

She's expecting another jab-and-retreat, but what she gets is a solid right in the middle of her forehead.

It feels like her legs have somehow melted into the canvas, because that's where she ends up, on her back, with more and more fingers appearing on the zebra's hand as he bends over her. She wants to get up, but the canvas is rather comfortable and her legs aren't responding. At ten, the zebra sweeps an X through the air and raises one of the opponent's arms.

61

She looks towards the stands, where her mother and the man are still talking, eyes only on each other.

Then, it's Zina over her, taking the lemon out of her mouth and removing the headgear. Zina has a wet towel and is smiling as she dabs this against her throbbing forehead. The wet towel feels so good.

*****

The first thing is the smell.

Pigs.

A farm.

Shit on her hands.

A rifle to the head.

She opens her eyes. Everything is blurry and slowly takes form. She's outside. It's Tuesday morning.

Someone is dabbing a wet towel against her forehead. It stings, making her wince, but she doesn't quite have the facility to move back to avoid the towel. There's some kind of breakdown between brain and body.

Next to her is a woman, dipping the towel into a steel bucket, then pressing it to her head.

It's hazy, but she can make out two people herding pigs back into the barn.

The woman, who looks about 60, but could be 20 years younger, doesn't smile. She tends to Mara with an air of servitude, providing this care as if expected to. The floral-patterned kerchief over her hair and flouncy, layered dress send her back in time nearly a century.

Things become clearer. Mara feels able to move more, to breathe. A deep inhale through her nose makes her realise that the awful smell is her. This shock makes her want to stand up in embarrassment, to put more distance between her and the woman. But she can't move. She's taped to the chair. To her right sits the big farmer, lumped in a plastic chair the legs of which are bending outward, and dressed now in a pair of dark green overalls.

Pig daddy, Mara thinks, wanting to be free of the chair so she can attack him.

The woman puts a large band-aid on her forehead, pressing it down hard enough to make Mara move backwards.

"Hold still," the woman says, with an accent.

The band-aid stuck, the woman stands up, grabs the bucket and heads into the house.

"Uh, thanks?" Mara turns to the farmer, who's holding her ID card in his meaty hands. "Get this tape off me. This is officially kidnapping."

"Mara Steinbach," he says in a rather high-pitched voice. "Any relation to Richard Steinbach?"

Mara looks around, then squints into the distance, towards the road. "Is this Moorfleet?"

"Tatenberg." He thumbs behind him. "Moorfleet's not far away. Other side of the canal."

So that's why I recognised the road coming here, she thinks. "You know Richard?"

"Everyone around here knows Richard."

She feels her strength coming back. She flinches against the tape, which holds firm.

"The question is," the farmer continues, "what's he to you?"

"He's my father."

The farmer chews on this, then takes out his phone. Mara can just hear a ring signal, then it's answered.

"Hello, Richard. It's Bernd."

Mara lets out a groan and struggles again with the tape.

"Yes, I'm fine, thank you. No, no trouble. Well, nothing significant. Not since you helped us out." Bernd looks at Mara as he says this, then turns away and watches his boys, still in pyjamas, herding the pigs. "Look, I've got someone here who says she's your daughter. Mara?"

She can hear her father's muffled voice, but can't catch what he's saying. She looks at the farmer's sons. The taller one is now driving a tractor, while the shorter one is looping a rope around a pig's legs. This pig is prone on the ground, not moving, and it appears the boys' solution is to drag the pig back into the barn using the rope and tractor.

"That's cruel," she says.

"No, sorry, Richard. I can't drive her over to your place. You'll have to come get her. Don't worry. She's not going anywhere. Right. See you soon."

Bernd pockets his phone.

"See? Now, tape off."

"You're going to stay like that until Richard comes."

"I think I'd rather you call the police."

"You would prefer to be arrested than see your father?"

"Don't turn it back on me," Mara says. "I know why you don't want the police. Nothing official, right? You wouldn't want them seeing this place and me being questioned. I've been assaulted and tied up against my will."

"I just defended my property from an invader."

"I'm not a threat. I'm not here to steal anything."

Bernd stands up, with the chair's legs springing back straight, making the chair hop once. "I can't believe you're his daughter. How far this apple fell from the tree."

"You don't know him as well as I do."

"I know he's a good man. Helped many of us out here. Never asks for anything in return."

"Not even a pig?"

"He's vegan. But you know him so well, you know that, right?"

"Still? I thought that might have just been a phase. But it makes me wonder why he would help you, given the state of things here."

"I'd say you're the one going through a phase. What the hell was all that about? Breaking into my farm."

"Honestly? I had no idea what we were doing. I agreed to protest, sure, I'll admit that, but I thought we'd be picketing out the front."

"You lot used to do that," Bernd says. "Camp at my gate and make a media circus. Richard made sure it stopped. Got an injunction. Or something. This is a government-subsidised farm."

"So that's how you become a local hero."

"He got all those cameras installed." Bernd points towards the front gate. "You're caught on it."

"That explains why all the others had balaclavas. I'm innocent in all of this."

"You attacked me with a rake."

"I was helping my friend. And like I said, I had no idea what I was getting into. I just reacted to what was happening. You fired the first shot."

Bernd shakes his head and starts to walk away, in the direction of his boys. The tractor-rope method is doing the trick, despite the horrific, protesting squeals of the pig.

"Get this fucking tape off me," Mara shouts.

Bernd stops and turns. "You know, you've got a real mouth on you. I would've thought any daughter of Richard's would be more polite and educated."

Mara's joyful realisation that she's speaking freely again, after years of holding her tongue, or trying to, on duty, makes her crank it up a notch.

"You prefer your women tending to you like servants? Keep a wife like you keep your pigs?"

"Now, hang on."

"Let me guess. She's not from around here. Shipped in from Poland or Belarus? Or further east? What did that cost you?"

Bernd waves a big hand in disgust at Mara and trudges away. She's left alone, taped to the chair, forehead throbbing, stinking of every possible pig-related odour, and waiting for her father. She can't imagine what might possibly be worse. The clouds gathering overhead promise rain. To get stuck in a downpour would just be the icing on the cake.

Fuck Susie, she thinks, who I saved so many times in juvie, and again today. She didn't even consider saving me. Just ran for it.

Trying to hold her head steady hurts too much. She cranes her neck back, to look up at the sky. This helps reduce the throbbing, but she has to close her eyes against the light.

She can't fight the tape, so she accepts that her father is coming and tries her best to be present in this moment.

Time passes.

When she moves her head back into position, she sees all the pigs are in the barn. Bernd and his boys, now dressed in green overalls of their own, head off to do other farm work. There's no sign of Bernd's wife, or partner, or mail-order fiancé, or whatever she is. But Mara does hear noises coming from inside the house, plus some occasional singing, which sounds Polish.

She looks towards the gate, wondering if her father even owns a car these days, while harbouring mixed feelings about wanting him to arrive and wanting him to keep his judgemental self out of this.

The sound of thumping footsteps makes her turn her head. Richard comes around the side of the house, eating an apple, a broad hat on his head. His rubber boots are covered in mud and he's wearing a huge raincoat that falls to below his knees. He stops in front of her.

"Oh, daughter of mine," he says, taking another bite of the apple.

"Did that apple fall from the tree all on its own?"

Richard nods. He looks relaxed, happy, pleased with himself. He has more white in his beard than the last time she saw him, making him look suitably professorial, and older. Out here, Mara thinks the beard-hat-coat-boots combo makes him look like a mad recluse.

"So did these," he says, pointing at the bulges in his pockets. "I'm thinking apple pie."

"Sounds great. Get this tape off me and I'll help you make it."

Richard picks up Mara's ID card and sits down on the plastic chair. He's far enough behind her that she has to twist uncomfortably to see him.

"While I've got you here, securely in place," he says, "maybe you can tell me what this is all about. What have you been up to for the last, hmm, how many, six months?"

"Keeping Berlin safe."

"Good luck with that. Berlin's addicted to turmoil. A city with conflict deep in its roots. A city that's not happy unless there's some kind of drama."

"Blah, blah, blah. Get to the point."

"You were in Berlin, and now you're here. On Bernd's farm. Tied up like a criminal. How did that happen?"

"I can explain."

"Bernd's a good man. His wife makes a solyanka to die for. What are you doing here messing with their lives?"

"I heard you helped him out," Mara says. "Have you turned yourself into everyone's go-to lawyer out here?"

Richard finishes the apple and tosses the core towards a nearby bush. "It's good to see you, Mara. How are you?"

"Fantastic. It's my favourite thing to be taped to a chair at Bernd the Butcher's farm."

"Yes. You look comfortable, twisting around like that. You're bleeding through the bandage too."

"Just get me out of here. I think I need stitches."

"I can get Remy to sew you up. He did a wonderful job with Felix a few months ago."

"Who's Felix?"

"My dog. He's running around somewhere in the cornfields

66

behind the house."

"Since when do you have a dog?"

"He was a stray Remy picked up."

Mara, fed up with contorting herself to talk to her father, looks forward. "Wait. Remy's a vet? You want to take me to a vet?"

"We could go to the hospital, but then you'd have to explain how this happened. Then the police might be called. My good friend Bernd might get in trouble. I don't want my good friend Bernd getting in trouble."

"Yeah, he's such a good guy, to knock me out with his rifle and make me his prisoner. So kind."

"I'm sure he had his reasons." Her father stands in front of her. "Hold still."

He produces a skinny-bladed knife, that might be used to gut fish, from his pocket, and cuts Mara free.

"You stink," she says.

"Speak for yourself."

"I've been rolling around with the pigs. What's your excuse?"

"I've been tramping in the mud. Come on."

Richard starts walking back around the house. Mara follows, rubbing at where the tape was stuck to her wrists.

"You don't want to use the front gate?" she asks.

"Not with the cameras down there. We'll take the back way." He stops to look at Mara's sneakers. "You might get dirty. In fact, you will get dirty. Fortunately, it won't make you stink more than you already do."

"Great."

"Try to keep up."

Richard leads the way. He whistles. Felix, an unidentifiable mixed breed sporting several shades of brown, comes running. The dog, filthy and loving it, knows where to go and gets ahead of them on the narrow track that follows a creek under the cover of trees. The water is tinged bright green and teems with insects. Felix snaps at the air trying to catch the horseflies.

Mara's shoes sink into the soft dirt, so far that she feels cold mud go over the lips of the heels and down inside the shoes. With the pig smell, the crud on her hands and the muck on her shoes, she resigns herself to being dirty, but can't embrace it quite as fully as Felix.

Richard sets a brisk pace, sticking to this sheltered path, which feels a long way from any road. Mara lets him get far enough ahead to prevent conversation.

When they reach the Tatenberger Schleuse, the only bridge over the Dove Elbe canal in Moorfleet, it feels like a return to civilisation. Richard's already over the bridge. Mara is tempted to let him go; to sit down at the next station and bus it back to St Pauli.

Or is there a chance Anthony is hiding out at the house?

She jogs over the bridge to catch up to her father, leaving a trail of mud behind her. Some blood trickles down her nose. She wipes it away with her sleeve.

"What about Remy?" she asks. "I need a cut-man, for animals or humans."

"You're in no condition to enter his examination room. He keeps it spotless."

"Call him."

"I will. From the house. I'm not using a phone out here."

"Thanks."

"You can get cleaned up there as well. Make yourself presentable before Remy arrives. All your old clothes are still there." He appraises her, then adds, "They should still fit."

They walk for a while in silence, which Richard breaks: "Feel free to tell me what you were doing at Bernd's farm."

"Let's just say Susie led me down another bad path."

"Hah. No surprise there. What are you doing hanging out with her?"

"Good question."

"That fabulous little fool. That manic pixie nightmare elf."

"Stop it."

"What kind of fool do you have to be to follow a fool like her?"

She can't stand it when he talks like this, as if he's orating to a full courtroom or lecture theatre; performing and loving the sound of his own voice.

They leave the road and take the straight dirt track to the house. It's only now, off the street and close to home, that Richard removes his broad hat. His hair is still dark and full, and seems at odds with the white beard, as if parts of his head are ageing at different rates.

The hulking, slightly aslant thatched-roof house is not a place of good memories for Mara. It's a monument to when things went wrong. A converted barn that required layers of clothing in winter;

68

that her father obsessively shaped into his own living space, clean and organised, with little thought given to her and Anthony. The move out here came when she was 15 and feeling different every day; when her only constant had been the firm smack of a glove against the heavy bag or an opponent's head. Then, a one-two combo that came from nowhere sent her spiralling down. First, Zina was transferred to Stuttgart for reasons that seemed consequential at the time, but which Zina never explained. Second, Richard left Lersner-Löwe and transformed overnight from a suit-wearing standard of law and justice to a rubber-boot-wearing conspiracy theorist who thought the government was watching him. Mara refused to change schools, which meant a one-hour slog on public transport every morning and afternoon to the Gymnasium in Othmarschen, until she stopped seeing the point in going. It was more fun to get in trouble and raise hell; to take all of Zina's training out of the ring and into the world, and do something bad enough to be sent away from the Moorfleet house.

Juvie, which was a relief. Reform school, which she didn't attend. A succession of low-paying menial jobs, none of which she could stick at. Tagging along with Susie and her leftist friends, to protests and football games, and pretty much living on the street, a day at a time, because she had no idea what else to do.

The entrance is shadowed by a rigged awning that flutters in the wind. The front door has three locks, and her father puts the keys in and unlocks them, working from bottom to top, hunched over like a crazy scientist entering his secret lab. He looks behind him with each lock click to see if anyone's watching.

Only Mara is watching, and what she sees is worrying.

Felix plonks himself in the basket by the door, panting, relishing an outdoor high as only a dog can.

From the way Richard lets himself in, and how he's dressed, the expectation would be that the inside of the house would be a chaotic reflection of that. But it's incredibly tidy.

"Shoes off," he orders, taking his own boots off and placing them in a paper-lined wicker basket. He hangs up his coat and digs the apples out of its pockets.

"I know the rules."

"Socks too. Straight into the bath with you."

"Sir, yes, sir."

Mara thinks her father has lost a fair bit of weight since she last saw him, which is further cause for worry.

"Don't get smart with me," he says. "Not after I just rescued you."

Mara gets down to her bare feet, which are also dirty. She follows her father on tiptoes, trying not to leave any tracks and scared to touch anything. Richard goes into the kitchen and drops the apples in the sink.

"I'll call Remy," he says, vigorously washing the apples, then his hands. "You'll probably have about half an hour before he gets here. Maybe a bit less. I want you ready and presentable."

"Are you trying to set me up with him? Can't he order himself a wife from out east, like Bernd did?"

"Your time in Berlin has damaged you. All these prejudices and this general nastiness. Bernd met Svetlana on holiday in Spain."

"Sure he did."

While the comment rankles, Mara thinks her father might have a point, that Berlin did change her, and not for the better.

"Where are my clothes? I don't think what I have on can be saved. Pig doesn't come out in the wash, does it?"

Richard goes to a closet and pulls out a large box. "You should find something in here. Don't be shy. Let Remy see your figure. You look good, Mara. You've filled out a bit. You're more shapely."

Annoyed, she pushes the sleeves up of her reeking, blood-stained hoodie and rummages in the box. "Where's Ant?"

"I knew it." Her father looks like he wants to punch a wall. "When Bernd called me, I sat here staring into my tea for a good hour thinking about what I would say, because I knew you would ask. Why don't you ask him yourself? Why aren't you out looking for him?"

"I tried calling. No answer."

They stare at each other, old battle lines being redrawn, both digging their heels in and getting ready for a fight. The remnants of all the arguments they had in this house seem etched into the ceilings and walls. The house scarred by shouting.

Mara, wondering how much her father knows, waits to be blamed for everything that's ever gone wrong with Anthony.

"Your brother left," he says, "A few months ago."

"What? Where's he living? Is he still going to school?"

"I can't answer that."

"Can't or won't?"

70

"I don't know where he is."

"You don't seem very worried."

"He's just doing what you did. Going wild."

"That's not how it was with me."

Richard paces around a little. "He was so set on the basketball scholarship. It was all he could talk about. Half his bags were packed. But then something happened. He started missing practice. He wasn't at school. Then he was gone."

"Did you try calling him?"

"What do you think?"

"I think you don't like using the phone."

"Of course, I called him. Every day."

Mara has found jeans and a hoodie in the box she can wear. "That makes me think he answered."

"He said he was fine. He was just … reassessing. Getting his priorities straight." Richard hands her a towel, flattened into a compact square. "He stopped answering a few weeks ago."

"Sounds like he met someone. Or made new friends? You know how he is. The marching Ant. If he starts worshipping someone, he'll follow them to the end. Until he finds someone else."

"He used to worship you."

"That was a long time ago."

Mara tries to recall the bodycam footage; to envision that second protester as a lanky, stretched-out, tomboyish, basketball-playing girl. Someone Ant would easily fall for.

"He's 18," Richard says. "He really can do what he wants. I'm glad he hasn't gone to America. That country's an absolute mess. He'd probably get shot on his first day on campus."

"You're so dramatic. Going to the States is the only thing he's ever wanted. College ball. The NBA."

"I can't force him. Lord knows I could never force you to do anything. Not even when you were 15. I'd say one thing and you'd do the opposite."

"I landed on my feet, eventually."

"But that doesn't quite track with you standing here with a split forehead, stinking of pig and messing up my floor. Does it?"

Mara turns and heads for the bathroom, no longer on tiptoes. She closes the door and strips off. Without a plastic bag handy, and surely not a piece of plastic anywhere in the house, she lays the inside-out

71

hoodie on the floor and puts the rest of her clothes on top. She ties this into a bundle using the hoodie's sleeves.

"Burn it," she says to herself.

The water is hot and feels good, until she puts her head under it and her forehead sends a stinging wave of pain through her body. Burning pain, coloured red. She manages to get the band-aid off and wash her hair. Finished, she towels dry, then balls up the towel to hold to her forehead, taking it away to inspect the wound in the mirror. It's a perfect crevice, from between her eyes almost to her hairline. Even with good stitches, she knows she'll be left with a scar.

Dressed, her figure hidden under baggy clothes, she presses the towel to her forehead and goes into the kitchen, where a man is sitting at the table. He's quietly handsome, about her age, but reluctant to meet her eyes. His shoulders slump forward, and his head dips a little, like he's trying to hide, or as if someone's just told him off.

There's no sign of her father.

"Are you the vet?"

"Yes, I'm Remy. Dr Remy." He stands up quickly, almost knocking the chair over. "Or just Remy. If you like. Whatever you want."

She removes the towel. "Why are you so jumpy? I'm the one with the front of my head cracked open."

Remy looks away. "That's a nasty gash."

"Can you fix it?"

Remy busies himself with his leather medical bag, which is large, old-fashioned and opens like an upright clam shell. The first thing he takes out is a bottle of vodka.

"Wow," Mara says. "Nothing says qualifications quite like Russian anaesthetic."

"This is for me." Remy takes the top off the bottle and has a swig. "I hate the sight of human blood." Another swig. "That's why I dropped out of medicine to focus on animals."

"They bleed too."

He has one more drink, then holds the bottle towards her. She takes it and has a mouthful.

"It's like battery acid," she says, coughing.

Remy starts taking things out of his bag, lining them up on the table. His hands shake a little.

"Are you sure you can do this?" Mara asks.

72

"I guess we'll find out. Do you have a spirit animal?"

"Pardon?"

"It'll be easier for me to imagine you as an animal. What do you want to be? What animal do you like the most?"

"A dragon."

Remy shakes his head. "That's not helpful. Can't you be a rabbit or a cat?"

"Fine. I'll be a cat. A tiger. Whatever it takes to get this done. Can we get started?"

"I'm picturing you as a tiger cub. How's your pain threshold?"

"I used to box. Hamburg champ, under 12s and 14s. There's a pile of trophies and belts, somewhere in this house."

"Impressive."

"I've been stitched up often enough to know what it involves."

Upon hearing this, Remy has another drink.

"Slow down, doc, or you won't be able to hold the needle steady."

"Please, don't hit me."

"I might roar at you, in tiger fashion."

"Just no hitting."

The local anaesthetic is the hard part. Remy runs through a gamut of disgusted expressions as he looks at, and then looks away from, Mara's forehead. But his hands are steady, even if his eyes aren't fully on the job. Mara grits her teeth and grips the chair, just about breaking the arms off as the needle goes in. But once it's out and her forehead goes numb, it's just a matter of coping with the horrible feeling of the thread being pulled taut through her skin.

Remy grimaces throughout, but there's a moment about halfway through where he becomes focused on his work, and it's just another wound to close. Proud of himself, he finishes up and toasts his handiwork with another gulp of vodka. Mara wants some too, but Remy closes the bottle and puts it in his medical bag.

"Not a good idea," he says, "with all the chemicals running through you now. Plus the concussion. How long were you out?"

"Long enough to be taken from a barn and taped to a chair. Hopefully, that was all that happened."

"Bernd's tame. He cries when a pig dies."

"That sure doesn't explain the state those pigs live in."

"You need to see a few more farms. That's a good one. The pigs are outside all day. They're only in the barns at night, to protect them

73

from predators. There are wolves around here, you know?"

"Well, that changes everything. I'll add Bernd to my Christmas card list. Anyway, thanks, Dr Remy, for making me whole again."

Remy sticks a large bandage to her forehead. "Give it two weeks. Maybe ten days. If you come back here, I'll take them out."

"We'll see."

"You could visit my surgery. Maybe, I don't know, see the animals. Or, just off the top of my head, come for lunch?"

Mara feels at the bandage. Her forehead is so numb it seems like the bandage is attached to nothing. "The status of my calendar escapes me right now."

"Don't scratch them," he says. "The stitches."

"Maybe you should give me one of those big cones to put on my head. To stop me from doing that."

"Ha. That'd be something." Remy hands her a stack of bandages, each in its own package. "Put a new one on every day. Like I said, happy to take the stitches out in a couple of weeks."

"I have a feeling Richard would want that. Where is he anyway?"

"He said he was going foraging. His word, not mine."

"Sounds just like him."

Remy packs up his gear.

"Why did you help me?" Mara asks. "I mean, if you can't stand the sight of gory human injuries."

"I owed Richard a favour. Your father's a really good man."

"So everyone around here keeps telling me. What did he do for you?"

Remy just smiles and shrugs. He lingers, perhaps waiting for an invitation to stay, but Mara wants him gone. She suddenly feels like she can't keep her eyes open. The weight of fatigue makes her dizzy. She manages to see Remy to the door and close it on him, then she collapses on the sofa, lying on her back.

The need to use the bathroom wakes her. She sits up, head hurting. The only light comes from the kitchen, just enough of a stream into the living room for her to navigate groggily around the furniture to the bathroom. She notices that its floor is spotless again.

Her headache is on the verge of crippling. It requires cradling her head in a hand, as some evil little miner inside her head tries to drill his way out through her forehead.

With no watch or phone, she has no idea what time it is. Her father never had any clocks in this house, not even when she and Anthony were kids with busy schedules.

It's night. Things become sharper, in the almost darkness.

She moves through the house. In the kitchen, she has a glass of very clear water – the tap has a strange device over it – and a piece of bland apple pie that kills what little appetite she has. The wedges of apple are so soft they feel rotten. She wonders how her father can be so obsessive and picky about his living space, but not about the food he eats, as long as it's vegan.

She finds her father in his study, which was her room. The desk lamp is on, casting a small circle of light on the big desk.

Richard is asleep in the chair, bending forward, his head cradled in his arms on the desk, the way a university student might nap in a library. His laptop is still on. She lightly rouses him and guides him to the sofa, where he lays down, head on a pillow. She covers him with the blanket, hating herself for not feeling the love she perhaps should.

Like the rest of the house, the room is very tidy and organised. Everything has its place. Along one wall, black arch files fill a shelf, each one labelled on the spine. It's too dark to read the labels, but she doesn't want to know the contents. All those theories and the pile of supporting evidence. No doubt one or more of those files is dedicated to what started it all off: her father's Holocaust theory, that the number of people murdered by the Nazis in World War II was actually much higher, and governments covered this up out of fear the potential retributions would set off another war. As if six million wasn't an incredibly high number already, worthy of revenge.

She sits at the desk and looks at the laptop.

The chair is warm.

Richard is working on some kind of article, or perhaps a paper for a university publication. The title is "Revolution and the Pursuit of Happiness". There is only one paragraph so far:

Throughout history, people who desired to change the world, to unseat leaders from power and instigate a new way, did so motivated primarily by their own personal situations. Rousing the masses requires broad thinking, to demonstrate the revolution is good for the populace, but each individual revolutionary joins a particular cause with their own situations front and centre in their minds. "What's in it for me?" "How will my life improve and that of my family?" And importantly, "Will I have more?" Which is why nearly all revolutions have been driven by economics. The very few have very much and those who have little want to change this, because they want to have their share; proof that a revolution is as much about greed as it is about equality. In the fair and just societies of modern Europe, where people seldom fall through the cracks and are left with so little they want to fight and get their share, it would seem the basis for revolution in any form no longer exists. This is not true. While people have money and security, it is now those very things that people want to react against. They have become prisoners of their own security, lulled into placidity and under constant surveillance. Governments and leaders, as well as companies and corporations, know this. It is security, financial and societal, that maintains the status quo and enables governments to implement soft forms of suppression. However, feeling secure is not a thing that people can believe in, nor may they think it's something wholly theirs. It is also not a given that security leads to happiness. Quite the opposite. Security leads to stagnation and depression. It is situational, not emotional. Money is a wonderful thing, but it doesn't make a person happy. Thus, the next revolution, which could easily sweep through Europe once condensed into a rhetoric – a community cause – everyone understands, will be about happiness. And the man who might be this revolution's leader is Milan Kollar.

She turns to look at her sleeping father and shakes her head a little.

"Seriously?"

She folds the laptop shut and leaves the study.

"Happiness? God."

The door to Anthony's room is still covered in hip-hop posters, plus the "KEEP IN" sign her father attached to the door years ago, hoping to ensure Anthony's mess didn't extend beyond this room.

The switch just inside the door clicks, but no light comes on. She finds a bike light on the shelf and sweeps its beam across the room. The trophies glint in the light. It's a bombsite of clothes, books, basketball gear, garbage and tech, and she wonders how her father manages to live with it. Keeping the door shut doesn't change how this room is.

It seems like a long time since Anthony was here.

But the bike light suggests there is a bike, somewhere. She locates the red rear light for it and heads out the house's back door. Sure enough, there's a mountain bike leaning against the wall, unlocked. It's too big for her, even with the seat as low as it can go, but she attaches the lights and starts pedalling, down the narrow track and out onto the road.

It feels good to be moving away from the house, but she rides slowly, still dizzy and hurting.

She takes the familiar Moorfleeter Hauptdeich cycle path that cuts the ride to Rothenburgsort in half. There are no streetlights, allowing her to see plenty of stars.

No traffic visible on the A1 as she rides towards the underpass. No noise, except the clink and clatter of the bike's stiff chain, which needs oil. No birds on the river to the right. No one else on this path. She assumes it must be very early morning, maybe not long after midnight.

As she rides, she thinks the whole time about the desire for happiness igniting a revolution.

The bike lights die when she reaches the Hafen City area. A digital clock near Lohsepark reads 0312.

Not seeing a single person on the ride makes her feel joyously alone, as if Hamburg is hers and hers only. Unlike Berlin, which seems to have a whole substratum of people who only come out at night.

Her solitary ride ends in St Pauli, where there are some people on the street and clustered around the bars. There's an atmosphere of people holding onto the night rather than revelling in it.

A pair of police officers outside Davidwache stop her for not having lights on her bike and want to give her a ticket. She explains the batteries died and she's almost home anyway, but they still order her to walk the rest of the way. The two cops follow her, to ensure she complies, which she thinks is a bit much, given what other crimes are potentially happening down the Reeperbahn's side streets.

It's a relief to arrive at Hamburger Berg. She hauls the bike up the stairs, the tyres leaving the odd black streak on the already dirty walls. There's space for it on the landing, but without a lock, the bike wouldn't last long. She parks it just inside the door, and it's good there, as one more thing in her apartment.

In the bathroom, she washes her hands and cups some water to drink. With one half of the bandage carefully peeled off, she gets a glimpse of Dr Remy's handiwork in the mirror. The stitches are neat, but she's not sure she wants him taking them out; though she could use that as an excuse, in ten days' time, to check up on her father. She presses the bandage back down.

In the living room, she writes HAPPINESS on one of the notepads, but can't remember the person Richard named as the revolution's supposed leader.

She's been gone nearly 24 hours and can't be bothered to look at her phone. She does check the flip phone, which has a message from Perceval: "Meet, 0700, Sternschanze station."

"Ah, fuck."

She replies: "OK. Bring a dog."

The alarm clock gets set for 0630. She kicks her shoes off, lies down on her back fully clothed and tries to sleep.

***

The trains rumble overhead, screeching in and out of Sternschanze station every few minutes. The noise makes her wince, but the pain is manageable; it's a dark shade of orange, vaguely warm. Not enough to require any painkillers. She's proud to have maintained that promise to Zina. But it sure was tempting for her last night to find an open pharmacy and get something for the pain.

The streets are already busy: vehicles, bikes, people, everyone up early and going somewhere. Again, she's fascinated by how dogs seem to be the on-trend accessory in the Schanze.

Perceval arrives on a yellow bicycle that has broad handlebars and a wooden box on the front. Inside the box is a tiny dog, shaking

78

ever so slightly. Perceval is wearing the blue tracksuit of a sports club. Near the left shoulder is ETC, the club's initials, and two table tennis bats crossed at the handles.

Mara and the dog look at each other.

"Morning," Mara says. "You call this a dog?"

"Her name is Madonna, and she is a hound of excellent pedigree."

"Take a look around. The local hounds are going to eat her for breakfast."

Perceval looks at her forehead. "You're injured. Explain."

"The result of being involved in a totally ridiculous protest, getting rifle-butted by a pig farmer and stitched up by a vet."

"An eventful first day." Perceval locks the bike to a pole. "Please confirm you are able to continue."

"I'm able. And willing."

"Excellent."

"It might come in handy," she says, pointing at the bandage. "You know, I've already taken one for the team."

"A badge of honour."

"Something like that. Can we walk? I want to show you something."

Perceval lifts Madonna out of the box and cradles her in his left arm. With the tracksuit and miniature dog, he looks like he runs a local hairdressing salon, or a cutting-edge graphic design studio.

"Lead on."

They head up Susannenstraße. Shops are getting set up for the day and locals walk quickly to work. It's a battle for space on the narrow footpath. Many people have their eyes down: over their phones or scanning the path to avoid stepping in something awful.

"The first night," she says, keeping her voice low, "I went to some of the old places. Like you suggested. The scene, at least as I used to know it, is no longer there. Maybe it's gone underground."

"Yet you still found yourself at this protest yesterday."

"I got lucky. I followed a group that came out of a bunker, and they ended up at another bunker, on Otzenstraße. Opposite the red church on the hill."

"The Friedenskirche. My mother used to take me there every Sunday."

"The bunker's off the street, down a short alleyway and behind an apartment building. It's very easy to miss it."

79

"Are we going there presently? Seems more like cycling distance."

"It's too far."

Mara guides Perceval down Schulterblatt and past the Rote Flora. Some people stare at Perceval, like he might be some kind of eccentric minor celebrity.

"Up here," Mara says. "Into the park. You can let Madonna run around a bit."

"She will do no such thing. She's adverse to exercise."

In the park, they sit down on a bench. Madonna sits quietly next to Perceval, looking like the entire world bores her.

In front of them is the huge bunker that's been turned into a climbing wall. Mara points at it.

"How is this of interest? Are protesters training as free-climbers for some nefarious purpose?"

"No idea. I think this bunker is used as a squat. The one on Otzenstraße was a meeting point, but a bunch of people spent the night there too. Young protesters. Leftists. I think a lot of them are squatting in the old war bunkers around this area."

"If you're thinking it might be the headquarters for Circus, you are quite wrong. They have a legitimate set-up on Große Elbstraße, near the river. It's called Elbe Help. A donation collection point. But it's Circus, no question."

"Why didn't you say this before? That could've been my starting point."

"You may start there now."

"Something definitely happened at the Otzenstraße bunker. Some kind of meeting."

Perceval strokes his dog. "That would make sense. Protest meetings wouldn't be possible at Elbe Help. That place is bugged all over. I'm certain they are aware of that."

"I got there too late. Whatever meeting they had was already over. But I ran into Susie, an old friend."

"Was it her you joined in protest yesterday?"

Mara nods.

"Very good. These people will converse. They will all know what you did. Your challenge now is to parlay that into more support."

"Right. Parlay."

"Begin by getting involved at Elbe Help."

"Do you know a woman called JJ? She was at the meeting, but not the protest. I think she's the Circus leader."

"Julietta Jabali," Perceval says. "A person of interest. You should make her acquaintance. You will find her at Elbe Help. She is very engaged with the refugees there. The youth volunteers as well. I suggest you apply for a position there."

"On top of the job I already have?"

"Do you require more money?"

"I'm good. For now."

Perceval checks his watch. "Anything else of note?"

"Two names. Gomez and Jesper. Gomez seems to be the leader of a faction within Circus. Younger, hardcore."

"And Jesper?"

"I don't really know who he is. But there's something about him that's off."

Perceval writes these two names on a small notepad with an equally small pencil. "Perhaps he has ulterior motives, like you. He's there for someone else."

"I hadn't thought of that. If he's a spy, who's he spying for?"

"Us, most likely." Perceval puts the notepad away. "Now, to more pressing matters. What about our suspect? What can you report?"

"You're not wasting any time, are you?"

"It is not a luxury we have. Yesterday, in the early evening, I attended a briefing for the next Fridays for Future protest. The police presence will be doubled. The thinking is this is an opportunity for a show of strength."

"Against a bunch of schoolkids who care about the environment?"

"I wanted to voice precisely this, but held back."

"What do you think? Should I join this protest?"

"Indeed, if the others from Circus are involved. I request you find out more regarding the plans for Friday. If Circus knows about the increased police presence, because be certain they have assets of their own, they may decide to bolster their ranks."

"I'll start at Elbe Help."

"Good strategy." Perceval scoops Madonna off the bench and stands up. "Please wait a few minutes, then leave in the opposite direction."

Perceval walks back down to Schulterblatt. When he turns right and disappears behind the Rote Flora, Mara gets to her feet and goes out of the park to Lippmannstraße. With a coffee and a

81

Franzbrötchen from a bakery, she starts the long walk to Große Elbstraße, taking the scenic route through the old cemetery that's now Wohlers Park, then over the pedestrian bridge to Walter-Möller Park. She passes another bunker, at Schomburgstraße, and wonders if that's also used as a squat.

At Fischmarkt, it's high tide. The river's brown water is lapping over the edge of the harbour walls and leaving silty puddles in the car park.

Outside the Elbe Help office is an unmarked truck, its doors open. She goes around the truck to the covered area, noting the "RO" on the license plate that signifies Romania, and has a quick look through the plastic bags and boxes of donations waiting to be sorted. She finds a well-worn black fisherman's beanie and puts this on her head, low enough for the bandage to be hidden underneath. She checks her reflection in the truck's side mirror; the beanie lends her an impoverished edge.

JJ comes down the stairs with a burly man Mara assumes is the truck driver. He climbs inside the back while JJ lifts a roller door on a storeroom of boxes, all of them taped shut with brown packing tape. JJ takes a box and carries it to the back of the truck. Mara copies her. There's a nod of recognition and appreciation from JJ, but nothing more than that. To Mara, it feels like there are clothes in the boxes.

It's hard work, made harder by JJ opening a second roller door on more taped-up boxes.

Once the truck is loaded, the driver, without saying a word, shuts the doors, gets in the cab and drives away. JJ and Mara close the roller doors, then stand there together.

"Thanks," JJ says at last.

"Glad to help."

"Do you need anything? I don't have any money on me."

"Maybe a drink?"

"Sure. Wait here."

JJ goes up the stairs to the office. Mara realises JJ might think she's homeless, or a junkie.

"Time to show the badge of honour," she says to herself.

When Mara hears JJ coming back down the stairs, she takes off the beanie and gives her hair a shake.

"What happened to your head?" JJ asks, handing Mara a bottle of water.

"I was at a protest yesterday. At a pig farm. We got caught by the owners. Well, I did."

"That was you? I heard about someone saving Susie from those farmers. I also heard they had guns."

"Don't I know it. I got the butt of a rifle right to the head."

"You poor girl." JJ steps closer. "Are you all right?"

Mara takes a sip of her water. "Yeah. Better today. I used to box. I can take a hit."

"Did you go to the hospital?"

Mara shakes her head. "Didn't want to get the police involved."

"Smart." JJ takes another step towards Mara and reaches out to her head. "May I? You're bleeding through the bandage."

"That's no surprise. I was stitched up by a vet."

"I think you better come upstairs and let me put on a new one. I used to be a nurse."

"Okay. Thanks."

Mara follows JJ up the stairs. In this old, warehouse-type building, Elbe Help occupies the first floor. There are disorderly cubicles at the entrance, crowded with young people sitting at computers and talking on phones. Stuff everywhere, spilling out of boxes: clothes, toys, books, bathroom products, consumer goods. It feels more like a start-up than a charity. Beyond the cubicles, long tables are set up with sewing machines, many of them buzzing away, men and women in just about equal number sitting in front of them. She spots Susie.

JJ leads Mara into a small office. While JJ looks for the first aid kit, Mara goes to the window. From here, she looks down on a T-shaped jetty where the tugboats are moored. They have huge rubber sides and names evoking strength, like "Atlas" and "Samson". Beyond the jetty is the broad expanse of the Elbe and the busy backdrop of the harbour, container ships in the docks and red-blue cranes unloading them. She can just make out the specks of people, on the ships' bridges and working on the docks, and they seem so tiny as not to be real. A ferry slices down the river's middle, its open top level packed with people and the enclosed lower lever empty.

JJ puts the first aid kit on the desk. "Sit down."

"Great view," Mara says, sitting on the desk's chair, the only one in the office. She tries to get a look at the papers on the desk, but can't make much out.

"I never get tired of it," JJ says.

"You don't know how much you've missed something until you're standing in front of it again. You can try to remember it, but it's only when you look at it and it looks back at you that it really hits. You know?"

"Humans are adaptable. Close your eyes." JJ sprays disinfectant on the bandage. "We learn to live without things. Did you grow up around here?"

Mara winces a little, as JJ slowly peels off the bandage, clotted blood pulling at the stitches. "Up on the hill. In Othmarschen."

"Ah. A local rich kid."

Mara grimaces, not with pain, but because she's not thinking hard enough about what she's saying. She's face to face with JJ. This is her chance.

"I wouldn't say rich," she says. "We managed. Then my father decided to stop working and moved us out of the city."

The bandage is off. It has a blackish-red line down the middle. JJ sprays disinfectant on the wound and this stings. Mara breathes out slowly, riding the pain.

"Relax," JJ says. "They're good stitches."

"Yeah, so, when we moved, then life really became a day-to-day proposition. My brother and I, we pretty much fended for ourselves, and Anthony was just a little kid."

"What about your mother?"

Mara notices that name-dropping Anthony results in no recognition from JJ, who is poker-faced as she dries away the disinfectant.

"She left. When I was nine."

"That must've been very hard."

"It was. But I think it was hardest for my father. He was never really the same after that."

JJ nods. "Children, you know. It's amazing how much they pick up on. So many adults think that children have no awareness of what's going on. But they get it. Maybe they can't put it into words, but they get it."

"Anthony was a baby when she left. I guess you could say I raised him."

"You guess?" JJ peels the back off a fresh bandage and sticks this on Mara's forehead with a gentle touch.

"I'm not sure I want to take full responsibility for how he turned out."

"How did he turn out?"

Mara fights the emotions she's feeling and tries to lock them down inside. "I don't know yet. It's too soon to tell. Thanks for the fresh bandage."

"The least I can do. You'll have a nice scar though. A vertical line, to make some corners with the horizontal worry lines you already have."

"Look closely and you'll see other scars." She points, with both index fingers. "Check out the matching set on my eyebrows."

"Boxing?"

"That area splits so easily. And it's trouble, because you bleed into your eyes."

JJ packs up the first aid kit, snapping it shut with a finality that Mara takes as a cue to leave.

"Sweat and blood stings," Mara adds, "when it combines."

"Do you still box?"

"No, but my old club is down the street. If it's still there."

"It is. We made a few punching bags for them, out of old clothes. That is, if we're talking about the same place."

"The giveaway would be Gus. He must be 80-something, by now."

The mention of Gus's name makes JJ smile. Mara can't help but stare, as the smile renders JJ strikingly beautiful.

"He's still there."

JJ moves aside, to allow Mara passage out from behind the desk and towards the doorway.

"Thanks for your help earlier," JJ says.

"No problem." Mara stands up. "Look, I'm not sure exactly what you're doing here, but can I pitch in? You can call Gus if you want. He'll vouch for me. At least, for the 14-year-old me who knocked over everyone in her age group."

"Do you know how to use a sewing machine?"

"Nope. But I'm dying to learn."

"That level of eagerness is much higher than anyone else shows in here. I think we better put that energy to use."

JJ leads the way out of the office. Mara follows.

They go between the cubicles to the sewing section. The buzzing grows louder. JJ stops at the table where Susie, sitting on three

85

pillows and wearing a shoe with a block of foam attached so she can reach the machine's pedal, is hunched over, her nose inches from her work.

"Can you give this novice a crash course?" JJ asks.

Susie doesn't look up. "Oh, come on, JJ. Why do you always ask me to do this? I'm busy."

"I think you owe her."

Susie stops. "Mara!"

She jumps up and hugs Mara, nearly making them both fall over because of that foam block under one shoe.

When Mara pulls back, she sees JJ already walking away.

"I was so worried," Susie says. "We thought, I don't know, you were in jail. Or something."

"What happened to the guy who got hurt? Is he all right?"

"We dumped him at the hospital. Said he was in a bike crash. Broken collarbone."

"Lucky."

"Yeah, that Rab and Matze saved him. Another minute on the ground and the pigs would've started eating him."

"Yuck. They already looked so over-fed."

Susie sits back down. "I'm sorry I took off like I did. I thought you'd get away. Deck the guy and run."

"Fists are no match for guns."

Susie lowers her voice to a whisper: "We need guns. We go out there with no way to defend ourselves. Look what happens. It's no wonder we get hurt."

Mara points at her forehead. "I guess I was lucky too."

"Did the farmer do that? Is it bad?"

"I'd say I'm in the ideal condition to learn how to sew."

Susie laughs. "It's easy. Sit down at this one, next to me. We're making these little onesies for premature babies." She holds one up. "Aren't they just so cute?"

Mara takes the onesie and looks at it. On the right shoulder, on the back, is a logo: a C inside three circles.

It's a beautiful Friday afternoon, with spring sunshine and blue sky. She joins a huge crowd gathered outside the FC St Pauli fan shop in front of the Millerntor football stadium. There are a lot of young people, excited and energetic. Even some small children, with their parents. Many tote the standard signs and banners: "There is no planet B", "Change the system, not the climate", "Act now or swim later", and so on.

The presence of these kids helps take the edge off, Mara thinks, lessening any sense of danger. The police wouldn't dare attack a protest group this young.

The faces in the crowd have the glossy sheen of middle-class health and security. No strugglers in this lot.

Having spent the last two days mastering the sewing machine at Elbe Help, Mara hangs with the people she worked alongside. This includes a dozen refugees from Afghanistan, Libya and Syria, some student volunteers, and a handful of retirees. They make an eclectic group, made weirder by some of them flexing their fingers and moving their wrists as they talk, their hands stiff and sore from sewing. JJ is nearby with a collection of teenagers; Mara recognises some of them from the cubicles of Elbe Help.

There's no sign of Susie, though Mara isn't looking very hard for her. Instead, she scans the crowd for Gomez and his group, but none of the people here look remotely like hardcore protesters. There's not a balaclava in sight. This is a relief, because even with the strong police presence, it makes her think everything will be all right. She's glad to march along peacefully, to be on this side of the protest.

In Berlin, she had worked numerous Fridays for Future protests, including the one last year that got totally out of hand and turned into a riot. The claim was that right-wing extremist groups had infiltrated the protest and caused disruptions for their own means. However it happened, once the violence and looting started, it spread quickly through the crowd; teens and students turned from peaceful to rowdy in an instant. The police had to respond; they couldn't stand there and let it all happen, despite the crowd's relative youth. Mara joined the lines as the police tried to disperse the protesters. This was deemed as an act of aggression and the protesters responded. After it was all over and she was nursing her wounds back home with Russell, she told him how scary it was that normal people could become violent so quickly and with little provocation, and that the components of an urban environment could so easily become weapons. Not just cobblestones ripped out of the street, but signposts and wooden slats broken off benches were used to attack the police. She even saw two guys lift one of those heavy stands used for temporary street signs and throw it through a shop window.

Looking over this crowd, she wonders if these kids could turn like that.

The walk begins across the broad expanse of Heiligengeistfeld towards Sievekingplatz. As JJ had explained at last night's meeting in the Otzenstraße bunker, large parts of downtown, including Valentinskamp and Jungfernstieg, would be blocked for traffic, allowing the protesters a clear route all the way to Rathausmarkt, where "the kids can wave their banners at city hall and be ignored." Gomez and his group hadn't been at that meeting, making Mara assume they won't be here today.

The mood is relaxed and convivial. More a social event than a protest. Many of the teenagers film each other with their phones; others stop to take selfies. Friends hang out together. The sun is shining. All these youngsters are enjoying being out of school and doing something with purpose.

Mara wants to feel like she's part of it, but she's an observer: police officer on the inside, protester on the outside, and on alert.

The police are waiting to block the traffic at Johannes-Brahms-Platz. A half-dozen motorcycle cops, plus four patrol cars. Horns sound out from the waiting cars as the protesters take their time getting across the intersection, some hurling anti-car epithets in return. But the atmosphere stays light. The horns and angry drivers seem to make the youngsters enjoy themselves more; the city has stopped just for them.

"Hey there, Mara."

"Oh, hey."

"Great to see I made a huge first impression on you. It's Jesper."

"I remember you. I just didn't expect to see you here."

"Why not?"

"You weren't at the meeting last night."

They follow the crowd as it's funnelled towards Valentinskamp.

"What meeting?"

"At the bunker. You didn't know?"

"I guess it was mostly people from Elbe Help, not Circus."

"Are they different?" Mara asks, fishing.

"JJ probably asked for support for all the kids marching today. She always wants that for protests like this." Jesper gives Mara a smile. "I heard you've been volunteering there. At Elbe Help."

"I'm expanding my skills. I'm now adept at using a sewing machine. It's actually been good to work with my hands again. Doing something worthwhile. We made onesies that were donated to a local hospital."

"Better than using your hands to break heads or put cuffs on people. Am I right?"

They look at each, still walking. Despite his aloofness, Jesper doesn't strike Mara as stupid. His sweet, goofy grin is now clearly one of knowledge.

"Susie told you," she says.

"Told me what?"

"You can stop that. I guess everyone knows now."

"I bet you look great in uniform."

"Not anymore. I'm out. I don't see why I should hide that. But I'd rather be the one telling people. Susie's always been a talker."

"She didn't say much about that farm protest. Word is you rescued her, then she didn't do the same for you."

She points at the bandage. "I was the one who got this."

A motorcycle cop zips past them, heading towards the next traffic block at Gänsemarkt.

"You do that too?" Jesper asks. "Biker cop?"

"I always wanted to, but it's hard to get in. Very much a male-dominated thing."

"No surprise."

They walk for a while in silence, shiny-windowed buildings on the left and the bohemian, arty Gängeviertel on the right. Jesper has proven to be a distraction for Mara; she hasn't been monitoring if any groups have blended into the crowd from the side streets. She notices now there are more people aged in their 20s and 30s. They don't appear overtly hardcore; quite a few of the new joiners have dogs with them.

"Why did you quit the police?"

"So I could break into pig farms and get my head split open."

"I warned you."

"No, you didn't," Mara says.

"I told you those eco protests are a waste of time. We should be concentrating on things that make a difference. Things that matter."

"Like climate change?"

"No. This is also a waste of time."

"You're wrong. This matters. The kids are taking a stand, and good on them. They could just sit at home and accept things as they are."

"Or stare at their screens and forget about it all."

"That too. But they're out here, trying to change the world."

"It looks great," Jesper says, "and I like the vibe, but it doesn't change much."

"That's so negative. But it sounds to me like you're just repeating the words of others."

"What the fuck?"

"You're parroting, Jesper. I know this kind of talk well, because Anthony does exactly the same."

"Who's Anthony?"

"He has this annoying habit of copying the rhetoric of the person he likes the most, which changes just about every week. He likes to march in these protests too, but I haven't seen him today."

As with JJ, there's no change to Jesper's face at the mention of Anthony. She's unsure about JJ, but her instincts tell her that Jesper knows Anthony.

They reach Jungfernstieg. Mara's section of the crowd merges with a hardcore group, dressed all in black and spoiling for a fight, waiting at the corner. Along the left side of the street, police vehicles are parked all the way down to the Europa Center shopping mall. The vehicles are the transporters Mara hates, full of police in riot gear in the back. She'd been in them a few times, fully kitted up, the vans sweltering with sweat and anxiety, in that awful atmosphere that seemed to foster aggression and violence.

As they move slowly forward, Mara sees a line of riot police already in place, on Jungfernstieg. They let the young protesters at the front through.

"This is bad," Mara says.

"You know what they're up to?"

As the riot police work to separate the protesters, people start to react against being stopped and pushed back. A few scuffles break out. Reinforcements arrive from the vans. A second line of riot police assembles across Jungfernstieg. Beyond them, kids, parents and people carrying banners continue on towards Rathausmarkt.

"It can't be so bad," Jesper says, as the crowd is halted by the police line. "They don't have any shields today."

"That's part of the strategy. To have both hands free. Attack and arrest."

"Really?"

Mara wants to do something, to maybe grab a bullhorn and tell everyone in the crowd to run for it. The police are clearly here for a fight, and the hardcore elements now mixed in with this crowd are going to give them one. Perceval thought a show of strength meant numbers; Mara sees now it means force.

But it's too late.

Instead of holding the line, the police move forward. All around Mara and Jesper, people are turning around and walking away, while others surge towards the front. Mara wants to run, but she can't with Jesper standing next to her; coward is a label she doesn't want.

The police are massively outnumbered, but are organised and armed. Their black batons swing in the air as they force the protesters back. Any resistance is met with arrest. The police have hoops of plastic cuffs on their belts and put these to swift use, leaving those cuffed on the ground as they continue to drive forward. The second line of police moves the arrested protesters off the street and sits them down on the kerbs. Further down Jungerfernstieg, Mara sees two mobile water cannons heading for this area.

The police are brutal.

Some of those fleeing the police have blood streaming down their faces.

With the police and their batons getting closer, Jesper grabs Mara's arm and pulls her off to the side, to make an escape. They reach the corner of Große Bleichen, where they are confronted by more police. An officer swings his baton at Mara, who braces herself to wear the blow on her left shoulder. There's no chance to think about how much that hurts, because the officer pulls back to swing again. She avoids his blow, elbowing him hard enough to knock his helmet off. She turns to help Jesper, but he's cuffed and being

91

dragged away. She leaps over the fallen cop and runs down Große Bleichen, weaving between the people on this swanky shopping street. She turns once to see she isn't pursued, but continues to run hard, taking a left on Poststraße, then ducking down an alleyway to compose herself.

They're staying on Jungfernstieg, she thinks. That's the order. Keep it contained. Make arrests. Don't leave the street and get isolated.

After a couple of deep breaths, she takes off her black hoodie – fished out from a clothes bag at Elbe Help – and stuffs this into a fancy Alsterhaus shopping bag she finds on the ground. Carrying the bag casually, she walks back down Poststraße towards Rathausmarkt, doing everything she can to get her adrenalin to subside and to appear like just another shopper caught up in this unexpected chaos.

People are going about their daily activities like nothing is happening one block away. Not even the sound of a helicopter can distract them from their shopping, coffees and conversations. Up ahead, Mara can see all the protesters the police let through, gathered in front of city hall, waving their banners and running through their chants, also seemingly unaware of the confrontation on Jungfernstieg.

There are police here, in regular uniforms, guarding the square. The scene is bizarrely calm; she can just hear the sounds of high-powered streams of water hitting asphalt and people shouting.

She detours down Alter Wall, the string bag swinging from a wrist, and finds herself in front of the offices of Lersner-Löwe. It's a potentially spontaneous visit, meaning a bit suspicious, but it's also Friday. She decides to chance it and rings the bell. It takes a few moments, then the door buzzes and she pushes it open.

While the firm's old Gänsemarkt office where her father had worked had a distinctly old-school maritime feel, with harbour prints on the walls and model containers ships under glass, this new location is decidedly upmarket. Everything says money, from the fancy key card entry to bypass the main door to the massive vases on pedestals. Lersner-Löwe has the entire top floor, city views in all directions. The gorgeous receptionist offers Mara a caffe latte, which comes in a tall glass with an equally tall spoon that nearly pokes her in the eye when she sips. The milk's foam is accented with cinnamon. She stays standing, scared to sit in the minimalist Swedish armchairs, which look too deep to get out of without help. She's also scared to touch anything. Just being in here feels somehow disruptive, even if the receptionist continues to flash her toothy magazine-cover smile at her.

Mara expects Nicola to come to the reception area, to this five-star foyer, but after around 15 minutes, the receptionist takes a call, then escorts Mara to the far end of the floor. The receptionist wears big heels with a high-waisted pencil skirt that would be uncomfortable to sit in but might cause a multi-car pile-up if she tried to cross a busy street.

Nicola's corner office is huge. On the glass desk is a massive monitor, more suited to editing films than writing up contracts. Mara lingers in the doorway. There's another vase, this one in swirly purple, on a pedestal in one corner. A cream sofa that looks like it cost more than a small car, plus a basket-type thing hanging from the ceiling that Nicola may sit in while pondering the world, when she's not suing it for all it's got. Nicola sits at the desk, facing away from it in her high-backed navy-blue chair. She's speaking on the phone in Italian, her phone cupped in her hand at chin height.

No files on the shelves. Not a sheaf of paper in sight. It reminds Mara of Spitz, his relentless sustainability kick and his creepiness, and it's a further reminder that she needs to get Russ onto Spitz and have him exposed.

She considers leaving. Nicola appears busy, and it doesn't feel right to be here.

"Si, darling," Nicola says into the phone as she spins around. "Ciao."

She puts the phone on the desk, next to two others, and beckons Mara to come into the office.

"Now this is a surprise." Nicola gets to her high-heeled feet and scoops up her trio of phones. "Perfect timing. I'm starving."

"I'm sorry for showing up uninvited. I was just in the area."

"I'm taking you to Parlament. I have a table there every Friday for lunch."

"I don't think I'm dressed for that place."

Nicola leans back on a heel. "No. That you are not. Especially if you're going to be seen there with me. I've got a reputation to uphold. Fridays are pretty casual at Parlament. But not this casual. What's in the Alsterhaus bag?"

Mara opens it, showing the well-worn hoodie. "Nothing better."

"That combines well with this whole chic-homeless look you're cultivating."

Nicola goes to the closet behind the desk. She takes out a thin grey jacket, holds this up in front of Mara, then takes it off the hanger.

"This'll work," Nicola says, handing the jacket to Mara. "If anyone asks, we'll say you're in advertising. A graphic designer. Something arty. Brand storyteller, maybe. Push the sleeves up."

Mara has the jacket on and does as she's told.

"Yes," Nicola says. "That's fine."

Nicola leads the way out of the office, then stops and goes back to the desk. She picks up her black key card.

"I'm always forgetting this. I don't know how many cards I've gone through in the last few years. Come on. Parlament awaits."

**

Stuffed from lunch, Mara takes the U-Bahn from Rathaus to St Pauli. Nicola's unstoppable propensity for talking about herself meant all Mara could do was eat, which was good, because it felt like she hadn't eaten properly since Russell made her penne carbonara a week ago. She worked through four courses, chewing and nodding, while Nicola caught up on a decade of bragging and poked at her salad as if feeling guilty for even having that.

Processing all of it, that monologue delivered like it was all nothing to boast about, is a challenge; mainly because she's trying to sift the important from the superfluous, with little of the former and a lot of the latter. There was never a break for Mara to steer the conversation in certain investigative directions; everything seemed to circle back to Flavio. Nicola's fiancé, the leading goal-scorer for FC St Pauli, was "destined to be picked up by a high-profile team next season." Then it was city-dropping, all the potential locations Flavio's magic boot might take them: Milan, Manchester, Barcelona, Madrid, Munich. But not Napoli, as Nicola can't stand Flavio's overbearing mother.

Still, the cellar under the Rathaus made a good hideout while the protest continued outside. It was also effective in pushing the events of Jungfernstieg out of her mind. But only temporarily. As the echo of Nicola's big talk fades and the U-Bahn comes out of the tunnel to run aboveground towards Rödingsmarkt, the protest works its way back into her thoughts; specifically, how the police were the aggressors, making the first move.

At the next stop, protesters are waiting to board the train. A few get in and sit near her. They rub at their wrists and talk animatedly about the injustice of it all. She doesn't recognise them, but they look like the hardcore types who run with Gomez. They were arrested, she concludes, but only held long enough to break up the protest. It was a catch-and-release display of power and force. A media drive for the police.

The train curls towards Baumwall, past the blood-red bricks of the Speicherstadt's old warehouses, before the Elbe and the harbour's vast expanse come into view. Achingly beautiful, and she's missed it. She looks out the window all the way to Landungsbrücken. She's still looking when the train goes into the hill under St Pauli and is surprised by her reflection: she's still wearing Nicola's grey jacket and looks very much like someone who works advertising. It's no wonder the protesters sneer in her direction. She expects them to get out at St Pauli, but none of them move. She had planned to exit here and go to the Otzenstraße bunker, but decides to stay with the protesters.

They're off the train at Feldstraße and move purposefully up the stairs, towards the Schanze. She follows them, keeping her distance. She has an inkling of where they are headed. Once on Schulterblatt, this group joins up with a few others, and they all head for the bunker with the climbing wall. Ten years ago, Rote Flora would have been the gathering place after a protest, but it's derelict and deserted. The protesters walk straight past it. It's the bunker that offers security now.

There are clumps of protesters loitering in the park. She spots lanky Jesper, standing near the bunker's entrance, talking with Gomez and JJ. They go inside and the rest follow.

Taking the hoodie from the Alsterhaus bag, she hastily pulls this over the grey jacket, dumping the bag in the bin. It's not comfortable, and she can feel something in the jacket poking her in the ribs, but she lifts the hood over her head and joins the line at the entrance.

Inside, she's surprised to find it's a massive dormitory. This main area, now crowded with people, has triple bunk beds all around the walls. She can't tell if that's where the beds always are, or if they've been pushed to the walls to accommodate all these people. Either way, 30 people could comfortably sleep here, with more on the floor.

She recognises some faces: from the first meeting, the pig farm protest and Elbe Help. Gomez holds up his hands and calls for quiet.

"We need to fight back," he says. "We need to go down and set fucking Jungfernstieg on fire. Who's with me?"

A few people cheer in support.

JJ moves through the crowd to stand next to Gomez. "Let's just take a moment to think about this. Going down there will just result in more people getting arrested. More people will get hurt."

"They started it. We're fighting back. We can't let the cops do this to us."

"Look around you," JJ says. "We're already hurt. We need to do this the right way. We can organise a protest for Sunday. If you go into the city and make trouble, they will just come down harder and we'll all end up in jail."

"Fuck no," Gomez shouts. "We go now and we go armed."

Gomez starts to move, but JJ puts a hand on his shoulder. He shrugs it off.

"Wait," she says calmly. "Think about what you're doing. It may not look like it, but we won today. You're right, Gomez. The police started it. The media was there and some of the press will document exactly what happened. If we now go down and set fire to the city, we'll lose the upper hand we hold. We can use what the police did today to get more supporters."

"All you ever do is talk about media and politics. It's all talk. I want action. I'm sick of being the victim. We're always on the end of it."

Jesper steps forward. "Hold up, G. She's right. We're in the box seat here. Plus, we've got a huge ace up our sleeve."

"What's that?" Gomez asks.

Jesper points at Mara and everyone looks at her. "Former police officer Mara Steinbach."

"Leave me out of this, Jesper," Mara says.

He moves towards her, slowly, enjoying his moment in the spotlight.

"She knew what they were up to today," he says. "She knew why they didn't have shields and why that meant they were going to attack. And she knew how to get away without being arrested."

Gomez folds his arms. "Why the fuck should we trust an ex-cop?"

96

"Because of what else she knows that can help us."

Jesper ends up standing right in front of Mara. She clenches her fists in the pockets of her hoodie, wanting to deck him.

"It's no secret," she says, feeling now she is standing on the stage with these other players. "The cops always have a strategy. I'm surprised you all don't know this."

"We know," Gomez says. "We want to know what you know."

"What they did today was the kind of thing used in extreme situations. I was really surprised to see it at Fridays for Future. What the fuck are they doing in riot gear at a demo like that?"

"What are you saying?" JJ asks. "It was premeditated? A deliberate attack?"

"What do you think? You don't show up with a dozen vans and a pair of water cannons to hand out flowers and balloons. It was a message."

"What was the message?"

"That if you protest anywhere from now on, this is what will be in front of you."

"Where the fuck is that coming from?" Gomez asks.

Mara shakes her head. "Because of last Sunday, you fucking moron."

"Hey, pig, don't you talk to me like that."

The way Gomez exaggeratedly bristles adds to the very theatrical feel of the situation. He's acting, she thinks, as is Jesper. It's an immersive production, with the audience standing at stage level.

"That dead cop had nothing to do with us," Gomez says.

"You were there," JJ says. "You were the ones fighting with the cops after the football, just because you lost the game."

"We didn't kill anyone."

"The cops don't know that," Mara says. "Don't you get it? One of their own has been killed. They want revenge."

"You know so much about this," Gomez says. "Tell us what they're going to do next."

"How should I know? I'm not in the police anymore."

"Wait," JJ says. "If the cops have a strategy for every protest, then getting our hands on that strategy would give us an advantage. We can know what they're planning."

"And use it against them," Gomez says. "Take those fuckers

down."

JJ turns to Mara. Her face is hard and determined. "You're going to get this for me. For us."

"JJ, I was an officer in Berlin. I don't know any Hamburg cops."

"You better find someone. Otherwise, some of the nice people in here might think you're still a cop, who was sent in here to spy on us."

The suspicion of a traitor in their midst changes the atmosphere amongst the audience in the stuffy bunker; they are suddenly aware who the villain is in this performance.

"It's always easier to put the blame on someone else," Mara says. "Right? Your protests fail, your group falls apart, and the first thing you do is blame an outsider for it."

Gomez walks towards Mara. "She's a spy. Leave her to me, JJ."

"Touch me and I'll knock out your front teeth," Mara says.

JJ holds Gomez back. "Stop giving into your first emotion, Gomez. Are you up for this challenge, Mara?"

"Yeah. All right. But let me just say that I don't know why I'm supporting a bunch of people who so easily turn on each other. Until all of you start working together, you won't stand a chance. What I saw today, and at that fucking pig farm, is that all of you are in it for yourselves. When things go bad, you run for it. Why don't you stand together?"

There's a moment of quiet in the bunker as these words sink in.

"That's bullshit," Susie says.

"I think Mara's made a good point," JJ says. She turns in a slow circle, addressing everyone: "We are fractured. We all need to help each other. We can't be fighting internally. That's just what they want. They want to see us divided."

A few people nod and clap.

"We'll protest on Sunday, against police brutality." JJ ends her circle back at Mara. "You will get those plans for us and we'll know exactly what to do."

"Yeah. Okay."

"I'll announce it tonight," JJ continues. "So the police will know it's coming. Now, everyone, go home and make some banners. Get ready for Sunday, because it's going to be big."

JJ stands next to Mara as everyone slowly filters out through the bunker's one door. As Jesper passes, he gives Mara a judging, distrusting look. Mara keeps her fists in her pockets to stop herself from pounding Jesper's face with them. Gomez is the last to leave; he smiles at Mara, but his expression is hard to read as he bumps her in the shoulder on his way past.

"Don't disappointment me," JJ says when they're alone. "Meet me here tomorrow night, at seven. Bring the plans."

Mara nods, then leaves.

She walks quickly to St Pauli. At the apartment, she grabs the flip phone and sends a message to Perceval: "Need a meet. Urgent."

Sweating, she takes off the hoodie, flings Nicola's jacket across the floor and paces.

"Fuck, fuck, fuck."

Her thought tree is growing limbs in a frenzy. JJ knows I'm undercover, she thinks. The way she looked at me. Those eyes. It's all a plan to expose me. She's known all along. Now Gomez wants to lynch me. If I could just change JJ's opinion, that would help convince everyone, and I wouldn't need to win Gomez over. Because fuck that weaselly little prick. JJ's the stakeholder. Gomez is nobody. I've got to get these plans. Somehow.

With so much nervous energy inside her, she starts punching at the air, like she's in pre-fight mode. Stepping forward, jabbing, swinging, ducking, weaving, taking down her invisible opponent with all those combos Zina taught her. It makes her wish she had a punching bag to work over. Gloves on, toes digging into the floor. Boof, boof, boof. Turn this panic into strength and sweat.

The flip phone buzzes. Perceval's reply: "Pink Dragon, 2200."

"What the hell? Why does he want to meet there?"

She's got a few hours, and she can't sit around here waiting until it's time for Lord Percy's lap dance. She needs to get active. Be productive. Burn off that massive lunch. She pulls the hoodie back on and heads down the stairs.

It's not that far to the gym on Große Elbstraße. She walks along the Reeperbahn, hood up. It's early evening and St Pauli is clicking into second gear. The packs of men crowding the streets have airs of hope and anticipation, that this will be a memorable night and they'll get laid. The pink-shirted hens' night girls wear silly hats and are still walking straight and having fun. The callers outside the strip clubs are just warming up, not nearly as aggressive and full-voiced as they'll be in a couple of hours. The buskers are young and good; later they'll be lousy and desperate. And through it all, there are plenty of people just going about their Friday business, because despite the neon-lit facades and decadent attractions, St Pauli is a residential area, with supermarkets, schools, playgrounds and even a few retirement homes.

She reaches the gym just as it's closing. Going through the door, boxers who are showered, in street clothes and shouldering sports bags come from the other direction. All men, all young. She feels their lingering eyes, giving her a quick up and down, and hates them for it. They're all out of her weight division, but she thinks she'd land a few telling blows, if given the chance.

"What are you looking at?"

"Nothing special," one of the guys says.

"Yeah? I don't see your picture on the wall."

With them gone, the atmosphere in the hallway changes. She can breathe and be comfortable there as she looks at the photos. The gym has had plenty of champs over the years, but none recently, judging by the photos. The largest pic is of a young Gus with boxing legend Max Schmeling. Next to it is her and Zina, the Hamburg belt held above her head by her skinny yet sculptured 14-year-old arms. Her left eye is a circle of purple and her right eyebrow has a row of stitch-tape on it. One of her best fights. Losing all the way, somehow hanging in, thumbs at her temples and taking so many blows to the body it got hard to breathe. Her opponent, 14 going on 22, was taller, stronger, better. Zina gripped the towel on her shoulder with one hand, ready to throw it in at any moment. But she kept moving, managed the pain and rode the punches. She went down twice, to a count of five, then eight. The zebra gave her that look, the one they all have: the slight raise of the eyebrows that asked, "Are you really sure you want to get back up?" But she got to her feet, put her thumbs back to her temples and pushed on, waiting for an opening. It came in the last round, Hollywood-style, with the hammer hovering over the bell. The big girl wanted the win, the knockout, the glory. She wanted the moment. Stupid really, because she was way ahead on points and could've just danced around until the bell. But some boxers need closure, to make their victory complete and obvious by rendering their opponent legless. The big girl's huge swing was a blur she just managed to avoid. But it opened up the right side and she landed a solid left into the ribs that cracked something and felt

100

really good. This got her opponent sideways and her elbows dropped instinctively to protect the point of contact, leaving her chin fully exposed. Without hesitation, she hit that chin as hard as she could, left foot pivoting to get her body weight going through the punch and sending that big girl perfectly backwards like her body was rigid and she was being tilted on her heels. The canvas rippled when she landed, and the zebra got to ten just before the bell rang.

"That's one I'll never forget."

Mara turns. Gus is standing next to her holding a broom. In the last decade, he's shrunk from being slightly taller than her to slightly shorter, even with the St Pauli beanie on his head. His baggy clothes look like they've been worn several days in a row, and he's really leaning on the broom, like it's a crutch.

"Hey, Gus."

"Of all the boxing gyms in all the world, you had to walk into mine."

"It's been too long."

They hug, but not quite properly. Mara puts an arm around him and draws him close, shoulder to shoulder.

"Good to see you, Mara. The one that got away, back again."

"Other things to fight for."

"Yes, looks like you're still fighting. What happened to your head?"

Mara touches the bandage. "Got the wrong end of the stick."

They both look at the photo.

"A fantastic bout," Gus says. "I don't seem to remember many fights anymore, but I remember that one, every single punch."

"Zina swears to this day that it was the fastest count she'd ever heard from a ref."

"It wasn't the knockout punch, or the rib-breaker. The end was the end. What was amazing was the way you kept at it. Your patience. Your will. Not many fighters have that."

"Taught well, taught right."

"You can't teach that stuff. You either have it or you don't. How is Zina?"

"She's good."

"Still in Stuttgart?"

"Yes." Mara looks at Gus. "I miss her."

"Get in line. Things weren't the same after her. She just left this ...

101

hole. I couldn't fill it with anything. The gym had a void. Still does."

"I know."

"Amazing how a person can leave and just about everything leaves with them." Gus lets out a tired, old-man sigh. "You want a drink?"

"No, thanks. My liver's still processing all the wine I had at lunch."

"What do you want then? I know purpose when I see it."

"You old fox. I wanted to see you, and I want a bag. Preferably one that's free-standing, because I don't have the tools to fix it to my ceiling. The building's so old it might make the roof cave in."

"No."

"What do you mean no?"

"No, I'm not giving you a punching bag. I want you to come back here and start working out with me. There's plenty of bags here."

"Maybe I'll start with the pair under your eyes."

Gus laughs, in that deep, natural way of a person who doesn't have much to laugh about anymore; a laugh that sounds like a rare gift.

"I remember that mouth," he says. "The only way to shut you up was to put in a mouthguard."

"Are girls even allowed in here? There's a real guy vibe, and not in a good way."

"You saw them leave? MMA boys. I had to diversify, to keep the gym going."

"Yeah, fights in the cage are all the rage," she says. "Too messy for me. All bluster and no style. A humanised cockfight."

"Still a purist, I see. That's good. Maybe you can help me get the girls back in. You could train them, like Zina did."

"Fill that void with me, huh?" Mara looks at the other photos. "I don't know, Gus. I got a lot going on right now. I'm volunteering at Elbe Help too."

"You are? Nice people there. But you could help them. The refugees, the girls especially. Teach them how to defend themselves. And how to attack."

"Maybe."

Gus leans the broom against the wall and starts walking down the hallway. "Come on. Let's get you into some gloves."

***

102

Mara takes the back way to the Pink Dragon, to stay off the Reeperbahn. But there's no avoiding packed Große Freiheit. She weaves through the boisterous crowd, towards where Perceval's Mercedes is parked half off the street in front of the Pink Dragon. While out of place on any other road, the car fits right in here. The bouncer moves aside to let her enter, perhaps thinking she's a new dancer, or going with the standard club rule that girls bring in guys, even in an establishment like this.

Inside, it's dark, smoky and hot. Low lighting. A lot of red. Nude statues in erotic poses. Circular booths. Bottles of fancy-labelled alcohol on display, though likely filled with cheap knock-off spirits. The centrepiece is a long dragon along one wall, decorated in glowing pink and glittering scales.

Strangely, for a Friday night, the place is just about empty, but there are two girls dancing languidly on the stage, in front of two guys.

She finds Perceval sitting in a booth at the back, far from the stage. With him is a guy who barely looks old enough to be in here. She slides in beside Perceval.

"This is the last place I'd expect us to meet," she says.

"I assure you, there is no safer location."

"There must be dozens of cameras in here."

"Indeed, but none are pointed at me."

"Who's he?" Mara asks, gesturing at the baby-faced blonde.

"This is Nils," Perceval says. "He is now officially helping with this investigation."

"Hi," Nils says, taking his right hand off his glass to wave. His drink has a chunk of pineapple wedged to the side, with two little umbrellas stuck in it. He leans forward to sip through a curly pink straw.

"I hope there's no alcohol in that drink, because you're clearly underage."

"He's more than ready for this," Perceval says. "I think he's an excellent addition and will be most useful."

"Sounds like you picked him up." She looks at Nils. "How are you enjoying high school?"

Nils laughs a little. "I'm 21."

"Right."

"That's enough," Perceval says. "Everything is in order. You should be glad. One more on our team."

"How did this happen?"

"There was something of a celebration today. Some felt the afternoon was a success and those involved decided to celebrate. That was where I ran into young Nils here."

"What success? They attacked and arrested people who were doing nothing wrong."

"Those involved think otherwise."

Perceval's phone buzzes on the table. He looks at it, and his expression changes.

"What is it?" Mara asks.

"Please make this brief. An emergency strategy meeting has been called. It appears there will be a protest on Sunday, against police brutality. Are you aware of this?"

"It's why I'm here. But I'm not saying anything in front of him."

"Don't be ridiculous. He's with me."

"Well, he's not with me. At least, not yet. He could be anyone."

Perceval and Mara share a look.

"Nils, be a good lad and wait in the car," Perceval says, his eyes still on Mara. "Be sure to keep people away from it."

Nils slides out of the booth with the huffy annoyance of a child sent from a room so the adults can talk. Once on his feet, Mara sees he's very tall.

"Woah, you're a giant. You play basketball?"

Nils doesn't reply. A scantily-clad girl in heels not even Nicola could stay upright in sneaks an arm inside Nils's elbow and escorts him to the door.

"He plays for SC Ottensen," Perceval says, "in Hamburg's top division."

"Good to know."

"You have five minutes."

"Why did you bring him in so quickly? He could be an informer, for all we know."

"Do you think I would recruit just anyone? You couldn't ask for a more impeccable background. His mother is a detective. One of the best. His father is a teacher, and his older brother is in the police."

"What about him though? Has he already been through the academy?"

"He's undecided," Perceval says. "That's why I suggested to his mother, who may I add is as tough as week-old bread, that he interns with me. Gain some experience."

"An intern?"

Perceval checks his watch. "You now have four minutes."

Mara leans closer and lowers her voice: "Whatever is decided at this strategy meeting, I need to know."

"Impossible. Please speak normally. There is no need to whisper."

"JJ, the Circus leader, she gave me an ultimatum. They know I'm police, was police, and she accused me of being a spy. I need to prove I'm with them."

"I simply cannot let you come to this meeting. You know that."

"I'm not asking for an invite. I just need you to tell me what gets planned. There's always a strategy. I mean, there's even a playbook they pull the strategies from."

"That book needs updating." Perceval is thoughtful for a moment. "You really think Circus will accept you into their fold if you complete this one task for them?"

"It's a test. If I get JJ on my side, the rest should follow."

"Doubtful. They are using you."

"What about your hierarchy theory? The new army?"

"Their sense of unity wasn't terribly apparent today. Everyone fled."

"You were there?"

"Not at street level. I was perched on a building roof, on Jungfernstieg."

"It was shocking," Mara says. "How the police behaved. Completely unprovoked. I was attacked as well. Did you see that?"

"Those at the top decided the message should be physical as well as visual. A last-minute change."

Perceval starts sliding out of the booth.

"Where are you going?"

"I have to get to this meeting."

"Will you get me the plans?"

"I will," Perceval says, now standing, "if you do something for me. I have not received anything useful from you, as yet."

"What about the bunker tip? And the names?"

"I need more than that. Meet me here for lunch tomorrow and we can do an exchange."

"This place serves food?"

"Yes. It's good."

As Perceval leaves, no girl goes up to him to try to keep him in the club or escort him to the door. He nods to the bartender, who nods back.

Mara slides Nils's drink towards her. She eats the wedge of pineapple, removes the straw from the glass and finishes the drink. It's very sweet and she doesn't taste any alcohol. Her right wrist hurts when holding the glass. Gus had her going for an hour at the heavy bag, and that was really satisfying. The aches feel earned.

The bartender is surprisingly small, making Mara assume the area behind the bar is elevated. He comes over to collect the glasses.

"Anything else?" he asks.

"Do I have to dance for it?"

"Only if you want to. But you look angry enough to rip the pole off its hinges. Something to calm your nerves?"

"How much for a shot of Sambuca?"

"Nothing," he says, smiling.

"That's very low for a place like this."

"You were in special company."

"Is that right? How special?"

"He didn't say?" The bartender smiles again. "He's so humble. Always has been. He owns this place."

"Very funny. You know he's police, right?"

The bartender nods. "If you're thinking he's corrupt, you're way, way wrong. Christoph is as pure as fresh snow."

"Then how does he get away with owning a strip club?"

"Nothing remotely criminal happens in here," the bartender says firmly. "The girls dance. The people enjoy it. Everybody drinks and has a good time. So should you."

"Okay. I get it. I just think it's unusual a cop would invest in a place like this."

"He didn't buy it. He inherited it."

As Mara processes this, the bartender goes back to the bar and returns with a bottle and two shot glasses. He stands at the booth, pours the Sambuca and pushes a glass across the table to Mara.

"Christoph's mother," he says, raising his glass, "is Penelope Perceval. God rest her marvellous soul."

He throws the shot down and goes to clean up the next booth.

106

Mara drinks hers as well, then leaves.

Outside, hood up, she's quickly down busy Große Freiheit, wracking her brain for something she could give to Perceval in exchange for the police plans. She hasn't seen anything incriminating at Elbe Help, and Perceval already knows about the bunkers. She should be trying to find Jesper, to get a lead on Anthony.

Patience, she thinks. Wait for the opening.

As expected, Hamburger Berg is rowdy. The numbers are about the same as during the week, but Friday night has an edge; a sense there are fewer consequences.

She gets into her building and takes the stairs two at a time, which includes leaping over a guy asleep near the second-floor landing. In her apartment, she lies down on the chaise longue with her phone. She swipes away the messages and notifications, then writes to Zina: "Big hello from Gus. Happy to say I'm back in the gym and loving it. Think I owe you a huge thank you for all the great stuff you taught me. Can you teach me how to coach as well? Love M."

It's tempting to search the internet for Penelope Perceval, find out who she was and what made her a legend. But she resists, because she would much prefer to hear this from Perceval himself, as a way of solidifying their relationship. It feels wrong to pry into what is likely to be a sordid background when she should be building ties with him, so he would be more inclined to do things for her without wanting anything in return.

She realises that Perceval is also now a stakeholder who requires managing, starting with some prime nugget that will make him give her the plans for Sunday's protest.

She wonders if Penelope once lay on this chaise longue, in this house that was once a brothel she owned.

Tired, she prepares for bed, brushing her teeth and changing the bandage. The stitches are already starting to itch.

The grey jacket is still on the floor. She picks it up and folds it, but feels something stiff as she does. The jacket has one of those security pockets on the inside, padded, with an almost hidden zip. She opens it, reaches in and pulls out a black key card.

Day 6

Dear Russ,

How are you? I'm fine.

God, I feel like I'm eight years old, writing to a pen pal I'll never meet.

Fair warning, pen-pal: this will be a massive brain dump. So much has happened in the past week. This letter is therapy for me. I'm going to just put everything down as it comes. It will be all over the place, as I am right now.

It's almost midnight. Tomorrow, there's going to be a massive protest in the Schanzenviertel. I have no idea what to expect. I'm planning to take a disposable camera with me and take photos. Though I don't really know how to do this without being seen. There's a good chance I won't have my hands free. I may well need them to be ready to defend myself.

JJ says we're protesting against police brutality. That's the brand for it. The headline grabber. The naming rights. "Today's protest is brought to you by police brutality." It's all for show. The whole thing will be about empowering the protesters. If this succeeds, you can blame me for it.

JJ is Julietta Jabali. She's the head of Circus, and she also runs Elbe Help, a charity that could be a front for something. Money laundering, maybe. JJ is my main stakeholder at the moment. I'm trying hard to win her over.

Exactly one week ago, I was in a street battle against right-wingers in Pankow. Now, I'm one sleep away from heading into battle with left-wingers (and whoever else decides to show up and mix in, maybe even some right-wingers). I could end up fighting with the police. I can hear you asking me, "How does that make you feel?" Conflicted, obviously. Not all the protesters are bad, and not all the cops are good. I was in the police long enough to learn that the majority in the force are good, but it's those bad ones who are memorable and make trouble.

Yesterday was the Fridays for Future demo in Hamburg. Did you see this? The police attacked the protesters, without mercy. As if it was a special battalion made up only of guys like Lauter. They let the kids, parents and banner-wavers through, then started pushing the

108

rest of us back. In Berlin, we had strict orders to hold the line and respond only when necessary. We were told never to instigate, which is what happened yesterday. A huge shift. I know, a police officer died at a protest, but I think a dangerous precedent has been set, which is what we're protesting about tomorrow and which will probably result in another huge fight.

Something Perceval said when I first met him continues to bug me. He said I got here just in time, as if he knew all this was coming. This makes me worry there's someone high up in the Hamburg Police, or maybe in the government, who is intent on using the police as a weapon. No longer serve and protect; it's attack and subdue.

There's a good chance tomorrow's demo will make all of this worse. Because we, the protesters, know what's coming. I managed to get the police's strategic plans for tomorrow. We know where the water cannons will be placed. We know how many vans have been organised, and how many squad cars. We know the designated points where the protesters shall be split and dispersed. So, now we have a plan that takes advantage of this knowledge. We'll be a step ahead of the police, and hopefully, this will result in us capturing two water cannons. If that works, it will be my fault, but also my achievement, and it will secure my place in Circus.

I didn't do this by choice. JJ forced me into it, as a way of proving I'm on her side. I didn't like being coerced in that way, but now I'm good with it. After yesterday, I want to see Circus win tomorrow, and I hope it results in the police backing off and doing the job they're supposed to be doing.

"How did I get these plans?" you're wondering. It was a trade. With Perceval. I brought him a pile of documents from Lersner-Löwe, the law firm that represents Circus. Yes, that's the same firm my father used to work for, and his father. I've included copies of those documents in here. Maybe you'll see more in them than I did. Perceval definitely thinks they're interesting. He keeps banging on about "following the money", like he's a detective in a TV show. He's probably right, because someone's paying the bills for Circus. Fancy high-heeled legal help doesn't come cheap. I can't see how Circus makes any income. Elbe Help is a charity, and that place is about as non-profit as anything can be. They take donations of clothes, toys and such, and organise them to be distributed to hard-up people. A lot of it goes east, to places like Romania, Bulgaria and Moldova.

109

From everything I've seen, they are doing good and commendable work. There are also refugees volunteering there, making clothes for the Circus fashion label (which also doesn't appear to make any money, because a lot of that stuff is practical and donated, like onesies for premature babies, which I'm now an expert at making).

Elbe Help was packed today. We went through every box and bag looking for yellow articles of clothing. This was JJ's idea, that we should all wear yellow tomorrow, to make the protesters clearly distinguishable from the police. She made this big speech about yellow being the colour of hope, friendship and optimism. It could become the protesters' new uniform. That would be better than protesters in black and police in navy-so-dark-it-might-as-well-be-black. Once the police attacked us yesterday, you couldn't tell the groups apart. The only differentiator was the helmets. And the weapons.

On that, I have a feeling a few protesters will be armed tomorrow. There are some bad elements in this group. People who are waiting for a fight, and some who want to loot the shops and set fire to stuff. Word is protesters are coming from all over the region, maybe even from Hannover, Bremen and Flensburg. You can bet they'll be hardcore and battle-ready. They won't come just for a quiet stroll through the Schanze.

I guess you're also wondering how I managed to get these documents from Lersner-Löwe. It was luck, but I'm going with the thought that I made this luck. I found an entry card in a jacket Nicola loaned me. Did I ever tell you about her? We went to school together, practically grew up like sisters, because our parents worked in the same firm, which was just Löwe back then. She was always getting me into trouble when we were kids. But she's a lawyer now. I guess that was always going to happen, and the only real question was what the journey would look like getting there. Maybe she understood this early on and decided to have some fun as a teenager, while she could. The key card got me into the office this morning when no one was around. No cleaning staff. Not even any cameras, that I could see. I wore a balaclava, just to be safe, one made by the people at Elbe Help. It has this plastic shield sewn in to protect the eyes from pepper spray and tear gas. Clever. Anyway, Lersner-Löwe is another paper-free office. I had to hack into the receptionist's computer. Okay, hack is a stretch, because the login details were on a green post-it note under the keyboard. I had this bizarre moment where it was all so easy, I thought it had to be some kind of trap. Like Nicola planted the card in the jacket for me to find. Even locating the right folders on the computer was a breeze. There was one labelled CIRCUS right on the receptionist's desktop. I printed everything, which wasn't much, as you can see, because the firm has only represented Circus for a few months. You're way smarter than me, so I expect you to make sense of it. Looks like Perceval's also way smarter than me, because when I left him at the Pink Dragon, he was completely absorbed in those documents while naked girls danced all around him.

He's a curious one, Christoph Perceval. You should do some research on him. Once we did the trade and he was satisfied with what I gave him, he became more talkative and invited me for lunch. I pushed him too, emphasised the importance of trust and the two of us building a relationship and that I needed to know more about him, starting with why we keep meeting at the Pink Dragon, which is a strip club on Große Freiheit. He owns it. Yes, really. Inherited it from his mother, who was a St Pauli lady of the night of serious repute, apparently. I'm currently living in the penthouse suite of Penelope Perceval's once-famous bordello. It's all apartments now. Still, if these walls could talk. I've commandeered some old furnishings I found in a storeroom, giving my place some additional colour and character.

Penelope Perceval's probably worthy of background research as well, to get some idea of where Christoph came from. It might help me manage that stakeholder better than I currently am.

But Perceval himself, I don't really know what to make of him. He plays table tennis. Competitively. Very smart, but he doesn't strike me as tough. He grew up surrounded by prostitutes and strippers, and went on to join the police. How does that happen? He might be gay. He can be whatever he wants, just as long as I can trust him. I don't think either of us is at the trusting point yet. He has a fascinating way of talking, like he went to a fancy boarding school 100 years ago. But he hasn't been terribly helpful so far. I've been fending mostly for myself. Maybe that's how it should be.

Of course, as already mentioned, the main stakeholder right now is JJ. I don't know much about her. She's American, from Tacoma, Washington. She's gorgeous, and must be at least 60. Doesn't look it though. She must've been a stunner when she was a student in Berlin, back before the Wall fell. That's when she got involved in the protest scene. The Cold War, nuclear threats, fingers on buttons, when the entire world was at stake. What's at stake now? That the planet's getting hotter and we might not have enough water to drink? That no one's happy?

Perceval wants me to get close to her, keeps saying I should make JJ my friend, or better, my mentor. I like JJ, because she reminds me a bit of Zina. I'm hoping to visit her in Stuttgart, when the G8 protest happens there in two weeks. It's already being talked up, by the protesters. Stuttgart could be massive, and what happens tomorrow might be a key indicator of how the police will prepare.

I've started boxing again, at my old gym. Gus, the gentle dinosaur that runs the place, is still going strong. He wants me to do what Zina did: coach girls. I find myself really wanting to do this, though I have no clue how to be a coach. First session is next Saturday, 0900. I better get prepared. I'm tempted to ask Zina to come up and help.

There's been no sign of Anthony. I confess I haven't been looking as hard as I should. He's not at home, because I was out there on Monday, and he hasn't been there in months. Richard's as difficult as ever, but he seems to have a lot of friends in his community, which makes it easier for me to let him be without feeling guilty. When I was there, I started reading this article he's writing, about modern revolution being driven by the pursuit of happiness. I wonder how many years he has before he starts to lose it. Maybe that's why Anthony moved out. He couldn't deal with Richard's conspiracy theories and paranoia.

I have no idea what kind of crowd Anthony's running with. He's always had the habit of following the person he admires the most, and that often changes. I'm wondering if he met someone and he started worshipping them, and that person is in Circus. He's not playing basketball, that I know, which is perhaps the weirdest thing of all. His coach says he hasn't been to practice for months. He rejected the scholarship to the States, the only thing he ever wanted. Why did he do that? I've dropped his name a few times around Circus people. No one has claimed to know him, but I think a few people do. I have a feeling he's still in Hamburg, hiding out somewhere.

Circus itself is a puzzle I haven't yet cracked. I can't figure out what they stand for and what they want. I've tried to speak with people about this. I get different answers. There are all these groups within the group, and it feels to me like the whole thing could fall apart at a moment's notice. There's no unity. Everyone seems to have a different bone to pick with the government or the police or whatever institution has wronged them. I get the feeling plenty of people are in it just to say they are in it. Like the students volunteering at Elbe Help because it will look good on their resumes. JJ's passionate, no doubt about that. She talks a lot about equality. She thinks Germany should introduce a universal basic income, among other things.

There is one person here from my old protest days: Susie. We met in juvie, years ago. She's all about saving animals and protecting the environment these days. I'm trying to avoid her, because she just drags me into trouble. But she did help me meet some others, including Gomez and Jesper. Write their names down. But now I see these names written down, they seem somehow unreal. Like, fake names. Gomez is the quasi-leader of a hardcore group within Circus. St Pauli fans. Disenfranchised youths, though they don't strike me as poor or from impoverished backgrounds. They all have really good teeth, to start with. Middle-class kids, slumming it. Gomez keeps talking about "taking action", but I don't know what form he means and what outcome he wants. He could be a closet right-winger for all I know. Jesper's hard to read, because I don't think I've seen the real Jesper yet. It feels like he's one of these guys who tries to be the way he thinks he should be in certain situations. Everything an act. I think he knows Anthony. Perceval put forward the idea that Jesper might be undercover, possibly also for the police. I'm not convinced. Something else is up with him.

My hand is starting to hurt from all this writing. I'm not pen-pal fit.

I'm finding it so strange to be in this protest scene without a clear mandate of what it's all about. It appears they're protesting just for the sake of protesting. One week it's climate change. The next week it's animal cruelty. Tomorrow it's police brutality. They jump onto whatever's topical, just to get a protest going, but there's nothing bigger behind it. It all feels so empty.

Maybe tomorrow will provide some answers. I plan to stick close to JJ throughout.

Now, though, it feels like Circus is waiting for something specific, a cause they can all get behind. Something to stick a flag into, if they had one. All these people at these meetings, who maybe 100 years ago would have turned to God or to the army or to certain ideologies for their beliefs and motivations, are floating with nothing. They don't seem to have a solid cause to fight for. What will happen when they do?

But even without unity and a clear mandate, this is still a community, and it has to be admired for being that. People are ending up here, at Circus or Elbe Help, for whatever reasons, and they are made to feel welcome. No one's turned away. It feels more than a bit like a family. It fills a gap in their lives, even if they can't put it into words. Protesting is a purpose. Right now, it's vague and disjointed and jumping from one cause to another. Could be this is just a problem of the leftist protest scene. No doubt, the right-wingers are absolutely clear about what they want and who is to blame.

I need more time. It's been less than a week. I need to get closer to the people here and have them get closer to me. To trust me. Getting those plans for JJ will help with this. My experience so far is that a lot of opinions are thrown around, but nothing sticks. I can hear you, Russ, saying something clever about how our arrogance is our worst trait. A whole country where every single person thinks they know it better. Yeah, yeah, telling others "you're doing it wrong" is one of our favourite pastimes. It can be I'm thinking too small here. You know, this isn't just a German thing anymore. It's human. Global. Perhaps the most accurate is to say it's digital. We've been rewired based on our last few decades of commenting on all things all the time.

But, what if someone comes along and stands there and tells everyone they're doing it wrong and this is how they should be doing it, and everyone listens? It feels like the protesters are waiting for just that person. For a leader. For a clear cause, delivered by someone charismatic. It's not JJ, or Gomez, or Jesper, or anyone I've met so far. Maybe this leader is someone who never comes, and these people continue to float aimlessly from protest to protest, fighting just for the sake of fighting.

What else? Before my hand cramps up and I nod off. Circus has a "no phones" rule at demos. This is because of bugging and tracking. They stay off social media as well. No phones at meetings, which are held in old war bunkers. No reception in there anyway. Elbe Help, meanwhile, is a bug-fest and under constant observation, according to Perceval.

On the bunkers, I've been amazed to learn how many of these still remain, out in the open or tucked away behind apartment buildings. The younger protesters use them as squats. There's one in the Schanze that's a huge dorm, like it's a frat house. Triple bunks. Climbing wall on the outside. I need to get in there and have a look around. Maybe Anthony's hiding out in a bunker, somewhere in Hamburg.

That's it for now. I need to get some sleep. Big day tomorrow. Time to change the world. The protesters coming out on top thanks to the devious work of an undercover cop.

Miss you, Russ. Take good care of yourself.

Love, Mara

The sky is overcast and the city is quiet as they walk from Dammtor station up Edmund-Siemers-Allee towards Schanzenpark. Their side of the road is blocked off for traffic. Uniformed police officers walk alongside the crowd, down the middle of the road, to ensure a safe separation from vehicles travelling away from the centre of the city. There aren't many cars, as it's Sunday morning.

"All yellows go together," JJ says to Mara.

The crowd isn't as big as Mara expected, maybe a few hundred people, spread out. No two shirts or pullovers are exactly alike in colour, but all the yellows blend nicely. Mara's own shirt, a gold polo pulled over her black hoodie, almost lends her a status of leadership she doesn't want.

"It looks good," she says, observing the crowd, seeing no hardcore elements here.

Mara and JJ are at the front with others from Elbe Help, walking in a line that extends the road's three lanes. They're close enough to each other to link elbows, if required.

The atmosphere is calm. A few people have banners. Some have written slogans on their yellow shirts in black markers: "Stop the violence", "End police brutality" and so on. One guy on a three-wheeled cargo bike has speakers in the front carrier section and is playing what Mara thinks is an inappropriate dance-type soundtrack, at low volume.

"A collective ray of sunshine," JJ says, "moving down this street."

"You were right about the colour. It adds something positive, and gives us some unity."

JJ smiles. "The diversion group comes in peace."

Mara wonders how many people in this crowd will join the fight, when it starts. She doesn't see anyone with a balaclava folded up onto their head like a winter hat. But that doesn't mean they don't have them, stashed in in a pocket, like she has. She also wonders what it must be like in the bunker on Schulterblatt, where Gomez and his group are waiting. Their objective is to take control of the two water cannons that will be stationed, according to the police plans, on the side street Oelkersallee at 1230. At last night's meeting in the Otzenstraße bunker, JJ had specified that no police should be harmed. Mara had scoffed at this, because a group can't capture a

116

water cannon full of police without needing violence in some form.

They cross the blocked intersection at Rentzelstraße. Mara checks the time: 1225.

According to the plans, the police vans and squad cars moved into position around Schanzenpark at 1215. Four vans at Schlump station and three on Altonaerstraße. Meaning at least 70 riot police close to the park. Plus three vans at Lagerstraße, to deal with any protesters arriving by train at Sternschanze station, and a further five vans at Budapesterstraße, near the football stadium, as reserve. But the water cannons are the key to it all, as Mara had explained last night.

"It's the cannons that drive people back," she'd said. "I've seen cannons send people flying if they get too close. It can even result in broken arms and legs. We get these cannons, it will turn things massively in our favour."

To her dismay, obtaining the plans hadn't won people over as she had expected. They were still cold towards her, with Gomez whispering to her on his way out that if it all turned out to be fake or a trap, she would want to get the hell out of Hamburg, because they would hang her by her feet from the Schanze bunker's climbing wall and throw empty bottles at her. But she wasn't going to take being threatened like that, and she spun him around and punched him right below his sternum, on that special point that knocks the wind out of someone. Gomez, doubled over and gasping for air, had the left side of his face exposed. He had been lucky that JJ had grabbed Mara's right elbow when the punch was already wound up to deliver the knockout blow.

"You have no idea what I risked to get these plans," she'd said as JJ pulled her back. "So don't threaten me, you fucking coward."

Halfway to Schlump, JJ looks at her watch and shows it to Mara: 1232.

"No turning back now," Mara says.

"You think they'll succeed?"

"No idea. If they don't, a lot of people could get hurt."

"You really think the police will be brutal at a protest against police brutality?" JJ asks. "That's the worst thing they could do for their image."

"Or it will exemplify the new approach. I hope you're prepared to spend the night in jail."

Mara watches a police officer using his radio. The officer's expression changes, like he hasn't quite understood what he heard.

Whatever the message, it doesn't matter now, because the crowd reaches the narrow entry point to Schanzenpark and starts pouring in, guided by the dozen police officers blocking the road. Suddenly, those officers are on the move, running past the protesters and towards Sternschanze station. Through the trees, Mara sees that the officers in riot gear are moving as well, jumping out of vans parked at Schlump station and running in tight formation towards the park's entrance. Mara assumes a fight has broken out at the other side of the park, with backup called for. She moves out of the crowd to get a better look and is knocked over by a police officer. He collects her on the point of her shoulder that was hit by the baton on Friday. As he bends over her, he's almost apologetic, like it was an accident.

For a moment, it seems like everything stops.

The officer holds up his hands, but doesn't extend one to help her up. Something goes off inside her. Some chemical reaction. Some primal response she simply can't control.

She gets to her feet and attacks the officer, leaping onto him and getting him to the ground, where she swiftly cuffs him with his own handcuffs. She pulls the balaclava out of her pocket and gets it over her head just as another officer aims pepper spray at her face. It hits the plastic eye cover and clouds her vision, but not enough to stop her from kicking him in the groin. She follows through with a solid right to his jaw as he keels over.

As she wipes away the pepper spray with the front of her gold polo, she sees fights have broken out all around her, and she's amazed to see how many protesters in yellow have joined in. They outnumber the police here, enabling them to fight two or three against one and to get each officer isolated. Most of those in riot gear are beyond this melee, running towards Sternschanze station, where smoke is already rising above the tree line.

Mara goes from one fight to another, pulling police officers off the protesters.

No one is being arrested. The police either knock a protester out or let them run. She sees JJ, in a balaclava, away from the fight and signalling for everyone to follow her up the small hill, towards the refurbished water tower that now houses a fancy hotel. Mara frees herself from the fighting and starts running. As she looks back, she sees protesters running in all directions, scattering as more police

118

pour in at the Schlump entrance.

When Mara reaches JJ, she's out of breath as she asks, "What are you doing?"

"Getting to the high ground."

"The fight's down there."

"We were losing that fight."

"It's a bad move. What are we supposed to do up here?"

Mara turns to see breakfasting hotel guests panicking and scrambling to get from the terrace back into the building, as if the protesters are coming for them. They knock tables and chairs over, as hotel staff try to guide them safely inside.

On the hill, there aren't many yellow-wearing protesters left. Mara assumes plenty of them used the break in the fight to make a run for it, around the side of the hill and back towards the Rentzelstraße intersection, away from the police gathered at Schlump. Looking up, she sees guests standing at windows, some with phones raised.

The police regroup at the bottom of the hill, in far greater numbers than before, many in riot gear. Despite the fights, few of the police appear hurt, while there is a scattering of injured protesters near the east entrance.

The police begin moving up the hill.

"What do we do?" someone asks.

"Run for it," another says.

"Where? They've got us surrounded."

"Don't resist," Mara says. "We haven't done anything wrong. They can't hold us."

Another group of protesters comes clambering up the other side of the hill, through the trees. They are dressed in black and all of them wear balaclavas. The riot police pursue them up the hill, with brutal fights breaking out in tight spaces.

"There's no reason for us to fight alongside those guys," Mara says loudly.

She's about to tell them all to raise their arms and submit to being arrested when a huge vehicle crashes through the narrow gap at the park's west entrance. The police fall back from the trees and return to the base of the hill, as if the water cannon is there to support them. But then the nozzle is pointed in their direction. The resulting spray sends many of them sprawling.

119

The protesters in black emerge from the trees and start cheering as the police are doused and driven back.

At the front of the cannon, a window is lowered and Gomez climbs half out. He pumps his fist in the air and motions for the protesters to come down from the hill and fall in behind the vehicle.

The remnants of the protest group in yellow merge with those in black as they head towards the park's west entrance, then down the narrow path leading to Sternschanze station. The water cannon leads the way, clearing the path of police.

Mara runs with the crowd, past the station and under the railway bridge. She sees a second water cannon, stationed at the north end of Schanzenstraße, keeping the police back. Up ahead, at the roundabout at Lagerstraße, she sees a large group of protesters in black clashing with police. While some of those in the crowd around her run for the roundabout, to join that fight, Mara detours up deserted Susannenstraße. It's no surprise that everything's closed on a Sunday, but she still thinks it's unusual there are no locals around, as if they were all forewarned. When she gets to Bartelsstraße, she stops and motions for those behind her to keep running.

"Get to the bunker," she shouts.

As they go past, she doesn't see JJ. But she does see one of the water cannons go roaring down Schanzenstraße, to join the protesters in black. Then she's running again, up to Schulterblatt and towards the bunker. This street is full of people, most with shirts or pullovers tied around their faces like bandit masks. In front of the Rote Flora, three cars are on fire. She hears the thumps of a helicopter overhead. Up and down Schulterblatt, storefront windows are being smashed and the shops looted. She thinks these people look nothing like protesters; some have the necks of their shirts pulled over their noses and hoods up as cover. No balaclavas. No yellow. No black. They look like regular people who have come here, possibly from apartments nearby, to ransack the shops while they can. They fill their arms with everything they can carry and disappear down side streets. Some load up shopping trolleys, with food, drinks and clothes. Two guys carry a massive TV together, its cables trailing on the ground. Even some of the protesters in black, as they head towards the bunker, stop to go into shops to grab six-packs of beer and bottles of spirits, holding these aloft like pirates clutching booty.

It's incredibly crowded in the park outside the bunker. Musical-festival crowded. Protesters drink and celebrate. Off to the side, there's a bonfire going and it's growing rapidly, as anything combustible gets thrown on top, including tables and chairs pilfered from the cafés on Schulterblatt. It's taken less than half an hour for things to get completely out of control, and in this brief moment, they can own this little patch of city and there are no rules or consequences. It feels like a sexless orgy, fuelled by alcohol and ego.

She knows it won't last. The area will be overrun with police once the water cannons run dry.

Many of the locals are standing on their balconies, watching and filming. Some shout that the protesters should stop stealing and fuck off.

As she pushes through the crowd in the park, she grabs anyone in a yellow shirt, to get them to follow her. Some do, some stay. She ends up standing with six others on Lippmannstraße, all of them still in balaclavas. From several hundred at Dammtor station, whittled down to this half dozen.

There are police cars at the traffic lights at Max-Brauer-Allee. Smoke is rising from various points around the Schanze. The bonfire near the bunker continues to grow.

"Take the chance now to escape," Mara says. "Before the police move in."

"But we won," one guy says. "It's over."

"This hasn't even started yet."

The only option is to run down Lippmannstraße, in the opposite direction of Max-Brauer-Allee. The group splits at Juliusstraße. Mara turns on this street, to avoid coming out at the police station on Stresemannstraße. Once onto Mistralstraße, she's alone. She takes off the balaclava and the gold polo shirt, dumping both in a garbage bin. Then she walks, slowly, trying to calm her breath, hands slightly shaking in the front pockets of her hoodie. At Paulsenplatz, there are kids on swings and families playing in the sand in the square's central playground; like it's a normal Sunday, while a few hundred metres away the Schanze is a battle zone.

She feels dizzy. The parents stare at her, looking at her forehead, not her eyes. She touches the bandage, feeling sticky blood.

A loud explosion makes them all turn and look towards the

Schanze. A plume of dark smoke rises above the buildings, causing parents to scoop kids off the ground and lift them down from swings, and start hustling towards the nearby apartment houses. The sound has brought residents out onto their balconies. Others lean out of windows and point towards the smoke.

Mara puts her hood up and skirts the playground.

"Mara," a voice calls in her direction.

She turns to see JJ standing on the narrow terrace of a ground-floor apartment. JJ has also dispensed with her yellow shirt and balaclava. The short stack of wooden boxes against the wall affords purchase for Mara to get up and over the terrace's steel railing.

"You all right?" JJ asks, taking Mara's shoulders in her hands.

"Yeah. I think so. You?" Mara removes her hood.

"You're bleeding."

"The stitches split, I think."

"I just got here. Let's go inside."

Among the collection of pot plants on the terrace, JJ grabs a fake-looking plant by the stem and pulls it out of its pot. Underneath is a set of keys in a plastic bag. JJ takes it, then puts the plant back in place.

One of the keys opens the terrace's glass door. JJ lifts the curtain for Mara to enter, then closes the door. It's dark inside, the curtains drawn on all the windows. The air is stale. Mara thinks no one's been in here for a while. JJ goes to the boxy old television set and turns it on, flipping around the channels until landing on live coverage of the Schanze. On the screen, a water cannon is in flames.

"That must've been the explosion," JJ says.

"They set it on fire once it ran out of water."

"Probably."

Mara suddenly feels incredibly thirsty. The kitchen is just off the living room. She doesn't bother with a glass, sticking her mouth straight under the kitchen tap instead. It hits like the joyous relief of a between-rounds squirt from Zina's water bottle. That memory stops her from drinking too much; to avoid being flooded.

"Mara?" JJ calls from the living room. "You need to see this."

They stand together in front of the television. The screen shows Schulterblatt, between Susannenstraße and the railway bridge, an aerial shot from a drone. The two commandeered water cannons are parked at either end, one smouldering and the other with its windows smashed and sprayed with fresh graffiti. The street is full of protesters, facing off against police in riot gear. The police have shields and batons. Their lines extend across the street; they are at least 20 deep. The camera moves back, widening the shot to show that three water cannons are coming up behind the riot police, who then part down the middle to let them through.

"We got out of there just in time," JJ says.

"I tried to get anyone I saw in a yellow shirt to safety."

"Did that work?"

Mara gives JJ a searching look. "There was only a handful of us left."

"We were the diversion. The peaceful protest. You can't expect those people to fight."

On the screen, the camera moves over the protesters, who hold baseball bats and lengths of wood and cobblestones ripped up from the street. One guy is holding a street sign pole like it's a knight's jousting stick.

"Just run," Mara says to the screen. "You can't win."

The protesters stand no chance. They try to throw cobblestones and bottles at the vehicles, but the water cannons send bodies sprawling all over the place, scattering them aside the way a high-pressure spray cuts a swathe through dirt. The first lines of riot police move in, between the cannons' jets. It's beautifully coordinated. Batons swing. Shields cut arcs in the air. Protesters go down. It's vicious. One-sided. Unfair. Quick.

"Oh, my God," JJ says.

"Disperse, secure, control."

The cannons pause to allow the police to arrest all the drenched protesters on the ground. Regardless of whether the protester is conscious or not, they're dragged onto the footpath in front of the Rote Flora and lined up, on their stomachs, hands cuffed behind their backs. The balaclavas are taken off and tossed aside. Mara sees Gomez, unconscious, blood trickling from his head onto Schulterblatt's cobblestones.

JJ turns the television off and goes into the kitchen. Mara follows, then watches JJ opening and closing cupboards and drawers randomly, like someone who doesn't live here. Mara finds a roll of paper towels, turned slightly yellow with time, and tears two squares off. She folds them and presses them to her forehead.

"What a fucking mess," JJ says, still searching the cupboards. "Getting those plans made no difference."

"I think it did for a while. We were just outnumbered."

"Yellow shirts or not, the problem remains a lack of unity."

"Who were those other protesters? Where did they come from?"

JJ shrugs. She finds a half-full bottle of vodka in the fridge freezer and puts this on the table with two glasses.

"Whose place is this?" Mara asks.

"Nate's." JJ puts a first aid kit on the table as well. "My son."

"Where is he?"

"Somewhere in the North Sea. He's an engineer. Works on wind turbines."

"Very noble."

"He'd be happy to hear you say that, because he spends most of his days unjamming rotors that have bits of dead birds stuck inside."

"Yuck."

"Yep." JJ pours the vodka. "The dark secret of not-so-green energy."

Mara takes the glass and looks at it. "This seems to be the go-to painkiller for anyone who wants to patch me up."

"They give it to boxers?"

"No, I mean the drunk vet."

"Sorry," JJ says, not sounding apologetic. "It's all I could find."

Mara throws down the vodka and holds out her glass for more. JJ obliges. They both drink; JJ sips while Mara gulps.

"You ready?" JJ asks, opening the first aid kit.

"No."

Mara sits down at the table, which is covered in a thin layer of dust, and takes the paper towel from her head. She inspects its contents, unable to look JJ in the eyes.

"What do you see?"

"An inkblot test, with my blood." Mara unfolds it. "I'm not seeing a red butterfly. Looks more like a, like, hmm, a basketball. You see it?"

"No."

JJ starts taking off the bandage.

"Aaah, okay. Now I'm seeing pain. Bright red pain."

The bandage off, JJ takes a square of paper towel and folds it twice.

"How does it look?" Mara asks.

"It's messed up. You shouldn't have been fighting with an injury like this. I can't fix the stitches, so I'll need to take them out, then tape the wound together."

"Wonderful."

JJ puts the folded paper towel on top of the open vodka bottle and tilts the bottle quickly over and back.

"Sorry," she says, sounding more apologetic this time. "I don't have any other disinfectant."

"Bring it."

"Brace yourself." JJ reaches forward with the damp towel. "This will sting."

Mara grips the chair, like she did in Richard's kitchen. The pain goes from red to white. Siberian white. Arctic cold. When she closes her eyes, she's there, on the frozen tundra, shivering, nothing but white in every direction. It makes her whole body shake momentarily.

"Hold still," JJ says. "Tilt your head back and tell me your pain level."

"On a scale of one to ten?"

"Yes."

"That's garbage. I'm not rating my pain like that."

"A lot of medical professionals swear by it."

"My boxing coach used to say one to ten is only for counting out the person lying on the canvas."

JJ laughs a little. She has nail scissors in her right hand and tweezers in her left. Mara notices JJ's hands are considerably steadier than Remy's were.

"Keep going," JJ says. "Talking's a great diversion. But hold still."

"Zina always said pain has colour. She was my boxing coach. Then my friend. Kind of like the sister, aaah, the sister I never had. Oooh. Then she was gone."

"What happened to her?"

"She moved away. I missed her so much, I couldn't really handle daily life anymore. I lost my structure and started making it up as I went along, with disastrous results."

JJ flicks pieces of black stitches onto the dusty table. "Interesting. Go on. Pain has colour. I like that."

"Yeah, so, ah, whenever I was hurt, she'd tell me to give the pain

125

a colour. To get a sense of how bad it was. White was always the worst. To see white felt like getting close to the end. Anytime I was knocked unconscious, I saw white just before I lost it."

"Maybe that's where the representation of heaven comes from," JJ says, picking up the vodka towel and dabbing it at Mara's forehead. "That pure place of white is the pain a person feels close to death."

"I never thought about it like that. It was all a code between me and Zina. Then it became an inside joke, where I tried to introduce a new colour each time."

JJ laughs some more. Mara finds it a lovely sound.

"I'd get to my corner," she continues, "banged up and finished, and Zina might say the colour of my pain was purple, which meant bruised and a bit bloody. She was never far wrong. But I'd get all clever by saying it was mauve or violet or something. I remember once saying it was periwinkle and we laughed so hard I couldn't concentrate anymore and got knocked out in the next round. Then it was all white."

"Periwinkle. Ha-ha. Even after that, you kept the game going?"

"Sure. Zina always said that it had to be fun. I mean, it could be a nasty business, trying to knock someone out. It had to be fun and challenging and strategic. If it wasn't those things, it would just be two senseless idiots trying to beat the crap out of each other."

"That's how it looks to me."

"No. It's a dance. More art than sport."

"Were you any good?"

"I won a lot of fights, but I was well-coached. Zina taught me right, from the first time I put the gloves on."

"It's hard to unlearn things you don't learn correctly the first time."

"Amen," Mara says. "What you learn correctly you keep forever."

"You floored Gomez with ease last night. With one punch."

"If you'd let me get in that second punch, he would've ended up in hospital."

JJ dries the wound with a fresh paper towel, then starts adding thin fingers of stitch-tape, crosswise. Mara winces as the tape pulls at the skin.

"Do you think you could teach other girls how to punch like that?" JJ asks.

"I'm planning to. Gus wants me to get that going at the gym."

126

"You could start with the refugees at Elbe Help. I have to say, it made me feel very good seeing you take Gomez down like that. Not just the punch, but the way you stood up to him. You weren't afraid. You weren't going to let him talk to you like that."

"Why should I let him threaten me? Then he'll just keep doing it. To me and to others."

"If our girls gain even a little bit of that by learning to box, it'll be great for them. They've spent their entire lives being subjugated."

"That's wrong. That's old power. Some book from a thousand years ago dictating how women should be. Fuck that."

"I agree. Though you want to be careful when and how loudly you voice that opinion."

"Which is a big part of the problem."

"You won a lot of admirers last night, because of that punch," JJ says. "Not because you got the plans, which I now see was a mistake."

"But that was your idea."

JJ takes a large bandage and puts this over the lines of stitch tape. "You saw the response. We tried to go big at the police, and they just came back at us bigger."

"We showed what's possible," Mara offers.

JJ cleans up the mess, sweeping the stitches onto a paper towel and putting everything in the bin. She stands up and leans against the kitchen counter, sipping her vodka.

"They started it," Mara continues. "On Friday, and again today. Remember that. There'll be lots of content from this. People were filming from the hotel, from balconies. The riot police getting floored by their own water cannons will be seen all over the world. All of us in yellow will be easy to see in the videos. The guys in black, not so much, but they were outsiders. Thugs who came to Hamburg just for the fight, I'm guessing. Plenty of the looters looked like locals. But the cops moved first. That cop knocked me down and I fought back."

"Maybe you should've stayed down."

"Seriously?" Mara stands up. "You're telling a boxer to stay down? The fight was on and I was in it. Maybe next time you should get involved before you just head for the hills."

JJ is shocked by this. "Are you saying I ran?"

"I don't know. Did you?"

They stare at each other.

"Thanks for fixing me up," Mara says, heading out of the kitchen.

"Don't worry. I'll see myself out."

The vodka on an empty stomach makes her feel pleasantly tipsy. It also sparks hunger. When she reaches Hamburger Berg, she orders a pizza and two beers from the Italian place on the corner, and has just enough money on her to cover it. She opens one beer and puts the second in the front pocket of her hoodie.

She paces outside the restaurant, drinking, so hungry she thinks the pizza won't make it across the street and up the stairs.

The fun feeling of vodka is quickly replaced by the anxiety of beer. She worries that storming out on JJ, after practically calling her a coward, was bad stakeholder management. No, she tells herself. It was the right reaction. It was honest and sincere, and it suited the heat of the moment.

She's finished the first beer by the time the pizza is ready and boxed. She consumes two slices on the way to her building. There, Nils is leaning against the wall, his head level with the top of the door's frame. Two drunk, and possibly high, guys stand near Nils, staring up at him like they can't quite believe a human can be that tall. One guy giggles a little, like he's hallucinating the whole thing.

"What are you doing here?" Mara asks.

"Waiting for you."

"Stand there long enough and people will start propositioning you. Especially anyone with a certain thing for tall skinny boys. Like these two might have."

"They don't even look like they're on this planet. Ignore them." Nils holds up his phone. "You've gone viral."

"Say what?"

Nils plays a video. The point of view is from high up and the zoomed-in, portrait-style video is grainy. Shot with a phone from a hotel room in the water tower, she assumes. She sees herself knocked down by the cop; it looks more vicious here than she remembers, almost deliberate. Then she's up and attacking him. It all happens very fast. The graininess of the video makes it hard for her to be recognised, but Nils appears to be convinced it's her.

"Nice moves," she says. "Look at that girl take him down."

"That's you, isn't it?"

Mara continues eating. "It could be anyone. Hard to tell."

"How does it feel to be a police officer who attacks a colleague like that, causing a mass riot?"

128

"A little louder, Nils, and the whole neighbourhood will know. It looks to me like that cop started it. The person in the video just responded."

"Are you really trying to tell me it isn't you?"

Mara holds up the open box. "You want some pizza?"

"I want you to tell me what happened."

"Show me the video again."

Nils plays it and Mara eats as she watches. The two drunks lean in to watch as well.

"See that?" she asks, pointing with half a slice. "He did that on purpose."

"Sure did," one drunk says.

"He changed his line and his elbow came out. That's intent. That right there is police brutality."

Nils pockets his phone. "There are videos of what happened today all over the internet."

"Tell me there's one of the water cannon blasting the riot police."

The two drunks drift away, back towards the nearest bar, arms around each other.

"I'm certain that's not what Christoph wanted when he helped you," Nils says.

"Christoph? First-name basis already? Good for you, Nils. You earned a slice."

"Too much fat," he says.

"You're way too skinny to be counting calories, Nils."

"He wants to see you."

"The lord of the manor is upstairs?"

"Yes."

"A house visit? This must be meaningful. It's surely a step up from the Pink Dragon. Here. Hold this."

Nils takes the pizza box while Mara opens the door.

"Come on," she says.

"He told me to wait here."

"It's clear you two are sharing everything. I think you better come up. I got a job for you."

Mara takes back the box and leads the way up the stairs.

"You look like you haven't eaten for days," Nils says.

"There's no hunger quite like post-fight hunger. Adrenalin is a massive calorie burner."

Inside her apartment, Mara finds Perceval sitting at the table, working on his laptop.

"Make yourself at home," she says.

"I will indeed. I admire your taste in décor."

Mara sits on the chaise longue, the pizza box balanced on her knees. Perceval moves the laptop so the screen faces her.

"It appears you had a productive morning," he says.

The screen shows a news clip from the protest, including the water cannon hitting the police. They all watch, Mara chewing and Nils towering behind the seated Perceval.

"Sundays are normally such slow news days," she says.

"You have certainly ensured that is not the case today."

"Don't lecture me about fighting my colleagues. Beanpole already did that."

"You started the whole thing," Nils says, bristling at the nickname.

Perceval raises a hand, signalling for Nils to be quiet.

"It was on whether I did anything or not," Mara says. "From what I saw, it had already started. Those cops were running to the Schanze, to fight a group of hooligans who arrived by train."

"Who were those protesters? Are you acquainted with them?"

"They weren't from Circus."

The pizza finished, Mara frisbees the greasy box towards the kitchen; it clatters against the doorframe.

"We will ascertain their localities, and their loyalties, once the arrest reports come through," Perceval says.

"It looked like you got a lot of them. I'd put whatever money I have left on them being from outside of Hamburg. Maybe even right-wingers. And speaking of money, I need some. I spent my last coins on lunch."

"Get a job," Nils says.

"This is my job. Why are you taking it so personally? That someone beat that cop down. Why does that matter so much to you?"

Nils paces around. The top of his head almost touches the ceiling.

"I do believe he is self-projecting," Perceval says. "It's a natural response. He thinks that it could have been him. Or his brother."

"I think he's imagined me into that video as well. Look. We were protesting against police brutality. What happens? The protesters are the victims of police brutality. There is something very wrong with all this. Who is ordering this police aggression? They are going

130

out there to break heads without provocation."

Perceval closes his laptop. "It's complicated. There are others involved."

"Is it political? We can't have politicians giving orders to the police like this. That is not what I signed up for."

"What, pray tell, did you sign up for?"

"To find the protester who killed the cop. What else?"

"I'm referring to you joining the police," Perceval says. "That was quite a change for you, at the time."

"It was either that or the army. Make no mistake, I wanted to change my life. I woke up one day and I knew I needed structure again. Like I'd had with boxing."

"They tried to recruit you while in detention. The army, I mean."

"Oh yeah. They had recruitment drives just about every week. But I didn't want to fight in any wars. Now, if politicians are ordering the police to fight, I'm not seeing any difference. The Hamburg government seems to be using the police as its own army."

"To a certain degree, you are correct," Perceval says. "There are politicians who consider themselves like parents and the citizenry their children. Which is why they believe, as parents, they should take a firmer hand with their out-of-control children."

"It would be better to sit down and listen to them. Hard discipline with kids always backfires. Forcing a kid not to do something just makes them want to do it more."

"Indeed. Not to mention that history has shown exactly what happens when a self-proclaimed father figure puts himself on a pedestal and tries to parent a land full of blonde-haired children."

Nils self-consciously runs a hand through his hair.

"That too," Mara says. "I thought things were bad in Berlin. There, it feels like everyone's wound so tight, any one small thing will set them off. But we always had the clear order to control situations. We were never to instigate. Never be the aggressor. From what I've seen here already, in less than a week, the Hamburg police are taking the opposite approach."

"Of course they are," Nils shouts. "A police officer died."

"That doesn't give them license to behave like this."

Nils is about to respond, but he gets the raised hand again from Perceval.

"That's enough. From both of you. You can argue all you want, it

131

won't change the facts. It is imperative we make an arrest."

Mara gestures towards the closed laptop and says, "You made plenty of arrests today. Maybe one of them is the suspect. Maybe you just need to ask the right questions and offer a few deals."

"There will be no deals. That has been made clear. The thinking is that putting the guilty party in prison for life will send the message needed to curb this current wave of protest."

"Or the opposite will happen. They'll rise up."

Mara goes to the kitchen to open her second beer.

"This is all just the beginning," she says, sitting back down on the chaise longue. "You, with all your theories and research and following the money, you should know this. Putting a guy in jail, or on the front page of the paper, it won't change a thing. It won't stop people from being angry."

"You may well be right. It could only exacerbate matters."

"What I've seen is that there are a lot of people spoiling for a fight. Every second day, there's a news report of some gathering getting out of hand. A rave turns into a riot. A stadium full of middle-class football fans suddenly morph into hooligans and tear the place apart. A flash mob of teenagers start out having fun but are soon smashing shop windows and looting. I mean, on my last shift, I was called to a basketball game that was just about to become an all-in brawl. And for what? One team thought the refs were favouring the other team."

"People are on edge," Perceval says. "You're saying the police attacking them will not help. I agree."

"I wish I could explain myself better. It's like they have everything, but it's not enough. Or it's as if having everything is like having nothing. Their lives are meaningless. They have nothing that defines them. We're the vague generation, drifting from one distraction to another."

"Vague. That's precise. But what you mean is that the police acting with clear force may turn them into a common enemy against which the vague generation could unite. A single target for a cacophony of groups."

"Yes. Who taught you to speak like that?" Mara has a drink while Perceval smiles. "What happened today might motivate more people to start protesting."

"That video of you will be used for recruiting," Nils says.

"I think you're reading too much into the power of a viral video,"

Mara says. "It might push people to attend a demo or two, but I hardly think it will get more people to join Circus. If anything, these videos show how easy it is to loot shops once a protest goes south. There'll be plenty of people looking to take advantage of that."

Perceval nods. "The police should be stopping that, rather than attacking people."

"The way you say that, it sounds to me like you know exactly who to talk to. You know who could have an influence on this."

Perceval stares at Mara. Then, his slight glance towards Nils makes Mara wonder if Nils's mother might be that person.

"If you keep throwing the first punch," she adds, "you better be ready for them to punch back."

Neither of them replies. The silence is long enough for Mara to drink more beer and regret having eaten so much so quickly. She wants to lie down on the chaise longue and sleep the rest of the day away.

Perceval putting €200 on the table comes across as a sign he's preparing to leave. Mara smiles, wondering how many times cash has been placed on that table.

"What do you need me to do?" Nils asks.

"What?"

"You have a job for me. What is it?"

"Yeah. Right. You play for SC Ottensen."

Nils nods.

"That means you know my brother. Anthony."

"Ace is your brother? He can really play." Nils turns to Perceval. "Had a scholarship to play college ball in the States."

"That he didn't take," Mara says. "He stopped playing. The coach wouldn't tell me why. Have you seen him?"

"Not lately. I noticed Janica pulled out as well, from the women's team."

"Janica?"

"His girlfriend. You didn't know that?"

A skinny, lanky basketball player, Mara thinks. That could have been Janica with Ant during the protest, behind him. She could be the one he's following.

Perceval stands up. "What is all this about?"

"I haven't heard from him for months. I'm worried. When you told me Nils plays for the same club, I thought he might know something.

133

Or he could ask around."

"How precisely will that help our investigations?"

"He's my little brother. I'm allowed to be worried about him."

"Fine. Nils will do this small thing for you," Perceval says, "if you do something for me."

"Nothing for free. Everything's a trade with you."

Perceval hands his laptop to Nils, who tucks it under his arm. "We are collaborating." He hammers this point home by interlocking the fingers of his hands and gesturing with this combined fist at Mara. "We are working together."

"Call it what you want. So? What is it?"

"I require you to get close to Julietta Jabali."

"You already said that, and I've been trying to do it."

"Try harder. Get closer."

Mara shrugs. "I don't think she's the big leader you made her out to be. When things got hot today, she ran."

"Even so," Perceval says, "getting into her coterie will perhaps help you find out who is actually the leader."

"The potential army's potential general? I can try."

"Do this outside of the Circus and Elbe Help worlds. She frequents an antiquarian bookstore at Fleethof."

"Does she? You seem to know a lot more about her than I do."

Perceval starts to leave.

"Wait a minute," Mara says, making them both stop. "Is that why you came here? To show me some videos and tell me to keep doing what I'm already doing?"

"Well, I wanted to ensure, to confirm, that you are in good health. Which I see you are."

"Huh. Thanks."

Perceval gives her a thin smile. "It cost me €200 to do so."

"Thanks for that too. I guess the room's rate is still about the same as it used to be."

Perceval heads out of the room. To Mara's surprise, the smile that Nils gives her is friendly, after he was hostile towards her earlier. It reminds her of how much stock people in Hamburg put on knowing each other. Nils softened the second she told him Anthony is her brother. She's not sold on the nickname "Ace" though.

The door closes and she's finally alone.

134

The long nap helps, but it throws her body clock off. At 1910, she's back on the streets, wide awake, walking through St Pauli to work off the vodka-beer-pizza heaviness and get some clarity. She heads for the river, going past the landing bridges and along the promenade towards the Elbphilharmonie. The big glass building juts out like a bizarre warehouse-greenhouse hybrid.

She walks through the Hafen City. It's a nice evening. People are out strolling. Some exercise: jogging, rollerblading and cycling. Groups sit close together on the steps of the promenade, drinking bottled beers and enjoying the harbour view. The clashes of earlier today – the Schanze a battle zone briefly in the control of protesters – seem like they happened in another city, or years before. It makes her wonder if these people even know what happened, and if they do, whether they care.

Of everything that happened today, what bothers her the most is the looting; that the minute the police lost control of the area, all these scavengers showed up with the sole aim of stealing. They seemed like ordinary people, just taking advantage, without remorse.

The thought eats at her: is this what we've become? Looting has nothing to do with protesting, she thinks, yet the two are now connected. Intertwined. All those people who descended on the Schanze to steal could have helped shop-owners defend their stores, like good local citizens. They also could have joined the protesters. But the looters didn't pick a side. They were only in it for themselves. They tore up the social contract and became one of the worst things she thinks a person can be in a fair and just society: a thief.

Lost in these thoughts, she finds she's walked all the way to Lohsepark. There's a hotel on the corner, with a large lobby bar that's empty. She goes inside and knocks on the wooden bar, to get the bartender's attention. The shot of Sambuca costs way more than it should, but it's Perceval's money, so she doesn't care.

The television above the shelves of bottles is showing footage from the Schanze, focussing on the looting of shops and the damage done by protesters. Broken windows. Gutted cars. The shell of the water cannon. Then, it's the protesters being loaded into police vans, cuffed and turning their faces away from the cameras. Owners stand amongst the ruins of their shops and give bewildered, sad interviews. The TV's sound is muted, but the closed captions are on. After the protest report, a handsome man in a tight suit is on screen, a bouquet of microphones in front of him. His name comes up as Thorsten Jawinski, Hamburg Minister for the Interior.

"My congratulations go to our local police force who excelled at getting the situation quickly under control," read the quoted captions. "Numerous protesters were arrested, and you can be sure these perpetrators of unnecessary violence will be brought to justice. Today was another fine demonstration that our police force remains effective and reliable, and that the citizens of Hamburg can feel secure and protected, thanks to the good work of our brave police officers. We will continue to work around the clock to clear the streets of anarchists and hooligans. As I've stated many times, I fully support peaceful protest and I consider it an integral part of democracy. I marched in protests when I was a student, and I encourage people to march now, but to do so peacefully. If they simply fight with police, burn our city, rob our shops and put the lives of others in danger, they will face the full consequences of the law. We want to have a city that is safe for everyone, where our children can grow up without the threat of violence and crime. Thank you."

As Jawinski walks away from the microphones, Mara spots Nicola following him out of the camera shot.

The news moves on to a report about a huge anti-immigration demonstration in Vienna.

Mara looks down at her glass. The shot of Sambuca has three coffee beans in it. She thinks of Russell, who got her onto Sambuca and who always drinks it with three beans.

"They represent health, prosperity and happiness," he'd said when they shared their first bottle. That was in the Charité hospital, a few days after the protest where Russell was beaten so badly he was left crippled, and she herself had been lucky to escape with a broken arm. They were recovering in the same ward, a few doors from each other. Mara didn't know why she wanted to visit him, this stranger she'd helped. There was no attraction, nothing sexual. But she felt drawn to him, wanting to know him and hear his story. What had happened to Russell was utterly unfair and she felt guilty she hadn't been able to help him sooner. She sat next to his bed the whole first day, watching him sleep. The next day she was there again, sitting this time in his brand-new wheelchair. He was awake and curious about his visitor. Their conversation came easily, without force and with comfortable silences. Russell put it perfectly, at the end of that second day: they had ancient chemistry, had maybe known each other through various lives. Some people might have scoffed at such a claim, but it didn't strike Mara as strange. It made sense. Russell was grateful, and he apologised for not being in better spirits. Mara said he had every right to be angry. Russell wanted to express his gratitude, and got a friend of his to sneak a bottle of Sambuca into the hospital, plus a bag of coffee beans. It was delivered on the third day, and they drank it from cloudy, scratched hospital glasses, three beans in each.

"I always eat them," he'd said. "One at a time. I learned about this in Italy. I'm not a believer, but I still say a little prayer with each bean."

As she munches on the first Sambuca-flavoured coffee bean in the deserted lobby bar, she hopes Russell is healthy and wishes that he will one day be able to walk again. With the second, she hopes Zina is prospering in Stuttgart and that her presence continues to have a positive impact on all those around her. With the last coffee bean, she stares at it in the shot glass. All the Sambuca is gone. Just the happiness bean remains. She thinks about the looters and their greed and selfishness, and she thinks about hooligans who just want to see the city burn.

"What's in it for me? What do I get from the revolution?"

She eats the coffee bean and says a prayer for Richard, and for all those revolutionaries pursuing personal happiness.

They cycle along the river, from Elbe Help to Tinaya's temporary refugee accommodation centre in Rothenburgsort. On the way, Mara gets more of Tinaya's story, the telling of which had started over the whirr and clank of sewing machines this morning, when Mara had decided to sit away from Susie and found herself next to a young woman who introduced herself straight away as "Tinaya from Afghanistan".

They talked and sewed all morning. Mara wasn't really in the mood for a life story, especially one this grim, but the ongoing conversation kept her in this section of Elbe Help, far away from JJ's office, without the pretence of appearing to hide. Mara hoped her self-imposed exile to the farthest sewing corner might force JJ to make the first reconciliatory move.

While Tinaya's story was hard to hear, it felt necessary. Mara also assumed she was getting a censored account, as hearing the blow-by-blow daily travails of a 15-year-old girl travelling from a small village outside Ghanzi entirely by land to Passau over the course of 18 months wasn't the kind of talk people had when becoming acquainted. But Tinaya wanted her to know it.

"The whole time," she'd said, as they sat by the river having lunch together, "I kept promising myself that when I get to Germany, I will learn how to defend myself. I've been here for over a year now and I haven't done it. I felt so vulnerable on that journey. All the other girls, they just want to marry someone with a German passport. Muslim, Afghan, German, it doesn't matter anymore. What matters most is the passport. Being automatically allowed to stay and to bring family members here, legally. To be safe forever."

"It's not as safe as you think."

"It is, by comparison. No. You can't even compare. How can you compare Germany to a country that will not even allow me to have a book in my hands?"

"That's wrong on so many levels. But from what you said, there were lots of girls making this journey."

"Yes. A few years ago, all the boys were being sent away. To Europe, to make the big money and send it back home. The boys were good in the beginning, if they made it. But they all start thinking selfishly at some point. They want the money for themselves. Or they suffer from prejudice and racism. Many of them try to go back."

"Why do the girls go then? I bet they're victims of prejudice as well."

"Many don't want to go. Their families force them. They save and save to pay the smugglers just for the first part of the journey. To get over the border. Then, they're on their own."

"I'm glad you made it. But don't you want to get married and have a family?"

"Yes, one day. I also want to help my family. Right now, I want to learn how to fight. Can you teach me?"

"I can try."

"That was you in the video. Everyone says it was you. I was there too, at the protest, but I ran even before I got to the park. I'm so ashamed."

"Don't be. That was a smart move."

"I want to stop running. I want to be a fighter. Like you. The policeman knocked you over, but you got straight up and beat him. It was so brave. I want to be this brave."

"It was stupid. My carelessness put all those people in danger."

"You're wrong. My name, Tinaya, it means warrior. This is me. This is who I want to be."

"I'm supposed to start training girls on Saturday. You can join, if you want."

"Yes. Thank you."

"Be warned. It's a long process. You need to be fit."

"I ride my bike every day from Rothenburgsort."

"That's a good start."

So, they ended up riding together, once the sewing day was done, Mara having decided to visit Richard. Tinaya had a small bike, which she said had been donated to Elbe Help and made rideable by Jesper, of all people.

When they get out there, instead of turning down the road to Moorfleet, Mara rides with Tinaya to the refugee centre, which is several double stacks of old shipping containers, converted into a residence.

"Four bunk beds in each one," Tinaya says, as they stop in front.

"Eight people in one container?"

"Not every bunk is taken, as many people come and go. The girls are kept separate, because bad things could happen if the rooms are shared."

Tinaya locks her bike against the high green fence that surrounds the containers. The one entry point is gated and manned by two beefy guards.

"All the more reason to learn how to fight," Mara says.

"Yes."

"You're welcome to bring as many girls as you want on Saturday."

"Okay. Thank you, Mara. And thanks for riding with me."

"It was on my way. My father lives a bit further from here."

As Mara says this, it occurs to her that a dozen refugees could live quite comfortably in Richard's house.

"That's nice. Are you visiting your father? Or do you live there?"

"Just visiting."

"Still nice. Family is important." Tinaya starts walking towards the line at the gate, where the guards are checking IDs. "See you tomorrow."

"Yeah." Mara wheels the bike around. "Hey, Tinaya. Thanks for telling me your story."

Tinaya smiles, then waves shyly.

Mara heads back the way she came, then cycles over the bridge at the Billwerder sluice and onto the back road to Moorfleet. No vehicles here, which is a relief. A few people are running, while others walk dogs along the dyke, but the dominant mode of transport is the bicycle, with everyone from commuters on electrics returning home from jobs in the city to Lycra-clad evening athletes on expensive racing bikes.

She's finding Tinaya's journey hard to imagine. 18 months is a long time for a teenage girl travelling through some rough country on her own. Because surely, along the way, there would've been numerous leeches and low-lifes looking to take advantage of her.

At the same age, Mara's life fell apart. She wasn't sent on a hellish, husband-finding odyssey by her family, but she did feel that her own family had let her down and she was on her own. The easy thing would be to lay all the blame at her father's feet, but Mara would be the first to admit now that a lot of the roads she went down were of her own choosing. That doesn't mean Richard has nothing to answer for; he was, after all, the one who made many of the decisions that so greatly impacted the foundation of her life, and did so without consulting her. That's the key point: he didn't ask. Nothing was

140

discussed. The move was forced on her, and she rebelled against it.

But if she's honest, it was Zina leaving that really changed things.

She turns down the narrow drive towards her father's house, telling herself not to be hard on him. He's just another person doing the best he can.

Felix runs out to greet her. He doesn't bark, something she noticed when she first encountered him.

She leans the bike against the wall, under the rigged awning. Raindrops start splatting against it.

The front door opens.

"Ah, Mara? Quick. Get inside."

"How did you know someone was here?"

"Sensors. I'm glad it's you. Now, get in before anyone sees you."

"Who's watching?"

"Everyone. Shoes off."

He ushers her in, shutting the door and securing the three locks. She wants to ask about the sensors, but decides to let it go. She slips her shoes off. The basket reserved for muddy boots has fresh paper in its lining.

"I'm so proud of you," he says, moving through the house. "Incredibly proud. I wanted to call you and tell you myself, but I'm not doing that on the phone."

They end up in the spotless kitchen. Richard puts the kettle on. Mara sits at the table.

"Where's this coming from?" she asks.

"Just mind-blowing, what you did. You're on the right team now as well. Finally. Standing up against oppression. Tea?"

"Uh, yeah. Thanks."

Richard takes a dishcloth and absently wipes the counter.

"They all followed your lead," he says. "This could be your future, Mara. You should consider getting into politics. Stand up to the conservatives like you stood up to that police officer."

"Oh, that video. Look, that was more reaction than action."

"Hamburg needs you, Mara."

"I'm not a full convert just yet, and I have zero interest in politics."

"The city is a few steps from becoming a full-blown police state. That's what Jawinski wants, for sure. He'll never say that outright though. He's too clever for that. He'll talk about security and community and wanting our children to feel safe on the streets."

"Jawinski? I saw him on the news."

"The people need to stand up to bullies like him. Don't look at me like that."

"What look? I'm not giving you a look."

"Like you think I'm crazy. He is a bully. I'd like to see you take him down. You really are your father's daughter."

This makes Mara shift in her chair. "I don't think we'll ever see politicians at the front line of a protest, on either side."

"You could be the first. Don't believe the image Jawinski presents. That man is a nationalist at his core. He wants to be mayor. God knows what Hamburg will become if he gets that. Then he'll set his sights on the Chancellery. First, he takes Hamburg, then he takes Berlin. History could repeat itself all over again."

"Stop being so dramatic." She wants to argue the point further, but her headstrong father can't be argued with. She considers the conniving Nicola to be a bigger threat than the glorified salesman in his tight suit. Is she pulling Jawinski's strings? Or does she have ambitions of her own, using Jawinski as a stepping stone?

"Given the way things are going," her father says, "I'm not being dramatic enough. Germany is on the verge of another self-destructive era."

While arguing with Richard is pointless, because he simply doesn't listen and can never have his opinion swayed, Mara knows he can be manipulated.

He brings the two cups to the table. "Coasters."

Mara takes two from the neat stack in the middle of the table and deals one to Richard and one to herself. She watches her father place the cup perfectly in the coaster's centre and swivel it so the handle is aimed towards her right hand.

"Thanks," she says.

What she dismissed as quirks for so many years are now presenting themselves as troubling. She wonders what kind of struggles are going on in her father's head. How can she make him realise he might need help?

"He was a student of mine," Richard says, sitting down. He puts both hands around his cup to keep himself from fidgeting. "Thorsten. A total regurgitator. The kind of student who kept his own opinions to himself and just said what he thought I wanted to hear. But even when he was saying those things, you could see in his eyes that he

142

didn't believe his own words. Too cunning and clever for his own good. I'd say dangerous, with his most dangerous quality being that he's good-looking. It's pathetic the way people are suckers for beauty, but it's a power we can't deny."

"People will always open a present when it comes in a pretty box."

"Yes, even if it's ticking."

"When's the next election?"

"Later this year. It hasn't been announced yet, but Jawinski will be a candidate. You can guarantee it. He's making all the right moves."

Mara sips her herbal tea, which is very good. "Do you think he's been giving the orders to the police to be more aggressive with protesters?"

"Not just with them. It's been amped up everywhere. Even out here. In fact, this little nook is a prime example of the shit Jawinski is stirring."

"How so?"

"Moorfleet has one police officer. Sten. His house is the police station. It's at the end of the street. Everyone around here knows Sten. You could always rely on him to be helpful and fair. Now, he's out there every day, ticketing anything that moves and watching everyone closely. He's turned Moorfleet into his own little police state. Believe me, Sten didn't change overnight, all on his own. Someone changed him."

"I seriously doubt that Hamburg's Minister for the Interior came out to the Moorfleet police station to tell its lone cop to clamp down on the locals."

"One order gets passed to another, on down the line," Richard says with conviction. "Oh, we're brilliant at that."

"At what?"

"Following orders. All through history, we have been the absolute best at doing what we're told."

"Not me."

"When it goes well, we're part of it and can bask in the success. When things turn bad, we can blame the person above us. 'Don't look at me. I was just following orders.' It's the easiest method of handwashing. No. They need to question. Go against the orders. Just like you did. There aren't enough people in Germany willing to defy

143

authority, but I'm glad now to say you're one of them."

"You sound like you're deep into this topic. Is this something you're writing about? Germany's history of following orders?"

"It's a component of a broader essay."

"About?"

Richard's smile betrays the slightest hint of disgust. "Is that why you stopped by? To interrogate me about my work? Are you worried I'll write something that embarrasses you again?"

And there it is, Mara thinks: her father considers that she herself would conspire against him, that she is watching him.

"You can write whatever you want."

"The university requires me to publish every year. You know that."

Mara sips some more tea. "Maybe you should write about this," she says, holding up the cup. "How to make the perfect cup of tea. It's very good."

"It's the water." Richard thumbs at the sink behind him, at the weird device on the tap. "Marleen makes filters. She lives two houses down. She came up with a system to purify water right as it comes out of the tap. Brilliant. Necessary too, because they're putting all sorts of crud in what's left of the groundwater these days."

"Something else you're writing about? Water shortages?"

"Marleen's also got this gadget for the shower. A timer that cuts the water off after two minutes. To stop people wasting it."

"You sound pretty proud of her too."

"She's a clever girl. From Estonia. We need innovations like this. The human race won't last long if we run out of water. That's something to get out on the streets and protest about."

"I'll be sure to raise it at the next meeting." Mara looks at her father, getting frustrated all over again and feeling like a teenager. "Look, I came out here to see you. I'm worried about you."

"Really?"

"I was in the neighbourhood and ..."

"With Remy?"

"Why would I be with him? No. I know someone who lives in Rothenburgsort. Tinaya. Nice girl. She's currently at the refugee centre."

"That monstrosity? They need to tear it down. Send all the refugees back home."

"What? I thought you'd be volunteering there. You always supported open borders. I remember that essay. 'The United States of Europe'. What happened to that thinking?"

"That was years ago. I was in a different place back then. I understand now that seeking refuge isn't the answer. Countries that take refugees in, like Germany did and still does, just compound the situation."

"I can't believe I'm hearing this."

"Listen and you'll learn something. By running away, a refugee is essentially supporting whatever regime is in place. These people should stay and fight and fix their own countries, rather than run away from them."

"You don't seriously think that? They just want to be safe and live their lives."

"To claim to be a refugee," her father says, his voice rising, "is to attribute blame. It's a way to externalise problems. It puts the onus on others to solve those problems for you. These people should take responsibility."

"And die trying?"

"Wouldn't you? The real problem is that 'refugee' has become a method of upward mobility without earning it. This whole thing about escaping persecution and tyrannical regimes is propaganda. You could almost call it rebranding. The refugees are cast as heroes who risked everything to escape, when really they're cowards who ran. If you want to get right to the truth of it all, they're people focused entirely on their own gain. The western world. Money. A better life."

"I never would've expected you to think like this. Why shouldn't people want a better life?"

"You're not listening, Mara, like always. Everyone can aspire to better themselves. They should. This, however, is a shortcut. One that makes everything worse. If they really want a better life and to change their own country, they would dig their feet into their dirt and fight for it. But no, it's easier to sneak away at dawn on a crowded raft at $10,000 a head."

"How on earth is Tinaya supposed to overthrow the Taliban? It's pitchforks against machine guns."

"Thank you. Afghanistan is the best example of what I'm talking about. A country that's stuck in the hamster wheel of fear and blame.

Around and around they go, century after century. It doesn't matter who's in power or who tries to invade. The leaders use fear and oppression to maintain power. The citizens blame the leaders for their bad lives. People leave. Power eventually changes hands. And the whole thing starts again. Whoever is in power believes they are good and doing the right things. In order to keep power, they have to ensure the people are scared of them."

"You're over-simplifying it. You can be so frustrating sometimes. The Taliban are evil. That's clear."

"Is it?" her father asks, in his element and thoroughly enjoying himself. "Do you think they sit around every evening and raise their glasses to evil? No. They think they're good. Gooder than good. Holy. They're doing Allah's work, bound for paradise when their time comes. If that means beheading anyone who disagrees and treating women like garbage, then so be it. They believe they are fighting the good fight."

Mara can't reply. She wants to leave, but outside the rain falls harder. It hits the kitchen window like someone throwing small pebbles against the glass.

"I'll take your silence as agreement," her father continues. "The thing is, all these people who disagree should be the ones picking up the knives and beheading the Taliban. You can be sure the Taliban are more than happy when their opponents leave, as it means they have fewer enemies to fight. I read a very interesting article a few months ago that described how the Taliban run the people smuggling industry in Afghanistan. So, not only do they get rid of the people they don't want, they make huge amounts of money in the process."

"Stop talking. I hate it when you talk like this."

"Like what?"

"Like this. Like a bigot."

"There's nothing bigoted about it. I'm just speaking the truth. If these so-called 'refugees' really believed in change, really wanted it, they would fight for it. No, no. Sneak away. Seek immediate gratification somewhere else. Let someone else save you through generosity. That's the real problem. People think that becoming a refugee is their last resort. The only and final thing they can do when all is lost. Wrong. It's the first move. The last resort, the very last act in a moment of desperation, would be …"

146

"Death? Your last resort, for all these people who just get in the way of the power struggles and ideologies of others, is a grave?"

Richard sits back, his point made. "Your words."

She realises that in an attempt to manipulate her father, he has manipulated her.

They stare at each other. Richard sips his tea like he's sitting on a golden egg.

"So that's where Ant gets it from," Mara says.

"Gets what?"

"This awful habit of changing his opinion every week. He just follows whoever he likes the most at any given time and echoes whatever that person says. So do you."

Her father's smugness turns to anger. "That's it. Take the cheap shot against someone whose argument is more convincing. Make it personal. It's an insult to me and Anthony."

"Who's where exactly?"

"I'm sure he's fine, wherever he is."

"Superb parenting, Dad."

He shakes his head admonishingly. "This is what you do when you're backed against the wall. You try to hurt people. Well, it hurts that you waltz in here and accuse me of being unoriginal, and a bad parent, and a bigot. All my opinions and beliefs have been shaped by my own thinking and experiences. I'm shocked you would think otherwise."

"I'm shocked you've gone from believing one thing to believing the opposite. I mean, you were there, at the central station, handing out bottles of water to refugees when they arrived. Now you're saying they should all be sent back. That's a huge change and I find it seriously worrying."

"This from the girl who went from breaking the law to upholding it, and who's gone back to breaking it again."

She wants to tell him the truth, that she's undercover and trying to save Anthony. All the sentences form in her mind; she just needs to open her mouth and it will all pour out, impressive enough to shut him up.

"Got you there," he says. "Of course, to be honest, I don't see anything wrong with people changing their opinions. You should be proud your brother is open to new things and new ways of thinking. It shows development and learning. Evolution."

147

"Compared to me. Same old Mara again."

"You said it. I think the saddest thing a person can be is someone unwilling to change. Or maybe even worse than that is someone who changes but then goes back to being the person they were before."

"You're saying I'm de-evolving? Ten minutes ago, you said you'd never been prouder of me."

Her father doesn't reply. The resulting silence is like all those other silences, during Mara's childhood and troubled teens, when they argued and she would try to catch him in his contradictions and outsmart him, but he somehow always won. Or at least, he made it seem like he won.

Mara looks out the window as the fat rain rattles against it, wondering how he manages to behave like he's talking sense even when spouting garbage. Is there a class for this at law school? *Introduction to How to Sound Logical When Waking Up One Day and Discovering You're a Racist.* But, she concedes, underneath it all, he makes a telling point about how it's important for people to change and to have those changes accepted.

"There's no denying it," she says, breaking the silence and keen to fight her way out of the corner. "In the end, we all become our parents."

"Well, that's just perfect. When all else fails, take the cheapest shot you can. I hope that feels good. What do you pugilists call it?"

"A knockout punch."

"No, no, no. Below the belt. It rolls right off me, because I'm nothing like my parents."

"But Anthony is like you, and he's a bit like your parents. How are they?"

"Unchanged."

Mara laughs.

"That's not funny, Mara. Not at all. You have no idea what it was like growing up in that house, with those people. Traumatising."

"Yeah, wealth is just awful. Isn't it?"

"It is when it's used to control people. To own them."

"What does that mean?"

"Exactly what I said. My parents use money to control people. Me. My family. They bought our house in Othmarschen without even telling me, just so they could control me."

"I didn't know that."

"Why do you think we left? It was also why I quit my job. I had to cut ties with them completely. Get out from under their thumbs."

"Why didn't you ever say this? About the house."

"Because it was between me and my parents. I didn't want to get you involved. You were too young anyway."

"I was 15."

"They bought the house not long after Anthony was born."

"What? After mum left?"

Richard shakes a finger at Mara. "Don't do that. Don't you try to connect all those dots, as if putting them together will make everything a neat, clear picture. It wasn't like that. Your mother was gone, in her head, years before. Don't forget she was often away for work for weeks at a time. It was just you and me. Then it was you and me taking care of Anthony. Those were good days. Hard, but good."

"Why did your parents buy the house?"

"Because of Anthony. My mother even said that, years later. Was proud of it, that they'd done a great and wonderful thing. Because the Steinbachs had a male heir. Yes, maybe they were trying to force themselves back into our lives now that Agnes was gone. Your mother never liked my parents. They certainly didn't like her."

Mara wants to ask why her mother left, but knows her father will simply leave the room if asked that.

"So, Anthony was a baby," she says. "Your parents bought our house. Then we lived there for another eight years. Why?"

"I wanted to move straight away, but you had started boxing and it was so important to you. I saw the way you looked up to Zina. I held on for as long as I could and saved enough money in that time to buy this place."

"Which you bought not long after Zina moved to Stuttgart. Were you waiting for her to leave?"

"Of course not. It just happened around the same time. I got the job offer at the university and that was my ticket out of the family business. I could get away from my parents. That's what I did."

"Without asking me if I wanted to move."

"It wasn't your decision," her father says. "This was between me and my parents. I think in the end we should've moved further away. Because I still can't get those two out of my life. Anthony being close to them just makes my blood boil. They still call too, but I don't answer. My mother writes these diabolical letters, like they were

149

written in 1936."

Mara looks around the kitchen, wondering how her life might have been different if they'd moved away from Hamburg.

The way Richard turns to the window with his arms folded suggests he's said all he will on this subject.

Mara decides to try a different approach. "So, what do you think of Janica?"

"Who's she?"

"Ant's girlfriend."

"He doesn't have a girlfriend," he says, turning back to face her. "I'm not entirely certain he even likes girls. I've always wondered if it's the homoeroticism of basketball that makes him love the sport so much. All those sweaty boys, rubbing up against each other and trying so emphatically to put a round thing in a round hole."

"Oh, come on."

"Don't be so shocked."

"Are you going to call me a lesbian because I used to box?"

"On the contrary, boxing has always struck me as the ultimate form of competition elimination. Winner marries the king. Or something like that."

"You're out of your mind."

"Sports have always had elements of eroticism," her father says, warming to the topic. "Going right back to the gladiators, and further. Only the strong survive, and the strongest gets to club the woman over her head and drag her back to his cave. The ancient Olympics even had the athletes competing with nothing on. A couple of guys wrestling in the nude is about as homoerotic as it gets."

"You're wrong."

"I've been waiting for years for him to come to me and say it. I was hoping for it. Because it just might be the kind of thing that gives my parents heart attacks. Simultaneously. The end of the Steinbach line, at last."

"He's not gay."

"How can you be so sure?"

"He would've told me."

"You really think you're still that close?" her father asks. "You don't even know where he is."

"You also don't know where he is." Mara stands up. "But I know who Janica is."

"If this Janica does turn out to be Anthony's girlfriend, you'll have to forgive me for being massively disappointed."

She's had enough and walks out of the kitchen.

"Where are you going? It's raining."

Shoes on, she unlocks the door and leaves it wide open. Then it's hood up and onto the bike. Pedalling away from the house, the rain feels somehow cleansing.

She rides hard, eager to put Moorfleet behind her, but the conversation continues in her head. She mentally says all the things she wanted to say to her father, predicting his responses, and getting so caught up in this internal battle, she barely notices the ride. She soon finds herself at Hamburger Berg, soaked and sweating.

When she gets off the bike, a set of headlights flash. They flash again when she looks in that direction. She goes to the car, a black hatchback. The window lowers.

"Nils?"

"Hey."

"What are you doing here?"

"Waiting for you."

He seems huge in the small car, with the seat way back. His gelled blonde hair brushes the glass of the sunroof, leaving streaks.

"Is Perceval upstairs?"

"He's not here."

"What do you want then? Can you make it fast? I'm freezing. I need a shower and to put on dry clothes."

"I think I've found Anthony."

"Really? Nils, you star. That's brilliant. Where is he?"

"Travemünde."

That single word is like a punch to Mara's stomach.

"What's wrong?" Nils asks.

"Nothing. It's ... oh, fuck. It's ... look, is this your car?"

"I certainly don't steal cars like you used to."

"You read my file. Now you know I was a screw-up who got straight."

"What's missing is the origin story," Nils says. "How it all began, how you ended up turning to crime and how you got out of it."

"You like those kinds of movies?"

"Yeah. I do. Maybe we could go sometime? See a movie."

"I'd rather you drive me to Travemünde."

151

"What? Now?"

"You doing anything?"

Nils shrugs his pointy shoulders. "I just finished training. I'm hungry. Why don't we have something to eat?"

"Okay, this has to stop, Nils. But, yeah, get us something to eat, for the trip."

"You're serious. About Travemünde."

Mara starts wheeling the bike away. "Give me ten minutes."

As she hauls the dirty bike up the rickety stairs, she wonders why Nils suddenly has a romantic interest in her.

The wet clothes get piled on the bathroom floor and left there. She's in and out of the shower in under two minutes, which would make her father's Estonian neighbour happy. She checks her phone while pulling on jeans and a fresh hoodie. The only thing worth reading is the message from Zina: "WTF are you up to in HH? I saw the vids in a morning briefing. Explain!"

She replies: "Will tell all in S. Visit soon. Promise."

She leaves the phone on the bed, puts on a fresh bandage and heads back down the stairs. Nils is in the car, sitting in the passenger seat, with that seat as far back as it will go, eating noodles from a colourful box. She gets in and moves the driver's seat forward. The distance between the two of them seems weird.

"We have to take turns," he says. "It's illegal to eat and drive."

She starts the car. "What a good citizen you are. Have a look at the German Criminal Code and you'll be amazed to learn about all the things we're not allowed to do."

"What's in Travemünde? Do you have family there?"

"Nothing in your precious file on that?" Mara puts the car in reverse and starts backing out.

"No. So, tell me."

"You don't want to know. Trust me, you really don't want to know."

***

The house is the second last up the tree-lined street of Helldahl, on top of a long rise and away from the beach promenade that visitors pound all year round, from the north mole to the yacht club.

As Nils stops the car in front of the house, he gives it an envious

152

look. The villa is faintly lit by old-fashioned streetlamps. Mara leans forward and grimaces. No lights in the windows and no car out front. But none of the security shutters are down.

"Must be awesome to have this in the family," Nils says.

"You'd think that. Depends on the kind of people who live here."

"I came to Travemünde as a kid, but we stayed in Priwall. On the other side of the water."

"The poor side, as my grandmother used to say. She probably still says that, and with even more contempt. She once campaigned to stop the ferries from running, to keep the poor people from crossing over."

"We took that ferry and walked around. I remember asking my parents who lived in these big, beautiful houses. Because a lot of them looked empty. Like this one."

"Holiday homes, most of them. This one has been in my family for almost a hundred years, on my grandfather's side. Do not ask me how that happened. All these places, the really nice ones, are never, ever for sale. They get passed onto the next generation."

"So, you and Anthony will get this one then."

"If I ever inherit this place, I will make it my mission to give it back to its rightful owners."

"What does that mean?"

"Ant would never let me sell it. Anyway, my grandparents are the kind of people who live forever."

"You must've spent lots of holidays here."

Mara laughs a little. "You'd think that too."

Nils scans the house. "I don't think anyone's home."

"They're probably on holiday. They have loads of money and go away a lot. Normally to shoot things. I don't think Ant's here."

"As I said, I only heard from a friend of Janica's that she'd gone to Travemünde with her boyfriend. Maybe they're staying somewhere else in town."

Mara looks at the house again. "He always liked coming here. A few times, he ran away from home and ended up here. My father had to take the train and get him. But he always let him stay for a few days, until Ant got bored and wanted to come home."

"I'd run away too, if I could run to a place like this."

"I'd lose all respect for you if you did."

Mara gets out and stretches, then puts the empty food containers

153

in a bin. A napkin floats to the ground. She picks it up and bins it. The street is completely free of litter.

Nils gets out as well. "What do we do?"

"No harm in having a look around." She opens the front gate and points at a white box attached to the ceiling near the front door. "The alarm's off. That's unusual. Someone's been here."

"Maybe the cleaning lady."

"Or Anthony."

Nils follows Mara towards the house. "Do you have a key?"

She goes to the side of the garage, to the boxy black key holder shaped like a massive padlock. The top flap slides down, revealing four dials, each numbered 0-9. She doesn't think the old code will work, but tries it anyway. 1-9-3-3. The notch moves down and the box opens.

"Wow," she says, stunned. "Unchanged indeed."

As she goes to the front door, Nils follows close behind.

"I'd prefer you to wait outside," she says.

"I need to use the bathroom."

"There's a forest at the end of the street. Go mark a tree."

"It'll just take a minute."

"Okay. There's one for guests, just inside the door. Use it and leave."

She opens the door and turns on the lights. Nils goes into the bathroom while Mara edges further into the house. The air is stale and musty. If Anthony and Janica were here, she thinks they didn't stay long. Like a well-trained police officer, she first checks the garbage in the kitchen. Empty. The fridge is also empty, turned off and its door left slightly ajar.

Every single thing, big and small, stirs up memories she'd rather not revisit.

The toilet flushes. Nils comes out and stands at the entrance.

"Any sign of them?" he asks.

She ignores him, moving from the kitchen to the dining area and down the three steps to the sunken living room. The huge tiger skin rug, replete with roaring mouth baring sharp fangs, dominates the room. She stands in the middle of the rug, wiping her feet and digging her shoes in. If Nils wasn't standing there, she would be seriously tempted to crouch down and urinate on the rug.

The living room is the same as she remembers. She scans it for

154

anything noticeably missing. Because if Anthony came here to ask for money and found an empty house, she thinks, then he probably took something that could be easily turned into cash.

"What are you looking for?" Nils asks, now standing in the dining room.

"I told you to wait outside."

"Maybe I can help."

"You can't."

"Is that real?" he asks, pointing at the rug.

"Stop asking questions and let me think."

"Did your grandfather shoot it?" Nils crouches down to inspect the tiger's head. "You said before they were on holiday, shooting things."

"If they were here, they would brag long and loud about all the innocent animals they've killed. Grandpa would tell you with full conviction that killing this tiger was the greatest day of his life."

"I'm kind of glad they're not here."

"If you'd stayed in the car like you were told to, you would've been spared all this. Now that you're in here, judge away. But don't judge me on this."

Mara takes the stairs up to the bedrooms. The wall along the stairway is covered in framed photos. Their wedding photo, both conservatively dressed for the swinging 60s. Her grandparents at famous places around the world, but neither of them ever smiling. Hunting shots, both holding rifles while standing with a leg up on a fallen beast. Her father, a single child, as a young boy, looking annoyed in a khaki boy scouts' uniform, like he was forced to wear it, and her father as a young law graduate, in robes. Incredibly, those are the only two photos of him on the wall. A puny Mara and an infant Anthony in a hole she had dug at the beach. A pre-teen Anthony surrounded by basketball trophies. Her grandparents posing with famous politicians. Her grandfather in a tuxedo receiving some kind of award. There are also older photos that she can't look at, but which still catch her eyes; grainy 1930s shots of great-grandparents she never met with big smiles, proud of the uniforms they're wearing.

No photos of her mother. Not even a wedding photo of her parents. But there is a small one at the top of the stairs, of Mara in police uniform. It was taken by Zina the day she graduated from the academy; she wonders how her grandparents got hold of it. She

155

reaches out to take it from the wall, but then decides to leave it there, as taking the photo might be a giveaway she was here. That was a great day, she thinks, remembering how happy Zina was. But now, she's just one more Steinbach in uniform, on a wall covered with family members in uniforms.

On the first floor, there are three bedrooms. The wooden floor creaks underfoot as she goes in and out of the two guest rooms, where there is nothing of value. Not even the main bedroom has any wealth on show; all the valuables are locked away in the safe, wherever that is.

"Anything?" Nils calls out from the bottom of the stairs, his voice echoing.

She goes down the stairs two at a time and passes Nils without a word. Then, she's taking another set of stairs that lead to the cellar. The stairway is lined with bottles of wine, laid flat, tops forward, labels up. The cellar itself has a 12-foot billiards table, covered in a shiny black sheet that almost reaches the floor on all sides. There's a wooden bar in one corner, long enough for three high-backed white stools. The pair of armchairs in the other corner are blood red. Behind them is a glass-doored gun rack, the rifles inside standing upright and ordered by size. It's locked, but all the slots are full, meaning no rifles are missing.

Nils appears. "Amazing how much you can learn about people just by the place where they live."

"You should know all about that. You're the one with a detective for a mother. Didn't she teach you any of this? Like putting your hands in your pockets so you don't touch anything."

"Yeah, when it's a crime scene."

"This is a crime scene. Anthony took something from in here, I'm sure of it."

Mara walks slowly along the mantlepiece that runs from the bar to the cue rack.

"There used to be something here," she says, pointing at the gap in the middle of the mantlepiece. "Something fancy. Like, a centrepiece."

She looks closer, seeing the faint outline of a circle where there is no dust.

Nils also comes over for a look. "A vase maybe. Or a candlestick."

She punches him in the shoulder, making him wince. "Yes. The

156

gold candlestick. It was always right here."

"Do you think Anthony took it?"

The loud knock on the door makes them both turn and look towards the stairs.

"Fuck," Mara says. "The lights."

"Must be a neighbour."

Mara nods. "It was a matter of time. You should've stayed at the front door, as a lookout. Now, stay here. And do as you're told this time."

She goes up the stairs and opens the door on a small woman, around 70, whose big hair is vaguely familiar. She purses her lips horribly together.

"Can I help you?" Mara asks.

"What are you doing in this house?"

"It was supposed to be a surprise."

The woman folds her arms. Mara is stunned to see she has a tattoo of a butterfly on the top of her right wrist.

"A spontaneous visit," Mara adds.

"Karl and Susanne are in Namibia."

"So that's where they are. Sorry, I didn't know that."

"I'm calling the police."

"There's no need for that. I'm Mara Steinbach. Their granddaughter."

The woman's dour expression slowly changes into a rather attractive smile. "Oh, yes. Mara. It is you. I thought you looked familiar. It's been such a long time."

"It has." Mara has no idea who this woman is.

"You were just a girl the last time I saw you. Look at you now. Such a beautiful young woman."

"Do you know when they'll be back?"

"In a week. I've been collecting their mail and keeping an eye on things. There have been a few break-ins lately. Can't trust anyone these days."

Mara points to the box on the ceiling. "Probably a good idea to get the alarm turned on again."

"I thought it was on."

"It was off when I got here."

"I'll take care of it. I'll be sure to tell them you were here."

"Thanks."

157

The way the woman stands there, with such firm friendliness, makes Mara think the woman won't leave until she herself leaves.

"Mara Steinbach. Such a troublemaker. I remember that. A crier too. You cried more than your baby brother. But you're all grown up now."

"I am. Anthony does most of the crying now."

"Hah. I doubt that, big basketball star that he is. I hear you're a police officer. How's that going for you?"

"Great. Great."

"We could certainly use more police around here. With all the break-ins." The woman looks at Mara's forehead. "But it must be dangerous. Did you get that on the job?"

"Oh, yes. All in the line of duty."

"Good for you."

The woman continues to smile thinly. There is just no getting rid of her.

"May I ask how you got into the house? Susanne would be very angry if you broke any of her windows. I'd have to get it fixed too. Or do they teach you how to pick locks at police school?"

"I used the spare key. In the security box."

"Did you? Be sure to put that back."

"I will."

They look at each other. Mara realises she has no choice but to expose Nils. She can't leave him there, locked inside.

"Nils?" she calls out. "Time to go."

"Is someone with you?"

"My boyfriend," Mara says. "This was the surprise. I ... you know ... I wanted them to meet him."

The woman leans to her left to look past Mara as Nils comes through the doorway. Then she cranes her neck slowly upwards.

"Oh my. Aren't you a tall and handsome young man. Such lovely blonde hair."

"Hello. I'm Nils."

"I'll get the keys," Mara says, going to the kitchen.

"It's so nice to meet you, Nils," the woman says. "I don't mind telling you that Susanne will be very glad to know Mara has such a fine male companion. You should come back in a week. She worried for years that Mara, well, how shall I say it. Susanne never thought Mara would bring a gentleman to visit."

158

Mara goes back to the door. She gently pushes Nils out of the doorway and locks the front door.

"We're very sorry for disturbing your evening," Nils says.

"It's no problem at all."

The woman loops an elbow around Nils's wrist and walks him down the path to the gate. Mara puts the keys back in the security box, leaving the number dials on 1-9-4-5. But she thinks better of this and scrambles the numbers.

When Nils and Mara are at the car, the woman waves from her front door, across the street. Nils waves back. They get in.

"Boyfriend?" Nils asks. "You don't even want to go the movies with me."

"It's all I could think of."

Nils starts the car. "Now what?"

"Back to Hamburg."

"I've really had it. Why don't we stay the night? Find a hotel. Separate rooms, I promise. Drive back in the morning."

"You can do that, if you like. But drop me at the train station. I'm not spending one second longer than I need to in this town." Mara softens her tone. "Sorry. Look, I can drive if you're too tired."

"I got it." Nils reverses onto the street. "It just seems like this was a total waste of time."

They drive down Helldahl, past all the old-timey streetlights that are supposed to be quaint but hark back to an era many would like to forget.

"It was good we came. Thanks for driving."

"How was this good?"

"We now know Anthony and Janica were here. They must've got lucky, were in and out before a neighbour saw them."

"Or they came in the middle of the night."

"They probably hocked that candlestick already. They needed cash."

"To travel? That means they could be anywhere now."

"Yeah."

"Why is it so important to find them? From what I heard, they're in love. It's bad they quit their teams, and Ace's a fool for rejecting that scholarship, but they're focusing on each other. That's the only thing that matters."

"You're a real romantic, Nils."

159

They drive onto the main road out of town, where Nils speeds up.

"What are you not telling me?" he asks. "Is your brother in some kind of trouble?"

Mara doesn't reply.

"If they've run off together," Nils continues, "there's not much you can do about that."

Mara stays silent. There's little traffic. The main road joins the Autobahn. Nils drives really fast down the outside lane, flashing his lights to make the slower cars ahead move out of the way.

"Fine," he says. "Keep it all to yourself."

They drive the rest of the way in silence. Once they're in Hamburg and driving through the centre of the city, Nils receives a call. He presses a button on the steering wheel.

"Hello?"

"Christoph here."

Nils looks at Mara, who shakes her head, signalling that Perceval shouldn't know she's in the car.

"What's going on?" Nils asks.

"Why am I on speakerphone?"

"I'm driving home. From basketball training."

"We've picked up some chatter. Apparently, there will be an important meeting on Wednesday. In Berlin. A gathering of clans, one could say. With representatives from numerous protest groups from Germany and abroad."

"Sounds big. Is it real?"

"We require the asset to attend this meeting. To observe and report."

Mara mouths "asset" to Nils.

"Do you have any details?"

"I hope to know more tomorrow. It could well be a ruse, as you suggest. It's highly unusual this communication is happening digitally. They are fully aware we are monitoring them. However, it could simply be time is too short for the verbal telegraph."

"Maybe they're not trying to keep this meeting secret. They want us to know about it."

There's a moment of silence, before Perceval says, "That's a very pertinent point, Nils. They have something to gain from us knowing."

Mara flexes her bicep and points at it.

"They're flexing their muscles," Nils says, without confidence.

160

"Indeed. A show of strength of their own. Perhaps an open attempt at unity. To show us they are coming together in a bloc."

"Isn't this what you've been waiting for?"

"It is. I will organise a meet with the asset tomorrow. Good evening, Nils. Continue driving safely."

Perceval ends the call before Nils can reply.

"Did you know about this?" he asks.

"No."

Nils turns onto Hamburger Berg, parks the car and switches the engine off.

"I always get the feeling you're not telling me everything," he says.

"Your asset is doing the best she can." Mara opens the door. "Thanks for driving."

"Maybe you can buy me a drink as payback."

"Look, Nils. What we're into here is already messy enough. I don't want to complicate things by getting feelings involved. I'm sure Perceval would agree with me on that. He wouldn't want you fucking the asset."

Nils stares straight ahead. "I heard what that woman said. You can just tell me you're not into guys."

"That woman doesn't know what she's talking about. If ever a girl turns you down, that doesn't automatically mean she's a lesbian."

"That's not what I meant."

Mara gets out and shuts the door. She doesn't look back. In the apartment, it's once again a relief to be alone.

She walks from the gym to the Pink Dragon, feeling the good kind of sore that results from a boxing session. Her calves are particularly tight from jumping rope, something she hadn't done in over ten years.

It's early evening and the Reeperbahn is busy.

She arrives at the Dragon a half-hour ahead of the scheduled meeting with Perceval, as she hopes to get another free meal. Perceval had been right about the food being good there, and she hopes to exploit their connection whenever she has the chance. Which is why she strides in, slides into a booth at the back and orders a schnitzel from the bartender.

"Give me a shot of Sambuca too. Thanks."

She doesn't watch the girls dance or observe the patrons. To look at each person, regardless of which side of the stage they're on, is to wonder how they ended up in this place on a Tuesday night, and that would be too many hypotheticals.

The bartender places the shot on the table.

"Was that you in the protest video?" he asks.

"Depends. How do you feel about it?"

"May strong women rule the world."

"I'll drink to that." She holds up the glass. "Got any coffee beans to put in this?"

He gives her a playful smile. "Does this look like a fancy cocktail bar to you?"

"There's plenty of cock in here looking to chase some tail."

"Ha-ha-ha. Oh, I like that. You need to start working here. Behind the bar, with me."

"Sorry. Too busy fighting the establishment."

"Well, if you ever tire of that, our door is open."

"Good to know. Meanwhile, you got anything to distract me from the evening's entertainment? A magazine maybe?"

He goes to the bar and comes back with a copy of *Der Spiegel*.

"Now that's highbrow," she says.

"I read every issue from cover to cover. That's the latest one."

He goes to the next booth and starts clearing away the empty glasses.

She checks the contents page and sees that Russell has an article in this issue. She flips straight to it.

Space: Our Final Frontier
Russell Wex

No, sorry, this isn't about the modern space race, where rich white men climb into (phallic-shaped) rockets and soar towards the stars for their own amusement and gain. The focus here is on personal space: where we set our boundaries and how our relationship with space, both historical and current, impacts our daily lives.

Because we Germans have always had an unusual relationship with space. Our country is small and densely populated. Space is a premium. We seem to both enjoy having our own space and relish the companionship of others. Mostly, we like company, but we're not so keen on those we don't like encroaching on our space. We all want a place where we can get away from each other, such as a holiday house, garden allotment or permanent location for a caravan. Somewhere we can kick back, be ourselves and breathe our own air, without anyone giving suggestions or orders.

Space has also been a defining point throughout Germany's history. In many eras, we armed up and marched off in search of more space, and were rightly sent back, at great cost to all those involved and who got in the way. Perhaps all those failures go some way to explaining why we remain fiercely territorial, both over our own patch of grass and our place in the wider world. Watch employees frequenting their company canteens sitting at the same tables every day. Observe debates over parking spaces turning into shouting matches, and even fistfights. Be amazed by your neighbour cutting back a tree the day it starts encroaching on their property.

But it's not only about having space. We want the best space. At beach resorts around the world, if there's a towel on a sunchair at dawn, you can be certain a German set their alarm extra early to place it there. If there's a view to be had from a restaurant or café, the Germans will want it. Along with this desire for the best place is the expectation to be first. The first on/off the train/plane. The first across the street. The first served in the bakery. The first opinion to be heard (often considered the best opinion as well).

All this, together with our growing lack of respect for the space of others, is leading to a new past-time in Germany: wheedling our way into the lives of strangers and invading their space. Whether it's stepping forward to demand first service, make snide comments or pass some form of judgement, we're the ones doing it. All these moments where we think we know things better, and feel the pressing need to share that, are times when we should back off, let people be, and stay out of their space.

Why do we want to tell everyone what to do? Why do we crowd some areas and expect other areas to be completely our own? An uncrowded train often sees new passengers getting on and sitting close to others, encroaching on their space. Restaurants seem to be set up for people to cluster together, the conversations overlapping and everyone getting annoyed, but no one does anything about it.

Watch how we try to absolutely own the public areas we use, from never giving way on the footpath to sitting in the middle lane of a three-lane Autobahn. Our determination to occupy is world-leading, and we remain stoic even when called out for it.

All this may be humorous – "Oh, the towels, that's so true" – and perhaps you're nodding your head and smiling, glad you yourself don't exhibit any such space-dominating traits. Well, sorry again, but there's a good chance you do. Maybe it's overt. Maybe it's subtle. Maybe it's something you never noticed, absorbed so much in your own space and not particularly aware that your actions might be bothering others. Maybe it's so deeply ingrained, you think there's nothing wrong with your behaviour. Maybe you weren't always like this, and your spatial evolution has been slow and incremental. You only in recent years started planting your personal flag and began owning your space, possibly as a reaction to how everyone else is doing it.

Because, let's face it, this isn't even something specifically German anymore. This could simply be how humans are now. We all want better lives. We all want to prosper. To be first. To have our own air to breathe. To do that, we need room to move. One can't spread their wings if locked in a cage.

In a limited space, we can't thrive.

But how do we reconcile this with eight billion people, and counting, who are determined to expand their own domains? How many of those eight billion, and counting, consider themselves locked in a cage and unable to fly? What are they willing to do to break free and go beyond the frontiers of their current, limited space?

Imagine eight billion people all trying to put towels on the best sun *chairs at the beach. What happens to all those who don't get one?*

The schnitzel arrives, served with potato salad. She thumbs through the rest of the magazine while eating. There's one article about Sunday's protest, but it's written in support of the police, and could almost be considered veiled PR.

Perceval enters and slides into the booth, just as Mara finishes eating. She angles her knife and fork on the plate to compliment the Dragon's chef.

"Good evening." Perceval looks at the plate. "I told you the food here is excellent."

"It is. The more I come here, the more I seem to like this place. Bizarre, really. I should be outside protesting for women's rights."

"This establishment is entirely above board."

"I'm sure it is."

"The employees are very well imbursed. No member of staff is forced to do anything they don't want to."

"Good to hear."

"All have health insurance."

Mara looks at the stage, where a dancer has managed to contort her body to wrap it around the pole like a snake. "I hope that covers physiotherapy. Where's Nils?"

"At training."

"Again?"

"Not basketball. Weaponry."

"What, like daggers, swords and maces?"

"Firearms."

Perceval moves closer to Mara, invading her space. She shifts away, laughing a little.

"What is amusing?"

"Nothing. Just something I read." She pushes the magazine to the side of the table. "What's with the meet? What have I done wrong this time?"

"You shall travel to Berlin tomorrow."

"Well, that's just an amazing coincidence, because I already am." When Perceval gives her a studious look, she adds, "There's a protester gathering. JJ asked me to come along. Just in case she wanted to give everyone the police perspective."

"I refuse to conduct any further thievery for you. Not after what

165

happened."

"I'm not asking you to. Even JJ admitted getting the plans was a mistake."

"Report back to me on your return from Berlin."

"That'll be Thursday, supposedly."

They stare at each other. Out of the corner of her eye, Mara can see the dancer is now hanging upside down from the pole by her ankles, fake boobs defying gravity, and wearing panties so minuscule they might as well be a fig leaf.

"Is that it?" she asks.

"You have nothing further? What about our suspect?"

"No leads. How's life in the basement? Does Nils like the office?"

"You should visit. The documents you obtained from Lersner-Löwe have opened several avenues for investigation."

"Progress. I'd like to hear about that."

"The financials are fascinating. There is a significant flow from Switzerland to Lersner-Löwe, as coverage for legal costs incurred by Circus. What we haven't yet ascertained is where this money is originating from."

"You need to show me all this. At your office."

"On your return."

Mara stands up. "Thursday. I'll see you then."

As she slides out of the booth, Perceval says, "Please accept an apology from Nils. He's very sorry for what he said."

"Do you know what he said?"

Perceval shakes his head. "In this case, I am but the messenger."

"Good intentions, but he should apologise to me himself. In the meantime, be a good handler and cover my bill."

She leaves Perceval at the booth. On her way out, she gives the bartender a friendly wave, and gets one back.

The train speeds east. They have taken over this wagon, bringing with them enough boisterousness and group strength to drive the other passengers from their reserved seats to the next wagons.

Mara sits at a tabled four-seater with Tinaya, who got permission to travel with JJ's help.

In the wagon, everyone keeps to their various groups. Gomez and his followers sit at the far end. Mara assumes Nicola, or a well-dressed Lersner-Löwe paralegal, got Gomez and those others out of holding in time to make this trip. They sit with heads close together, like they're conspiring, and drink beer from cans. The rows ahead are occupied by Susie, Rab and Matze, and a few other eco-protesters Mara recognises from the pig farm fiasco. Mara and Tinaya are in the middle of the wagon, somehow faction-less, in a kind of no-man's-land. JJ and the other older members of Circus are a few rows behind. The spatial divides feel meaningful.

"I brought you a present," Mara says.

"Really?"

She hands Tinaya an old tennis ball. "I know. I shouldn't have spent so much money on this, but I saw it and immediately thought of you."

"Uh, thanks?"

"This is your first step to becoming a fighter," Mara says. "You need to squeeze this ball, every chance you get. Both hands."

Tinaya takes the ball and starts squeezing it with her left hand.

"It'll make your hands and wrists stronger. They need to be really strong to handle the stresses of repetitive punching."

"It's easy."

"That's a beginner's ball. I stuck a needle in it to take the pressure out."

Tinaya moves the ball to her right hand, which isn't as strong as her left.

"Work with that ball until it falls apart. Once you've had a few boxing sessions, we'll move you up to a normal ball."

"Okay. Thank you."

Tinaya looks at the ball as she squeezes, like it's the best present she ever received.

Susie falls into the seat opposite. "She making you do that too?"

167

Tinaya barely looks up.

"I thought it was crazy." Susie sits way forward, resting her elbows on the table. "But it works. It's also somehow meditative and relaxing. Maybe I'll come along on Saturday as well, get back into it."

"I could use an extra trainer," Mara says, assuming Susie will shirk the work and stay away.

"What does it pay?"

"Nothing but the good feelings that result from helping people learn something new."

"That's not enough." Susie rubs her thumb and index finger together. "Money talks, Mara. That knock to your head make you forget that?"

"I guess it did."

"How is it? Looks like it healed up."

"It's better," Mara says. "First day without a bandage. I can walk around again without everyone thinking I had a frontal lobotomy."

"You know I wanted help. I would do that every day of the week. But they had guns. No point in both of us getting caught."

"You ran away?" Tinaya asks. "You could have helped her?"

"When things go bad," Susie says, "it's everyone for themselves. That's the rule."

"Why is that a rule?"

"Hey, I didn't make it. I'm just following those orders."

Tinaya moves the ball back to her left hand and squeezes it with serious vigour. "That allows you to be a coward. You had the chance to save Mara, but you just wanted to save yourself. Now you hide behind this pathetic rule."

"Slow down, sister. It was way more complicated than that."

"I would've stood by Mara if I had been there. And I'm not your sister."

"The whole thing was misguided from the start," Mara says, jumping in before Susie can reply. "I still don't understand what the point was to all that."

"Bad planning." Susie sits back and holds up her little hands. "Not my fault."

It never is, Mara thinks.

"Anyway," Susie continues, talking to Mara, "you were full of fight on Sunday. Those vids are awesome. The way you took that cop down. Amazing."

168

"She didn't run," Tinaya says.

"I did in the end. Right before the cops moved in to take the Schanze."

"When we had those water cannons, I thought we could conquer the whole city," Susie says wistfully. "I was in one of them. The power, it was ... like riding in a tank, and we forced the cops back. I tell you, we need our own water cannons."

"Shame it all didn't end as well as it started," Mara says.

"I said we should drive that fucker all the way to Rathausmarkt. But G wanted to help out the other protesters."

"Who were they?" Mara asks. "Those protesters in black. Where did they come from?"

Susie shrugs. "Somewhere up north. Or east. I don't know."

"Did Gomez organise that? They looked hardcore to me, like right-wingers."

"So what if he did? They were fighting with us. They were on our side."

"Yeah? They didn't speak German. It sounded like Danish to me."

"Must've been Jesper then," Susie says. "He's from Kolding."

"Is that right?"

"Where's Kolding?" Tinaya asks.

"Denmark," Susie says, inflecting the word enough to make it sound like Tinaya is an idiot for not knowing.

Mara leans to her left to look down the aisle. Jesper is in the Gomez section. Their eyes meet. Jesper smiles. Mara waves for him to join them.

"All the football fans know each other," Susie says. "Whether they're fighting or not. Maybe Jesper knows some of them in Kolding."

"You think he negotiated some kind of deal with hooligans?"

"Why not? They came down and joined us. We'll go up there at some point and help them. Wouldn't be the first time. There are plenty of guys just living for the weekends and looking for a fight to join. Doesn't matter where it is or what it's for."

"If that's true," Mara says, "then all that's needed is some kind of network to connect everyone. In Germany and neighbouring countries. Not just Denmark. A whole bunch of reciprocal agreements. You fight with us, we'll fight with you."

"Word is that's what this meeting in Berlin is all about."

Jesper strolls down the aisle and sits next to Susie, opposite Mara. Tall Jesper and small Susie sitting next to each other, both with close-cropped blonde hair, makes them bizarrely look like siblings, Jesper the older brother protecting his little sister.

"Ladies," he says, attempting to sound suave.

Tinaya smiles shyly and keeps her head down. Mara notices she has stopped squeezing the ball and is hiding it in the cup of her hands.

"How was jail?" Mara asks.

"Awful. Weren't you there?"

"I got out of the Schanze, just in time. With JJ."

"Lucky you. But I'm sure you know exactly what holding pens are like."

"Inside and out," Mara says.

"She's been arrested plenty of times," Susie says. "Probably more than you."

"Leave it, Susie. Those guys, Jesper, on Sunday, all in black. Did you recruit them?"

Jesper grins, but doesn't reply.

"Why do you care about that?" Susie asks. "We were all fighting together."

"For what? What are we fighting for?" Mara points at Jesper. "What do you want? What is all this about?"

Jesper turns to Susie. "Now that's what I call being direct."

"You should answer her," Susie says. "Or she'll knock your head off."

"Yeah. Supergirl from the video. She took that cop down with such ease, you might think the whole thing was staged."

"Fuck you, Jesper," Mara says. "You don't look banged up at all. Not a hair out of place. You look to me like you should be working in an office somewhere. Pushing pens around."

"An office?"

"I don't know. I look at you and I think, trainee architect."

"That's good. Architect. Can't I be a doctor instead? Or a lawyer?"

"I think shapes are more your thing. Blocks and lines. You don't seem to have much of a handle on right and wrong."

"What the fuck?"

"Even Gomez and his supposedly hardcore pack of bros," Mara continues, "you put them in some better clothes and they could be

170

working at advertising agencies and start-ups. Something techie. Gaming, maybe."

"Is that why you waved me down here? To insult me?"

"No. But at least answer the question. What do you want? What's this all about? I'm new, so you're getting the impressions of an outsider. To me, what you're doing all seems so empty." Mara turns to Susie. "Ten years ago, we went to all those protests to close down nuclear power plants. We travelled all over Germany. You remember? That was a clear, meaningful thing to protest about."

"We got arrested in Stuttgart," Susie boasts.

"We did. I like to think it all made a difference. Those protests reignited the debate. Some of those plants have shut down since then." Mara shakes her head a little. "Sunday just felt like an organised brawl."

"Sure it was," Jesper says. "We were protesting police brutality. Getting their water cannons upped the ante considerably. Then the fight was really on."

"Don't forget a cop died just over a week ago. The police could've been out there having their own demo against protester brutality."

Jesper moves in his seat. "It's pretty clear what side you're on."

"I'm on the side that wants to have something clear to fight for. I want to make a difference."

"Our protest last Monday made a difference," Susie says.

"Did it? Free the pigs? Is that going to be the defining moment of our generation? I'm sorry, Susie. But I really hope not."

"What do you think it should be then?" Susie asks snidely. "If you think you're so smart."

"This is exactly what I'm asking. Both of you, and you don't have an answer for me. If those thugs came down from Denmark to ..."

"Thugs?" Jesper asks.

"Whatever. Hooligans. Bikers. Right-wing extremists. Mama's boys. Call them what you want. They travelled a long way to stand with us, and it looked like they enjoyed themselves. The fighting and looting. But it all seems to me to be grounded in nothing."

Jesper is about to respond, but Mara cuts him off, anticipating his reply.

"No. Don't do that. Don't try to say something grand about changing the world. And don't play the eco card. Bikers and hooligans don't care about the planet. Climate change is for

171

teenagers. For tweens who want to skip school. It's the long play. Making incremental reductions in percentages that we won't be able to see the impact of for another 50 years or so. I'm talking about now, Jesper."

Jesper stands up. "I'm not going to sit here and let you lecture me. Maybe you'll hear the doctrine you want in Berlin."

"It's such a secret that you can't tell me?"

He turns and walks to the far end of the wagon.

"He doesn't know," Mara says to Susie. "Nobody can tell me what this is all about because nobody knows."

"Not everything requires a purpose, Mara."

"Seriously? What's the point of protesting if it doesn't have a purpose?"

Susie slides across the seat and stands up. "Sometimes you have to fight because fighting's what's needed."

She follows Jesper down the aisle and plonks herself on Rab's lap.

Mara watches her. "There she goes, running away again."

Tinaya starts squeezing the ball once more, but half-heartedly, like her mind is elsewhere. "He's so cute," she says to Mara, her voice barely above a whisper.

"Yes, he is. But don't be fooled by the attractive packaging. You don't know what's inside."

The train starts passing through the outskirts of Berlin. Mara sits back and looks out the window, thinking it feels like a year since she left. One thing she'd like to do is see Russell; hard to organise that without a phone, and she's not willing to ask anyone to borrow theirs.

When they all get off at the central station and go up the escalators, Mara hangs at the back. Tinaya stays with her. Then Mara sees a familiar face working behind the counter of a coffee shop and goes inside. She orders two milk coffees.

"You're Danny, aren't you?"

"No, the nametag's wrong," he says sarcastically.

"I'm Mara," she says, as brightly as she can muster. "We met at one of Russell's dinner parties."

"Yeah, you're the roommate," Danny says, smiling now. "How is Russ? Haven't seen him in a while."

"He's good. Look, this is weird, I know, but I forgot my phone at home. Can you contact Russ and tell him I need to meet him?"

172

"Uh, sure. When and where?"

As the protest conference is happening at the hotel they're all staying at, near Alexanderplatz, she needs a location nearby.

"Maybe, uh, Leise-Park. Next to the Cemetery Museum."

"No idea where that is," Danny says. "New cruising spot?"

"Russ knows. At nine tonight."

"Okay. Mara, right?"

She picks up the coffees. "That's it. Thanks, Danny."

He's on his phone as Mara heads out of the coffee shop.

"Where is everyone?" she asks, handing a coffee to Tinaya.

"Is that for me?"

"If you keep squeezing that ball with your free hand, then yes."

"Everything already hurts. I can't feel my fingers."

"That's good pain. It means it's working. So? Where did they all go?"

"Upstairs. To the S-Bahn."

"Is this your first time in Berlin?"

Tinaya sips and nods. "The first time I've been allowed to walk around here."

"Then that's what we should do. Walk. We can see some of the sights on the way." Mara points towards the Washingtonplatz exit. "Come on. I know the way."

"Do we have time?"

As they walk, Mara says, "I'm guessing this gathering will be the kind of thing that takes a while to get going. If it ever does."

"Why do you say that?"

"Because there'll be lots of people wanting to speak and be heard. I bet there'll be arguing too, and not much order. I mean, you heard Jesper and Susie. They don't even know what they're protesting about. A whole movement without any kind of a mandate."

"Is that why you asked Jesper?"

"I'm just trying to get a handle on this."

"Maybe nothing is what they want," Tinaya says. "Just make chaos."

"Chaos is something. It leads to anarchy, a total breakdown of society, which is what happened in the Schanze before the police moved in. That anarchy looked terrible to me."

The station is very crowded for late morning on a Wednesday. They move through the throng and get outside. Mara takes Tinaya towards the Reichstag, then through Brandenburg Gate and down Unter den Linden.

"It's all so beautiful," Tinaya says.

"Yeah, here. Berlin puts on its best face in the areas popular with tourists."

Alexanderplatz, with its concrete, glass and dated world clock, has a certain retro charm. They cross the square and reach the hotel, which is a very business-like, three-star cube. A harried JJ is waiting in the lobby.

"Where have you two been?" she asks. "The meeting's about to start."

"We walked," Mara says. "I wanted to show Tinaya a bit of Berlin."

"There's no time for that. We're here for one purpose only. To attend this conference. Now, this is your room card." JJ hands the card to Mara. "I've got you two sharing. This better be okay, because I don't have time to rearrange things just to make people happy."

"It's fine," Mara says.

Tinaya nods.

"Follow me." JJ walks quickly out of the lobby and down a long hallway. "There's no time to go to your room. You'll have to put your stuff in the corner. We're behind schedule as it is."

They pass closed doors, which Mara assumes open on smaller conference rooms. The sound of many voices gets progressively louder. The hallway ends at a set of double doors, behind which conversations hum.

"There's a good chance you'll be called on to speak," JJ says to Tinaya. "I think you're the only one here with refugee status. They might want your opinion. Is that all right?"

"I can't speak for everyone," Tinaya says.

"Just do your best. Expect some pushback. There's a real cross-section of folks in here."

"Including people who want refugees to be shipped out?" Mara asks.

"I've spotted a few nationalists and some alt-right-wingers. Be warned. Phones?"

Mara and Tinaya shake their heads.

"Good. Find a seat and get comfortable. This could be a long afternoon."

JJ opens the door. The collective volume of voices floods out. JJ goes inside. Mara and Tinaya stay in the doorway.

"So that's why she brought me along," Tinaya says. "To represent."

"They'll probably call on me too. You'll do the refugee perspective, and I'll do the police perspective. Hey, that makes us the experts here."

Tinaya likes this. "The guests of honour."

"Oh, yeah. VIPs. Don't be scared of anyone in here. I got your back."

Mara leads them into the crowded conference room. They weave between the clumps of people. Every seat is occupied, whether by a person or by a bag or jacket. They go to the back of the room and find a spot half sitting on a windowsill, tailbones on the edge. Mara is surprised to see many people her age and younger, having expected that any leaders of protest groups would be more of JJ's vintage. She plays a little mental game, trying to determine where people have come from and which way they lean based on how they look, dress and act. She estimates there must be at least 100 people in attendance.

The room has been set up for a presentation, the chairs lined up in rows, theatre-style.

It looks and sounds like every single person in the room is talking. But these voices slowly die down as a young man at the front gently taps a microphone. He's rather short. His dark hair is combed back from a chiselled face spotted with acne. He appears confident and assured with the microphone in hand, and in no hurry. His other hand slides into the front pocket of his pants as he waits until the room is quiet. Once it is, he lets the silence hang momentarily in the air.

A few people cough. A woman at the front clears her throat with the exuberance of a life-long smoker.

It's very stuffy in the room. Mara turns and tilts open the window behind her, letting in the faint hum of traffic from Otto-Braun-Straße below.

"Welcome, everyone, to this momentous occasion," the young man says in a smooth voice. "I'm really happy we're all here and that you made the effort to travel to Berlin on such short notice."

"Who are you?" someone shouts.

"I'm certain many of you know who I am and the organisation I

175

represent, as I've been travelling around the country and continent to meet with you face to face. For those of you who don't know me, I'm Vilem Kollar."

A round of applause follows this. There's also a murmuring of "Kollar", as people repeat this name to each other.

Mara briefly closes her eyes, trying to recall where she heard that name before.

"Thank you," Vilem says. "I also want to get to know all of you. I had thought we might keep things relatively secret, but then I discussed things with my father and decided that if we're all going to become allies and work together, we should all know each other."

More applause.

"Now, we have a lot to get through today and I'm certain we will all be on the same page by dinner." Vilem takes a few steps to his left. "I want to start by showing you a video."

The lights are turned off. The screen at the front of the room comes on.

"You've probably seen this already, but it's worth another watch, because it is just that good."

It's the grainy video from Sunday's protest.

"Not again," Mara says, feeling the eyes of those in the room who know it's her.

"That's just brilliant," Vilem says, facing the screen. "Take that bully down. I can never get tired of watching this. Just three days ago, and check out the views." He points at the number, as the video ends. "Over a million."

Half of the lights come on.

"A million," Vilem repeats. "That's not voyeurism. That's not a video going viral just because everyone wants to see what everyone else is watching. That's a million people who want to do exactly what this protester did. Fight back against oppression."

More applause. Some cheering this time.

"One million viewers. Supporters, all of them. You know what I think that is? That's an army, waiting to be mobilised. In a few more days, those views could double. Another army."

Vilem's use of military words has Mara listening closely.

"The people are ready," he continues. "We've had enough. You all know this. We've been kept in cages for too long. We've been held down, told what to do, oppressed. It's up to us to free ourselves. So

176

we can live the lives we want, free of oppression and the limitations of established systems, none of which work. We can be the ones who change Germany and Europe for the better. Help everyone get the lives they deserve. Specifically, take the power away from the elites and ensure a fair distribution of wealth."

"How do we do that?" someone near the front asks.

"If you knew that, you would've done it already," Vilem says. "Look, you can't fight oppression single-handedly. In your groups, your factions, your gangs, you're all outnumbered, disjointed, and up against an enemy far better equipped and organised than yourselves. No one cares about your little protests and battles. The people on the streets just think you're all troublemakers. Not worth listening to, even when you've got something important and relevant to say."

Vilem walks to the side of the room, then back to the middle. The room is silent. All eyes are on him.

"We need to think bigger," he says. "We need to unify. Turn the minority into the majority. Because together, we can be stronger. Together, we can achieve big things. The stronger we are, the more unified we are, the more people will join us. There are millions of people out there waiting for a movement to get behind. Something that's bigger than themselves. Something they can be part of. We can be that movement."

Vilem gestures towards the screen, where the video is replaced by a presentation. The first page has MODRA in big blue letters.

"Now, I appreciate we don't all quite share the same political beliefs. Without question, there are people in here who want very different things. However, what we all have in common is we want to see the established powers removed. We want to get rid of the old leaderships and political structures in our countries which are only in place to exert control over the population. In order to succeed, we need to put our differences aside and focus on our commonalities. We have to stop thinking in terms of right and left, and start thinking in terms of right and wrong. We need to do what's right for our countries, for our people. Together, let us fight the good fight."

As Vilem points at the screen, Mara is amazed to see everyone in the room hanging on his every word.

"It's time to join Modra. It's time for all of us to stand together under one name and join forces at one protest. A better future starts right here."

177

The screen moves to a photo of the leaders of the G8 countries, their flags behind them.

"Stuttgart," Vilem says. "This will be where we protest together for the first time. It will be a landmark day, what we start working towards from now on. It will be the first day in our war against oppression."

Vilem faces everyone and waits for a response. The polite applause quickly rises into jubilation, with shouts and cheers.

Vilem smiles and nods appreciatively. He holds his right fist in the air.

"Let's end oppression," he shouts into the microphone.

***

She goes up to her room to retrieve her backpack, steal a towel and leave a note for Tinaya. It's a relief to be out of the hotel restaurant, which had become too drunkenly jovial for her liking; the kind of edgy enjoyment that can quite easily result in disagreements if one wrong word is said, one wrong look given, or one joke taken the wrong way. She thinks Vilem's quest for common ground didn't make much progress, after a rousing and promising start. Through the course of the afternoon, she participated in meetings and focus groups that degenerated into stand-offs and arguments. Two guys even left one meeting to fight outside, presumably in the car park. But as afternoon turned to evening, they all seemed to agree that moving to the hotel bar and drinking it dry was a group task they could all embrace. The alcohol helped, though, because it loosened Susie's tongue enough for her to disclose that she knows Anthony and that he is in Linz, and this startling revelation sparked Mara into action.

She takes the stairs down to the lobby, avoiding the elevators and the restaurant.

Outside, she heads down Otto-Braun-Straße, between the prefab high-rises built during the time of East Germany. The bland concrete has long been painted over with bright colours that are now faded. A cool wind funnels between the apartment blocks, strong enough to make it look like the buildings are swaying.

Berlin is in its evening transition. There are plenty of people on the streets, going out or going home, distinguishable by attire and

178

attitude.

Mara sees a police car mixed in with the traffic flowing towards Alexanderplatz. She puts her hood up and keeps her head down, turning left down Prenzlauer Berg and taking the first entry to Leise-Park. She once chased a pickpocket into this park and lost him amongst the old tombs and gravestones. It feels spooky now, as a gloomy darkness falls, with no one around. She finds the Cemetery Museum at one of the park's exits and stands in an area of streetlight where Russell is sure to see her.

She regrets choosing this meeting point.

A police car comes slowly down the street and stops just beyond the beam of the streetlight. It's the same car as before, and Mara now recognises the license plate as a vehicle from the Kollwitzkiez station. Two male officers get out and walk towards her.

She wants to run, but when she sees it's Lauter and Brennhof, she digs her fists into the pockets of her hoodie and stands firm. They approach, walking with hands on their guns and belts, like cowboys.

"You there," Lauter says. "The park's closed. Get your drugged-up arse out of here."

"I'm clean."

Lauter gets closer, bending a little for a look under the hood. "You're trespassing. Move it. Now!"

"I'm just standing here, waiting for someone."

"We'll take you in," Brennhof says. "You can sober up in the holding pen."

"I'm not drunk and I'm not on drugs."

"Maybe you're waiting for your dealer. You're here to buy drugs."

Lauter steps back and looks her up and down. "Steinbach? Is that you?"

She takes the hood down. "Lauter. Brennhof. Why don't you both just move along?"

"What happened to you?" Brennhof asks.

"I heard you quit the force," Lauter says, "but you look like you're living on the street. Are you sure you're all right?"

"I'm fine."

She thinks his concern should be genuine, but there's something in Lauter's expression that's really worrying her. Those eyes. Like he's picked out the lobster in the tank he wants to eat.

"Why did you quit?" Brennhof asks.

179

"Burned out. Too many long nights. Just couldn't do it anymore."

"I hear you. They're hell."

Lauter takes a few steps closer. He's undressing her with his eyes, while checking to the left and right to see if there's anyone else around.

"We miss you," he says.

It's like those moments before a bout begins. The fight's coming. Everyone knows it. Get ready. Lauter's going to attack her, she's sure of it. She knows that look. That hunger. She also knows that Brennhof won't do anything to stop him.

"I don't miss you, Lauter," she says.

"You always had a mouth. Any time you talked, I knew you weren't one of us."

"I wanted to be a police officer. But I never wanted to be like you."

She can't fight them both. She needs to get one of them down, then fight the other. She lets the backpack fall from her shoulders onto the ground and puts her hands at her sides.

Be patient, she tells herself.

"That hurts, Steinbach." Lauter holds his hands up a little. "Hey, we're not going to arrest you. You can trust us."

"Then get in the car and drive away."

Brennhof stays where he is, but Lauter comes closer.

"With that attitude, I think we should take you in. Arrest you for trespassing."

"It's a public park."

Lauter takes out his handcuffs and spins one of the loops around his finger. But he's not very good at it, glancing down to make sure they don't fly off. That's her chance. His eyes are averted long enough for her to step forward and punch him in the side of his face. Lauter's a head taller, so the punch loses its momentum and power once her fist gets higher than her shoulder. But it's still good contact and it sends him reeling backwards. Brennhof comes to his partner's aid, stepping forward and reaching for his baton. The smaller Brennhof is closer to her weight division, and she knows from their training sessions that he's not very good with hand-to-hand fighting. A quick low-high, ribs-chin combo knocks him out. Suddenly, her arms are pinned from behind by Lauter. She struggles. He's strong enough to lift her in the air, so her feet kick wildly. Then he muscles her to the ground, getting her face down in the dirt, a knee on her back, high up

180

near her neck. He pulls her left arm behind her. Click. Then the right. Click.

He's got her.

The knee is released. She strains to look behind.

"I've wanted a piece of you for the longest time," he says, taking off his belt.

"I will get you for this, Lauter."

"No one will believe you."

He reaches down and under her to get her jeans open. His hands are large, his long nails scratching at her skin. She squirms against him, which earns her a painful blow between the shoulder blades.

"Hold still."

He yanks her jeans and panties below her hips. She tries to scream, but a hand grips the back of her head and pushes her face into the dirt, causing her to inhale bits of sand and dust, and choke on them.

"Shut up, bitch."

She feels him, probing. His feet kick at her ankles to get her to spread her legs.

"You should've gone out with me when you had the chance," he says. "But I'm going to nail you anyway, and you'll like it."

She can't breathe. She's fading.

He has her and there's nothing she can do about it.

There's dirt in her lungs, but she can't cough it out.

She holds her breath, wanting it to be over.

It's like being held underwater, trying to get to the surface, but a hand keeps her down.

Then, the air around her seems to crackle and pulse. Lauter is suddenly a shaking, heavy weight on top of her; his erection like a blunt instrument pushing into her lower back.

She hears tyres rolling across stones and the squeak of wheels; sees the outline of a wheelchair through eyes clotted with dirt.

It's Russell.

He leans out of his chair and tries to get Lauter off her, lifting his shoulder enough for her to slide out from under his still-shaking body. She manages to sit up, bare arse in the dirt. She coughs and spits.

"Get these cuffs off me. The key's in his pocket."

Lauter is lying on his back, twitching, his pants open and his limp

181

manhood exposed. Russell gets the keys, looking with disgust at what he sees up close.

Mara struggles to her feet. Her jeans and panties are around her ankles. Russell moves around behind her and unlocks the cuffs.

In this intimate moment, he softly and reassuringly says, "Breathe."

The cuffs clatter to the ground.

Mara coughs and spits some more. "Thank you."

Russell moves back, giving Mara space to pull up her clothing. She wipes a sleeve across her mouth and nose, then takes one deep, cleansing breath. Brennhof stirs. She takes the cuffs from the ground, puts them on him and knocks him back out with his baton. Then, she turns to Lauter, who's now on his hands and knees, trying to get his motor skills back. He's groping at his pants like an old man who doesn't quite know how to dress himself anymore. She takes three steps towards him, gaining momentum with each step, and kicks him as hard as she can in the stomach.

"You fucking prick!"

She stands over him and kicks him again.

"Mara."

Lauter balls himself up on his side, so she takes his baton and drives the end of it into his ribs, enjoying the sound of the crack. Lauter grunts with pain.

"Mara! Stop it."

She's about to hit Lauter in the head with the baton when Russell positions himself in the way.

"It's enough," he says.

Mara can barely get the words out: "He tried to rape me."

Lauter rolls on the ground, one arm wrapped around his ribs, the other trying to get his pants up.

"Nothing happened," he manages to say.

"It's over now." Russell takes the baton from Mara's hand. "Don't take it any further. We got him."

Mara paces around a little, coughing some more and trying to calm down. "What did you hit him with?"

Russell holds up a taser.

"What are you doing with one of those? That's technically a weapon."

"Do you have any idea how often people try to rob me in this city?

182

It's like the wheelchair makes me everyone's easy target."

Mara goes to her backpack and takes the bottle of water from it. She rinses her mouth out and washes her face.

"Come on," Russell says. "Let's get a taxi and go home."

"I can't," she says, taking Brennhof's cuffs and putting them on Lauter, who has coughed up a small pool of blood.

"Why not?"

"I need to get to Linz."

"Austria? What's there?"

Mara mouths "Anthony". She gets Lauter up and into a sitting position. He looks at her with utter hate, like she's the villain in all of this, the one who should go to jail.

"So close," she says, more composed now. "But you're done."

"It's your word against mine," he says weakly. "I'll say we got attacked by a couple of addicts. I was tased by this cripple. He's the one who's fucked."

"Slow down," Russell says. "I'm a journalist for *Der Spiegel*. Maybe it's not the kind of thing you read, but it's a very popular news magazine. These glasses I'm wearing, they're smart glasses. They take photos and record videos. Very handy, especially for a cripple, because I get targeted a lot. Which is why I also carry a Taser. Everything these glasses see goes straight to a secure server. Including this very conversation."

"You're bluffing."

"Why would I try to bluff you? I got it all."

Lauter's shoulders sag. He coughs some more, grimaces and spits blood in the dirt.

Russell looks at Mara. "The question is, what are we going to do about it?"

"That's easy," she says. "We make him your bitch."

"I was thinking something along those lines."

"You could use his inside information to bring down the Berlin Police's number one slimebucket. Hans Spitz. Because the whole sexual harassment and abuse thing, no one wants to hear from us women anymore. But, if a man comes forward as your trusted source, calling out his boss for his bad behaviour, then everyone will surely listen."

"No one cares about Spitz," Lauter says. "He's been exploiting his position for years. It's no secret."

Mara folds her arms. "And yet all those people are still too scared to say anything. You'll be the one to change that. You could be a hero."

"It'll make the front page, I'm sure," Russell says.

"The public loves a scandal, especially in an institution that's supposed to uphold the law and protect people."

Russell gestures towards Lauter. "Is this the guy you always hated doing shifts with?"

"Yeah. The male supremacist who always told me to smile more. Shocking to think that the whole time we were out there policing the streets, all he ever wanted to do was rape me."

"With that in mind, I think you should give him one more kick. Right where it hurts. Kick all those nasty thoughts right out of him."

"Agreed."

"No," Lauter says, his voice breaking. "Steinbach. Please. You got me enough. We're square."

"We'll never be square." She looks down at his exposed manhood. "But relax, little man. I didn't feel a thing. You, however, are going to feel this."

She slams her right foot into his groin. Lauter lets out a howl of a scream that would turn the bodies in the nearby tombs, and rolls onto his side.

"We better go," Russell says. "Someone definitely heard that."

"A scream like that, they might think a little girl is in danger."

"I'll see you soon," Russell says to Lauter. "I'll come to the police station to interview you, under the pretence I'm doing some kind of diversity story. Be ready to tell all."

They leave the two police officers cuffed and lying on the ground.

Mara shoulders her backpack and helps Russell push the wheelchair off the dirt path and onto the concrete footpath. From there, Mara walks at Russell's side.

"All right?" he asks.

"No."

"You will be."

"Thanks, Russ. Really, massive, huge thank you."

"I'm sorry I didn't get there sooner."

"You showed up just in time."

"I finally got to pay you back."

"That was never required," Mara says. "But I'm really glad you did."

184

They cross the street and head down Friedenstraße, alongside Volkspark Friedrichshain.

"Do you want to talk about what just happened?" Russell asks.

"I want to get myself cleaned up. I want to wash that scumbag off me."

"Understandable. You can have a shower at the train station, I think."

"Let's go there."

"This will be a good thing," Mara says. "I'm going to make sure of it. If you expose Spitz and shine a spotlight on the misogyny and sexual harassment in the Berlin Police, then I will always remember what happened tonight as being a good thing."

"It would be a huge story."

"Did you really get everything on video? I'm not sure I want to see it, or have it go public."

Russell smiles. "Lauter was right. I was bluffing. These are just glasses. Hopefully, the threat will be enough to get him to play his role. I'm amazed he fell for it so easily."

"He's not very bright. Plus, the police are basically watching everyone all the time."

"Maybe that's why. Everyone's watching everyone. That's the world we're living in right now."

"You sound like my father."

"You mentioned him in your letter."

"Did that arrive already?"

"Yesterday. When Danny texted me that you wanted to meet, I was thrilled. I've got a million questions."

"I bet. But let me ask the first one. Have you heard of Modra?"

Russell shakes his head. "Is that a person or a company?"

"I'm not entirely sure. I think it's a foundation. Maybe even a charity. Or one of those shady non-profits that attract people with extremist beliefs. You need to find out. Because this Modra thing, well, whoever they are, they're gearing up to take over, starting with Germany."

"You're joking. You make it sound like they want to overthrow the government."

"That's just for starters."

"There's no way they can achieve that," Russell says, as they veer down Platz der Vereinten Nationen. "I would say it's not even

185

something achievable anymore. Not in Europe. This used to be Leninplatz, by the way. There was a massive statue of Vlad the Red down there. You could say he was the last true revolutionary."

"I know it sounds far-fetched. Like those preppers always getting ready for doomsday. But Vilem Kollar thinks otherwise. You need to research him too. He's barely out of his teens, but he's an outstanding public speaker. Charismatic and clever. He could be your next Lenin."

"Who was he speaking to?"

"He organised this conference, a kind of showcase for Modra, and invited leaders of protest groups from all over Germany. Some others flew in, from Spain and Serbia and Italy, I think. Left and right, and just about anyone with a beef against their government. Some separatists too, for good measure."

"How'd it go?"

"As you'd expect," Mara says. "A lot of arguing. Kollar is trying to unite all these groups under the Modra banner."

"If he succeeds, that could be a powerful group. But what would happen if they won? How would they divide the spoils? They'd just end up fighting each other."

"This was discussed all afternoon. They're probably fighting about it now."

"Not you. You're going to Linz. You really think Anthony's there?"

"Don't know. But I absolutely have to try. This is the strongest lead I've got so far. If I don't find him, I'll go to Stuttgart and visit Zina."

"That I support," Russell says.

They skirt the huge roundabout of Strausberger Platz and continue down Lichtenberger Straße. Russell grills Mara about her first week in Hamburg. She pushes his wheelchair so he can take notes.

As they go up the elevator to the Jannowitzbrücke S-Bahn station, Mara says, "If you can manage it, you need to get to Stuttgart for the G8 meeting."

"That's politics. Photo ops. Not my area, and mobility required."

"Better get in contact with whoever's covering it. Kollar said this protest will be day one of his war against oppression. Whatever that means."

They wait on the crowded platform.

"You touched on that in your letter," Russell says. "That you don't

186

know what the protesters stand for. Now you have it."

"It's still not clear to me. Oppression's a pretty vague thing. As if this is an umbrella to put everything under. Like terror, or something similar. A word to justify it all. But that doesn't qualify as a clear mandate."

"Which in itself is fascinating. As if the word was chosen following research surveys and focus groups."

As the S-Bahn rolls in, those waiting cluster along the safety line, everyone wanting to be first on. Mara and Russell get in the last wagon, which has an area for bicycles, prams and wheelchairs. Someone is playing the accordion further down the wagon; a morose Russian tune.

"The protesters are like chameleons," Mara says. "Changing their colours to suit whatever they're protesting on a given day. Green one day, yellow the next. Brown for football games and black for fighting with police."

"Sounds like Kollar plans to turn these chameleons into soldiers. Get them wearing one colour all the time."

"You're brilliant, Russ. Already writing this story. And after tonight, you're a superhero too."

"I thought that was you. That video."

"It was in the heat of the moment. The cop knocked me down. I had to do something."

"It was impressive."

"Kollar's repositioned it as a recruiting video. For the Modra army. Speaking of which."

The train enters Alexanderplatz station. She sees Gomez, Jesper and a few others waiting on the platform. They bustle onto the train. She puts her hood up and turns away from them.

"What's the matter?"

"Some guys from Circus got on the train. I can't let them see me."

"Why not?"

"They think I'm still at the hotel," Mara says. "I don't trust them. Not these guys."

"You think they're going out or heading back to Hamburg?"

"I don't know. Maybe they'll try to take over Circus while JJ and the other leaders stay here."

"A coup? Has it come to that already? Look, just keep your back to them and push my chair. You'll be amazed at how this thing makes

187

a person invisible."

"Except to thieves."

Russell laughs. "I've missed your humour. The apartment's not the same without you."

"I bet you don't miss me banging the heavy bag."

"Actually, I do. I always found it meditative. Like Zen drumming. Believe me, you left a massive void in your wake."

"Don't try to fill it."

"No chance."

The train pulls into Berlin's main station. Mara positions herself behind Russell's chair and watches out of the corners of her eyes, to see which direction Gomez and Jesper will go once on the platform. They exit and go right. Mara and Russell need to go in that direction as well, to get to the elevator, but they're the last off the wagon, and Gomez and Jesper are far ahead.

"Was one of those guys Gomez?" Russell asks.

"The skinny guy who looks like an upright reptile. The pretty boy was Jesper."

"Oh, yeah. The blonde. I noticed him. You like?"

"Hard not to, despite the idiocy that spills out of his mouth."

"Send me some photos when you get the chance. I think I need to study Jesper more closely."

They ride the elevator down, then go to the nearest ticket machine. Mara gets a one-way to Linz. The train is supposed to leave in ten minutes but is running half an hour late.

"Night train?" Russell asks.

Mara nods. "But just a seat. Can't afford more than that."

"You need some money?"

"No. Perceval gives me pocket money. Not enough, but I can't be seen to be well off. His intern, Nils, says I should get a job."

"This is your job. You're risking everything for these people."

"I know. I said the same thing. I think Perceval wants me to cultivate an aura of poverty. But there should be some extra cash coming my way. From Gus. He's got me lined up to train some girls at the gym."

"That's really good."

Mara points at the WC Fresh. "I'm going to have a quick shower. You don't have to wait."

"I'll meet you back here in ten."

Russell rolls away.

The spare, sterile interior of the shower and toilet section reminds her of the communal bathrooms of juvie. She wants to be in and out of here quickly.

She takes her bathroom bag and towel from her backpack.

Dirt falls onto the tiled floor as she gets undressed.

It's wonderful to get clean. The steam from the hot water helps her cough more dirt and gunk out of her lungs.

Her thoughts keep going back to the moment, cuffed on the ground, her face in the dirt, Lauter groping at her. Those nails of his. But she fights this, focusing on how she beat up Lauter and Brennhof, and how she gave Russell a big story that needs to be told.

That's the primary focus: her friendship with Russell and what he means to her.

When she exits the WC Fresh area, feeling a lot better in clean clothes, Russell is waiting. He holds up four mini bottles of Sambuca, two in each hand.

"No coffee beans," he says. "But we can still drink to our health, prosperity and happiness."

This makes her smile.

Sleeping is difficult on the train. It's tempting to sneak into one of the unoccupied sleeper wagons and lie down properly, with the door locked, but the conductors and security guards are up all night, patrolling the aisles. No doubt they deal on every one of these journeys with people trying to secretly upgrade from a cheap seat to a sleeper. Mara thinks the guards are exercising a bit too much power; one guy has already been brought back to the wagon she's in, dumped in his seat and had a gnarled finger pointed at him in warning.

It's a train of two halves, divided by wealth and status. But she thinks there's an important gender aspect to consider. This darkly lit train, rolling through the German countryside in the early hours of the morning; it doesn't feel safe. Not in this wagon. Not with these solo transients, all of them men, scattered around the seats. They have either too much luggage, like they're between homes, or not enough, like they're on the run. This is not a place for women travelling on their own. Sleep too deeply, she worries, and one of them might try something. Two have already made advances disguised as idle small talk, hoping to join whatever the train version is of flying's mile-high club. Neither took her polite request to be left alone very well, slouching back to their seats like there's something wrong with her. If they only knew what she'd gone through a few hours ago.

Fucking Lauter, she thinks. That guy is poison.

As the train heads south, then veers south-east, it hits at a lot of stations, staying at each one for longer than it would during the day. A bit of buffer time, in case any passengers need to be roused before their stop, or at it. When the train makes these extended breaks, many passengers get off to smoke on the platform, pacing aimlessly around or clustering in small groups.

She drifts in and out of sleep, not willing to give in fully to her fatigue, and snapping awake each time to be back on alert.

At Bamberg, Erlangen, Nuremberg and other places along the route, people are awake at this hour to get on the train, while others wait on platforms to meet bleary-eyed passengers. She wonders about these people. Where are they going? What have they left behind? What do they believe in? Are they happy?

Everything feels vague and out of focus. The pre-dawn fog that clings to the countryside seems like it's inside the wagon; but in here it's just a muggy cloud of male sleep-breath.

She's not a huge fan of trains. There's something about the way the train doors shut with a vacuum-type seal that she finds imprisoning. It's a reminder of juvie, where the doors closed in that same way, sucking the air from the rooms and locking all those supposedly bad girls inside. Then there's the lack of comfort crapshoot; a full train can make the journey unbearable for everyone, while one passenger can turn an empty wagon into an uncomfortable, unwelcoming space. Like when some drunk guy vomits on the floor. Or someone gets on with a bag full of junk food and consumes it all loudly. Or there's someone who's just plain scary and unhinged, like they escaped from a mental institution. And worst of all, those weirdos who just stare at the other passengers.

Regensburg comes and goes, looking attractive from the train window in the dawn light. Then Straubing and Plattling, places she's never heard of and will never visit. The short platforms and small stations remind her of when she rode the trains with Anthony, out to towns and villages so he could play in regional basketball competitions. They would stop at obscure stations where the platform wasn't long enough for the train, which would have to stop once, let people off and on, then move forward enough to allow those in the back part of the train to get off. Well before he was ten, Anthony was showing serious promise, dominating games and causing rival coaches to execute plans to put him out of action. She could barely believe it when witnessing it for the first time, a coach telling a kid to deliberately injure Anthony. Nor could she believe the shouts from parents in the stands who wanted to see just that very thing happen. Her brother, reduced from a person to a number. "Foul number 13 as hard as you can." "Take that 13 out of the game." But Anthony was too smart and skilled, was a few steps ahead of the other players, able to get through the games relatively unharmed. The better he played, the further they had to travel. Richard never came along; he had no interest in the sporting endeavours of his children. But Mara enjoyed going with Anthony, as those trips felt like little adventures. Until he decided to go by car with friends and their parents. Or with the coach. By that time, she had her own stuff going on. Namely, all the different ways she could get in trouble; be bad enough to attract the attention of Zina and make her move back to Hamburg. When that plan didn't succeed and after several stints in juvie, Mara went to Zina, joining Susie for that southern trip to protest at nuclear power plants in Baden Wurttemberg. They skipped school, missed important exams, drank too much, smoked weed, raised hell in villages that didn't deserve it and were eventually arrested in Stuttgart. Then she had Zina's attention. Zina got her out and Mara stayed with her. They argued all week, almost coming to blows a few times, but Mara rode the train back to Hamburg a different person. No more protests. No more Susie. No more lashing out to get attention. It was time for structure, to do something good in the world, and Mara knew that joining the police was exactly the right move.

She notices there are now teenagers on the train, toting matching schoolbags, clumped in small groups and talking in whispers. One boy spins a basketball on his finger.

She thinks it's disappointing that Anthony has potentially thrown away a sporting career, the only thing he ever wanted. He's sure to have his reasons, as she did when taking off the gloves, but it still seems a waste. It reminds her of something Zina once said, about how being good at something is a burden as much as a gift; the pressure is immense, whether the talent is taken as far as it will go, but never to the top, or left by the side of the road and carried emotionally as an opportunity wasted. For Mara, her main regret is not knowing how good she could have been. Good enough for the Olympics, like Zina was? The fact she'll never know is her own fault. She can't blame Zina for quitting boxing.

Anthony will try to lay blame, she thinks. Point fingers at others, shirk responsibility. If he has rejected the scholarship and given up basketball, then it's all on him.

At Passau, while the train is stopped for a frustrating amount of time, two middle-aged men, who look homeless, sweep through the wagons with large garbage bags, picking up cans and bottles that can be exchanged for a refund. She thinks of Tinaya, who made it to this border town after that arduous journey from Afghanistan and spent three months enclosed in a refugee centre before being moved on to the next place. Erfurt? Or was it Jena? Someplace in the old east. She can't remember, but it would have been bad either way, trying to get established in a city that doesn't have a great reputation for welcoming foreigners. Then another city, and another, and finally Hamburg. She's amazed a person can survive all that, at such a young age; be riddled with trauma and still manage to get through each day without breaking down. She's envious of how hopeful Tinaya is for the future.

Eventually, the train continues east, crossing into Austria. No border controllers get on to check passports.

Now, plenty of people on the train look like commuters, clear-eyed and fresh. The presence of school children and working people shift the balance in the wagon, taking it from late-night seedy to morning routine. It no longer feels dangerous, and Mara thinks that now she can get some sleep. She asks the woman in the seat across to wake her when they get to Linz. The woman doesn't appear enthused about this responsibility, but complies, enabling Mara to sleep an hour.

Once there, off the train, stretching and sore – what hurts most is her right foot, from kicking Lauter, a good kind of pain, orange and warm – she's unsure which way to go and how to tackle finding someone in this foreign city. From the size of the station, Linz feels like a big place, where a person could easily get lost.

Two people, she thinks, because Janica has to be with Anthony.

She joins the current of people flowing from the platform to the exit. The passengers stepping down from the sleeper cars look well-rested and perky. They pile their luggage on trolleys, like people on grand tours of Europe. She puts her head down and tries to focus on Anthony; to get inside his head. What would he be doing, mid-morning, in Linz? Not sleeping, because he's always been an early riser, having spent his childhood getting up at dawn for conditioning runs and strength workouts.

Or has that changed? Is Janica not a morning person?

She buys a large black coffee. The pastries on offer look tempting, but she thinks the coffee is about all her train-churned and lack-of-sleep-effected stomach can handle right now.

A map from the tourist office. A course set for the old town. No idea where to start looking. So, she just wanders around, up the alleys and down the narrow roads. Straddling the Danube River, Linz turns a beautiful face to the morning sun. The cluster of old buildings on a thumb jutting into the river sit against the stunning backdrop of snow-capped mountains. Churches, squares and scrubbed clean

193

cobblestones. Healthy-looking people. Blue sky. Clear air. A youthful, vibrant vibe. A sense that if there's anything bad happening in the world, it's not happening here and it never will.

It's ridiculously spotless. Almost sterile. A city seemingly with the hygiene mandate of a hospital. Dirty from the overnight journey, Mara thinks she could bend down, touch the footpath with her open hands and they would be cleaner than before.

She looks at everyone, trying to decide who might be a potential accomplice. Who's hiding Ant in one of these well-kept buildings? Come on, she thinks. I'm 18 years old, on the run, scared, in love, trying to constantly impress a girl, maybe low on cash again, but a thousand kilometres from grandma and grandpa. How to make money?

Get a side hustle going.

Basketball.

Trick shots.

Betting.

At the main square, she starts asking people if there are any outdoor basketball courts in Linz. The locals are friendly and smile with shiny white teeth, but don't really know.

Try the university.

Try the Stadtpark.

Try along the Danube.

She crosses the river, which is a putrid grey-brown colour in stark contrast to the natural surroundings and the chemically-clean old town. She questions more locals on the way and gets more doubtful responses.

Maybe near the pool.

Maybe the football stadium.

Maybe the skate park.

"Where's that?" she asks.

The teen points to the riverside path. "Just follow that. You can't miss it. Fair hike, though."

She goes that way, lacking a better option. The path takes her past a strange-looking market area, then a collection of football fields, where the goal positionings make it seem the fields overlap. But these green spaces seem to promise further sporting pursuits, so she keeps going.

A bench facing the river offers respite. Her feet hurt from walking.

194

Sitting there, she feels like she's seen the whole of Linz in the last few hours; could write postcards with the inside knowledge of someone who's been there for a week.

Focus, she tells herself. Anthony. What are you doing right now? Where are you? Why Linz, of all places?

At a bench about 50 metres away, a big man sits down, doing so in a way that suggests he's killing time. He looks fit and burly enough not to require a rest. He doesn't look like a tourist, or a local. No dog. No bag. No newspaper. He just stares straight ahead.

She wonders: is he following me?

So caught up in navigating Linz and trying to find an outdoor basketball court and getting into Anthony's head, it hadn't occurred to her that someone might be on her tail. Because Susie surely said something. That blabbermouth. That selfish girl who's not to be trusted.

She waits for the man to look in the other direction, then stands up and starts walking further along the river, weaving between a row of trees for added cover. There's a playground, which looks clean even from this distance, and a broad expanse of concrete that might be used for seasonal events, like a fun fair or Christmas market. Under the rail bridge. A pair of empty beach volleyball courts where the sand has been raked into neat grooves. Lots of grass, cut low and very green. And a basketball court, next to the skate park.

There's nobody.

The broken glass, empty beer bottles and takeaway food containers overflowing from the trash cans make her think this is an evening place, popular with youths and well out of the jurisdiction of the clean police.

She needs to come back later.

The big man from the bench has lumbered along the river in her direction, but he doesn't approach the skate park. He keeps walking, strolling really, aimless, hands in pockets, like a man with a whole day to fill and no idea how to fill it.

She heads away from the court and gets directions to a supermarket where she buys a packaged salad and a bottle of water. Back at the skate park, she sits at the top of a small half-pipe, legs dangling over the side, and eats.

It's a lovely day, warmer than it should be in the mountains in spring. She finds it very nice, to sit there, take in the view and have nothing to do. The last ten days have been incredibly hectic, and it feels like big things are now at stake, following Vilem Kollar's rousing speech in Berlin. An end to oppression. Revolution. Overthrowing the government. A war with the police.

So hard to believe.

The time passes.

At one point, she sees the big man come back, having perhaps reached a certain turnaround point.

The skaters start drifting in after 1500, coming straight from school. She moves to a bench shaded under a tree, closer to the basketball court. The players arrive one by one and shoot around in disorderly fashion until a small guy gets a game going, his stocky stature reminding Mara of that troublemaker in Friedrichshain and making her wonder if he was ever arrested in the end. It's two-on-two, then three-on-three. Very scrappy, with a lot of missed shots. Once there are half-court games going at both ends, the players assemble for full-court five-on-five. Again, it lacks cohesion and skill. The use of the whole court basically turns the game into endless fastbreaks. None of them can get up and down the court fast enough to play in half-court sets.

No sign of Anthony.

As afternoon becomes evening and better players show up, the quality of play improves. The games are more physical. One player suffers an injury to his left ankle and needs to be helped off the court. He lies on the ground, foot up on a bag while exhaling a dusty cloud of marijuana smoke towards the sky.

The skate park is busy with teenagers, with a surprisingly even gender split. The girls are given plenty of space to skate and are very much part of the scene. The basketball court is all male.

The teens not skating gather in groups and have competing hip-hop soundtracks playing from portable speakers. The music lends this place an edgy Americanised vibe that she thinks is undeserved and wrong.

She wonders if Susie lied about Linz; sent her on this fruitless chase and was back in Hamburg right now laughing about it with Rab and Matze. Or she lied because Gomez told her to. The best thing to do is forget all of it and go to Stuttgart. Visit Zina. Tell her what's going on and regroup. Zina will know what to do.

But then she sees him, sauntering towards the court, holding

196

hands with a lanky girl who walks with the confidence of someone who likes the body she's in. They're both in dark tracksuits and peel these off when they get courtside. A couple of players running back on defence veer to that side of the court, to give Anthony a hand-slap and to signal he should join their team for the next game.

Mara finds it interesting, and impressive, that Janica is dressed to play, going so far as to put a hand on Anthony's shoulder for balance as she stretches her quads one at a time. She's pretty in the way that young athletic girls tend to be; slim and powerful, with the brightness and positive attitude that comes from being fit and good at something. She ties her long brown hair back into a ponytail. Anthony looks surprisingly lean, with a helmet of hair rendering him almost unrecognisable.

The game ends. The players disperse to fetch water bottles from bags and take long drinks. Anthony dribbles the game ball to the far end and warms up with an effortless two-handed dunk. Janica trails after him and positions herself under the basket to catch the ball as it goes through and pass it back to Anthony, as he hits jump-shot after jump-shot with the ease of a robot programmed to do that singular task. His motions are fluid and confident, to the point of arrogance.

Now that Mara's found her brother, she doesn't quite know what to do. To move towards the court would alert him to her presence. If they tried to run for it, she wouldn't be able to keep chase with two ultra-fit basketballers.

As a new game gets going, she decides to let them play. It's not much of a contest. Anthony and Janica basically play two against five, and really enjoy themselves. Mara's watched enough basketball to know they could sub in three no-hopers and still win. Janica is easily the second-best player on the court, and by far the most physical; both know the game in ways the others don't. They've been well-coached and well-drilled, from a young age. Mara can relate. Her boxing training comes through whenever she needs it, without ever needing to think about it.

Taught well, taught right, she thinks, missing Zina.

The game ends. A new team of five takes the court to be on the receiving end of Anthony and Janica's tag-team punishment. Two defenders follow Anthony everywhere he goes on offence, but all this does is open up the court for the others. Anthony is able to get them the ball in positions where they can't possibly miss, and he looks unselfish doing so. Even if they miss the unmissable, he still gets there quickly enough to clean up and score.

Mara thinks Anthony has improved since she last saw him play, though his fitness isn't at the same level. By the third game, he starts to tire, losing some pace, getting lazy and making mistakes.

That's her opening.

She gets up from the bench, goes out of the shade and walks down to the court. The play is at the other end, Anthony's team on defence. She stands under the hoop, on the baseline, leaning against the hoop's metal support. Janica gets a steal – whacking the ball from a player's hands, who's too scared to cry foul against a girl – and outlets the ball to Anthony on the break. He just beats two players to the hoop, but only has the legs for a lay-up, not a dunk. When he lands, he's looking right at her.

"Maz? What the fuck?"

"Hey, Ant. Having fun?"

Anthony grabs the ball to prevent the game from continuing without him. "What are you doing here?"

"Looking for you. What are you doing here?"

"Holiday."

They stare at each other. Anthony, who didn't give school much priority during his childhood quest for basketball glory, is slow on the uptake. But something clicks in his head, because he throws the ball at Mara, who defends herself in instinctive boxing fashion, fists at her temples. The ball caroms away towards the skate park. Anthony runs for it. He's across the court and picking up his stuff, as is Janica, before Mara even gets moving.

They sprint towards the river, easily pulling away, running with legs that have done thousands of suicide sprints. As Mara pursues them, she realises Anthony hadn't got tired during the game; he was bored. Her backpack bounces and makes running awkward, even with the straps pulled tight. She's no match for them, but follows anyway, in dogged police officer fashion, towards the rail bridge. After they're under that and in its shadow, they stop and turn. Mara keeps running, sees them, then slows to a walk, catching her breath.

"Anthony," she yells out. "I'm not here to arrest you. I want to help you."

Anthony looks at Janica, who shakes her head slightly.

"Come on, Ant. Just talk."

Mara holds up her hands, to show she's unarmed and means them both no harm. He takes a few steps forward. The way his body relaxes on the spot makes her think she may yet save him from the wrath of the Hamburg Police. Save them both. But then a figure comes out of the shadows, moving quickly, with purpose, something in his hands. It's the walker from before. There's someone else behind him, but she can't see him clearly.

She puts a hand up to protect herself, but he's too quick.

***

Her eyes open slowly. The room comes into focus. White walls, the paint flaking. Small windows, high up near the ceiling, as if in a cellar, or a room half underground. She's lying on the floor: cold tiles, a bit damp.

The pain is at the back of her head. She tries to reach for it, but can't. Her hands are taped behind her back. Duct tape, she concludes, feeling its stickiness pulling at the skin of her wrists.

Here she is once again, concussed, taped up, caught. Somebody's prisoner.

There's daylight coming through the windows, which makes her worry she's been out all night and it's a new day. They would have had to drug her for that, whoever they are.

A door opens. She turns her head to see the walker enter, carrying two chairs.

"You," she says. "You were following me. Who are you?"

He doesn't reply. He sets the chairs up, one facing the other, and lifts her to sit on one.

"Hey. Gorilla. Can you talk?"

He smiles a little and lets out a gorilla-ish grunt. There's something in the way he does it that makes her think he has no intention of hurting her further. He's being playful, not intimidating.

"How's my head?" she asks.

"No blood."

He has a deep voice, accented. Russian or Balkan maybe. He has a very round head. Darkish skin and lots of brown hair, especially on his arms; hair that's thick enough on his forearms to require combing. It goes up to the sleeves of his shirt, hinting that it goes over

199

his shoulders as well. On seeing it, she regrets calling him a gorilla.

"Thanks, I guess, for not making me need stitches."

"Only a gentle tap."

"Didn't feel like it."

"Just some funny monkey business."

"Sorry," she says. "About the gorilla comment."

He takes a bottle of water and places it on the other chair.

"Can you open that?"

"Knockout brings the thirst. Just need to know the right place. Don't have to hit hard. Right spot, then boom, lights out."

This makes her think he boxes. Or used to. He has the physique. His round shoulders slump forward from a meaty neck of which any light heavyweight or above would be proud. He also has that weird hunched-over walk that results from years of shuffling forwards, backwards and to the sides in short, controlled steps.

"Switches," she says. "My coach called those spots switches."

"Yes. That's good. But only off, not on."

He leaves the room. She stares at the water bottle, wondering if she can hold it between her knees and unscrew the top with her teeth. But any movement of her head forward makes her feel dizzy. She tilts her head so it doesn't throb, and tries twisting the tape off. It doesn't yield. Its stickiness pulls at her skin.

The second chair alludes to a second visitor. The bottle of water is bait.

She kills the time with conjecture, running through a list of what the thug might have hit her with. Anything metallic would have made a wound. A fist to the skull would have hurt, even for a thug like him. It had to be something wooden, like a baseball bat. Something blunt and pliable, with a bit of give. Why was he following me? Who is he?

The door opens again and another man enters. She watches him walk slowly to the chair. He's around 50, with brown hair turning grey, and a lean physique that shows he applies himself to staying fit. Not a weightlifter or gym junkie, because he's too streamlined. A runner maybe. Or a cyclist. The strong shoulders look like a swimmer's. The safe bet is all three: a triathlete. No. An ironman, who came to it later in life as some form of middle-aged rite of passage.

He's wearing a casual, dark blue suit, no tie. His white shirt has three buttons open on a hairless chest. He picks up the bottle and sits in the chair. He holds the bottle up to his narrowed eyes, tilting it slightly to look at the water, like it's something valuable; the way a jeweller inspects a diamond.

"Who are you?" she asks.

Despite the situation and circumstances, she's not scared. There's no sense of danger. He doesn't appear to be here to interrogate her or inflict violence. She stares at him, committing as much of his face to memory as her foggy brain will allow. He crosses one leg over the other, nestling the bottle in the V his thighs make.

"Thirsty?"

"For knowledge. A name. A place. A reason why your goon knocked me out and brought me here. Wherever here is."

"You're quite safe. This is my compound."

"Compound? That makes it sound like you're some kind of recluse. Or a drug lord? Fuck, compound. Like something surrounded by a huge fence and guarded by guys with machine guns."

"My estate then," he says, amused.

"Not better. Now you sound like you're rich from money you didn't make. You inherited this estate and now lord over it like you earned it yourself."

He smiles. "I heard you like to use humour as a defence. When you're nervous."

"Who told you that? Anthony?"

The smile fades. "Here's what's going to happen," he says firmly. "You're going to be taken to the train station where you will board the next train for Hamburg. You were never here. You never saw me. You never saw anyone. Do you understand?"

"Why show your face to me, then tell me I never saw you?"

"To make you see the intent in my eyes and the people I have at my disposal."

"Oh, you're trying to intimidate me. That's why you brought me to your lair when you could've just dumped me on the train."

"Putting you on the train would've meant you were in Linz. But you were never in Linz. Right?"

"Right. No Linz. No Austria. No you. Whoever you are."

"Good."

"Didn't see Anthony. Or Janica. But can you at least tell me they're all right?"

"They're fine." He moves to stand up.

201

"Wait a minute," she says. "There's still a lot I'm not really getting."

"If you'd prefer to stay down here, I can accommodate you, but you won't see me again. I think you'd much rather continue your new life in Hamburg. Wouldn't you?"

"New life? How do you know about that?"

He gets to his feet and places the water bottle on the chair.

"You seem to know a lot about me," she says. "I know nothing about you. A bit unfair, don't you think?"

"That's the idea."

He walks out.

The thug shuffles back in, a mesh bag in his hands. He stands in front of her and holds it up.

"Seriously? This place is such a massive secret you need to blind me?"

"You take the bag. Or I give you another gentle tap. Your choice."

"I'll take the bag."

"Smart. Too many concussions, not good for you."

He puts it over her head, with the gentle hands of a father dressing a child. The bag is dry and scratchy against her face, and smells faintly of food. Onions or potatoes. It makes her wonder if the thug doesn't do this often, and he had to improvise with something he found in the kitchen. Her vision isn't completely blacked out, but nothing is discernible through the tiny gaps in the mesh strands.

He gets her up and walks her out of the room, a hand at her right elbow, but not gripping too hard. No stairs, which she finds weird, given the basement feel of that tiled room. Outside, the temperature is considerably cooler than before. Gravel underfoot, scrunching. A car door opening. The thug helps her in.

"Lie down," he says. "Not a good look to have a bagged passenger on the back seat."

She complies. "Yes, sir."

He lifts her legs in and closes the door. Then another door opens and the car rocks a little as he settles his large frame in the driver's seat.

The car goes forward. More gravel. A pause. Then asphalt.

She starts counting, but soon gives up, because the car gathers serious speed and any attempted estimate of time into kilometres becomes pointless.

202

The thug hums a tune to himself. Some nursery rhyme-sounding ditty. It makes her sleepy.

The car slows down and negotiates the stop-start situations of a city centre.

At a traffic light, he reaches a hand back and pulls off the bag. The mesh strands grab at her hair and mess it up.

"Can I sit up?"

"Yes."

She does so. Wherever that compound is, she thinks, it's somewhere on the outskirts of Linz, close to an Autobahn. That assumption gets a narrower focus, because when the thug pulls up to the station, she sees that she's actually in a place called Wels. Meaning the mystery man's place is likely somewhere between Linz and Wels, near the Autobahn, and closer to Wels.

The thug takes a camping knife from the glove box. She turns to let him cut the tape. As they both get close to each other, she sees he has a gun holstered under his left arm.

It's a relief to have the tape off. She rubs at her sticky wrists.

"You need money?" he asks, passing her backpack from the front seat to the back.

This takes her by surprise. "Uh, yeah, sure. Who'd say no to that?"

He gives her a crisp €100 note.

"Thanks."

"No Linz," he says, waggling an index finger. "Go home."

"Aye, boss."

She assumes it wouldn't matter anyway. Anthony and Janica are gone. But the question remains: why did they go to Linz? Because of the man in the blue suit? Is he some kind of supporter? The Circus patron funnelling money through Switzerland to pay all the legal bills?

"You go now."

"Sorry. I thought the door was child-proofed and you needed to open it from the outside."

"It's not locked. You're free."

She gets out, slowly, as she's still dizzy. The car is a grey, medium-sized SUV that wouldn't stand out anywhere. The thug gives her a wave, then pulls away.

It's 1935. It means about 90 minutes passed from when the thug clipped her under the bridge to being dropped off here.

She shoulders the backpack and enters the station. The ticket machine eats the thug's note for the trip to Stuttgart. The schedule shows it's the last good connection, leaving in ten minutes, via Salzburg and Munich. She's glad not to have to do another seedy night train.

She hustles to buy a big bottle of water.

On board, she takes a seat behind a middle-aged couple, both reading. She hopes their proximity will allow her to sleep for some of the journey.

She drinks half the bottle, ignoring everything Zina ever said about hydration management, and tries to process the day. Nothing makes sense. But she thinks identifying that suited guy will help. She needs a picture, even if it's just a sketch, to show to Perceval and to run through all the databases. She hopes Zina will be able to help.

Day 12

The train arrives at 0250, 45 minutes late. The 16-platformed Stuttgart station, a significant hub for trains from all directions, has the level of activity in this early morning hour of a place that never has a moment's respite. There are lots of people, standing in groups and even sitting on the ground, while some rush to catch trains or be somewhere. Walking from the platform to the exit, she's approached by seven different people asking for spare change, at intervals that hint at choreography.

Outside, downtown Stuttgart is quieter, with all the action limited to the station, above ground and below. She starts walking, bone-tired, dragging her feet, foggy in the head, like she went the distance only to lose on points. It's tempting to spend more of the thug's money on a taxi, but as Zina's place is not far from the station, she decides the walk will do her good.

She cuts through the Schloßgarten. Barriers have already been set up, in preparation for the G8 meeting in a week's time. Despite Vilem's rousing call to arms, she can't envision this place as any kind of battleground. But she does notice how the barriers have been positioned, in a staggered maze meant to herd protesters away from key areas and prevent them from getting anywhere near the leaders. Barriers placed in this way also helps separate the protesters, making it easier to arrest them.

Up the long hill to Diemershalde, feet hurting, every step an effort. She hopes to hell that Zina is home and that she won't be angry with her for showing up at this ridiculous hour.

A hug, a shower and a bed; that's what she wants. She'll tell Zina everything later, after she's had a chance to reset. To get earthed here. Because Zina will know what to do; break things down to the essentials and offer the kind of insights that make everything seem simple and doable.

Just step forward and punch.

At the top of the hill, she yawns loudly. It's a couple of years since she was last here, and she's unsure of the way. On turning, she sees a man halfway up the hill duck into the shadows.

She wonders if she really saw him, or if her fatigued, recently concussed mind is playing tricks. Either way, better safe than sorry. She keeps turning around, feigning to find the way. Awake now, paying attention.

Her walk is deliberately slow as she zig-zags a few streets; not trying to lose him, but to draw him closer. To draw him out.

She thinks he could be the second man from under the rail bridge.

The rising adrenalin helps her become more alert. But after a hellish 36 hours, the last thing she wants is another fight.

On Gaisburgstraße, she sneaks down an alleyway just before Zina's building and hides behind a dumpster. A large rat scurries away. Crouched down, back against the wall, she looks through the gap between the dumpster and the wall and sees a pair of jeaned legs pass the entrance to the alley. Then the man stops and backtracks.

A quick scan of the immediate area reveals no viable weapons. She just has her fists. Slowly, she slides her backpack off her shoulders, letting it make a soft thud as it hits the ground. This gets the man's attention, and he edges into the alleyway, following the sound. His shadowy outline is lean and tall, and somehow familiar.

She lets him get just past the dumpster, then pounces. A full force left into the ribs, to bend him over. A downward right to the side of the head, to stun him. Then a left uppercut to the chin that sends his head back and knocks him out. He crumples to a heap on the ground.

It's Jesper.

She hears a gun click.

"Don't move!"

Mara holds up her hands and turns around slowly. Zina, barefoot and in an untied dressing gown, is standing at the entrance to the alleyway, gun drawn.

"Z, it's me."

"Mara? What the ...?"

"I can explain."

Zina lowers the gun and steps forward. "What have you done to this guy?"

"He was following me. Help me get him inside."

"In my apartment? No. I'm calling it in."

"Don't do that. I know him. Just help me."

"Who is he?"

"It's a long story."

"It better be a good one," Zina says, putting the gun in the dressing gown's front pocket, causing it to sag down on one side.

Mara retrieves her backpack. Then they each get under an arm and lift him up. It helps that he's almost conscious again, able to find his feet.

"Looks like you hit his chin switch," Zina says. "Got him out long enough for a ten-count."

"The ace in the three-card trick. The one you taught me. Ribs-cheek-chin. Left-right-left."

"Should I be proud of you?"

They walk Jesper out of the alleyway. His head hangs forward. He's dazed, not quite sure where he is.

"How did you know I was out here?" Mara asks.

"I heard a noise. We had a bunch of break-ins. Thieves entering the building from behind, using this alley."

"Are you keeping watch?"

As they negotiate the front door, going through sideways, Zina says, "I was still up. You're lucky I didn't shoot you."

"I had it all under control. How was I to know I was being followed?"

"By someone you know. He doesn't look the predator type. Too pretty."

"I'm noss," Jesper manages to say.

They get him up the first flight of stairs and into Zina's apartment, where they sit him down in a kitchen chair. He wipes the blood from his mouth and looks up. Zina and Mara stand over him, both with their arms folded.

"Good insensions," he says. "I swear."

Mara wants to punch him again. "Now you're a bodyguard?"

"Come on. Is me. Jesser."

"As in a court jester?" Zina asks. "Making jokes and amusing everyone? Little bells on your shoes."

"He's got a nice fat lip."

"Sure has. It won't last because ..."

"The mouth heals the fastest."

Mara and Zina smile at each other. The smile from Zina wipes away a lot of the hell of the last 36 hours.

"Well, fat lip or not, he talks too much," Zina says. "We should shut him up."

"Yeah, he might yell for help. Got any tape?"

Zina opens a drawer and takes out a big roll of brown packing tape. She hands it to Mara who sets about taping Jesper's ankles to the chair's legs and his hands behind his back.

"Please," he says. "I sell you everysing."

Mara tries to put a piece of tape over Jesper's mouth, but he moves anytime she gets close. Zina points the gun in his face and this makes him hold still. The tape goes on and Mara forcefully presses it down, making Jesper groan with pain. His watery eyes plead for mercy. Mara thinks he looks genuinely scared.

"Right," Zina says to Mara. "Let's have it. Who is he? Why was he following you? And why are you here?"

"Okay, I know you're annoyed, and I'm sorry for just showing up."

"You should've called."

"I would have, but I've been on the road without my phone the last couple of days." Mara takes a breath. "This is Jesper. From Kolding. In Denmark."

"I know where Kolding is."

"I met him in Hamburg, about a week ago. He's part of the protest scene. So am I." Mara holds up a hand. "I can explain that too. We're in this group called Circus."

"A court jester in the circus. What a shock."

"It's not really a circus. That's just the name. And it's not really a group. More like a gang, and there are gangs within this gang. I'm sorry. I'm not making much sense. I'm tired. Believe me, I'm really happy to see you, Z, but I just want to go to sleep. My trip started in Hamburg. I had to fight off two cops in Berlin. Then I took a night train to Linz, where I got knocked out and temporarily kidnapped. Now I'm in here. All the time, Jesper was following me."

"Why?"

Mara turns to Jesper. "Yes. Why?"

He mumbles under the tape, trying to say something.

"You should know better than to follow women," Zina says. "Look what happens when you do."

Jesper mumbles some more, what sounds like pleading. The way a sheep might bleat before having its throat slit.

Mara steps forward to take the tape off, but Zina stops her.

"Leave it," Zina says. "Whatever he's trying to say, it's a lie. It's written all over his face."

"What do we do with him then? I don't want to keep watch on him all night."

Zina takes a glass from a cupboard and fills it with water. From a

208

drawer, she takes a small container of something and adds a few drops of this to the water.

"There's no point talking with him until you've told me what you're doing in Hamburg." Zina gives the glass a bit of a swirl, then hands it to Mara. "Give him this. He's probably very thirsty."

Mara takes the glass to Jesper, but he shakes his head, eyes wide, not wanting it.

"Relax, honey," Zina says, very sweetly. "It's just a painkiller. In drop form. I can't swallow pills, that's why I have these drops. I'd say you're really sore after being beaten up by a woman. This'll help."

Jesper's eyes soften. Mara pulls some of the tape off and helps him drink.

"Sanks," he says, once the glass is empty.

Mara presses the tape back over his mouth, then turns to Zina. "I'm really sorry I ..."

Zina calmly holds up a hand. "Just wait."

Jesper's head starts to drop, until his chin is on his chest and he's out.

"That was a roofie," Mara says. "You almost had me convinced for a second there."

"You're too trusting. Still. When are you going to grow out of that?"

"Hopefully never. I want to be able to trust people."

"Have a shower and meet me in bed. Put a towel under his chair, in case he wets himself."

Zina walks out of the kitchen, gun in her right hand, dressing gown billowing behind her.

***

She's woken by a noise somewhere in the apartment. She's very comfortable, under two blankets and with Zina's bed all to herself. But another noise makes her sit up and fling the blankets aside.

With no more clean clothes to wear, she pulls on a pair of Zina's jeans and takes a shirt from one of the drawers.

In the kitchen, she finds Jesper on the floor, attached to the chair and lying on the white towel that's now stained yellow. His jeans have a damp triangle around the groin area.

He sees her and mumbles under the tape.

"Should've put down two," she says, stepping around him to open the window. "You stink."

More mumbling.

She bends down to pull the tape half off.

"Aaah, thank you," he says, sucking in air. "I could barely breathe."

She tilts her head to look at him, so their eyes are level.

"Help me. Please."

"Why were you following me?"

"Come on. I'm disgusting. Let me clean myself up."

"A great big man-baby who can't control himself."

"You're the one who drugged me. I woke up like this."

"That was Z. Not me." She stands up and opens another window. "Look. Tell me everything. Don't lie. And maybe then you can have access to the bathroom."

"Okay. Deal."

"Why were you following me?"

"I'm not from Kolding. I'm from Copenhagen."

"Why did you lie about that?"

"To sound tougher. Kolding's got some hardcore groups. Copenhagen's got a royal family and a freaking mermaid."

"Go on."

"I'm an actor."

"That I can believe. Aspiring, I guess."

"No, for real. I've done some ads, and some online stuff. My hair was longer then. No one in Circus knows this. Me telling you my biggest secret shows how desperately I want to get clean."

"How does an actor end up a protester?"

"About a year ago, I was up for a big role in a film, as the leader of a protest group. The director liked my look, but she didn't think I was convincing enough. I needed first-hand experience. So, I went to Hamburg and got into the protest scene. For research. Tried to go all method."

"With a new name as well?"

"I didn't get the part, but by that time I was deep in. I couldn't just go back to Copenhagen. I'd made all these connections to groups in Denmark. Some dangerous people, too. It would've been very suspicious if suddenly I pulled out of all that and then they saw me on TV. They would've come after me, for sure."

"Imagine what they'll do when they find out it was all just

210

research for a part in a movie you didn't get."

"Gomez can be seriously scary when he wants to be."

She laughs. "That lizard doesn't scare me. He's all show. Keep going."

"There's not much more to it. I stayed in Circus. Made friends. I kind of started to believe it, and enjoy it. Now, with Vilem, it's all so much more. There's the meaning you wanted."

"He's a good talker." Mara puts the kettle on and finds the instant coffee. "Taught well, taught right. I'm not sure there's much substance under that surface though. He's good packaging."

"Can I have a coffee?"

"I thought a shower was at the top of your list of demands?"

"It is. But I've got this awful taste in my mouth."

"Yeah, drugs will do that. Roofie residue."

"Mara, please."

She spoons coffee into a mug and pours the water. "No coffee for you. Focus on what great research this is, for when you get offered a role where you're kidnapped and interrogated. You'll nail that part."

"And beaten up, and roofed, and left to lie in my own mess."

"That's right. So many quality experiences. Expanding your range." She sips her black, sugarless coffee, holding the mug close to her nose so coffee is what she smells. "What do you know about this guy Vilem?"

"That was the first time I'd met him."

"You seem pretty taken with him, like his brainwashing worked."

"Brainwashing?"

"What would you call it? He basically gave you a script you all can read from. So you can all be on message when you talk."

"He spoke the truth," Jesper says. "About what we're fighting for."

"Right. Which is?"

Jesper is thoughtful for a moment, then says, "It's all about fairness. A fair distribution of wealth and taking power from the elites. We're ending oppression."

"See? Brainwashing. You're just repeating what Vilem said."

"Well, he's right. We've been oppressed for too long. Worst of all, we don't even know it. It's time for everyone to wake up. We just need to work together."

"Wow. You're definitely on message."

"Get as many people on board as we can and take control."

211

"Pitchforks against machine guns," she says, smiling. "Cobblestones against water cannons. I like our chances."

"We take control at the top and it all filters down. Vilem's got a plan."

"Says the man who couldn't even beat up a girl. Lying in a mess of his own creation and talking about revolution."

"We showed everyone what's possible. Last Sunday. You showed it."

"I wish people would stop referring to that. I was just defending myself, like anyone would. It was instinctive."

"You're part of it now, whether you like it or not. Change is coming. It's coming to this city and it's going to be huge."

"More brainwashing. Have you seen the barricades? The cops are getting ready to crush any protest."

"How do you know?" Jesper asks. "Your friend. She had a gun. Is she a cop?"

"Why were you following me?"

"Is she your mother? You never said you were adopted."

"I'm not."

"Stepmother? You two seem close. Like family."

"Answer my question or I'll leave you on this floor until the G8 protest."

"Fine. I'll tell you. It's no big deal. It was Gomez. I saw you at the station, in the elevator. With some guy in a wheelchair. Susie told Gomez you were asking about Anthony. About Linz. Gomez ordered me to follow you."

"Why would Gomez care that I'm trying to find my brother?"

"Come on. Really? Stop playing that game."

Mara sips some more coffee. "What game?"

"You know it's him in the video. At the protest. Him and his girl, Janet, or whoever."

"You think I went to Linz to arrest him?"

"What else? You're the cop."

"Not anymore." She finishes the coffee and gives the cup a rinse. "I don't know what video you're talking about. All I know is that I haven't heard from Ant for months. My father doesn't even know where he is. Of course, I was going to look for him. Like any sister would."

"You chased after him like you wanted to arrest him."

212

"Ah, so that was you under the rail bridge. With that goon who knocked me out. Who is he?"

"I don't know."

"You're not in the position to lie, Jesper."

"Honestly. I don't know. I was given a number to call. In Linz. In case I needed any help."

"Blue suit," Mara says.

"Huh?"

Mara puts it together: Jesper was following her, but the thug was there to keep her from getting close to Anthony. That means the guy in the blue suit was protecting Anthony.

"Listen," Jesper says. "You can't tell anyone about my background. The acting. That has to stay here."

"The easiest way to ensure that is for you to stay here. Right where you are."

"Please. No."

"But I'm certain Z doesn't want a stinking mess in her kitchen permanently." She takes a knife from the drawer. "Don't try anything ambitious."

"So you can deck me again? And roof me?"

"I thought we established this is all an acting masterclass."

"You are awful. I never expected this from you."

She bends down and cuts the tape at the chair's legs, then frees his wrists. He rolls slowly onto his hands and knees; he stays there momentarily as the feeling comes back into his limbs.

"Wonderful. The big man-baby is learning to crawl."

"I had no idea you were this cruel."

"Only to people who follow me. Use the towel. Like a nappy. Don't get anything on the floor."

"Where's the bathroom?"

She points. From the roll of heavy-duty trash bags under the sink, she tears off two and hands them to him.

"What do you want me to do with this?"

"Put your clothes in there. The towel too. Double-bag it, so you can take it all with you when you leave. You can take the chair as well. I think you ruined it."

"I hate you."

"That's what you get for following me. I'm glad to have helped you learn this important lesson."

213

He starts crawling towards the bathroom, the back of his jeans stained a colour too horrible for her to look at.

"Be sure to clean up every bit of mess you make in there," she says. "I'll see if I can find you something to wear."

***

After Zina finishes her shift, and after Mara completes her detailed confession about being undercover in the protest scene, they debate, over dinner and with both kitchen windows still wide open, how to travel to Hamburg. Zina needed little convincing to come as well, keen to help out with the first girls' training session at the gym. Mara is happy to have Zina along for this, as her plan for the session hadn't gone further than giving them tennis balls to squeeze and doing some rope-skipping.

It feels really good to have a friend in her corner again.

In another debate, about Anthony, Zina convinces Mara to forget about him for a while, saying that he'll come back into her life when he wants to be found. Until then, it's probably best she stops looking for him, as trouble seems to be following her, and finding him might just result in the police getting to him first.

They decide to take the train. Zina buys the tickets, selecting the high-speed connection to Frankfurt, then a switch to the NightJet.

Once they're away, make the change and settle into their twin bed couchette, Mara marvels at how different it is to the seated wagon of the train to Linz.

"I feel like I'm on a spaceship," she says.

"When you wake up, we'll be there. You just have to go to sleep."

"It wasn't like that on the last night train I took. I didn't let myself sleep."

"That's why you slept so deep last night. You were out before your head hit the pillow."

"The concussion probably had something to do with that. Second one in ten days."

"What was the first one?"

They lie down on their narrow beds, opposite each other, with about a 30-centimetre divide. Mara tells Zina about the pig farm protest that went so horribly wrong and resulted in her getting rifle-butted by Bernd the farmer.

214

"So that's how you got that line on your forehead."

"In hindsight, it was worth it."

"You wanted to prove yourself," Zina says. "Understandable."

"It worked. It got me in."

"After one protest? Doesn't sound like they need much convincing."

"I think they'll take anyone. Still, it was an example of a bad thing happening that had a good result. That's been a bit of a trend lately."

Zina rolls onto her side and pulls the blanket up to her chin. "Give me another example."

"That video. Then Jesper following me. I can't believe he's an actor."

"I shouldn't have drugged him. He's tarnished my place forever."

"My fault. For bringing him inside."

"I thought he was dangerous."

"He's my bitch now," Mara says. "Because I know his big secret. Although, he could be far more dangerous than I first thought."

Zina's eyes are closed. Her head slowly goes deeper into the pillow. "Why?"

"Because he's a convert. He had nothing to do with the protest scene, and now he's all in. He's looking at this Vilem guy like he's the saviour. The second coming. I think that's dangerous. That normal, reasonably intelligent people can be so easily influenced and changed, and potentially made to do nasty things."

"Wouldn't be the first time in this country."

Mara stares at the ceiling. The rocking movements of the train are lulling her to sleep. Zina already sounds gone, letting out a few snoring-type noises.

Then it hits.

"Fuck!" Mara says.

Zina opens her eyes and props herself up on an elbow. "What?"

"Linz. Nazis. Albrecht Löwe. My grandmother's father. He was a lawyer in Linz and a member of the Nazi Party. He moved his family to Hamburg after the war. To leave the past behind. Sort of."

"Any family still there?"

"No idea. Maybe Anthony went looking for them. He's always been closer to Grandma and Grandpa than me. I can't stand them. Same as my father. He's waiting for them to die."

"Left and right only go together in boxing combos." Zina lays back

215

down. "It's good you're going to coach girls for Gus. I'm super happy to help you get it started."

"Thanks, Z."

"My biggest regret is leaving his gym, and Hamburg. And you."

"What happened?"

Mara turns to Zina to get an answer, but she's asleep. It's calming to watch her, the white blanket going up and down at her side. Mara sees little scars, around Zina's eyebrows and one under her chin, earned from a trophy-gathering boxing career of her own.

Mara turns out the light. She takes Zina's tablet from the little table under the window, punches in her code and searches for Modra. It turns out to be a foundation, based in Vienna, promoting clean water for everyone. There's nothing special about the website. It has a few photos – smiling kids with their hands at gushing taps and third-world farmers in lush fields – and some large-font copy about the importance of water and why access to it should be everyone's right. But there are no names anywhere; getting into contact requires filling in a very standard-looking form and proving you're not a robot.

She wonders why a clean water foundation would try to rally protesters all over Europe to bring down their governments. Then she wonders how any single thought could sound as ridiculous as that.

A search for Vilem Kollar yields nothing. That in itself is strange, given he presented himself as the leader of Modra, yet has no online presence.

She thinks: is that not his real name? Are there bigger players behind him?

"Blue suit," she says to herself.

Zina's tablet has a facial composite program. Mara gets this open and tries to reconstruct the face of the guy with the compound outside of Wels.

"Hey. Wake up. We're almost there."

Mara opens her eyes. "Already? I feel like I just fell asleep."

"Come on. It's Hamburg. Blue sky and sunshine."

"Awesome."

"Can I have my tablet back?" Zina asks. She's sitting on the edge of her bed, in fresh clothes, backpack near the door, ready to get off.

Mara passes the tablet to Zina, who unlocks it and looks at the sketch.

"Are you in love with this guy? You were hugging this thing so hard I couldn't take it from you."

"That's the guy from down near Linz. We need to find out who he is."

"The lord of the manor."

"Wherever that manor is." Mara sits up and rubs her eyes. Through the window, she sees the new buildings of the Hafen City.

"Yes, it's beautiful," Zina says, following Mara's gaze. "Now, get moving. You've got about two minutes."

Mara starts getting dressed. Suddenly, the couchette seems cramped.

Zina gestures with the tablet. "Good looking."

"He hangs out with a big galoot. Not sure what their relationship status is."

Zina looks out the window as the train passes over the final bridge towards the station. The brownish Elbe extends west, cutting canals between the old warehouses of the Speicherstadt.

"Ah, Hamburg. My pearl. You got a place here?"

"I do. You're going to love it."

"Where is it? Walkable from the station?"

"St Pauli. So, yes." Mara closes her backpack and pulls on a hoodie.

"Cool. I need to move. We can get breakfast on the way."

"Deal."

Zina opens the couchette door on an already crowded hallway. Mara smiles.

"What?"

"Space," Mara says. "It's an absolute premium these days."

"And wanting to be first. I read that article, too. Love Russell's work."

They're the last to exit their sleeper wagon and get stuck in the funnel of people on the platform jostling for the escalator. Suitcases requiring escalator steps all of their own slow everyone down, while every second person takes a moment to steady themselves before making the short leap onto a moving step, as if riding an escalator for the first time.

Mara and Zina, both toting small backpacks, take the stairs. Outside, they head down the hill to the Binnenalster, then walk waterside towards Jungfernstieg. The northwest wind is just strong enough to blow a cloud of mist from the lake's central fountain that hits them both refreshingly in the face.

"I have missed this place," Zina says. "Look at it. I'm wasting away in Stuttgart."

Zina has a spring in her step that Mara struggles to match. She feels like she's chasing Zina, across Rathausmarkt and past the Lersner-Löwe office on Alter Wall, where that silver Maserati is parked out front. When they're over the bridge to Fleethof, Zina points to a table outside a café that's next to an antiquarian bookshop.

They sit down. Zina orders them coffee and croissants.

"Nothing heavy," she says, once the waiter's gone. "Just enough for a kick."

"I'm glad you're here, Z. I don't have a clue what to do with these girls."

"Have any of them boxed before?"

"Doubt it. I got Tinaya squeezing a ball already. She's mad keen."

"Let's keep it simple." Zina takes sunglasses from her backpack and puts them on. "Work from the ground up. Feet and body position."

"Elbows tucked. Thumbs at the temples."

"You got it. You don't need me." Zina looks around. "It's so good to be back. You showing up was just the shot in the arm I needed. Last time I escaped Stuttgart was when I visited you in Berlin last year."

"No holidays?"

"No money."

That Zina says this with both pride and regret makes Mara think Zina is still sharing a big chunk of her salary with members of her extended family, in Germany and Ghana.

Breakfast arrives. Zina adds half a teaspoon of sugar to her coffee and a very slight pinch of salt. She sips.

"Even the coffee tastes better here. Good water, not like the sludge down south."

"Time to move back, Z."

"Every transfer I apply for goes straight into the shredder. How long have we got, before training?"

"About an hour. Should we go straight there?"

"Your place is on the way. Let's dump our stuff. I don't want to move around St Pauli with everything important in my pockets."

"It's pretty tame these days."

As Mara sips her black coffee, she sees JJ come down the hill from the church and cross the bridge to Fleethof. She grabs a menu and holds it up to her face.

"Who are you hiding from? Protester paparazzi?"

Mara moves the menu enough to peer around the side of it. She watches JJ enter the bookshop, which has just opened. Then, Perceval crosses the bridge as well and follows JJ inside.

"Hey?" Zina asks. "What's going on?"

"I just saw JJ. The Circus leader. The woman I told you about."

"Why don't you want her to see you?"

"Perceval's tailing her. They're now both in the bookshop."

"Let's switch seats," Zina says. They do so. "Keep your back turned. I'll tell you what's happening."

"I think they're the only two in there."

"Plus the owner, who is now talking to JJ. They seem to know each other. He's laughing. She's smiling. God, she's beautiful. They might be flirting. Do people flirt in bookshops? Seems inappropriate. Hang on. She's leaving. Perceval's moving into her path. And, he executes a bump-meet. Badly."

"Amateur."

"Books fall," Zina continues. "They both bend down to pick them up. He's no amateur. He's now holding a book and they're talking about it. Common ground. Small talk. Smiles. Perceval thumbs towards the café next door. JJ nods. This looks very romantic."

"Perceval's all business. I think he boxes for the other troupe."

"Absolutely nothing wrong with that." Zina lowers her voice: "They're heading for the table right behind you."

Mara mouths, "Fuck."

Zina tilts her head back and to the left, implying they should leave in that direction. Mara nods and puts some cash under the sugar container. They finish their coffees. Having swapped sides at the table, they end up carrying each other's backpack. Zina's is rather heavy. They walk down Admiralitätstraße, Mara leading the way until they're around the first corner and out of sight.

"What have you got in this bag?" Mara asks. "Your rock collection?"

"Give me that. Weakling."

They swap backpacks.

"Why didn't you want them to see you?" Zina asks.

"Just JJ. Because I'd have to explain why I left Berlin, and I'm not in the mood to do that today. I don't give a flying fuck if Perceval saw me."

"He had the clear view. JJ was facing the other way. You have to assume he saw you."

"Maybe."

They head up the long hill to St Pauli.

"JJ probably already knows I was in Linz," Mara says.

"And Stuttgart. Your admirer would've checked in by now."

"My admirer?"

"The handsome court jester."

"He hates me. Even more than he did before."

"Nuh. Even under that extreme duress, you could see in his eyes he's hot for you."

"Hot for me? What year is it?"

Zina punches Mara in the shoulder. "Careful. Don't talk to me like I'm some old mother hen."

"You punch like one."

Mara puts an arm around Zina's shoulders and half hugs her. They walk this way, stepping in unison, all the way to Hamburger Berg.

***

Outside the gym, Tinaya and five other girls are waiting, toting their gear in a variety of bags that include well-used plastic and paper shopping bags. One girl has a battered backpack that looks like it was carried all the way from Afghanistan. Tinaya waves to Mara from a distance. Her hands are empty, and Mara sees that the girls are each taking turns to squeeze the tennis ball.

"What going on?" Mara asks, when she and Zina reach the door. "Why aren't you inside?"

"It's locked," Tinaya says.

The muffled sound of angry German hardcore rock comes from behind the door.

"Do you have a key?" Zina asks.

Mara shakes her head. "Gus knows we're coming. He set the whole thing up."

Zina goes to the door and bangs a fist on it. "Gus? Open up, Gus."

After a few seconds, the door is cracked ajar, the music pumping out. Gus's old head appears.

"Zina? What a pleasant surprise."

"Yeah, I love you too. Let us in."

"I can't. Not today. The MMA boys have taken over. I tried to tell them, but ..."

"Gus," Zina says flatly. "Move."

"I don't like them either. Believe me. I want them gone."

"But you like their money. How things have changed."

Gus holds the door open. Zina and Mara enter, but Tinaya and the girls stay outside. Mara motions for them to follow, and they're tentative in doing so.

The music is ridiculously, offensively loud.

Once down the hallway and in the main workout area, Zina folds her arms and looks around. There's plenty of grunting and pads being whacked. A lot of posturing and flamboyance. The horrible smell of sweaty feet. The half dozen MMAs are in their early 20s, in varying weight divisions.

Zina locates the portable speaker and turns it off. The grunting and smacking of pads suddenly stops.

"Sorry, guys," she says. "The gym's already booked this morning."

The guys laugh. One turns his back and continues to punch and kick the heavy bag, as if Zina doesn't exist. He's barefoot. Mara notices they all are, which in part explains the disgusting smell.

"Yeah, booked by us," says a lean guy in a tight muscle shirt. "Off you go, back to the jungle."

His shirt has a V of sweat from the neckline to the LONSDALE emblazoned on the front. He has the pale, mean look of someone who would be more at home in an underground fight club.

"Get out, all of you," the guy adds. "Back to your own countries and your kitchens."

Mara turns to see Tinaya and the girls shuffling to the hallway with the stoic resignation gained from a young lifetime's worth of being denied things.

"Stay where you are," Zina says, stopping the girls. She peels off her tracksuit top, her cut torso rippling beneath a green singlet.

Mara hears the girls behind her take sharp intakes of breath. At 43, Zina looks spectacular.

"Gus," Zina says. "Get me some suitable gloves."

The old gym owner smiles ever so slightly, then ambles towards his office.

"You guys don't seem to know much about tradition, but we'll do this the old-fashioned way. Do it fair. You guys want the gym. We booked the gym. The best solution, because you don't want to be gentlemen and leave, is to settle it in the ring."

The guys laugh some more.

Gus comes back and hands Zina a pair of gloves. She nods a thank you.

"Who's it going to be?" she asks. "Who's brave enough for this ... rumble in the jungle?"

More posturing, more grinning, but no one steps forward.

"Looks like they don't want to fight a girl," Zina adds, "at least in the ring."

"If you don't accept the challenge," Gus says, "you forfeit. You'll have to leave. Gym rules."

"Okay, yeah," says the guy in the tight muscle shirt. He isn't the biggest of them, but he's somehow their leader. "But no boxing. MMA rules."

"I challenged you," Zina says. "I get to pick. And by our rights, the gym is booked for us. We box, like real athletes. None of this barefoot, pit bull shit."

The use of pit bull seems to spark something. "I got gloves," he says. "Get ready to feel pain."

As Zina puts her gloves on, she says, "Sounds like you don't have any problem with hitting a girl. Like you've done it plenty of times before."

"Only girls who ask for it."

222

"I guess that's all of us, right?"

Mara gets close to Zina and helps her with the gloves. "No hand tape?"

"Look at this idiot," Zina whispers. "Everything on the right. Total one-sider. This won't take long. It's tempting to draw it out and give him some punishment, but we've got coaching to do."

"You don't have to do this. There's nothing to prove."

"You and I both know I absolutely have to do this. I've been fighting pricks like him my whole life."

"Then nail him. Nail him good."

Zina looks towards the girls huddled together. With their shopping bags, well-travelled backpacks and faraway stares, they look like they're waiting to board a rubber boat to cross the Mediterranean.

Gus climbs into the ring with difficulty, watched by the MMAs, none of them holding the ropes wide for him. Lonsdale shirt is already in the ring, gloves on, an elbow leaning on the pads of one of the corners. No helmet. No mouthguard. Still barefoot. He clearly thinks this is all a joke and it will be over in under a minute.

Mara widens the ropes to give Zina, also without a helmet, access to the ring. Once inside, she executes a backwards lap, skipping around, loosening up, very light on her feet. Gus gets them in the centre, though Zina's opponent takes his time getting there, then stands with the slouched shoulders of someone bored by the whole thing. Gus goes through the formalities, listing the rules, with first to five points, no breaks, and getting them to touch gloves.

The guys ringside yell encouragement to their man as Zina and Lonsdale shirt square off. The girls gather in a line along the other side of the ring, their faces full of fear and awe, some on their toes to see over the first rope.

The fight starts. Zina's body position is textbook perfect. The guy shuffles forward, gloves high and wide, the left wafting out in front, like he doesn't really know what to do with it, and the right already pulled way back. Zina dances left, opening herself up to that right. He swings it straight at her and she evades it easily. He puts so much into that first punch, he loses his balance and is forced to steady himself with the ropes. He regroups, embarrassed, and comes back more aggressively, that right glove pulled even further back, and his upper body twisting that way to generate more power. Zina, on her toes, keeps moving to her left, circling the ring like she could do it all day and never get tired. He swings again and misses. On his way through, Zina pops him in the ribs with a sharp left. A hello punch. A welcome-to-your-beating punch.

"One," Gus shouts, scoring the point.

The guy tries to take it up a gear, more serious now, intent on avoiding humiliation.

Mara knows that's exactly what Zina wants: to get him thinking about anything other than strategy and technique.

He moves forward, gloves tighter to his head, and tries to spar more traditionally, leading with the left to open up space for the right. Zina avoids every punch, seeming to know each time what's coming.

It's beautiful to watch. Mara is reminded how boxing is done with the whole body. People who say it's all fists and unhinged aggression have no idea what they're talking about. Proper boxing, how she was taught, is artistry; a powerful, strategic ballet that starts at the toes and goes all the way to the top of the head, where every movement has purpose and meaning.

Zina just dances around the guy, playing with him, being patient.

Another big swing misses. Zina puts more weight into the punch this time, getting him high on the jaw with another left as his right side is exposed again.

"Two," Gus shouts.

The guy shakes it off, looking surprised at how much was in the punch. He's angry now, fully in the wrong mindset. He wants to hurt Zina.

Mara knows: you don't box angry. Any pre-fight threats are usually just for show, adding to the soap-opera element of boxing as entertainment. But once in the ring, the two fighters are in it together, and may the best one win. There should never be any anger, as that distracts the boxer from the task at hand.

But Mara thinks it's not only about who gets the gym this morning. This guy's motivation is coming from a different place. His whole belief system, everything he defines himself by and identifies with, is on the line, right here. Mara wants Zina to knock the ugliness out of him.

Any semblance of rhythm he had is gone as he attacks without strategy or skill. He's dogfighting now, trying to stand and deliver

224

from two bare feet planted parallel. A big right, half a left, another right. The gloves whoosh through the air as Zina dodges them with ease and continues dancing left. He's breathing heavily from all the effort, sucking wind, but moves forward, with a right coming from a huge wind-up. It misses, and Zina delivers a three-card trick in a flash: left to the ribs, right to the jaw, and a left with everything to the side of his mouth that sends his chin to his shoulder and his eyes to the back of his head. He's out in mid-air. The ring shakes as he lands. Blood drools from his mouth, adding a fresh stain to the very stained canvas. Gus bends down and hooks an index finger into the guy's mouth, to keep him from swallowing his tongue. The finger is covered in blood when he withdraws it.

Mara thinks the guy would spit out a couple of teeth, if conscious.

Zina turns to the girls, whose mouths are five little O's of shock and adoration.

"The changerooms are down there," she says, pointing with the left glove that did all damage. "Three minutes. No more. Go, go."

The girls hustle in that direction.

Three of the guys grab their bags and leave. The two remaining drag their fallen comrade, who's conscious again, from the ring. Mara picks up their bags while they each get under a sweaty armpit. At the door, the guy nearest Mara gives her a narrow-eyed look, like he's already planning some kind of revenge. She drops the three bags on the ground, closes the door and locks it.

***

The training is fun. Mara and Zina start by teaching the girls simple footwork; how to stand and how to move. A bit of bag work. Some rope-skipping. Push-ups. Sit-ups. Bare fists against open palms to get the feel.

Gus helps for a while, but runs out of energy and falls asleep sitting upright on a bench.

Despite their high motivation, the girls aren't very fit, and Zina doesn't push them. After an hour, they're flat on their backs on the big stretching mat.

A pounding on the door makes Zina and Mara look at each other, both thinking the MMA guys have come back, perhaps with reinforcements. Zina hustles the girls into the changeroom while

Mara goes to the door. She unlocks it and opens it on a pair of male police officers: Callenberg and Gornau, according to the names on their uniforms.

"We're sorry to disturb your training," Callenberg says. He's the older of the two and strikes Mara as decent, while Gornau has the shifty eyes and aggressive stance of someone with an agenda.

"We had a report of criminal activity going on here," Gornau says.

"Since when is boxing against the law?"

"The report involved illegal immigrants." Gornau really adding spice to "immigrants" confirms to Mara that he's the more dangerous of the pair. "This gym is part of a people smuggling operation."

Mara laughs. "That's a good one. Am I the head of this operation?"

Gornau steps into the doorway, filling the gap with his large frame. "Are you? Bringing illegals into this country is no laughing matter."

"That little miracle when Germany threw open its doors to a million refugees seems so long ago."

"They weren't refugees. They were migrants, sneaking in while they had the chance." Gornau pushes the door further open and walks down the hallway. "They took advantage of our generosity."

"Which appears to have run out."

"Gornau, go easy," Callenberg says. "Let her explain."

But Gornau's already down the hallway and into the main area. Callenberg gives Mara an apologetic look.

Suddenly, Gornau pulls out his gun. "Don't move!"

The gun is pointed at someone in the main area. When Mara gets there, she sees the target is Zina.

"On the floor," Gornau shouts. "Now!"

Mara positions herself in front of the gun, causing Gornau to take a few steps back. "What the fuck are you doing?"

"On the floor! Both of you!"

Mara turns to see Zina slowly move to the left, to block the door to the locker room.

"Who are you hiding in there?"

"Nobody's hiding anyone," Mara says. "There's a group of girls in there, all with legitimate refugee status. We're teaching them how to box. Put the fucking gun down."

"Quiet. Callenberg, restrain her."

"Don't you touch me," Mara says. "What is wrong with you two?

226

We haven't done anything wrong."

There's a moment when no one moves. The silence is broken only by Gus letting out a few old-man-type snores.

"Let's all just take a breath," Zina says, and her calmness amazes Mara. "My name is Zina Koranteng. I'm an officer of the Stuttgart Police. Lower your weapon and let's handle this professionally. Like the colleagues we are."

"You're not my colleague," Gornau says. "You ..."

"Gornau," Callenberg says, interrupting just in time. "We'll check their IDs, sort this out. Put the gun away."

Gornau doesn't move.

"I'm going to open this door," Zina says, pointing behind her, "and let the girls come out. They're just teenagers. They'll show you their papers and everything will be cleared up. Please, holster your weapon."

"Do it," Callenberg says, though his voice lacks authority.

"I'm not opening the door until you put that gun away," Zina says. "We can stand here all day, if you want."

"When you guys should be out there policing the streets properly and stopping actual crimes," Mara says.

Gornau looks at Mara. "I really want to shut you up."

"I'd like to see you try."

"Mara," Zina says. "That's enough. These officers are just doing their jobs, responding to an anonymous tip."

"Anonymous? You don't think just maybe it was the one of the MMA guys from earlier?"

"Let's not escalate things."

Gus coughing a few times in his sleep has the interesting effect of diffusing the situation slightly. Gornau puts his gun away, but keeps one hand near it, and motions for Zina to open the door. The girls file out, changed, with their papers, cards and passports in their hands, ready for inspection. They look young and scared.

"It's all right," Zina says. "Just a misunderstanding. You're not in any trouble."

She gets them lined up in front of the ring. Callenberg keeps watch while Gornau takes a long look at each of the girls' documents. He's disappointed when everything is in order.

"Thank you," Zina says. "Well done."

Gornau nods and takes a few steps backwards.

227

"Thanks for your cooperation," Callenberg says. "False alarm."

Callenberg puts a hand on Gornau's shoulder, as a prompt for them to leave.

"Wait," Gornau says. He looks at Zina. "Where are your papers?"

"Not on me. I know better than to walk around St Pauli with all my important stuff on me."

"That's a problem." Gornau smiles. "Maybe you don't have any papers at all. You're the illegal one."

Mara steps forward. "Hey, moron. Take out your phone and search for Zina Koranteng, Olympic Games. Not only is she a police officer, she boxed for Germany."

"No way," Gornau says. "There's no chance she represented my country. Look at her. She's not even from Germany."

"Gornau," Callenberg says. "Take it easy."

"She was born in Bremen," Mara says, barely able to keep her voice even. "German mother. And didn't you hear? She's police. She was busting heads and arresting actual criminals in this very area when you were still shitting in nappies."

"You shut up, or I'll arrest you for abusing a police officer."

"While you're in the process of doing that exact thing, right now. Your partner should arrest you."

"Where's your ID?" Gornau asks.

"Everything's at my apartment in St Pauli," Mara says. "Zina's ID. Mine too. We can go there right now."

"So, you also can't identify yourself."

"I'm Mara Steinbach, formerly of the Berlin Police."

Gornau scoffs. "You two are crazy. Police? Both of you? Please. You should both be locked up. In a mental institution."

"What is wrong with you?" Mara asks. "Is this what you call serving and protecting? You're making way too big a deal of this. I know you just want to help your friends ..."

"What friends?"

"Those guys who were here when they shouldn't have been, then got humiliated by a person they consider inferior."

Gornau shrugs. "I don't know what you're talking about. But I've had enough of your talk. You two can't identify yourselves. You're both under arrest. Callenberg, cuff her."

"You touch me and I'll knock your front teeth out."

"Mara," Zina says, her hands already out in front of her, "don't resist. That will just make things worse. We'll sort all this out."

Mara lets Callenberg cuff her. Gornau steps forward to do the same with Zina. But Tinaya jumps forward and is a whirlwind of fists as she tries to protect Zina. Gornau takes a step back, withdraws his baton and hits her on the side of the head. Then Zina is onto Gornau, tackling him to the ground and overpowering him. But Callenberg goes to his partner's aid and gets Zina's hands behind her back where he loops on a set of plastic cuffs.

"That's definitely going in my report," Gornau says, as he lifts Zina off the ground.

"You brutally hitting an innocent bystander will go in mine," Zina says.

As the two police officers march them out, Mara shouts, "Gus!"

She sees him wake up just as she reaches the hallway.

Outside, Mara expects to see the MMA guys, waiting to come back in. But there's just a police car. She and Zina are shoved in its back seat.

***

The holding pen of the Davidwache station has two drunks passed out on the long bench. Through the glass, Mara sees Gornau working in slow-motion at a computer, typing with single fingers. Callenberg sips coffee and chats with another officer.

Zina rubs at the welts on her wrists.

"You all right?" Mara asks.

Zina nods. "Looks like they got the order, too."

"What order?"

"There was a briefing, last Monday. I thought it was just for us, with the G8 coming. Exercise more control. Check IDs. Profile, if necessary."

"I can't believe it. A formal order for racial profiling?"

"It wasn't mentioned outright, but let's say it was heavily implied. Approach anyone who looks suspicious, that's what they said. Foreigners being the key focus. For some of us in that briefing, things became very uncomfortable."

"You think the Hamburg Police got the order too?"

"I assume now it was nationwide. Maybe it originated here. After what happened on Sunday."

229

"Jawinski. He acts like he's the head of the Hamburg Police."

"Maybe it came from him and went all over the country. To get back control."

"By turning Germany into a police state and playing right into the hands of protest groups in the process. This is just what they want. To fight against oppression. Now, the police are giving it to them."

Zina looks at Gornau. "He's going to take all day to type my name, and probably get it wrong."

"Who should we call? You know, to help speed things up. I don't want to sit in here all day."

"Your man Perceval?"

"That could blow everything up. He'll deny he knows me. Maybe Nicola?"

"The Lersner girl, your friend?"

"Not my friend anymore."

"The girl who somehow styled her hair to cover her horns. How can she possibly help?"

"She's a lawyer."

"Oh, that fits."

Mara smiles. "She also represents Circus."

"I never liked her. She got everything so easy. I don't want her help."

"Me neither." Mara groans. "I guess that leaves Richard."

"I bet he's just waiting to help you out."

"Yeah, to come here and throw his intellect into everyone's face."

"Call him."

"He probably won't answer. He avoids using the phone."

"They can send a car then. It's not like they have anything else to do." Zina sits back against the wall and folds her arms, resigning herself to a long wait. "I can't believe I used to work here. Things have really changed. Look at this place. All men, all white. Back in my time, we were a real mix. The poster station for diversity. The sons and daughters of immigrants. All here because we wanted to be the change we wanted to see in the world. We had these awful tan and brown uniforms. With green ties and leather jackets."

"Better than the uniforms now. Might as well be in black."

"Agreed."

Mara goes to the glass and knocks on it. Gornau ignores her, but when she has Callenberg's attention, she mimes making a call, shaping her left thumb and forefinger into an L. Callenberg puts down his cup and approaches the holding pen.

When the door is opened, Mara says, "I need you to contact Richard Steinbach. My lawyer."

Callenberg nods. "We'll sort this out. Don't worry."

Mara gives Callenberg the phone number and address, then sits back down on the bench. "He seems all right. His partner's from another era."

"The police are attracting more and more guys like Gornau. And girls too. In fact, the girls are worse. There's nothing nastier than a female nationalist."

"For sure. You should see my grandmother. A sweet little old lady she is not."

"I thought about quitting last year. But I don't know what else to do."

"Move to Hamburg and become a boxing coach. You and me. We take over Gus's gym. I think poor old Gus is on his last legs."

"No family either."

"Just a long string of ex-boyfriends."

"I love Gus. I wish I'd never left."

Mara looks at Zina. "You know, you're taking this really well. They have totally fucked up and racially abused you. They've broken so many rules, and done it against one of their own."

"Believe me, I really want to smash Gornau's head against the keyboard he has no idea how to use. But it won't change anything. This has been my life. No one ever looks at me and thinks I'm German. In Bremen, it wasn't so bad. But when we moved to Chemnitz, it was terrible. It was verbal, it was physical. Even if it wasn't so overt, you could still see it in people's eyes. Small little acts of racism, day after day after day. They weigh on you. Heavily. You've got to be very strong to handle that. I learned how to box just so I could get rid of my anger and defend myself. It didn't really help, though. You fight one off and they come back with three. Or they do something cowardly, like smash the windows of your house or spray vile graffiti on the walls."

"But you won everything. Didn't that help? Everyone loves a winner."

"You'd think that. But not even when I fought my way up to qualify for the Olympics. That was such an amazing experience. But

231

when I came back, people abused me for not winning a medal. I'd let everyone down. I was too lazy, didn't train hard enough. Wasn't tough enough. I was German when I won and black when I lost."

"I'm so sorry, Zina."

"Don't be. That's how it was. How it still is. Maybe it's even worse than before, because people who suffer from racism often move away the first chance they get. Like I did. Which, I guess, is kind of the whole idea of it. Drive away the people you don't want. Tribal thinking. Wanting to spend all your time with people who think, look and act just like you."

"I don't want to live in a world like that."

The door to the holding pen is opened and two young black males are pushed inside. Mara wonders if they're drug dealers, from the crews who loiter around the Onkel Otto bar, a few blocks from the police station. Then she catches her own prejudice and tries to remove the thought from her head; they are just two guys, maybe put in here unfairly, like she and Zina were. They sit down on the bench.

Zina smiles at the new arrivals and gets a nod from both in return. "People have always sympathised and said I must have it hard, being not one or the other," she says to Mara. "Half-and-half. Not totally dark, but not white enough. The point is, it's not about how I look or who I am. It's all about who's looking at me."

"People shouldn't see a colour at all. Every skull looks the same with the skin removed."

"How was it in Berlin? At your station."

"White and beautiful."

"Now who's profiling."

"Stating a fact. There are only white people, and everyone at the station is good-looking. Healthy and fit. I think the head wants it that way. He chooses his people based on their looks."

"Which station is that again?" Zina asks, her face falling flat.

"Kollwitzkiez. I was in Schöneberg, which was great, because it was close to home and it was a quieter area of the city. But then I got transferred, a couple of months ago. For balance, they told me. You know, gender."

Zina stares straight ahead. "Who's managing that station?"

"A real creep. Hans Spitz."

Zina grunts out a laugh.

232

"What?"

"You just can't keep bad people down. He likes a pretty face, does Captain Spitz."

"You know him?"

"He's the reason I had to leave Hamburg."

"You said you were transferred."

"That was the official line," Zina says. "The truth is I was exiled. Because of Spitz."

Callenberg approaches the door and opens it. "Your lawyer's on the way. Needs about half an hour, he said."

"Thanks." When the door is closed, Mara adds, "Yay, Richard to the rescue."

"Eventually."

"You can use the time to tell me what happened between you and Spitz. Because you leaving Hamburg pretty much ended my boxing career."

"Don't do that. If you stopped boxing, that's on you."

"I'm not saying it's completely your fault."

"You already needed a new coach. I'd taken you as far as I could. You'd plateaued."

"I was the Hamburg champ."

"For your age group. Don't look so shocked. You knew it too. You'd stopped getting better and didn't have the drive to get up another level."

"Wow. Don't hold anything back, Z."

"That's the truth."

"The way I remember it, you just left me. I couldn't box without you."

"There was nothing I could do about that. You have no idea the place I was in."

"Tell me about it."

"You made your own choices," Zina says. "Anyone who wants to be really good at something should never lack motivation. If you wanted it, you would've found another coach and got on with it."

Mara folds her arms and doesn't reply.

"Maybe with you, the timing was wrong." Zina softens her tone. "You were 15. It's a difficult age. I'm sorry. But there was nothing I could do about it."

"What happened? Help me understand, because it's always felt

233

like you just left me."

Zina looks through the glass at the Davidwache station's collection of desks. There are no women working today, and the station has a very masculine feel, as if the only women who come in here are cleaners, complainers and criminals.

"I know that's selfish thinking," Mara adds, "but that's how I remember it."

"Spitz and I worked here. Back then. He was on his way up and did a lot of the admin and organising. He was very ... hands-on. With all the women, not just me."

"He hasn't changed."

"Please tell me he didn't get to you."

Mara shakes her head. "He tried. I know he got to others in Kollwitzkiez. Stations are small places. Everyone knows what going on."

"But no one's ever brave enough to do anything about it."

"He would frame everything like an exchange. Do this for me and I'll do this for you."

"The strategy is to make you culpable, part of the exchange. Then no one talks because they're scared of being exiled. Like I was." Zina sighs. "He's just the worst kind of predator. A strategist who masks everything in friendliness. If you think he's getting too touchy-feely or abusing his position and you say something, he goes all innocent and claims he's just being friendly. Like there's something wrong with you. Then he talks to others and suddenly you have the reputation for being a bitch. A whiner. Someone's who not committed to the team. So you find yourself doing weeks full of night shifts, including every Friday and Saturday night, which was just wild around here in those days."

"Just because you turned him down? What about the others?"

"He made plays for them too. When he succeeded, we all saw the changes. Getting the best shifts, holidays signed off at the best times of the year. I made it clear I wasn't interested, but he still kept at me. With guys like Spitz, it's all about the hunt, not the feeling of power when he's fucking you. It's the thrill of the pursuit. Some alpha male caveman mentality that's etched in their DNA, in the kind of men who haven't evolved at all."

"Not all men are bad, sister," says one of the young guys.

"No, and not every snake is poisonous. But you want to stay far

234

away from the ones that are."

"Snakes, poisonous or otherwise, shouldn't listen in on private conversations," Mara says.

The guy smiles and shrugs. "Look where we are. We're all in here together. We all hear everything."

"What are you two in for?" Zina asks.

Another shrug. "I'd say, general darkness."

"We didn't do anything," says the other. "Just hanging out at the wrong place."

"What happened to this guy Spitz?" the first asks. "You take him down, sister? I hope so, because it sounds like he deserved it."

"Stop calling me sister. I'm Zina. She's Mara."

"Hello. I'm Kamran. This is Adu. He's new to Hamburg. First time getting arrested. I keep telling him to relax. This will be part of his life."

Adu shakes his head bitterly. "This is no life. It's unfair."

"You'll get used to it, Adu," Kamran says. "As long as you never break the law, they have to let you out. Anyway, I want to know about this Spitz man."

Zina turns to Mara. "Does he still limp?"

"That was you? Tell me that was you."

"Believe it or not," Zina says to Kamran and Adu, "I'm a police officer. I used to work here. With Spitz."

"What are you doing in here?" Adu asks.

"Like you. Darkness. I didn't have my ID on me. I do that sometimes, go out into the world without any ID, to see what will happen. To sort of gauge where Germany is at with its racism. Especially with the police."

"You don't need to try to do that," Kamran says. "It's all in the eyes. You got that right. It's about who's looking at you and what they think."

"Things were different when I worked here. Spitz was the only arsehole. The rest of us, we were like family. Very diverse. We were social too, having barbecues and parties. We couldn't not invite Spitz. And he was clever about that too, because it was often him doing the inviting. Hosting the events at his place. He was really generous like that, until it became clear what his motives were."

"He wanted the benefit of home turf," Mara says. "A controlled environment. His own cave."

"True. It happened at his place, at the Christmas party. He was all over me. Kept saying I was his present that he couldn't wait to unwrap, like that was a funny and charming thing to say. He brought me drinks all night, then got all offended when I wouldn't drink them. Criticised me for being uptight and no fun. He even suggested I was a lesbian."

"Ah, that old pearl."

"Things went fully bad when he followed me into the bathroom. He had a real go, but I fought him off."

"She used to box," Mara says to Kamran and Adu. "Went to the Olympics."

"How are you in here with us?" Kamran asks.

"Spitz was a fitness fanatic," Zina continues, appearing to enjoy the memory now. "Amateur cycling. He used to brag about going to events around Europe. It only took two punches to get him down, and he had a couple of weight divisions on me. When he tried to get up off the floor, he was on one knee. He grabbed my dress. I turned and kicked his other knee, which went at a whole different angle. He screamed with pain and I ran for it."

The glass door is opened by Callenberg. Richard is standing behind him, in that massive coat of his, and broad hat, an e-scooter over his shoulder, upside-down.

"Some things never change," he says.

"He's talking about me," Mara says to Kamran and Adu. "It's not my first arrest either."

"Nice to see you, Richard," Zina says. "Thanks for coming."

"How can I help?"

"I need you to go to my apartment around the corner and get our IDs," Mara says. "Callenberg has my keys and the address."

"Grab my tablet as well, please," Zina says.

Richard nods. "Very nice to see you, Zina. You haven't changed at all. Except for where you find yourself in this constabulary."

"I've been regaling everyone about my good times here."

"Give me ten minutes," Richard says.

"Wait," Mara says. "Before you do that. Can you get these guys out? They haven't done anything wrong."

"More victims of the police state. I'll see what I can do."

They all watch as Richard talks with the officers who brought Kamran and Adu in.

"Is he a lawyer?" Adu asks.

"He looks like a mad scientist," Kamran says.

Mara laughs. "He's mad, but he's also a lawyer. The best kind. An absolute expert in conspiracies."

Richard comes back to the glass door and motions for Kamran and Adu to stand up. They both shake hands with Zina and Mara and say "thank you" several times.

"At least one good thing has come of this mess," Zina says, when the door closes again.

"This seems to be a trend that's happening a lot to me. Bad things that eventually have a good outcome. Like ending up in here and getting your story about Spitz, which you still need to finish."

"Yes. Sorry. I should've told you years ago."

"What you need to do is go to Berlin and tell it all to Russell. He's working on a story about Spitz. We've got an insider in the Kollwitzkiez station. Your story is exactly the context Russ needs to show how far back this goes and how the police have long enabled Spitz and guys like him."

"I'm not using my name."

"You can be anonymous. Russell will know how to work around that."

Zina nods slowly. "You're right. It's time. It's way past time. I'm really glad I told you all of this."

"But not how it ends. You wrecked Spitz's knee. Then what?"

"This is the really bad part. Spitz reported me for misconduct. He actually wanted to have me arrested for assault. Can you believe that? There were so many interviews. In the end, it was my word against his, and you get one guess as to who everyone in this male-dominated club believed. I threatened to go public. I wish now I had. The real problem was that no one at the station said anything, including the girls Spitz had already hunted and gathered. I had no one in my corner. That's what hurt the most."

"Fuck."

"What they wanted most of all was to avoid any kind of scandal. You know, stop the police from having anything remotely like a me-too moment. The solution was to exile us both. Spitz east and me south."

"I'd hardly call Berlin an exile. He runs Kollwitzkiez now."

"While I've been in Stuttgart ever since, still working the streets.

237

Every transfer request rejected."

"I'm so sorry, Z."

"It's a man's world."

"We've still got Gus," Mara says. "I hope he helped Tinaya."

"I'm certain he did. No poison in him."

They sit in the holding pen in silence until Richard returns. He has their IDs, which he shows to Gornau. Callenberg opens the door and is gushingly apologetic, especially towards Zina.

At Gornau's desk, Zina takes the tablet from Richard. She unlocks it and swipes away Mara's sketch.

"I must've got your name wrong," Gornau says with a shrug. "These foreign names have such complicated spelling. Anyone would've made that mistake."

Zina shows Gornau photos of her at the Olympics.

"What medal did you win?"

"I'm going to report you," Zina says.

"Good luck with that. We did everything by the book. You were the ones without IDs in a hostile environment protecting potentially illegal immigrants."

"Yeah, shame on us for training young refugee girls how to defend themselves. They have no reason to feel unsafe in this country, right?"

Gornau chews whatever he wants to say, but keeps his mouth shut.

"Come on, Z," Mara says. "Let's get out of this dump."

Outside, Richard puts his e-scooter on the ground and places one rubber-booted foot on it, ready to ride off. With the Reeperbahn backdrop, he looks to Mara like a highly mobile homeless person.

"Thanks, Richard," Zina says.

"The all-new German police state strikes again. Happy to help."

"Can we repay you with lunch?"

"No, but you can show me your tablet again."

"The Olympic photos?" Zina asks.

"That sketch."

Zina brings it up on the tablet and shows it to Richard.

"Who made that?" he asks.

"I did," Mara says. "This guy ... he ... I met him in Linz. Do you know who he is?"

"Yes." Richard points at the screen. "That is Milan Kollar."

238

They enter the Pink Dragon. The small bartender, clearing glasses from a table, gives Mara a smile, then nearly drops the glasses when he sees Zina.

"You're hired," he says. "Again."

Zina looks around the strip club that feels well-soiled at 0915 on Sunday morning. "To do what? Clean?"

"No. No. No. A dancer. You should be on that stage." The bartender does a lean-back, to take all of Zina in admiringly. "In or out of your police uniform."

"Sounds like you remember me?"

"How could I possibly forget the most beautiful creature I've ever seen. And I've seen a lot of dazzlers in here."

"Right," Zina says, amused by the bartender's seasoned charm. "I bet you give this line to all the girls who come in here."

"He didn't give it to me," Mara says.

"You were off limits," the bartender says. "In here with Dragon royalty."

"Well, she's off limits too, because she's with me. Anyway, where is the king of the pink?"

"Far corner. Hiding in the dark. Sambuca?"

"For breakfast?"

"Call it a very late nightcap."

"No, thanks. But yes to coffee. Please."

"For me as well," Zina says.

The bartender smiles his assent, in a smitten way that makes it seem he would do just about anything for Zina.

Mara leads the way to the dark corner where Perceval is in the booth with Nils.

"You've been here before?" Mara asks.

"Long time ago," Zina says. "On patrol."

On seeing Mara, Nils slides his gangly frame out from behind the table to greet her. "Mara, hi," he says. "How are you? Look, I'm really sorry for what I said last time."

"What did he say?" Zina asks.

"Called me a lesbian when I refused to go out with him," Mara says.

"The pick-up line that never fails."

"It came out completely wrong," Nils says. "I'm sorry. I never meant it like that. I take it back."

"Stop apologising, Nils," Perceval says. "We have more pressing matters."

The table is covered in paper, as if Perceval is totalling up the Dragon's Saturday night take.

"It's all right, Nils," Mara says. "But learn from it."

Perceval looks straight at Zina. "Who may I ask is this?"

Mara sits down and Nils follows. Zina remains standing, tablet in hand.

"This is Zina," Mara says. "Koranteng. From the Stuttgart Police. I know her and trust her."

"Our insider for next weekend?" Perceval asks.

"Yeah. Right."

"Mara told me everything," Zina says. "I'm here to help."

Perceval looks at Mara. "I specifically requested that you not talk to anyone about this highly classified operation."

"I had to improvise." Mara gestures for Zina to give her the tablet and sit down. Zina complies.

"Extrapolate," Perceval says.

"You mean, like, explain? When I was in Berlin, I got a lead on the Kollar family. Vilem Kollar was the key speaker at that protest group meeting. Yes, Nils, write that name down. And this one, Milan Kollar. I'm guessing they're father and son." Mara swipes at the tablet and shows them the sketch. "That's him. Milan. He has a big place somewhere between Linz and Wels. Keep writing, Nils. Modra. This is the organisation that's trying to bring the protest groups under one umbrella. Left and right. Hardcore and peace-loving. And anyone else with a passing interest in bringing down the government."

"Fascinating," Perceval says. "What is Modra? Some kind of militia?"

"It's a clean water foundation, doing good work, as far as I can see. You need to dig into it. I think it's Modra that's funding Circus. Somehow."

Nils stops writing. "Why would a water charity fund a protest group?"

"It's a front," Zina says. "People can donate money to Modra and all the foundation has to do is complete a few water-related projects. It could be a way to launder money or use charitable donations to fund protests."

Perceval nods. "Possible. You seem to know a lot about this."

"Modra may be a non-profit," Mara says, "but Milan is loaded. My father says he's seriously wealthy, from something with hydroponics."

"What's that?" Nils asks.

"Growing plants without soil," Zina says.

"You can't find anything about this guy online." Mara stares at the sketch. "It was my father who identified Milan, from this. I didn't know who he was when I met him. My father wouldn't say how he knows Milan, but he said it's most probably not his real name. He did tell me he believes Milan's a Bosnian Serb who was involved in the massacres of the Balkan Wars."

"Srebrenica?" Perceval asks.

"I don't know. My father has some pretty outlandish ideas sometimes, and I'm not sure I believe this one, as Milan didn't speak with an accent. He also thinks ..."

The bartender places a pot of coffee on the table, along with a small jug of milk, a sugar dispenser, four pink cups and four teaspoons. Nils starts pouring.

"Could you bring me some salt?" Zina asks.

"You take salt in your coffee? We're made for each other. Forget about the job offer. Marry me. Today."

Perceval gestures for him to leave them, then asks Mara, "Putting this Bosnian theory aside for the moment, what does your father think Milan Kollar is up to?"

"It's pretty wild."

"Elaborate, please."

Mara sips her black coffee. "Okay, but don't judge me on the craziness of my father. He's been researching Milan for a while and has this theory he's planning a big Europe-wide revolution. Starting in Germany and Austria, and then spreading across the continent. A kind of peaceful change, where the people take over. Vilem talked about this too, in Berlin, but I couldn't really believe it. They want to bring an end to oppression. To free the masses. Everyone's happiness becomes the priority, and it's achieved through fair distribution. That's their rhetoric. Wild, isn't it?"

"The country is bordering on a situation where huge change is possible," Perceval says. "Don't believe the media. The economic

241

situation is dire."

"So bad you think the people want to hang the Chancellor from a pole outside the Reichstag?"

"Why not? History shows people will go to any length to get what they want." Perceval waits for the bartender to deliver a saltshaker and a basket of croissants, then adds, "You should have said something sooner. You dallied too long with this important information."

"It's all just a crazy theory, from my crazy father. I wanted to meet you yesterday, but you said you had some ping pong thing."

"Regional league match, in which my team was victorious. I played sublimely, in singles and doubles."

"Congrats."

"You met this gentleman?" Perceval asks. "This Milan Kollar?"

"Yes."

"Detail your impressions. Shall he be Europe's next revolutionary?"

Mara shrugs. "I really don't know. It all sounds completely far-fetched to me. I had trouble keeping a straight face in Berlin. It was laughable. This guy Vilem was trying to get antifascists and right-wing extremists to work together. Can you imagine that? The idea is that once the government is overthrown, the country can be divided up, into left and right, with everyone living where they want to based on their politics."

"Left Germany and Right Germany?" Nils asks.

"See? It's just ludicrous."

"Is it?" Zina asks. "Germany sort of has that divide already."

Mara scoffs. "Why not just build another wall and be done with it?"

"One needs only to analyse how the citizenry votes in local and national elections," Perceval says.

"I spent much of my childhood in Chemnitz." Zina adds a little salt to her coffee and stirs it in. "There's no doubt in my mind what flag that city will fly if the country ever gets divided up like that. But even places in the west are cut along political lines. There are areas of Stuttgart that support the nationalist right. What happens to those people if this revolution comes? Will they be forced to move?"

"We're getting way ahead of ourselves," Mara says. "None of this is going to happen. A bunch of protesters can't overthrow the

242

government in a modern country like this."

"We are also drifting from the task at hand," Perceval says. "Our objective is to find a murderer. You were to position yourself in JJ's orbit, not go galivanting across Europe chasing leads on revolutionaries."

"I'd say you've got JJ covered. I saw you yesterday at the café at Fleethof. You two looked like you were hitting it off."

"I also observed you both, trying to sneak away like amateurs."

"Hey, careful," Zina says. "You're the one who pulled off that clumsy bump-and-meet."

"I executed that to perfection. You witnessed the result."

"What were you doing with JJ?" Mara asks. "Extrapolate."

"Making contact."

"What does that mean?"

"It means he's trying to turn her," Zina says. "Get her working for him."

"What? JJ would never work with the police."

"False," Perceval says. "She has been an informant before. The Stasi successfully recruited her when she lived in West Berlin."

"How do you know? Did she just tell you that over coffee at your first meeting?"

"I got access to the file. The Stasi had the modus operandi, and it was very successful at the time, of entrapping or bribing American students and workers in West Berlin. Particularly those who struggled for money. You can be sure that her becoming a nurse was the result of Stasi intervention. She moved to Hamburg, I assume, to put that troubled past behind her."

"A Stasi informer? That doesn't seem anything like her."

"Doubtless, she wouldn't have wanted it. The Stasi would have stooped very low to secure her services."

"Still, it was up to me to get close to JJ."

"It was taking too much time. Your efforts thus far have been helpful, especially with Lersner-Löwe, and now this Modra lead seems promising, but you have made zero progress in finding the suspect. This is why you are with us. The G8 meeting is less than a week away, and I can feel the guillotine waiting impatiently above my neck."

"I wouldn't worry too much," Zina says. "The high command's plan is to pre-empt anything from happening next weekend."

Perceval starts gathering up his papers. "I'm aware of that. The order passed my desk before it was circulated. Place any potential troublemakers in holding and prevent others from travelling into Stuttgart."

"A blockade?" Nils asks. "Is that possible? Isn't Stuttgart too big for that?"

"Protesters are going to descend on Stuttgart from all directions," Mara says. "That's what Vilem's called for."

"There has been almost no digital chatter regarding the G8 and attendance thereof," Perceval says.

"They're probably staying off their phones. We were specifically told on Wednesday not to take our phones to Berlin. At that meeting, Vilem also clearly stated that the G8 protest shall be the first day of the war against oppression. God, I can't believe I just said that."

Perceval is thoughtful as he watches Zina sip her coffee. "You know something, do you not? You're withholding."

"The blockade's a bad idea," Zina says. "We don't have the resources for it."

"That's not it. I am pleased to have you as part of the team, but I need proof of your commitment."

Zina finishes her coffee. She takes a croissant from the basket and bites into it.

"Look where you are," Perceval says. "I've spent much of my life watching people lie to me. Or withhold the truth. You, colleague, are sitting on vital information."

"Aren't you clever?" Zina sits back and folds her arms. "I bet that's not working out well for you, being clever. Those high up normally prefer people who do as they're told."

Perceval smiles. "What do you know?"

"It's not knowledge or information. It's just a rumour. I'm hoping that's all it is. I'm close with some people who are part of the riot police in Stuttgart. Apparently, there was a briefing with a select group, after what happened here last weekend, where they were told to ensure the police keep their distance from certain water cannons during the G8 demos."

"You're fucking kidding me, Zina," Mara says.

"What?" Nils asks. "What does that mean?"

"It means they're planning to add chemicals to the water," Mara says.

"Most probably a dye to mark the protesters or something that burns," Zina says.

"Turn the whole cannon into a giant can of pepper spray. How can they even think of doing something so inhumane as that?"

"Keep your voice down," Perceval says.

Zina leans forward. "Like I said, it's just a rumour. Probably just scare tactics, to keep protesters away."

"Because the police know the protesters are monitoring them, with informers of their own. Perhaps you are one. Tell this rumour to us, and Mara goes off and tells the rest of Circus."

"How dare you question my loyalty," Zina says. "You don't know the first thing about me."

"Not yet."

"Well, enjoy your Sunday reading my file. But let me tell you this. What's not a rumour is that the water cannons will be heavily guarded before they're called into action. There won't be a repeat of what happened here last Sunday. Reinforcements are being called in from across the region."

"Do you know the numbers?"

"I'm sure you can find that out. You seem to be an expert when it comes to paper and figures."

There's a moment of silence as they all look at each other. Despite Perceval's accusations, Zina smiles as she eats her croissant.

"I knew your mother," she says. "From when she came into the Davidwache station, to rescue any girl who'd been mistreated by a pimp and ended up in the holding pen. What I remember most about her is that she was funny. You don't seem to have inherited her sense of humour."

"This is neither the time nor the place for witticisms," Perceval says.

Zina glances around. "It used to be."

"Look," Mara says. "Why don't we just arrest Gomez in connection with the murder? You said yourself it's making the arrest that's important. That's what matters. A report in the media. A press conference. Even if it eventually turns out to be the wrong person, it'll take the heat off. You get Gomez, lock him up for a while and divert the pressure."

"Do you believe it was him?"

"He's always going on about taking action and giving protesters

245

weapons. Maybe with the right interrogation, he'll confess. Maybe he knows who it was and will offer that person up, as part of a deal."

Nils seems to like this idea. "How do we find him?"

"Don't let her tarnish your sense of justice, Nils," Perceval says. "What she's talking about is assuming guilt and having him prove his innocence. She has it the wrong way round."

Mara ignores Perceval and speaks to Nils: "There's a Circus meeting tomorrow night at the bunker on Otzenstraße. You can get him when he comes out of there. He'll have some people around him, so make sure you're prepared for that. Whatever you do, don't storm the bunker. Follow him and arrest him somewhere else."

"That's a brilliant plan. Christoph? Let's do it."

"We will consider this," Perceval says.

"Then we're done here." Mara slides out of the booth.

Nils tries to be a gentleman again, standing up with Mara and Zina, but gets ignored by both of them.

As they leave, the bartender says, "The door's always open and my offer still stands."

"In your dreams," Zina says, politely.

Outside, Mara points at the Mercedes that's parked half on the footpath. "That's our friend Perceval's car."

"Sweet," Zina says. "That was Penelope's."

"You need to tell me about her, and what you two did together."

They walk down Große Freiheit, which still has drunk people staggering out of bars and a few guys passed out against the walls of buildings.

"I'd rather you tell me about this bunker business," Zina says.

"There's not much to it. The protesters use old bunkers in the area, as meeting points and squats."

"That's new. I remember most of the bunkers were considered unsafe to be inside. Can you show me?"

***

She walks from the central station back to St Pauli, taking the scenic route through Planten un Blomen, the park straddling the edge of the city's business district, along where the old town walls used to stand.

As expected of a sunny Sunday afternoon, the park is crowded.

But this doesn't prevent Mara from getting some much-needed me-time. She steers clear of the groups and processes the last few days. They seem piled on top of each other, with barely enough time to make sense of things before new stuff happens. She had her first session as a boxing coach. She was arrested. She finally got the full story from Zina about leaving Hamburg, including Spitz, plus all the other times she was harassed.

Poor Zina, she thinks.

And tracking further back: Stuttgart, Jesper, Milan Kollar, Linz, Anthony, Lauter, Vilem Kollar, a revolution of the left and right. From a routine of police shifts and sleep deprivation to an improvised life where each day serves up unexpected challenges and ludicrous plans.

As she walks, she notices the park has plenty of police on patrol. They're selectively checking IDs, going on skin colour and clothing. She finds it strange to see police officers in this setting, among families and children enjoying their Sunday in the park. This calm, green space where any uniforms look out of place. The police presence is having an adverse effect. They should all feel safe, but it feels more like they're being watched, profiled and monitored.

She leaves the park and crosses Heiligengeistfeld. There's a football match in progress at Millerntor. The packed stadium heaves with cheers and refrains, the grandstands appearing almost to vibrate with noise. FC St Pauli, regardless of their success on the pitch, attracts a huge crowd at every home game, the club's predominantly middle-class fans donning hoodies for a day to show their lefty allegiance before returning to desk jobs tomorrow in freshly ironed shirts and slacks. The opposition fans can just be heard singing their chants from the north end. She wonders how far they've travelled to be here and whether the two clubs' hardcore fans have already clashed pre-match. Will they stand side-by-side next weekend in Stuttgart? Fight together in order to divide Germany into the physical embodiment of the political spectrum's widest extremes?

At Hamburger Berg, there are clusters of FC St Pauli fans standing outside the bars, half looking through windows and open doors at the game unfolding on screens. The match itself seems to be of secondary interest. More important is the social occasion, like it is in the stadium; a chance for people to meet, drink, talk and laugh. They

247

can let go of everyday life and responsibilities, for a couple of hours, be different versions of themselves, and be part of this tribe. And this moment of communal bliss is made all the more blissful if St Pauli scores goals and wins.

Nils's spindly frame is crowding the door to her building.

"You again," she says, worrying he's getting a bit too stalkerish.

"Hey."

"Are you here to apologise some more?"

"My mother says you can never say sorry enough. Or thank you."

"Smart woman. What do you want, Nils?"

"Christoph sent me," he says, keen to give his presence purpose.

"Can't get a moment alone, can I? Did he break-and-enter again upstairs?"

"He's at the office. He asked me to bring you there."

"It's Sunday."

"He said he messaged you about it."

Mara holds up her hands. "No phone. Been outside all day, walking around with Zina."

"Where is she?"

"On the way to Berlin. I just dropped her at the station."

"You were supposed to come to the office on Thursday," Nils says. "We waited all day for you."

"In that miserable basement? Must've been awful."

"Christoph was really worried. He thought something had happened to you."

"That level of care wasn't exactly on full display this morning."

"He's under a lot of pressure. You should cut him a break."

Key in hand, Mara pushes past Nils and opens the door. "Can't all this wait until tomorrow?"

"We've got important information on Milan Kollar."

"That was quick."

"Christoph wants your eyes on it. He wants your opinion. Today."

Mara sighs and pulls the door shut. "Fine. Let's go."

Nils leads the way to his car. He goes to the passenger side, to open the door for Mara, but she waves him off.

"That's not helping you, Nils. I can open my own door."

"Sorry."

He jogs around the car and gets in the driver's side.

"The city's pretty quiet today," he says, as they back onto the

248

street.

"Football. A lot of the people who would be protesting are drinking beer from plastic cups at Millerntor."

"I guess it means the game has caused a temporary ceasefire."

"Or it's the calm before the storm."

As Mara says this, they drive down Budapesterstraße, past a long line of riot police vans parked bumper to bumper near the stadium. A water cannon is stationed at the entry to the Rindermarkthalle shopping centre, a ring of police around the vehicle.

Nils looks at the cannon as they pass it. "Do you really think they'll put something in them, in Stuttgart?"

"Zina and I were arrested yesterday. At gunpoint. I think anything is possible with the police right now."

"What about ...?"

"Nils, do me a favour. Just shut up and drive."

He quietly seethes as he steers the car down Schanzenstraße and turns onto Max-Brauer-Allee. As they head northeast, they pass the Schanzenpark and the hotel in the water tower perched on the hill.

That protest was one week ago, she thinks, unable to quite believe it. Because it's two night trains, one evening train, a concussion, a kidnapping, an arrest, and an attempted rape ago. She vows to get Lauter once Russell is done with him. She wonders if, once the story is published, there will be a whole group of women lined up to get Lauter and others like him.

She knows she will have to confront that experience at some point: being powerless on the ground, naked, under Lauter's boot, cuffed and breathing dirt. A good start would be with a proper revenge. She was lucky Russell arrived when he did, but she refuses to concede this as being a good thing. No person should ever end up in such a position in the first place.

As they drive through Rothenbaum, she thinks there's something seriously wrong with men. Not all men, because Russell Wex is a pure diamond. But still, she can't help wondering just how many women throughout history have been raped. She imagines sitting down to talk with every one of them, getting each woman's story, working through it with them, and maybe getting clarity after all those discussions as to why a man would do such a thing. The Spitzes and Lauters, and all those monsters like them. The whole history of humanity littered with them. That's the revolution she wants. Get all

249

the sexist, chauvinistic, abusive pricks against the wall and fire. A culling of creeps. So women everywhere can go through the world without wondering who's following them, or which person they trust might try something nasty. So they can walk safely through parks alone and ride trains at night and learn to box and have a career and do everything on their own merits and no longer have to make horrid journeys from Afghanistan to Germany to live in comparative safety.

Sitting in this car with Nils behind the wheel, she fights the desire to kick him out of it. Nils taking her to the office in Alsterdorf isn't remotely like Lauter having his boot on her naked arse, but she still wants to be the one driving. She's sick of men, the influence they still wield and the power they abuse. "Oh, would you like to be promoted? Sure, just take your clothes off and suck this. Don't want to suck it? Then make me some coffee, or you're fired."

They pass through Hamburg's affluent north: Harvestehude, Eppendorf and Winterhude. Broad boulevards lined with Jugendstil buildings that survived all the bombings and fires and have been passed down from one man to the next.

While she thinks the world urgently needs to be cleansed of slime like Spitz and Lauter, she actually thinks it's those around them who need the most attention. The enablers. Like Callenberg, who just stood by while Gornau behaved like a racist arsehole, then even helped him. Looking the other way, doing nothing, saying nothing, just following orders. Those officers who Zina worked with at Davidwache, guys Zina considered family, they weren't brave enough to speak out against Spitz and stand at her side. In such situations, to ignore is to abet. That's what the protest movement should be really about: getting people to stand up and call out bad behaviour rather than look the other way. The police are watching. The government is lying. The economy is failing. Plenty of people don't have enough food and water. Rich people continue to get richer. And everyone just lets all this happen, and even enables it.

She thinks that's a call to action to embrace. Not the war on oppression. She wants to fight the war on enabling.

Because if everyone at Kollwitzkiez station protested against Spitz, he would have to be removed. Russell wouldn't need to write an exposé and hope *Der Spiegel* publishes it. The officers, men and women, could do the exposing themselves. If they wanted to. If they were braver. If they were willing to move from the audience to the stage.

Nils parks in front of the bland office building on Sydneystraße, next to Perceval's car, but with a wide enough berth so there's no chance either car will be scratched by the opening of doors.

"Here we are," Nils says.

"Thanks. For driving me and for the silence. I appreciate that you honoured that. I needed to get my thoughts in order before my brain gets bombarded with more information."

Nils smiles, and looks sweet when he does.

They get out. Mara is interested to see that Nils doesn't have a key to the building. He rings the bell, then pushes the door open when it buzzes. He goes to hold it open for Mara, then decides to walk through it first, dipping his head under the frame. They go down the stairs to the basement. It feels damper than before.

Inside the office, things have changed dramatically since Mara was first here. She's forced to enter along a side wall, as the floor is covered with papers, printouts, maps and photos. Perceval is in the middle of it, crouched down, blue plastic covers on his shoes, like he's investigating a crime scene.

Nils gently places a hand on Mara's shoulder, to stop her. He gives her covers for her shoes, then puts a pair over his own massive sneakers. Mara puts the covers on and carefully steps into the room.

"I thought detectives used walls for this kind of thing," she says.

"I find it easier to comprehend things and identify connections from this angle," Perceval says, head down.

"Like looking over a ping pong table?"

"Please stop saying that. Ping pong is for drinking games. Table tennis is one of the world's most challenging sports."

"Sorry."

"But, yes, there are analytical similarities."

Mara looks at the floor, unsure what to give her attention to. "So? What's new?"

"It's good that you're here, and also good you were absent last week. We weren't ready for you. After this morning's conversation, we've made significant steps."

"Milan Kollar?"

"He's essential, but one part of it." Perceval points at a white printout with MODRA on it in big letters. "This is the key to everything. The nucleus. The connector. Our investigation now

251

surmises that it all starts with Modra."

"Someone from Modra killed the cop?"

"Why do you say that?"

"Not me. You. If this is all about Modra, then isn't that as well?"

"We're thinking much bigger than that single crime."

"Interesting." Mara starts looking at the photos on the floor. "When just this morning I thought you might gear up to make an arrest."

"That is now planned. Tomorrow evening."

"How did you get these photos? They're from the protest last Sunday. Before things went ballistic."

"I put those together," Nils says. "From body-cam footage, drones and social media."

"My father would be so happy to hear that." Mara stands next to Perceval.

"Step carefully, please," he says.

"What do you know about Modra?"

"A water charity, as you explained. Listed in the Zurich registry, under the name Agnes Kollar. About her we can find nothing."

"Agnes?" The mention of her mother's first name has Mara listening closely, wondering if it's just a coincidence.

"We think she doesn't exist," Nils adds. "She's just a front."

"Why make up a fake person using the Kollar name?" she asks.

Perceval stands up. "Good question. I would say to both claim and deny, whenever required. What's interesting is Zurich."

"You already mentioned the Swiss link. Is this part of that? Don't lots of charities and foundations run through Switzerland? As a way for rich people to hide their money."

"Indeed. They want to avoid tax bills, while also taking advantage of the non-disclosure of banks. My assumption is the accounts for Modra are brimming with funds."

"Based on what?"

"Look at this." Perceval takes a few tip-toe steps to his left and points at documents on the floor. "All these companies are water suppliers. Bottled water. Across Europe. What they have in common is the mandate to donate a certain amount from each bottle purchased to a foundation providing clean water in third-world countries."

"Modra," Nils says.

"It's an integral selling point and important for the reputations of all these brands. A consumer can buy the bottled water and feel like they are doing something good."

"But?" Mara asks.

"The money goes to Modra, that we know. We've found numerous water projects, where some of that money is used. But what about the rest of it? If Modra is funding Circus and other protest groups, it could mean all the people buying bottled water are in fact funding an organisation that may have the intention to overthrow governments in Europe."

"People who don't like tap water are financing the revolution?"

Perceval smiles. "Wonderful irony, don't you think? Bottled water being one of the biggest scams in the history of capitalism."

"Modra's funding Circus, right? Those payments to Lersner-Löwe were from Switzerland."

"We are thinking along the same lines. But I can prove nothing. Oh, Switzerland, how do I hate thee. Always claiming neutrality while reaching your hands into the deepest pockets."

"Do you have any contacts? People you can lean on?"

"We would need someone in the bank," Perceval says. "An insider. It could take months to find someone we can trust. We simply don't have the luxury of time."

"We'd also need probable cause," Nils adds.

"Yes, we need actual proof a crime is being committed, linked directly to Modra. Or the intent to commit a crime. We have only conjecture, at this stage."

"I think Vilem Kollar has declared his intent," Mara says. "To do something big in Stuttgart. Isn't that enough?"

Perceval shakes his head. "Organising a protest isn't a crime. Neither is getting all the protest groups united under Modra. It looks to me, if anything, like it's branding. A corporate move. To raise Modra's profile."

"How does that help? For recruiting?"

"I don't know. I need to do more research."

"What about Milan Kollar? What do you know about him?"

"Very little. Just one thing. Nils, check the printer, please."

Nils steps carefully, on his toes, looking like an uncoordinated, giant ballerina, towards the desk. He takes the bundle of paper from the printer's tray and shuffles it neatly together. He tip-toes back and hands the bundle to Perceval.

"What's that?" Mara asks.

"A patent. Registered at the European Patent Office." Perceval checks the date on the front page. "Almost 15 years ago. For 'A Method to Grow Produce in Standard Homes and Apartments without the Need for Soil.' Milan Kollar is one of the names on this patent."

"Hydroponics. So my father was right about that."

"It appears so."

"Is this Kollar's company? Or is it another thing shrouded in Swiss mystery?"

"My assumption is he's a genericist."

"A what?"

"He doesn't make any products of his own," Perceval says. "Nothing consumer-facing. No public profile. No website. No presence. Perhaps not even an office. It may all happen at the Kollar estate near Linz. He creates innovations and sells them to large companies. It would be incredibly lucrative."

Mara reaches out for the printout and Perceval hands it to her.

"It all would have begun with this," Perceval continues. "A hydroponics patent. A company saw this, a behemoth, perhaps. Braun or Philips. They bought this from Kollar and made the product themselves."

"Why?"

"To save them spending millions on R&D. Companies do this all the time, to cut corners, expand their product portfolios and beat competitors to market. I believe Kollar has continued with this, without ever registering another patent. He sells the innovations directly to a company, which then registers the patent as their own."

"What about further back? The Balkan Wars? Is he a Bosnian Serb, like my father said?"

"We don't know. It's likely not his real name. Under another name, he could've been anyone who did anything."

"Modra is the Serbian word for blue," Nils says, sounding very proud of himself.

Mara shrugs. "So? Blue. Water."

"I thought the Serbian connection was important."

"Maybe Kollar just liked the name," Mara says.

The three of them look at each other, unsure what to do next.

"Is that it?" Mara asks. "You don't have more? All you have are assumptions and theories and fake names."

"And paper," Nils adds.

"We're trying to unravel a massive conspiracy here."

"Which this morning you didn't take seriously," Perceval says.

"Okay. Seeing all this here is making it more of a reality."

"We must ensure this all stays with us, for the moment. Until we can prove our assumptions are correct."

Mara holds up the printout. "Can I take this?"

"Certainly. Nils, please escort Mara home."

"No, thanks. I don't need an escort. I'll take the train. You guys need to prepare to arrest Gomez tomorrow. Focus on that."

Mara walks to the door, takes the blue covers off her shoes and heads up the stairs. Outside, the fresh air is good. She rolls the printout up and starts walking for the Alsterdorf station, the tube in her right hand like a baton.

She thinks about Agnes Kollar: not a common name, Agnes.

Afternoon has given way to evening. The streets are free of traffic and the platform at Alsterdorf is scarily empty. Across the tracks, there's a large billboard for the Hamburg Police, showing three officers who together tick every diversity box. They're smiling, proud, keeping the city safe. Why not become one of them?

The train bound for the city centre rolls in, a smattering of passengers on board, all of their heads bent over phone screens. She boards, finds a clean four-seater and sits, placing the tube of paper on the seat opposite, where it unfurls, enticing her to read it. But the info-screen has her immediate attention, as the news-ticker moves between the headlines of the day: FC St Pauli losing and fans fighting with police post-game; a massive demonstration in Paris in support of the right-wing National Rally political party; Stuttgart getting ready for G8, with images of barricades, water cannons and police patrolling the main station and centre in large numbers; a flash-mob party in Dortmund that turned into looting once police tried to disperse the revellers; and Thorsten Jawinski speaking at a special security conference in Amsterdam about modern justice. Then the ticker starts up again and runs through the same stories.

She thinks Jawinski has a particularly punchable face.

The stations come and go.

The train remains just about empty, and she keeps on alert. When she switches at Kellinghusenstraße, there are more people on the train and they bring with them a more raucous atmosphere, partygoers on their way to St Pauli, many of them already drunk. They are all dressed in going-out clothes, and their air of festivity doesn't quite fit this Sunday evening.

To turn her attention away from them, she picks up the printout and starts reading:

A Method to Grow Produce in Standard Homes and Apartments without the Need for Soil
Introduction:
Water is the planet's most precious resource. Huge amounts of water are wasted each day on high-intensive farming in developed countries. Like oil, water is a finite resource. The well will eventually run dry. When once wars were fought over gold, Gods or glory, they soon could be fought over water.

Introducing methods for the growing of produce using a vastly reduced quantity of water, or even no water at all, will have a significant impact on our water dependence and help create a more equal, peaceful and just world. It will also enable available water to be distributed more widely across the Earth, to ensure the health and prosperity of more people, especially in places where water is already scarce. Such methods will also enable people to easily grow their own produce, with minimal water, establishing a road map towards self-sufficiency and global water security.

Throughout the course of human evolution, water has defined us. Settlements have always been established at water sources, be they rivers, lakes, seas, oceans or springs, and some of our greatest innovations have been connected to water: Egyptian irrigation methods, Roman aqueducts and China's Grand Canal. The move from the waterwheel to the steam engine was the defining moment of the Industrial Revolution.

Human prosperity is inexplicably linked with water, as is human decline. Empires rose and fell based on water and its available supply. When the river runs dry, or it is poisoned by an enemy, human survival is greatly jeopardised. Without water, there simply is no future.

The patent here concerns a method to grow produce for human consumption without using soil, while also using far less water than traditional field crop production. Many methods for hydroponics

256

already exist. The innovation here concerns the nutrient-filled liquid used to support the growth of terrestrial and aquatic plants. The liquid is created by filtering the nutrients from the excrement of standard farm animals, including pigs, sheep and cows. Thus, this innovation enables a farm, large or small, to become a circular method for the production of vast amounts of food, greatly reducing the amount of water used and making intelligent use of animal waste. Even a household with one pig or goat, for example, could deploy this device to readily supply themselves with additional food.

Through further innovation, the device could be adapted to grow produce using no water at all. The excrement filtered into a nutrient-filled liquid could then be made into spray form to be atomised on plants grown using aeroponics technology.

Mara puts the printout in her lap.

Now that is seriously clever, she thinks. Who wouldn't want that?

The people boisterously moving around her and singing lines from trashy pop songs get her attention. They crowd around the doors as the train pulls into the brightly lit St Pauli station. She retubes the printout and follows everyone off the train. She weaves between the drunks on the stairs and ignores the guy who invites her back to his place to freebase with him. She walks to Hamburger Berg, wanting to be in the apartment and away from everything and everyone, but wondering all the way if that pig farm out in Moorfleet is actually a fancy new hydroponics farm. If not, it should be, and Susie and all her eco-warrior friends should be working there, not trying to shut it down.

Day 15

There's a meeting in progress when Mara enters the office of Elbe Help. People are gathered in a layered half-circle that fans out in front of JJ. Mara stands at the back, behind Tinaya, who is wearing a headscarf and squeezing the tennis ball Mara gave her.

"Okay," JJ says. "Get to it. Form some work groups and we'll review your designs at lunchtime. Remember, Vilem specifically gave this task to us and we need to come through for him. We have to make our submission by COB today. Nothing I saw on Friday was good enough, so let's get creative."

The groups head off to various corners. Tinaya turns and sees Mara.

"Hey, you got out. Are you all right?"

"Yeah, fine. No dramas. What about you? How's your head?"

"No stitches, but a big bump." Tinaya proudly points to where Gornau struck her. "Gus wanted to take me to the hospital, but I didn't want that."

"Another file, another system."

"Exactly. Gus bandaged me up and my friends helped me get home."

"I'm sorry for what happened. Don't judge every cop for the behaviour of those two. And don't judge every man based on the guys who were in the gym."

"That was the best day. Zina showed me what I can do. What I can be."

"She's good at doing that."

"I didn't run. I stepped forward to fight. The first time in my life."

"You did. Looks like we tapped into the warrior inside you. But you need to be careful when dealing with the police. You could get deported."

"I know. I will be."

Mara looks around. "What's going on? What did I miss?"

"The flag competition. It started on Friday. Do you want to join our group?"

"Sure. What's the flag for?"

"Modra. Vilem announced it at breakfast on Thursday, before everyone left. You missed that. Your family emergency."

"My father is being very demanding at the moment." Mara

258

watches JJ go into her office. "Listen, I'll catch up with you in a second. I just want to say hi to JJ."

"Okay. We'll be at the back."

Mara goes to the open office door and knocks on the frame.

"Hello, stranger," JJ says. "What happened to you?"

Mara wonders how much JJ knows. "Family stuff."

"You weren't the only one to sneak away on Wednesday night. Gomez and his crew skipped out as well."

"Really? I thought this was all exactly what Gomez wanted. Action."

"You'd think that. Where were you on Friday? Your family's in Hamburg, right?"

"I was in Stuttgart. A friend down there, she needed my help."

JJ nods, but doesn't smile. "So, not family after all."

"Zina's pretty much my surrogate mother. Or the big sister I never had. Accurate to say she probably fills both those roles. I definitely consider her family."

"How's the city looking ahead of the G8?"

"Battle ready," Mara says. "Lots of barricades, with a staggered setup, to separate protesters and isolate them."

"That old technique. You need to share this info at the meeting tonight."

"But that's if anyone actually gets into the city. There's a rumour the police could put a blockade in place. Create a ring around Stuttgart, to stop people getting in."

"Is that right? How do you know?"

"From Zina," Mara says, deciding it's best not to lie. "She's police."

"Good to know. You have a contact down there."

"Zina's my friend, not my … informer."

This word hangs in the air between them as they stare at each other. JJ blinks first, turning her attention to some papers on her desk.

"If there's a blockade, we could travel a day earlier, to beat it," JJ says.

"Or we don't go at all."

"I'm also uneasy about it. You should voice your reservations tonight, and we'll gauge the consensus."

"Okay. I'll do that, if anyone listens."

JJ smiles a little. Mara starts to leave.

"Your input is more valued than you think," JJ says. "Personally, I'm glad to have another voice of reason at the meetings."

"I hate that video, though. I don't want to be the poster girl for Vilem's war on oppression."

"Understandable, but you do have leadership qualities. You've started something with those boxing lessons. Some great feedback already. You could be inundated with girls soon."

"Thanks."

"Maybe you can teach me a few things."

"You better start squeezing a tennis ball."

"So that's why all those girls are doing that."

Mara holds up her fists. "You need strong hands and wrists for repetitive punching, to prevent injuries."

"Good to know."

Mara goes to the window and looks out over the harbour. "What's with this flag thing?"

"It's Vilem's attempt at unity, after things didn't go so well on Wednesday. I will say that things were far more productive on Thursday morning. Most of the hardcore people had left by then."

"Including Gomez."

JJ nods.

"I guess the thinking is that all these groups will feel closer together if they march under one flag," Mara says. "Right?"

"Yes."

"Well, better get to work."

"It's good to see you, Mara."

"Yeah, you too."

"You've been here barely a week and already you've had an impact. Keep going with that. Those girls really look up to you."

"I'll see if I can help them make the best flag."

Mara leaves JJ's office and walks over to where the sewing machines are. Susie is there with another group, their heads over some flag sketches, and the two of them exchange nods.

When she reaches Tinaya and the girls, it looks like they've been waiting for her.

Mara leans in close and whispers, "Guess what? Modra is the Serbian word for blue. That's a good base colour to start with. Don't you think?"

260

Mara walks with JJ from Elbe Help to the Otzenstraße bunker. On the way, she asks JJ about Berlin and her life as a student there. But JJ expertly dodges each question by steering the conversation back to Mara's experiences as a police officer. Their talk feels lively and intimate, but when they reach the bunker, Mara realises JJ has revealed very little about herself. She has the overwhelming impression JJ has much to hide.

As they head down the narrow alley to the bunker, Mara doesn't see any signs of police presence. But she's certain they are there, lurking in the shadows and sitting in unmarked vehicles parked not far away.

Inside, Mara sees tonight's meeting is being held in the main area. It's crowded and noisy. Tinaya and her friends got here early to hang their winning Modra flag on the wall and proudly stand on either side of it. While the flag will certainly look better when professionally produced, even this rough piece of sewing and patchwork looks good. It has four colours and a pall design: the horizontal Y-shape in the middle is blue, to represent water and unity; the triangle inside the Y is white, for health and peace; the top section is yellow, for hope and prosperity; and the bottom section is red, signifying earth and strength. The flag brightens up the concrete bunker and gives the meeting a stronger sense of purpose. They now have a definitive symbol to identify with, one which proves they are part of something bigger.

JJ goes to the front and stands on the small stage, where the bad punk band shouted at a teenage audience two weeks ago.

There are familiar faces present, plus plenty of new ones. As Mara moves through the crowd, people point at her and talk behind their hands. It's a predominantly young crowd, nervous, edgy and excited. Mara decides to stand next to Tinaya, whose headscarf is now bundled around her neck, with her loose hair tumbling over it.

Mara is fascinated again to see how much older Tinaya looks without the headscarf; that it's somehow like a child's bonnet, presenting the allusion to youth and innocence.

On the stage, JJ raises her hands and lowers them slowly, trying to get silence. It takes a while for this energetic group to quieten down. Once she has their attention, she starts talking about Modra,

261

the new flag and the plans for Stuttgart, including the option of not going.

Mara looks around, not really listening. Jesper is standing near the stage, with Gomez. An actor, she thinks, still not quite able to believe it. Is he still acting? Or was it all a lie, and claiming to be an actor was just a cover?

Gomez and JJ start arguing loudly about going to Stuttgart. Mara really hopes Perceval succeeds in arresting Gomez. He's no leader; just an attention-seeker. The kind of person who clears his throat before talking; whose first few words are always louder than the rest of the sentence. She also suspects he's only in this for himself.

"This discussion is over," he says, taking the stage, his voice projecting far better than JJ's had. "We're going. No question. Tell your friends. Show them our flag. This will be the biggest protest in Germany's history. No, the biggest protest in the history of Europe. We're going to take over the city."

Gomez mimes a mic drop and many people cheer him.

JJ gestures to Mara, to get her to come to the stage, but Mara holds up her hands, not wanting to get involved. There is no swinging this momentum. Nothing she can say will stop these kids from travelling to Stuttgart. They're not even listening to JJ anymore, as she tries to explain about the barricades and the high risk of being arrested. The rising crescendo of voices drowns her out and people turn away from the stage to organise their own plans for Stuttgart. They talk about G8 like it's a music festival: how to get there, where to meet, what to take, who else to invite and what to do afterwards. Mara hears a girl talk of driving on to France if her parents lend her their car.

The meeting ends abruptly. People have bags to pack, gear to sort, supplies to buy and cars to borrow. Gomez and his group are among the first to leave, pushing through the crowd like rock stars towards the bunker's one exit. On the way, Mara sees Gomez signal to Jesper and point in her direction. Jesper comes over to her and tilts his head towards the exit.

"Gomez wants to talk to you," he says.

"Good for him."

"Outside."

"No."

"It's not a choice," Jesper says, trying to sound tough.

262

"Ah, Johnny, I think it is."

He gets closer. "Don't say stuff like that. Not here."

Mara looks past Jesper, to where Gomez is waiting near the hallway. "Why can't he ask me himself? Who the fuck does he think he is?"

"Just come with me. Please."

"He's scared of me, right? Scared I'll deck him, in front of everyone again."

"Trust me, he's not scared of anyone tonight."

She looks at Gomez again, then at Jesper. "Are you telling me he's stupid enough to walk around St Pauli, dressed like that and behaving the way he does, with a weapon? Is he so dumb as to carry a gun?"

"Not so loud."

"He strikes me more as a knife guy. Just waiting for the moment to stick that knife in your back. You know the police are under orders to spot-check anyone they think is suspicious, don't you?"

"How do you know that?"

"I was arrested on Saturday. You didn't hear? Strange that, because in Circus everyone is talking about everyone else. Me and Zina spent Saturday in Davidwache."

"What for?"

"Zina for having the wrong skin colour and me for trying to defend someone with the wrong skin colour."

"But she's a cop. It's Zina that Gomez wants to talk about."

"So, you told him about her," Mara says.

"She can help us. In Stuttgart. She can give us all the plans."

Mara wants to punch him. "You don't know her at all. She's not yours to use."

"But she would help you. Just ask her. Look, Gomez won't leave you alone about this. He'll follow you home."

"He'd regret that, believe me."

"Just walk with us for a bit."

Mara starts helping Tinaya take down the flag, and realises Jesper's not going away.

"Hear him out," Jesper adds. "You might be surprised by what he has to say."

"Okay. Fine."

If Gomez does have a weapon, she thinks, that will give the police

263

further grounds to take him in for questioning.

She gives Tinaya a hug goodbye, then walks towards the exit, with Jesper behind her. Gomez and his group start moving as well. Outside, they all head down the hill in an organised formation: three guys walk in front, with another four at the back. Between these two lines, Mara walks with Gomez and Jesper on either side of her. She's at the centre of this moving circle, hemmed in, Gomez way too close for her liking.

"We need the plans," he says. "Contact your friend down there. Zelda, or whatever her name is."

"I'm not doing that for you. She won't help, even if I ask her."

"I'm giving you an order. Obey it."

"I don't take orders from you. Since when are you the leader of Circus?"

"She trusts you. I know how close you two are."

"Yeah, you know so much. You can't even get her name right."

"I know where she lives. Maybe I should talk to her myself."

"I dare you to. Did your little lackey tell you what happened to him down there? What the fuck was that about? Sending Jesper to follow me."

"He was there to protect you."

"You should've sent someone else to protect him. He woke up on the floor in a pile of his own filth."

"That's not what happened," Jesper says.

Between the guys in front, she can see vacant footpath. To her right, there's no sign of any movement from across the street. She really hopes Perceval is here, with reinforcements to arrest Gomez as was planned, but until they come out, she's enjoying riling him up. If the police are nearby, they're doing a brilliant job of staying concealed, perhaps waiting at the end of the street, down near Paulinenplatz.

"She's exaggerating," Jesper adds. "I was in control of the situation, G."

Mara laughs. "Yeah, taped to a chair, in full control."

"Shut up," Gomez says. "Left."

The group turns down Bleicherstraße, away from Paulinenplatz.

"You told JJ about the barricades," Gomez continues. "You know the plans already. Tell me everything and I'll let you go."

"Fuck you. I'm not your prisoner. Try to kidnap me and I'll shout as loud as I can."

"I've got one very good reason why you shouldn't do that."

This confirms for Mara that Gomez has a weapon of some kind.

"Look, the barricades are standard," she says, changing her tone and thinking it a good idea to de-escalate the situation by giving him something. "The police know the number of protesters will be huge. You heard Vilem on Wednesday. He wants people to come from all over Europe."

"He's all words. The countries just have to close their borders, then no one will get there."

"Seriously? They won't do that. This is a protest, not a pandemic."

"We want to get the water cannons again. We need the locations."

"The cannons will be massively guarded. They've learned from what happened here and are ready for it. You can be sure of that."

Bleicherstraße ends at Thadenstraße. Mara assumes the group is heading for the bunker behind Rote Flora. She hopes Perceval has this route covered.

"Wait," Gomez says, bringing them to a stop.

They are about 20 metres from the end of the street. Up ahead, Thadenstraße – a key access road between the Schanze and Altona that's usually busy with vehicles, cyclists and pedestrians throughout the evening – is bare. Gomez is suddenly wary. Mara is surprised by his level of awareness, and wonders if he may be smarter and more perceptive than she gave him credit for.

It happens quickly. The police appear from seemingly nowhere on Thadenstraße and jog towards them, guns drawn. Gomez turns around, and Mara does as well: another half dozen are coming up behind them, their guns also raised.

Perceval moves between the line that came up from Thadenstraße, gun in his left hand, at his side.

"David Wollenknecht," he shouts. "Stay where you are. The rest of you, please disperse. We just want Wollenknecht. Anyone who resists will be arrested."

"For what?" Gomez yells. "We're just walking around. We haven't done anything."

Perceval gets closer, flanked by two officers. Mara sees Gomez take a slight step behind her. The others in the group seem torn between protecting Gomez and saving themselves. They choose the latter, raising their hands halfway up and moving slowly away from

265

Gomez.

Perceval holsters his gun. "There's no need for a confrontation," he says calmly. "There are residents here. Children are sleeping in these apartments. The street is blocked, Wollenknecht. There's no escape."

Gomez's left arm wraps tightly around Mara's neck and she sees he has a knife at her throat.

"Nobody move," he shouts. "Guns down, all of you."

"G, what are you doing?" Jesper asks.

Mara stays still.

"You keep out of this."

"It's Mara. She's one of us. Put the knife down."

"Shut up, Jesper."

The adrenalin rises quickly. Mara knows she needs to act now.

The line of guys in front parts to let Perceval take a step closer.

Gomez points the knife at him. "Stay back!"

With the knife away from her throat, Mara butts her head backwards, into Gomez's chin and he staggers back. Then she spins to her left and uses this momentum to smash her right fist into his left eye. As he moves back with the punch, she kicks the knife from his hand and starts working his body, lefts and rights into his ribs and gut. When he slumps forward, she pushes her left hand into his right shoulder, to prop him up, and drives her right fist into his stomach, getting as many punches in as she can before she's dragged away by a couple of cops, lashing kicks out towards Gomez, who's on his knees. He coughs blood onto the footpath.

"Let me go," she shouts.

The police circle around Gomez. His hands get cuffed behind his back. The others in the group have scattered. Except Jesper, who doesn't appear able to move.

The cops continue to hold her.

Perceval picks up the knife. He inspects it, then hands it to another officer who bags it.

Gomez continues to cough and spit blood.

"You fucking arsehole," Mara says. "You pull a knife on me? Fuck you!"

Perceval holds up a hand towards her, but doesn't look at her. "Either contain yourself, young lady, or you will be further restrained."

Mara struggles against the officers holding her, full of rage.

"It's over," one of them says. "You did good."

This helps her calm down a little.

"David Wollenknecht," Perceval says, standing over Gomez, "please be informed you are under arrest for the murder of Peter Marten."

"Who the hell is that?"

"Officer Peter Marten, killed at the protest two weeks prior, a few hundred metres from here."

"What? That wasn't me. I swear. It wasn't me."

"Yes, carrying a dangerous weapon is a definite sign of innocence." Perceval signals to the officers. "Take him away."

"Wait. It wasn't … it was her brother. It was Anthony."

Two officers lift Gomez to his feet and walk him towards Thadenstraße. Most of the other officers follow.

"It was her brother," Gomez shouts again.

When prompted by Perceval, the cops let Mara go. She gives her right hand a shake, then inspects it. The skin has been scraped off the first knuckles, from making contact with Gomez's very bony eye socket. Blood weeps from the wound.

Perceval walks straight past her without making eye contact.

"Hey," Jesper calls out. "What about her?"

Perceval stops and turns. "She defended herself. What she tried was ridiculous, but I admire her for freeing herself so swiftly."

"She beat him up, and you just let her do it. You all just watched. Arrest her."

Perceval pivots and walks away.

Mara looks around and sees that there are heads in the windows of some of the apartments. One woman, her window open, gives Mara a round of applause. A few of her neighbours join in. Mara raises her bleeding right hand in appreciation. After giving her details to one of the cops, and answering some standard questions, she starts walking back to Otzenstraße.

Jesper, also done with answering questions, hustles to catch up with her.

"Get the fuck away from me," she says.

"Mara, wait."

"I'm warning you. Don't make me, Johnny. My hand's killing me."

At the end of the street, Jesper grabs Mara by the arm, to make her stop. When she does, he immediately lets go and steps back. He holds his hands up, palms towards her.

"Why didn't you say something to the cops?" he asks.

"What should I say?"

"The truth."

"The truth? You're a fucking actor."

"You know it wasn't Gomez. It was Anthony."

"It wasn't Anthony, believe me. And now, we both know that Gomez isn't Gomez. He's David Wollenknecht. Sounds like a typical son of privilege."

"They'll beat the crap out of him," Jesper says. "They're calling him a cop killer. They will go at him. You can prevent that. Do something."

"What can I do? I don't even know for sure it was Anthony, and I sure as hell don't know where he is. I just think I saw him in the footage. That's all I have. I could've gotten the truth from him in Linz, but your buddy knocked me out. Remember? So, if anything, Gomez getting arrested is your fault."

Mara walks off. Jesper follows her.

"Stay away from me," she says. "You're poison. So is Gomez, or David, or whoever the fuck he is."

"I'm sorry, Mara."

But she's not listening. She wants distance, some ice on her hand and something strong to drink. As she walks, quickly, almost running, she hopes the knuckles aren't broken. She'd bet a lot of money that Gomez's left eye will be swollen shut in an hour.

At Hamburger Berg, when she sees Nils standing by the doorway, she wants to turn around and run. It's been too many people and too many things in one day.

"Go away," she says, opening the door to her building.

"Perceval sent me to keep an eye on you."

"I don't need your protection."

"No, you definitely don't. I saw how you took down Wollenknecht."

"That was training. Go to the academy and you'll learn useful stuff like that too."

Mara enters her building, Nils behind her.

"Why didn't you say Anthony's the suspect? He's the one in the video."

"Maybe talk a little louder, Nils. Let the whole building hear you."

She goes up the stairs, her footfalls echoing. Nils takes the stairs three at a time.

"You recognised him straight away," he says. "That's how all this began."

"I thought it looked like him. I wasn't sure. That's why I needed to find him. To confirm it wasn't him. Anthony's no killer."

"He ran. It must be him. Was he in Stuttgart? Is that why you were there?"

Mara opens her apartment door. "I don't know where he is."

Inside, with the door closed, Nils paces around, annoyed. With his lanky frame and large feet, his presence seems to fill the apartment. Mara wants him gone.

"You should've told Christoph everything," he says. "From the start. You're compromised."

"Of course I'm fucking compromised!"

"You can't keep working the case."

"I have to. Surely you can see that. There's no walking away. Just this morning I helped design the flag everyone's going to be marching under this weekend."

"What flag?"

In the kitchen, Mara runs cold water over her right hand and winces as the water stings the wound. She sees red and shuts her eyes against it. Visualising Gomez's closed and puffed-up left eye makes her hand sting pleasurably and changes the pain's colour. Yellow, she thinks. Sunshine yellow.

"Mara, what flag?" Nils asks.

"The Modra flag," she says.

"You made it? That's a contribution, but it's not the same as having a personal stake as big as your brother being police enemy number one."

"So, that's it. You're not here to protect me. You're here to fire me. Can't Perceval do that himself?"

"It was fully incorrect to withhold that vital information."

"God, you're even starting to sound like him." She turns the water off and carefully dries her hand on a tea towel.

"No, I'm not. But I'm right about this being personal now. You can't continue."

"Nils, every police officer starts every shift with something personal at stake. If the motivations aren't personal, it becomes hard to even put the uniform on. You'll learn that, if you ever wear one. What you do has to matter to you personally. Otherwise, you're just a bully breaking heads for those in charge."

"I never thought about it like that."

"Any police officer who goes out there trying to save the world is really just trying to save themselves. They're trying to right their own wrongs by helping others."

In the living room, Mara finds Nils sitting on the edge of the chaise longue, his knees like twin mountain peaks.

"Make yourself comfortable," she says.

"Christoph is questioning Wollenknecht. He said it might take a while. You're next."

"Fantastic. A dawn interrogation at the Pink Dragon. I can't wait."

"He already thinks Wollenknecht will make a deal, because he shouted so quickly about Anthony. Be the witness, which means Anthony will be hunted down."

"That fucker would sell anyone up shit river to save himself."

"If we get to Anthony first, maybe we can make it easier on him," Nils says, with genuine concern.

"Am I right that you know him better than you've been letting on?"

"He's younger than me, but he often trained with the older age group. I've been playing with him for years. Such a talent. I kind of hate him that he's stopped playing. If I was that good, I'd focus on basketball and nothing else."

"I don't know where he is, Nils. I'm getting the feeling you think I do, but I don't. Honestly. He's gone."

"It's been two weeks already. They could be anywhere in Europe by now."

"What about Janica? What do you know about her? Does she have strong ties to Hamburg?"

Nils shrugs. "I don't know her that well."

"If you don't like girls," Mara says with a smile, "you can just say so."

Nils laughs a little. "I'm really sorry I questioned your sexuality."

"It's all right."

"I have to be honest and say I'm massively intimidated by you. You make me nervous. Things I don't want to say just slip out. I don't

270

normally make those kinds of mistakes."

Mara goes to the window. "On that, maybe arresting Gomez was a mistake."

"I don't think so. We should've done it sooner."

"In a way, it doesn't matter now. I think we've got bigger problems."

"Like what? The G8 demo?"

"I don't know. Maybe. There's something else. Something I'm missing."

"Modra?"

She opens the window and looks down on the street below. The bars are busy, predominantly with men, their voices carrying up to the top floor of this old brothel. She wonders how many women leaned out of this window and scoped the man-packed street below.

"Mara?"

She thinks about Zina and her simplified method for boxing success, which can be applied to just about anything: want it like you want nothing else in the world, and don't want it all.

"Just let it go," she says.

"Let what go?"

"Are you hungry, Nils?"

"Actually, yeah. All that excitement made me very hungry. We can order something."

"At the police's expense?"

"I think so, if we talk about the case."

"Deal. But we're going out. Let me have a shower and then we'll hit the streets."

The gurgling of a coffee machine wakes her.

Her head hurts. It takes a while to get her eyes fully open.

The hands of the alarm clock are at 0605.

The coffee machine continues to whirr and splosh in an enticing fashion. It draws her further out of sleep. She wonders how Nils procured the machine at such an early hour, finding it flattering that the kid never stops trying to impress her.

She rolls over and up, bare feet on the floor. The pillow comes with her, stuck to the back of her weeping right hand. Once separated, the white pillowcase has a yellowish mess of coin-sized circles dotted around it.

She's in underwear and a bra, but doesn't remember undressing. Her clothes are in a reassuring pile on the floor, typical of the way she leaves them. She remembers Sambuca, lots of it, and a really good seafood meal at some tiny place just off the Fischmarkt.

Her hangover is awful, but somehow pleasant; a reminder that it's sometimes good to let go, drink too much and just forget about everything for a few hours.

Standing, woozy, she lifts the blanket up and wraps it around her. A mobile cocoon.

A few careful steps. Things come more into focus.

The coffee machine splutters some more.

Nils helped her up the stairs. Or did she help him? They were both so drunk. Yet, he's already up and has coffee on the go.

In the living room, she's surprised to see Nils all over the chaise longue, lying on his stomach, limbs outstretched either side and his back at an awkward angle; like he fell asleep during missionary sex. Or he tried to hug the chaise longue, but gave up halfway. His long toes grip at the floor, flexed and ready to burst from the blocks when the starter's gun is fired. Just in underwear, his skin is pale to the point of translucence. Any slight movement ripples a muscle somewhere on his elongated frame. But he's not bulky. He's lithe and defined in the way tall, skinny athletes are; the muscles, tendons and sinews are stretched as far as they can go, the strands and fibres almost visible underneath the skin.

"Good morning."

She turns to see Perceval standing in the kitchen doorway,

sipping coffee with a slowness that suggests he spent a long night interviewing Gomez.

"Morning."

"Coffee?"

She nods. "You are a champion for bringing that machine and everything that goes with it."

"I didn't source it," Perceval says. "It was in the storeroom, across the landing, along with a couple of packs of coffee. I simply cleaned it up and got it running."

"It was there the whole time? I don't know how I missed it."

"Sometimes you need to know what you're looking for and have an inkling where it might be hidden."

Perceval pours Mara a cup and hands it to her.

"Some salt perhaps?" he asks.

"Hell no. Don't put anything in it."

"I'm just joking."

Mara sips the coffee, wondering how old the coffee might be. "Too early for humour."

"I do believe an explanation is in order."

"Did David Wollenknecht continue to point the finger at Anthony Steinbach?"

"Without any prompting. A deal has been requested, by your friend Nicola Lersner."

"Not my friend."

"She made quite the entrance, in full eveningwear, like she'd come straight from the opera. She sashayed down the hallway like it was a fashion show runway."

Mara smiles, envisioning that scene, knowing how much Nicola would have relished the attention. "What will it mean, Wollenknecht being a witness? No one in Circus likes a snitch."

"His assistance will go on the record as an anonymous tip. Lersner negotiated that. It will only become a problem for Wollenknecht if your brother turns out to be innocent."

"He is innocent. Anthony's no killer. Trust me on that."

"Still, he is your brother and you knew it was him all along."

"Oh, I'm sorry if I hurt your feelings or slowed down your precious investigation because I love my brother and want to protect him."

"Your assumptions are incorrect," Perceval says. "Additionally,

273

your sarcasm is unwarranted. It seems perfectly reasonable to me that you would have some kind of personal connection to all this. I thought maybe an old friend you wanted to assist. Or perhaps it was a clever way to switch sides?"

Mara takes another mouthful of coffee. It's helping with the hangover. The previous evening becomes clearer; mainly, that she enjoyed hanging out with Nils, once they put police matters aside and behaved like people.

"It's also perfectly reasonable to put family first," Perceval continues. The way he glances around the kitchen makes Mara think he made his own share of sacrifices and compromises for family.

"I had to do something."

"Nevertheless, you need to understand there will be a nationwide search for Anthony Steinbach. Have you seen him?"

Mara considers her options: lying now would come back to haunt her if they catch Anthony at some point, while telling Perceval the truth may help make up the ground she's lost to him by withholding the information in the first place.

"Yes," she says. "Last Thursday. In Linz."

"So that's what led you down there."

"He was on the run. He had help, some bodyguard who knocked me out. That was the last time I saw him. I have no idea where he is and no way to contact him. I'm sorry."

She finishes the coffee and puts the cup on the counter. In the living room, she drapes her blanket over Nils and heads for the bathroom. Perceval follows her.

"A little privacy, please," she says, trying to close the door on him.

"Can you imagine how much nakedness I saw in this house during my youth? You can trust me to avert my gaze. We need to keep talking."

She lets him in.

"How did that little brothel boy grow up to be a cop?"

"Like many things in life, I was inspired by love. However, if ever I write my autobiography, 'Little Brothel Boy' will be the title."

"I'd read it."

Mara gets in the shower and pulls the curtain closed. She removes her underwear and bra, and drapes them on the curtain rail. The water is hot and good and feels like velvet. She can see Perceval's outline behind the curtain, leaning against the wall near the sink, phone in his hand. The bathroom feels cramped with him in there, but strangely comforting.

"When you say love, you mean romantic love, right?" she asks. "You followed someone to the academy."

"Not that kind of love. More akin to what's driving you to protect Anthony."

"Ah, the infamous Penelope Perceval. You did it for her."

"I did indeed. All she ever wanted for me was an honest life. What could be more honest than law enforcement?"

"You might want to revisit that. You know, given the direction law enforcement is going in. Racial profiling and chemicals in water cannons are not what I signed up for."

"Not to mention this latest scandal."

Mara moves the curtain enough to poke her head out. "What scandal?"

"Your housemate in Berlin is keeping busy. A story he wrote is fully consuming the press today."

He shows her the screen of his phone. The headline reads: *Spitzkrieg – Harassed Officers Bravely Step Forward to Expose High-Ranking Sexual Predator in the Berlin Police.*

"Russell Wex," she says loudly, closing the curtain, "you goddamn motherfucking superhero!"

"Are you his source? The one quoted in the article? I know you lived together."

"I'm not. But I know who is, and he's next on my to-do list."

"He? That's interesting. The source is male. This story has already instigated a shitstorm of epic proportions."

"Colourful. I knew others would come forward once Spitz was exposed."

"Your friend Zina," Perceval says, "she worked with Spitz at Davidwache. I checked the files. They both were transferred at the same time. That's no coincidence."

"It was a punishment. For Zina." She turns off the water. "Towel, please."

She sees Perceval's outline take a towel from the rack and reaches through the curtain gap to take it.

"Thanks. I want to read this story. I hope they lock that creep away for a very long time, and that everyone in prison knows he's a cop and a predator."

"He wouldn't last a week."

Mara wraps the towel around herself and gets out of the shower. "Good."

"Ah, you're looking much fresher now," Perceval says.

"Careful. That kind of talk will have you lined up to be next."

The way Perceval grimaces makes Mara wonder if he's been more on the receiving end of harassment and taunts himself in the police.

Nils stands in the bathroom doorway, his clothes clutched to his bare chest.

"This is turning into a family meeting in the bathroom," Mara says. "You want to have a shower too?"

Nils nods. "If possible."

"Don't worry if the boss watches," she adds. "He's an utter professional. Think of him like a doctor."

Perceval smiles and shakes his head a little as he leaves the bathroom.

"Do you have a towel?" Nils asks.

"Under the sink." Mara reaches up and takes her underwear and bra from the curtain rail. "Best not to think about what the towel's experienced in its extended lifetime here."

Mara goes into the bedroom and gets dressed quickly, in the hoodie-jeans combo that's become her St Pauli dress code. She finds Perceval in the living room, sitting at the desk, eyes closed. She takes his phone and starts reading Russell's story. The first paragraph has a level of detail about the Kollwitzkiez station and how Spitz manipulated female officers that only could have come from Lauter. She worries Spitz might try to get revenge on Lauter if he's revealed as the source, which would prevent her from getting revenge first. Or will Spitz go after Russell?

"Did he ever try to get close to you?" Perceval asks, his eyes still closed.

"Nothing concrete that would hold up in court. Just seriously sleazy."

"Yet another middle-aged white male using his position and authority for his own sexual means. Why do men continue to think they can behave like this? It's the benchmark of awfulness."

Mara continues reading. "Amen."

"Give me an insider's example of his particular brand of sleaze."

"The typical I'll-take-care-of-you-if-you-take-care-of-me."

276

"Shameful. What year is it? Let people achieve things on merit, not on sexual favours."

"Get this. He runs a paper-free station. He's very proud of that, is Captain Spitz. The only paper in his office is a box of tissues, placed on the corner of his desk, next to an old armchair."

"Disgusting."

"When he's looking to make … an exchange with you, he'll glance at it. Russell could write a whole series of articles just about that box of tissues."

Perceval opens his eyes. "Wet-wipes are better suited to such usages, with no bathroom nearby. Tissues stick and are messy."

"Now that's the voice of experience." Mara hands Perceval his phone. "Have they already arrested Spitz?"

"Not that I'm aware of. There will certainly be an internal investigation. He will likely quit. Or be forced out."

"Heaven forbid he should actually pay for these crimes."

"Am I hearing worry? For your Russell, perhaps?"

"Sure. His name's all over this."

"Spitz will go after the source, not the messenger. This was clearly an inside job."

"That's why you asked if it was me."

"Yes. Now, about Linz. I gather you didn't go there to find Milan Kollar. You went there to find Anthony."

"Correct. Milan was an unexpected bonus."

Mara explains everything that happened in Linz, including that Jesper was there.

"Gomez must know how to get in contact with Milan," she says. "Jesper had a number."

"It will most likely be invalid now. A burner. It matters not. We know where Milan is. This estate you described. We obtained a satellite image online."

"You located him? Why aren't you down there arresting him?"

"For what exactly?" Perceval asks. "He is a person of interest, but he has committed no crime. On the contrary, he is clearly doing good things for the world."

"Yeah, using pig shit to grow plants. Really clever, I have to give him that."

"You read the patent."

"If I show that to Susie, she'll want to have all of Milan's babies."

277

Perceval smiles thinly. "Where do you get his humour? Your father, he is smart, but he's not funny."

"Crazy is sometimes funny. Some of his theories are hilarious." She sighs. "Look, I'm really sorry I didn't tell you about Anthony."

"No need to apologise. I would've done the same in your position. It's family."

"What now?"

"Are you travelling to Stuttgart?"

Mara nods. "Thursday. Early."

"Good. Business as usual. This is far from over for you. We need you to keep doing what you're doing."

"What about Anthony? You have to believe me when I say it wasn't him."

"The innocent shout their innocence, as Wollenknecht did. The guilty run. They always run."

Mara wonders if it's Janica who the police should want. There was more than a touch of spite in the way she bullied those guys on the basketball court in Linz. Is she more prone to excessive violence than Ant?

Perceval stands up. "I apologise for my outburst at the Pink Dragon on Sunday morning. I was feeling a certain amount of pressure, from above. This has been relieved with the arrest of Wollenknecht. In hindsight, we should have done this sooner."

"Which would've exposed Anthony."

"Indeed."

Nils enters the living room, dressed, rubbing at his hair with a towel. He smiles at Mara.

"Keep going," Perceval says to Mara, and he walks out.

Nils carefully hangs the towel on the door handle, smiles once more at Mara, then follows Perceval. The door closes and it feels like some special gift to be alone. But she's due at Elbe Help in an hour.

***

They stop at the bridge to say goodbye.

"It's a shame you can't travel to Stuttgart," Mara says.

Tinaya shrugs. "Maybe it's for the best."

"You don't want to get arrested."

"What I think is the worst of all is that you won't be here on Saturday morning."

278

"Go to the gym anyway. I'll tell Gus you're coming. He can run the session. Teach you some old-school stuff."

"I can call him. I have his number."

"Okay. Do that. He's a good one, old Gus. You can trust him."

"I've heard that before."

"Gus is different. Don't let any negative experiences lead you to misjudge good people. Gus is gold."

"You're right. I need to look forward, not back." Tinaya starts to pedal away. "See you tomorrow."

"Hey, wait."

Tinaya wheels around and comes back.

"What are you doing now?" Mara asks.

"Watching the paint peel from the walls in the refugee container, like most evenings."

"I need to teach you how to shadow box. Then, you can turn every wall into an opponent."

"Box my shadow?"

"Are you free right now? For an hour or two?"

Tinaya checks her watch. "I just need to be back by curfew."

"They have a curfew? Like you're kids and you've got to be home before the streetlights come on?"

"We're lucky we get to go out during the day. I stayed in some places where we couldn't leave the building. They locked our room doors at night. Like in a prison."

"You deserve so much more than this, Tinaya." Mara turns her bike towards the bridge. "Follow me. There's someone I'd like you to meet."

They ride onto Elbinsel and take the back road to Moorfleet, getting passed by people on bikes that cost more than a year's worth of Tinaya's benefits money.

At the entry road to her father's house, Mara stops.

"Where are we?" Tinaya asks. "It's so nice out here. So peaceful."

"I used to live here."

"Lucky you."

"Yes and no. I'd like you to meet my father. He's very worldly and open. You don't need to wear your headscarf."

"Uh, okay."

Tinaya removes it, furling it into a scarf around her neck. She shakes her hair loose. Again, Mara is amazed by the transformation.

279

"You have such beautiful hair," Mara says.

"That I shouldn't hide it under my headscarf?"

"That's not what I mean."

"I don't want to wear it. My friends also don't want to wear theirs."

"Then why do it? You don't seem overly religious, if I may say so."

"I'm not. With the headscarf, it's a problem either way."

They start walking their bikes down the narrow entry road.

"Because of religion or prejudice?" Mara asks.

"Both. If I wear it, people judge me and look at me negatively, like there's something wrong with me. They question why I would allow myself to be covered up like this. Or worse, am I hiding a bomb under my clothes?"

"That's ridiculous."

They reach the house and kick the stands down quietly on their bikes as Felix is asleep in the basket near the door.

"If I don't wear it," Tinaya continues, "I get subjected to horrible abuse, mostly from young Muslim men, but also from old Muslim women. They demand I cover myself up, as if I've broken a sacred rule."

"You want to avoid that more, I bet. Their doctrine-driven hate rather than a white person's prejudice."

"Wouldn't you? Who do you think is more dangerous and harmful?"

"Hard to compare, but I'd say they both are."

The door opens. Richard stands in the doorway.

"Mara? Quick, inside. Who's this?"

"My friend, Tinaya. We volunteer together at Elbe Help."

"That's very good of you. An excellent organisation, that one."

"We're also the heads of the flag design department," Mara says.

"No idea what you're talking about, but get inside. Both of you. Shoes off."

They enter and comply. Richard closes the door. Tinaya watches with trepidation as the three locks click into place.

"Don't worry," Richard says. "That's to keep the enemy out, not to keep you in."

He moves past them.

"Flags, flags, flags," he continues. "Symbols and structures and banners. Brands, all of them. Tea?"

"Yes, please," Mara says. She tries to smile at Tinaya, to show everything is okay and it's safe to be here.

In the kitchen, Tinaya sits at the table and Mara leans against the counter.

"Excuse the mess," Richard says, as he gets busy making the tea.

Tinaya looks around the spotless kitchen. "Mess?"

"This is my father, Richard," Mara says.

"Pleased to meet you. You have a lovely home."

Richard, holding the kettle, looks at Tinaya suspiciously. "I think you are telling the truth. So, thank you."

"You're welcome?"

The kettle filled, via the bulky filter on the tap, Richard places it on the stove.

"Thanks for helping out on Saturday," Mara says. "With me and Zina, and those two young guys."

"Police state, Mara. I told you this. Last time you were here, I told you. This is our future. I've been saying this for years, but nobody listens."

"I'm starting to listen."

"We're all being watched. We have to do something about it, or it's just going to get worse. I take it you're going to Stuttgart."

"A lot of people from Elbe Help are going. But I think the focus will be on wealth distribution and monopolies rather than the police state."

"That's the wrong focus. Surveillance is what you should be protesting against. I told this to my students today. But Stuttgart was all they could talk about. G8 this and G8 that. They couldn't even name the eight countries in it. They just want to be part of the protest. Post everything online and brag they were there."

"He lectures at the university," Mara says to Tinaya.

"Part-time. Pretty soon no time."

"What happened?" Mara asks. "Did they cancel your contract?"

"I quit. Oh, it was brilliant. One of those great moments when you take total control of your own life. It gets me out of that … institution. This will be my last semester. And thanks to all the gods."

"What will you do instead? You're too young to retire."

The kettle boils. Richard pours the tea and says, "I was so angry with you on Saturday, Mara. That you were arrested and that you called me. Why call me?"

281

"Because you're my father."

"That policeman. Gornak."

"Gornau."

"Yes, him. What a horrid piece of work he is. How did they make him a cop? He should be in jail."

"I'd say his type is at the top of the police's recruiting list right now."

Her father nods. "No doubt. The police state needs men exactly like him."

"There are worse people in the force."

"Plenty of them can't keep their dicks in their pants. What is going on?" Richard hands a cup to Tinaya. "Use a coaster, please."

Mara steps forward to take a cup. "You saw that story?"

"I can't decide who's more evil. The right-wing policemen locking up black people for no reason or senior officers systematically raping policewomen."

"I'd say you can draw a very short line from guys like Gornau to guys like Spitz," Mara says. "They're shit that all belongs in the same bag."

"It's dangerous to generalise like that, but may they all be first against the wall when the revolution comes."

As they sip their tea, Mara glances at Tinaya, who appears more amused than shocked.

"I quit the university specifically because of my encounter with Kamran and Adu," Richard says. "Nice boys, those two. I know. Don't start with me. The last time you were here, maybe I said some things you didn't like, about refugees fixing their own countries. I made some good points, I know I did. But both of those boys were born here. Like Zina. They hold German passports. They are German, like us. I don't buy into this whole legacy thing, that some people consider themselves more German than others simply because they've been here longer. Kamran and Adu are my countrymen. But it's amazing how so many people don't think like that. When they look at Kamran and Adu and Zina, they don't see a comrade or a nationality. All they see is a skin colour. That's wrong. I was wrong."

Mara smiles and squints up at the ceiling.

"What?"

"I'm trying to remember," she says, "trying really hard to remember the last time I heard you say that."

282

"Always with the jokes. But this is serious. We're losing our country. It's in the hands of the wrong people and we have to change that. Germany is ceasing to be a country. It's becoming a system, one that's focused on oppression."

"Are you coming to Stuttgart too?"

"I'm thinking about it. Give me an appropriate flag and I'll carry it."

"It just so happens we have one." Mara turns to Tinaya. "Why don't you show him what we made yesterday?"

Tinaya puts her cup on the table and reaches for her bag. Richard moves to the table and puts Tinaya's cup onto a coaster, perfectly in the middle of it.

Once the flag is unfurled, Richard claps a little.

"It's beautiful. What's it for?"

"This is the new flag of Modra," Mara says. "We'll be marching under it this weekend."

"Modra? The water charity?"

Mara is about to tell him about the Kollar connection, but a noise comes from the back of the house.

"What was that?" she asks.

"Just Felix," her father says. "He sometimes wanders around the house like he's lost."

Mara thumbs towards the front door. "He's asleep outside."

"Probably just the wind then. Or an animal." Richard looks at Tinaya and adds, "Deer come up to the windows out here and tap on the glass with their noses."

Mara looks at her father, but he can't meet her eyes. He positions himself in the kitchen doorway.

"Is ... is Anthony here?"

"Of course not. I haven't ..."

Mara pushes past her father and goes down the hallway towards Anthony's room. The door is locked. She bangs on it.

"Ant? Open the door."

Sounds come from inside the room. She pounds on the door again. When it's not opened, she leans back for leverage and kicks at the door, close to the lock.

In the room, Anthony is struggling to shift his big desk, to move it enough to fully open the window behind it. As Mara steps into the room, he starts throwing things at her: a couple of schoolbooks, then a stapler. She fends it all off. He charges at her. She makes a small sidestep and uses his momentum to trip him over and get him prone face-down on the floor, hands behind his back and her right knee on his neck.

"Get off me," he shouts, squirming on the floor.

She puts her whole weight on him. "What are you doing here? The whole country's about to start looking for you."

"I didn't do anything. It's a fucking conspiracy."

"Let him go, Mara," Richard says, standing in the doorway and looking more concerned with the state of the broken door than with his fighting children.

Anthony is starting to wheeze. "I can't ..."

Mara releases some of the pressure on his neck. "You will stand up and tell me what's going on. All right?"

He nods. "Yes. Fuck, yes."

"The police state has come to my home," Richard says.

"I'm not in the police anymore."

"It doesn't look like that from here. Can the police buy me a new door?"

"Ant, are you ready?"

Mara lets go of his hands and stands up. Anthony moves onto all fours, then sits on the floor, his back against a bookshelf that has far more trophies than books.

"Explain yourself," Mara says.

"He's your brother, Mara. You should trust him. Support him."

"Not when he just lies to me and runs away." She looks at Anthony. "You can't stay here. A witness has named you as the suspect in the protest murder. They're going to scour the country looking for you, and you can be sure they'll start right here."

"What witness? We were in balaclavas."

"Gomez ratted you out. He was arrested last night. He named you to save his own skin."

Anthony shakes his head. "No way. G would never give anyone up."

"He was shouting your name before they even had cuffs on him. And this was right after he held a knife to my throat."

"G's my friend. He wouldn't do any of that. You're lying."

"You choose your friends so badly, Ant."

"Fuck you, Mara."

"Where's Janica?" She looks around the room. "You're not sleeping here, so where are you staying? Somewhere nearby?"

"With Bernd," Richard says.

"Bernd? Pig farmer Bernd? Bernd who cracked my forehead open with his rifle Bernd?"

"They're safe over there. No one knows, and I trust you to keep it a secret as well. Protect your brother, Mara."

"Don't you get it? They're not safe anywhere. Someone has to fall on this sword, and it's going to be Ant unless we do something."

"The cop just collapsed," Anthony says, almost in tears. "I didn't touch him."

"Then why did you run? I've been trying to find you everywhere. Why did you go to Travemünde to steal that candlestick?"

"How do you know about that?"

Richard laughs very loudly at this.

"Why go to Linz?" Mara paces over Anthony. "Why set me up to be knocked out by some thug who works for Milan Kollar?"

"Who's he?" Anthony asks. "What happened in Linz, I had nothing to do with that."

"You didn't try to help me either."

Anthony looks at the floor.

"Jesper told you to run for it. Am I right? Did he also tell you to do that after the protest?"

"The police claiming it was murder is a fucking lie. He fell, all on his own."

Mara tries to remember the footage she saw in the Kollwitzkiez station: the bodycam angle, Anthony and Janica in front, the angle changing as the officer falls, Anthony leaning down to see if the officer is all right, then Janica pulling him back and them both running.

"Did you have a weapon?" she asks.

"No weapons. Those are the rules."

"The Circus rules, which Gomez never follows."

"He fell, I swear it. Like a soft centre taking a charge in the lane. We weren't even close. He must've had a heart attack or something."

"It's a cover-up," Richard says. "The police state protecting their own."

Mara holds up a hand. "Slow down. It takes a lot to cover something like this up."

285

"While providing exactly the reasons to clamp down on protesters and citizens and give police greater power."

"You can't keep something like this secret," Mara says. "There are too many people involved. Too many levels. Someone would talk."

"Or all those involved want the same thing, to use this to their advantage. Meaning, it's no longer a conspiracy. It's a mandate. A strategy. I bet Jawinksi has been waiting for precisely this opportunity, and now he's grabbed it with both of his power-hungry hands."

"You think he wants a country controlled by the police? By guys like Gornau?"

Richard smiles. "He would never frame it like that. You have so much to learn, Mara."

Anthony moves to stand up, but Mara points at him to stay on the floor.

"Educate me, if you're so smart," she says to her father.

"He'll talk about keeping people safe. That's what the narrative will be. Providing security, especially for the middle class. The precious German baby-making middle class. Enabling children to walk safely to school and all that."

"You have to help me, Maz," Anthony says, sounding like he's finally understood the gravity of the situation. "You got to get me out of this. And Janica. We just want to go back to how things were. We want to play basketball again. I want that scholarship. I don't want to be on the run."

"Hard to go to the States when you're in jail here."

Anthony cries properly now, like an overgrown child. "It's all lies. I don't want to go to jail."

"You need to act on this, Mara," Richard says. "Talk to someone. They're just trying to manipulate everyone, and it doesn't matter whose lives get destroyed. You have to expose this."

"You want me to go to the police and tell them they've covered up a murder of one of their own just so they can extend their policing powers? I just march into police HQ and shout that they're all liars."

"What about Zina? Ask her to help."

"I can't do that. Not right now. She ... she's got her own stuff to deal with."

Anthony hugs his knees, looking suddenly very small. "Please, Maz. Help me."

286

"Okay. I know someone in the Hamburg Police, and I think we can trust him. But we need to get you out of sight. Preferably out of the country. Does anyone know you're here? Did you talk with anyone from Circus?"

Anthony shakes his head. "No one."

"Phones? Computers? Anything trackable?"

"We're off the grid. Have been for the last two weeks."

Mara turns to her father. "What about the cameras, at Bernd's gate?"

"They've been using the back way. The same route we took."

"Good. Best not to leave the farm at all. For now."

"We're working on the new greenhouses," Anthony says.

"What greenhouses?"

"Bernd's expanding into hydroponics," Richard says.

Mara smiles. "No shit."

"Plenty of shit. That's the problem. Bernd's got the solution."

Anthony stands up. "They're going to filter it and use it to grow plants. Without needing any water."

"Milan Kollar is the guy who invented that," Mara says.

"They should give him the Nobel Prize." Anthony starts stuffing clothes into a sports bag. "It's world changing."

Mara thinks her brother has found a new favourite person to follow. "More than protesting?"

"Absolutely. We joined Circus to try to change things. They talk and they walk and go to football games and fight with the police. But they don't change anything. This guy's going to revolutionise food production."

"There's a lot more to it than that." She watches her brother pack. "Who told you to run, Ant? Was it Gomez?"

He doesn't reply.

"Hey. This is important. Whoever said this might be in with the police and know about the cover-up. They could be playing for both sides."

Anthony zips the bag shut. "It was JJ. She told us to get out of Hamburg. But we needed money to do that."

"Goering's candlestick," Richard says. "I wish I could see their faces when they know it's gone."

"Sorry," Anthony says.

"Don't be. I love you, my son. I fully support that. Feel free to go

287

back to Travemünde and steal other heirlooms. Saves me dealing with all that when they're gone."

"They're good people. You're way too hard on them."

"I'm not nearly hard enough. But I'll take your support of them as a way of volunteering to take care of all that crap once they're dead and buried. You can have their bunker in Travemünde."

Tinaya appears next to Richard. "I'm sorry to interrupt, but it's getting dark outside and I need to go home."

"Why?" Richard asks.

"She has no lights on her bike," Mara says.

"What about me?" Anthony asks. "What do I do?"

"Go back to the farm. I'll come out there tomorrow, and I'll have a plan. I promise."

She stands outside Elbe Help, back against the wall, hands in pockets, face turned to the morning sun. As others arrive, greet her and ask what she's doing, she gives them all the same honest reply: waiting for JJ. Many of them will be up for an early start tomorrow, for the long haul to Stuttgart, and they trudge up the stairs with limited enthusiasm. Understandable, she thinks. Why waste time sorting musty clothes and sweating over sewing machines today when they could potentially change the world in a few days' time?

It's annoying that JJ is late, as it's making Mara late for her meeting with Perceval. But it gives her time to consider how to convince JJ to come with her. Of all the alternatives, she thinks the truth is the best.

A bus stops further down the street. JJ gets off with a few other Elbe Help volunteers. They walk together, chatting.

"Mara?" JJ asks at the entrance. "Is something wrong?"

"Can I have a word with you? Alone."

JJ nods to the others, who form a single file to go up the narrow stairs.

"What's happened?" JJ asks.

"Can we walk a bit?"

"Not until you tell me what this is all about. I feel like you're cornering me."

Mara wonders if JJ holds her responsible for Gomez's arrest. "It's about everything. Modra. Jesper. Gomez. My brother. The Kollars. A cast of millions."

"That's a lot."

"But we can't talk about any of it here. It's not secure."

"Let's go upstairs."

"That's really not secure. You don't know that? The police are watching this place, very closely."

JJ seems unsurprised by this. "How do you know that?"

"I just know. It's not exactly a secret. We watched places like this in Berlin too."

"Then let's go to one of the bunkers."

"Also not secure. The police are onto them after they got Gomez near Otzenstraße. He's probably blabbed about all the bunkers you use."

"He must've told them something. He'll be released today, so I heard."

"You have good lawyers."

JJ folds her arms. "I'm getting very hostile vibes from you, Mara. Gomez was absolutely out of line to pull a knife on you."

"You know about that?"

"He was wrong to have a knife at all. But you seem very edgy this morning."

"Come with me and I'll explain."

"Where?"

"St Pauli," Mara says. "A place called the Pink Dragon. We can be off the grid there."

"You're sure of that?"

"If you want the answer and to hear everything else I have to say, you need to go there with me."

"I don't like this cryptic kind of talk."

"You think I do?" Mara steps closer to JJ, then starts pointing around them. "There are cameras at the bus stop. A few more on the streetlights. We can't talk about anything out here."

"Fine. I'll give you half an hour."

JJ starts walking and Mara hustles to catch up. They go down Große Elbstraße, side by side, in silence. Neither says a word on the 20-minute walk to the Pink Dragon. When they're outside, Mara tells JJ to turn off her phone.

"You must have a good reason for choosing this place," JJ says.

Inside, the club is empty, except for the bartender.

"Hello, Mara," he says. "Where's your gorgeous friend?"

"Back in her secret tower."

Then he sees JJ. "Ah, you brought another stunner. Hello there."

"Save the charm," Mara says. "Where is he?"

"Christoph? Not here."

"What? We have a meeting."

"No one's been in here for hours. Very quiet last night. The police were up and down Große Freiheit all evening, checking IDs and arresting people and telling suspicious people to go home. Let's face it, everyone looks suspicious in this area. By midnight, the Reeperbahn was just about deserted."

"But the Dragon kicks on. You're still open."

"My dear, I don't know how to do anything else. Christoph pays us exceedingly well, even when we're not doing anything."

Perceval and Nils enter.

"Speak of the dragon master," Mara says. "Unusually late."

"Sorry," Perceval says to Mara, ignoring JJ. "We were delayed. Meetings, briefings and paperwork."

"Wollenknecht has blown this investigation wide open," Nils adds, giving Mara a smile.

Perceval signals to the bartender. "Maurice, be a good man and escort this lady out. This is a private meeting."

"She's with me." Mara moves towards the nearest booth and slides in. "You can both drop the act that you don't know each other."

"It's clear that you all know each other," JJ says.

"If you didn't know that already, JJ, now you do. Yeah, we're Team Dragon."

Perceval and JJ glance at each other.

"Maurice," Mara says, glad to have finally learned his name without having to ask for it, "coffee times four, please." Then, to Perceval and JJ, "Sit down. Here's the deal. I'm going to talk and you're both going to listen."

Perceval sits first, followed by JJ. They book-end Mara in the booth. Nils waits at the bar for the coffees.

"I don't want any of you to interrupt me," Mara continues. "Just stay quiet and let me speak."

"Can we even talk in a place like this?" JJ asks. "It doesn't seem secure to me."

"It is, Julietta. This is my place."

"Interesting."

"JJ, stop it," Mara says. "We all know who we are. You know I set up Gomez to be arrested. And you know that Anthony Steinbach is my brother."

"You've been an informer all along?" JJ asks.

"Takes one to know one, right? Now, stop talking. Both of you."

JJ starts to move out of the booth. "I don't have to listen to any of this."

Mara grabs JJ's arm. "Sit down. A lot of this concerns you."

JJ slides back into the booth, but takes her time about it; long enough for Nils to come over with the coffees and put them on the table. Mara looks at the contents of her pink cup and pushes it away.

"No milk for me," she says.

"Oh, I forgot about that." Nils goes back to the bar. "I'll have that one."

"Thanks. You stop talking as well, Nils. All of you, do something out of character and just listen."

"This better be good," Perceval says, leaning back and gripping the curved table with his hands.

"I'll get right to the important part. The dead police officer, Marten, he died of natural causes. My brother is innocent. The police claimed it was murder just to clamp down on protesters and introduce tighter restrictions, which clearly had an impact on business here last night."

"That's madness," Perceval says. "The police would do no such thing. Can you imagine how many people a project like that requires?"

"You're not supposed to be talking." Mara sips the black coffee Nils hands her. "This is massive and it means everything. My brother told me he didn't touch Marten. He wasn't even near him. He had no weapon. No intent. No motive. He was just a teenager at a protest, at the wrong place and the wrong time. Marten collapsed. That's what Anthony said. He would pass any polygraph on that. Marten just fell over, dead. Maybe a heart attack, or something else. Wearing all that riot gear is hard on the body, believe me. You sweat a lot. Anyway, key people in the police have used this death for their own purposes. My theory is that Jawinski's behind it. By claiming it was murder, Jawinski could then introduce emergency measures to be brutal with protesters and start random ID checks. The police could have the power to lock up suspicious individuals. Namely, anyone who isn't white or right."

"How do you know this?" Perceval asks. "About Marten. Where's the proof?"

"Anthony told me. I believe him. He has no reason to lie about it."

"He's wanted for murder. He has every reason to lie about it."

"Where is he?" Nils asks. "Have you seen him?"

Mara ignores them and turns to JJ. "Ant said you were the one who told them to run. Him and Janica. Which means you didn't believe them when they said they didn't do anything."

"It didn't matter if I believed them or not," JJ says. "The word was a cop was killed. I've been around long enough to know what that means. The police were looking for two suspects. Anthony and Janica

292

were caught on camera. Their only option was to run. They haven't done that very well, because you found them."

"Twice. You should've believed them and helped them more. They're practically kids."

"This explains why you came into my life, out of nowhere," JJ says, "when all my instincts told me to be wary of you. Even with the balaclava on, you recognised your brother and wanted to save him."

"Wouldn't you?"

JJ turns to Perceval. "Did you know all this? That she's family?"

Perceval shakes his head. "This came to light later. The operation would not have begun if her familial connection had been made clear at the start."

"So, you're still in the police, Mara? Or are your just an informer for them?"

"I don't want to be part of a police force that arrests people for no reason, like they did with me and Zina on Saturday, and that uses an officer dying on duty for their own devious means."

"Not to mention the harassment scandal," JJ says.

"This is all the stuff we know about," Mara continues. "How much more is being hidden from us? How else are the cops breaking the law? What else is in the planning?"

Perceval picks up his cup, then decides he doesn't want any coffee. "These are all just words until we can prove there has been a cover-up."

"Demand to see the autopsy report. Though that's probably been doctored too. You need the body."

Perceval scoffs at this. "This is beyond preposterous. You want me to waltz into my boss's office and demand that our fallen comrade, just given a hero's funeral attended by politicians and all those in the upper echelons of the Hamburg Police, be exhumed and sliced open, independently, under the pretence of a conspiracy in which they are all partaking?"

"Yes. You got the balls to do that?"

"It has nothing to do with courage. It's insane. It's career suicide."

"If you don't, my brother will spend the rest of his life in jail for a crime he didn't commit. Can you live with that?"

A slither of a grin appears on Perceval's face. "We don't have him yet."

"It's only a matter of time before he's caught. Someone will tip the

293

police off. That's the whole point of a police state. Everyone scared of the police."

"Are you scared?"

"Yes, of what they might do. History has shown plenty of times what happens when the wrong people are given way too much power and latitude."

"You're getting too far ahead of yourself. All the focus is on Stuttgart this week." Perceval looks at Nils. "You shall stay with Mara for the rest of the day, in case her brother makes contact with her again."

"I won't let you arrest him," Mara says. "I could just as easily go public. Russell could write the story. He's on a roll right now. He exposed Spitz. He can expose this as well."

"Must be useful having a journalist catering to your every whim," Perceval says.

"Were you involved in that, Mara?" JJ asks.

"My mother said it's all speculation," Nils says. "Clickbait based on fabrication. One person's word against another's."

"Your mother's wrong, Nils. Way wrong. I worked with Spitz. I know exactly how he operates. Everything in the article is true. I bet some editor even dulled it down for mass consumption. Maybe the next time you talk to your mother, ask her how she rose to such a high position in the boys' club that is the Hamburg Police."

"What are you implying?" Nils asks. "That she fucked her way to the top?"

"I'm just going on what I know. I don't know her story. I do know that my best friend, an outstanding police officer, rejected Spitz's advances and tried to report him, then got exiled to Stuttgart for her trouble and hasn't received a single promotion since. Maybe she'd be in your mother's position now if she'd played along."

Nils shakes his head. "I don't believe any of this. Women have it so ..."

"Nils," Perceval says firmly, "given the company you are with and the place you are in, you shall consider your words very carefully."

"No," Mara says, "please finish, Nils. Tell me how easy I have it, being a woman. Tell me how great it is to be on a night train and not dare fall asleep, in case one of the men on board tries something. And that's me, a trained police officer with a boxing background. I'm scared on that train. How do you think it must be for women who don't have the skill set that I have? Easy? You have no idea what it's like for women, Nils, day after day after day."

"Try being a woman of colour," JJ adds. "Do you know how often I get told to go back to Africa? Seriously. People say this, out loud. I can't begin to imagine how many people think it and don't say it. In all my life in Germany, whenever I go somewhere and people don't know me, they expect I'm there to clean their toilet, or something like that."

Nils holds up his hands. "I'm sorry. I mean no disrespect. My mother has earned and deserved everything she's got, and I'm sure she had trouble with men along the way. I just don't want to believe the police are all bad. They can't all be bad. They're supposed to protect people."

"My father believes they're moving to take control of the country," Mara says. "A full-on police state, from the Chancellery down. I'm not sure we're quite at the point, but it feels like it's not far away. Which is why this cover-up needs to be exposed."

"Not possible," Perceval says. "This isn't some piece of Hollywood cinema where one simply pushes the weakest domino and the rest fall and the villains are captured. This is real life, and whenever good actually conquers evil, in real life, it feels like an anomaly. Even if this conspiracy were true, these people will take their lies to the grave. Not only that. There would be people involved at all levels. They would all believe it to be the right thing to do. Thus, they would perpetuate the lie to protect themselves, each other and everything they believe in. They would base so many things on that single lie that it would become truth for them. Do you follow? What you are calling a lie is their truth. To ask your friend Russell to write about this would mean destroying his career. Without any proof, no one will believe him. They will call him the liar. He would lose all credibility."

"He could write Anthony's story," Mara says, lacking conviction.

"Even worse. The wild accusations of a wanted man. A murderer saying anything to save himself. No one will swallow that. No media outlet will publish it. There is no evidence of any wrongdoing on the police's part."

"The evidence is six feet under."

"And there it shall remain."

"I won't let you send my brother to jail for something he didn't do."

Perceval's supportive smile surprises Mara. "Then you should make sure he's somewhere no one will find him."

Mara stares into her half-drunk coffee.

"Sounds like you have an idea where that could be," JJ says.

"It certainly means moving him from his current location. Because Mara knows where that is, and under the right kind of duress, she will part with that information."

"Now you threaten me?" Mara grips the cup; she wants to throw the coffee in Perceval's face. "After everything I just told you."

"I'm not threatening. I'm stating facts. If the police are in fact manipulating cases, then what happened with your brother may just be the beginning. Once that snowball starts rolling down the hill, it will get increasingly harder to stop."

"If they can get away with this," JJ says, "they can get away with anything. A country run by the police and their informers. Like East Germany was. Everyone spying on everyone else."

Perceval nods. "Arguments could be made that we are already there. The difference being that the citizenry makes everything about themselves readily available for consumption and analysis. There's no need for the spying methods of old."

"What do you mean?"

"The Stasi would marvel at the surveillance powers of the internet." He takes out his smartphone, which is turned off, and adds, "People conduct every aspect of their lives with the most accomplished informer in the history of spy-craft in their hand or pocket. They sleep with it. They sit on the toilet with it. They take it everywhere and tell it everything."

"Big Brother is watching," JJ says.

"No one is watching anyone. Sitting in attics or vans with headphones on, listening in. None of that. It's all data analysis. A single algorithm can accomplish in a split second what it took thousands of Stasi officers several years."

"But not with Circus," Mara says. "The no phones policy. The bunkers, where there's no reception."

"Yes, this is most impressive. Someone had the foresight to ensure the protesters could get off-grid sometimes. I'm sure many break this rule, but it becomes very hard to track people without their pocket informer."

Nils takes out his phone, also switched off, and stares at the blank screen, appearing to wonder what the gadget knows about him, where all that information is being stored and how it might be used.

"I would like to add," Perceval continues, enjoying the conversation, "that none of what I explained was ever public policy. Neither the government nor the police ever introduced mandatory smartphones for everyone. I'm certain there would be mass protesting against the insertion of tracking chips into bodies, but people eagerly line up to buy the latest phone which will track their every move. With the internet and mobile coverage, people have willingly, and in many ways knowingly, put themselves under total surveillance."

"Some people have even profited from it," JJ says.

Perceval nods. "Indeed. Today's influencer is yesterday's informer."

"I think you would like my father very much," Mara says.

"I do."

"You've met?"

"I attended some of his classes. At university. A smart man. I'd say ahead of his time, but that might be construed as a way of justifying his craziness in the present."

Mara stares at Perceval. "That is so accurate."

"His lectures were very entertaining. He was detailing the complexity and outcomes of self-inflicted surveillance long before it become anything remotely like a topic for public discourse."

"I guess someone heard him, back then." Mara slaps the table as it hits. "Jawinski. He was my father's student. Maybe he took those crazy theories for face value."

"Or he saw the potential in them."

Another silence. This time it's JJ who speaks first.

"I'm not sure why you brought me here, Mara. What has any of this got to do with me?"

"It's your fault for telling my brother to run when you should've helped him. You made him guilty. You've played a big part in all this. Did you say he should go to Linz?"

"I might have suggested it."

"Because of Milan Kollar? You know him, don't you?"

JJ doesn't reply.

"I assume she does," Perceval says. "It would only take a few minutes of research to link Julietta to Linz. Train tickets, flights, hotels, phone tracking, scanning photos online where Julietta is in the background. The data would reveal all. It would surprise me if they didn't know each other. This is not the first time an enterprising person with leadership ambitions has tried to unite various radical groups."

"You think Milan has tried this before?" Mara asks.

"We're researching this. Nils has proven extremely good at finding connections. Demonstrations that descend quickly into looting appear to have commonalities. We're also looking further back, to some unusual activities in the Balkan Wars. Nothing substantial yet, and the fact it's pre-internet makes things harder. There were a few examples of rival groups committing atrocities together."

"Milan Kollar potentially being a Bosnian Serb," Nils adds.

"Do you really believe that?" Mara asks. "That was my father's crazy idea."

JJ stands up. "I've heard enough. Mara, I'll make a deal with you. I'll keep it secret you're working with the police if you don't tell anyone about my involvement with Anthony. I'm not going to be an accessory once he's caught. I'm not going to prison for him. That silence extends to you two."

"That's great leadership," Mara says. "Throw my brother right under a herd of dancing elephants."

"I don't see any other option."

"Fine. Save yourself. It's what you do best."

"That's not fair. You don't know anything about me."

"Maybe I'll start by reading your Stasi file."

JJ gives Mara an angry look, then storms out.

Once the door is closed, Perceval says, "It appears your cover remains intact."

"By making JJ hate me again?"

"Your feistiness with Julietta was exactly what was required. For what she did to your brother, your response was fully warranted. Good work. Now, we need you at the G8 demonstration."

"What for? To be honest, I don't want to go."

"You must."

"What am I even doing now? This was all about finding the suspect, and we did that, only to discover that the suspect is actually

298

a scapegoat for a bigger conspiracy. But you won't do anything about it."

"I'm sorry. I can't."

"You know about Milan Kollar and where he is. You know about Modra. You have these Swiss bank accounts. What good am I now?"

"You have done superbly, especially for a rookie."

"Thanks."

"I'm impressed with your instincts. You have said all along that you feel something big is coming. Perhaps not this weekend, but soon. Being present in Stuttgart may be essential to understanding what this big thing might be. We need you there."

"I want to know," she says. "I'm just tired of fighting."

"You can't give up yet. There's nothing we can do about Anthony. Only you can save him."

"Are you suggesting I try? You'll let me?"

Perceval nods.

Mara looks at Nils, expecting some whiny objection, but he also appears in agreement with this.

"How long have I got?" she asks.

"Jawinksi wants to make this his moment. His press conference is at two. That's when he will take centre stage to announce David Wollenknecht will be released and Anthony Steinbach is the prime suspect. From then, the search will be underway in earnest."

"What about the second protester?"

"Do you know who that is? Yes, you know. Well, there's no interest in that person. The one caught on camera is the one we want."

"We're going about this all wrong. Anthony's innocent."

"Nils, please leave us." Perceval waits for Nils to slide out of the booth and walk out, which he does less sulkily this time.

"You can bet his mother did something to get ahead," Mara says, once the door closes. "That's pretty much the only way a woman can in this world."

"Trust me. She didn't. His mother is a wonderful, kind, fearsome woman. Also, it's dangerous to generalise in such fashion. Men like Spitz are the exception, not the rule."

"The whole thing with Zina and Spitz really shocked me. How long it's been going on. I thought we were past that kind of abusive manipulation."

Perceval looks around the Pink Dragon. "All throughout history, plenty of women have used sex for their own means."

"But that's deception, and cunning. Spitz is a predator. He's violent. A caveman with a club. Basically banging women over the head and dragging them back to his cave by their hair."

"Not anymore. He's finished. I wager there will be a knock-on effect. Others will be exposed. Others will go into hiding. The article was timely and impactful. You should be very proud of Zina. What she did was brave."

Mara lets out a long sigh. "So, what about Anthony?"

Perceval inspects his nails. "You know, the Baltic Sea is beautiful at this time of year. Especially in the old Soviet republics, which have become wonderful locations for reinvention. The basketball is also of a high quality, though they certainly have their share of classy table tennis players."

"Good to know."

"Riga is a personal favourite. The Perceval name is known there."

"Is it?"

"My Aunt Esther lives in Jurmala, near Riga. I really should visit her. Maybe I'll call her instead."

"Is she also in the family business?"

"Oh, yes." Perceval gestures towards the immense dragon on the wall. "There's a Latvian Dragon, of a different shade. Everyone knows it. Aunt Esther often complains she can't find good help these days. If you know anyone there looking for a job, she would be happy to meet them and help that person out."

"Good tip," Mara says, standing up.

"Have a safe journey to Stuttgart."

"I'm going tomorrow."

"Indeed. Ticket on a train at dawn. Along with the Circus leader who you so cleverly exposed yourself to."

"That was clever?"

"You have established mutual need. This is an excellent basis for cooperation, maybe more." Perceval smiles warmly. "Perhaps our paths will cross in the south."

"I hope we all just get out of it alive."

"We will. But if you even want to get there, you will not succeed on the train."

"That's the blockade? Rail?"

300

Perceval nods. "Limited resources combined with an expectation of a younger demographic. Also, the result of data analysis of tickets purchased to date. There will be roadblocks and ID checks, but the main focus will be the central train station."

"I better think of something else." She starts to walk away, then stops. "Hey, uh, thanks."

***

It's important to stay away from cameras, which means avoiding train stations and buses. A taxi would also potentially be traceable. The only option is to ride to Moorfleet, on the back roads, hood up over her head.

On the ride, she thinks about Latvia and how to get her brother there. Anthony would get picked up if he tried to fly, and probably wouldn't get further than the Germany-Poland border on the train. It's too far to hitchhike, and cars would get stopped at the borders. That leaves the ferry, from Travemünde.

It all seems complicated. Unreal. The problems of other people. But what eats at her is that helping Anthony escape is solving a problem that's the result of another problem. She's disappointed Perceval won't help with proving Anthony's innocence.

But, the more distance she puts between herself and the Pink Dragon, the more she realises Perceval is right. Trying to expose the cover-up without solid evidence would be pointless, and it would end Perceval's career. The lie has become truth, already. Marten was murdered by a protester. A witness has named Anthony as the perpetrator. The search is on. That is the version of events that has gone into the records, signed off by those at the top and everyone involved.

She needs to get Anthony out of Germany.

At her father's place, she explains the situation and what she and her father need to do. He's ready for action, and appears to have been waiting for this moment. He dons his full-length coat, grabs his broad hat and leads the way down the narrow path to Bernd's farm.

As they walk, Mara is relieved that her father is on board and willing to help. Had he been of a different opinion, they would have argued for hours, fruitlessly, because she would have had no chance of making him see things differently.

301

That doesn't matter, because they agree that getting Anthony out is the only option.

"The real problem will be separating the young lovers," her father says, as they skirt around the back of Bernd's house.

"That's the best thing for Janica. Only Anthony will be named, but if she's caught with him, then the police might jump at the chance of playing up the role of the second protester."

"Expect them to dig their heels in. They're young. They think this is it. The big love. Nothing can tear them apart, and anyone who tries to just makes the need to stay together even stronger."

"Was that how it was with you and my mother? Your parents were trying to keep you apart?"

"We weren't 18. Janica doesn't work for the BND, as far as I know. But we were definitely in love."

"I really wish you'd tell me what happened."

Her father doesn't reply. He goes to the door and knocks on it.

"You make it sound like the BND was the reason she left," Mara says. "Was it?"

"You talk some sense into your brother. I'll organise a vehicle."

Mara shakes her head at her father, hating his stubbornness and selfishness; that he has always denied her the truth. But at least he's here, trying to help. She wonders if it's worth asking Perceval, who loves a good file, to research into Agnes Steinbach of the German Foreign Intelligence Service.

The same plastic chairs are in front of the house, including the one she was duct-taped to; dirt is clinging to where the duct tape once was. Getting rifle-butted feels like ages ago. But she thinks it's not so bad. After several years in Berlin when she drifted from shift to shift and the days blended into months, and it felt like she missed two seasons each year – it was either cold or warm – having time slowed down like this has given her a stronger awareness of the present. It has also made her more present. The way a boxing bout can seem like it stretches for hours when it only lasts about twenty minutes, and every second matters.

Bernd opens the door and ushers Richard inside. Mara waves at Bernd, who responds with a single, non-committed nod.

She assumes the greenhouses are being built behind the barns and heads in that direction, bringing the neck of her hoodie up over her nose and mouth to combat the smell. When she gets to the end,

302

she hears the faint sound of an engine struggling to turn over; it makes the clickety-clickety-click of a battery problem.

The first greenhouse has the beginnings of a skeletal frame. Bernd's sons are there, working under the supervision of a builder. At the back of the frame, she sees Anthony on a ladder Janica is holding. He's shirtless and hammering something into place. She thinks their closeness and the way her brother looks very much at home working here will make it that much harder to get him to leave.

"You again," the older of Bernd's sons says. "Another protest?"

"I'm here for Anthony," she says.

"Who's that?"

"The guy on the ladder. My brother."

"He calls himself Jordie."

"Then I need Jordie. But not the girl, whatever she's calling herself."

The older brother turns to shout, but Anthony is already down from the ladder and coming towards them. Janica, walking at his side, hands him his shirt, suggesting to Mara that their relationship dynamic may not be what she assumed it to be.

"Did you fix everything?" Anthony asks, pulling his shirt on.

"Follow me."

Mara walks back around the barn, to get some distance from Bernd's sons and the builder. Anthony and Janica follow, holding hands.

"Can we go home?"

Mara stops. "I need to talk to you alone."

"Anything you say to me you can say in front of Jani. We have no secrets from each other."

"If you both want to stay out of jail, this will need to be your first. Janica, it's very nice to meet you, properly this time, and I'm sure you're a great girl, but you can't be in this conversation. That's for your own safety."

"So, you didn't fix anything," Anthony says. "I'm still wanted and the cops are still lying."

"I can't change the whole country, Ant. We've got to deal with what's in front of us." She steps closer to her brother. "Look, if you care about Janica and want her to be completely left out of this, you need to do exactly what I say."

Anthony looks at Janica and nods a few times. She walks back to

303

the greenhouse.

"Jordie?" Mara asks, once Janica is out of earshot.

"I thought I needed a cover."

"You should've thought a bit harder. I mean, a basketballer named Jordan?"

"Jordie," Anthony corrects.

"Yeah, that makes all the difference. You don't need it here anyway. Bernd knows who you are."

"I'm pretty sure you're about to tell me I can't go home, so I'm sticking with the name."

"Fine. Do that. You're going to need it, where you're going."

"Where am I going?"

Mara tells Anthony everything she knows: about the naming of the suspect at Jawinski's press conference in a few hours, how the police are probably already gearing up to storm the house, once they get the go-ahead, and how flying or taking the train are out of the question. The only option is to take the ferry to Latvia and stay in Riga, where Esther Perceval will be able to help him.

"Who's she?" he asks.

"A friend's aunt, and we can trust her," Mara says, hoping that's the case.

"I don't want to run."

"You don't have a choice."

"We can go public. Tell the truth in the media. Your friend, the journalist, he can do it."

"No one will believe it. The entire police force will deny it. They'll call you crazy. Russell would be ruined."

"I could get a lawyer. Grandma and Grandpa would help. They're connected. They know lots of important people."

"Given the values they hold so dear, once you're made public enemy number one, they'll probably disown you."

Anthony runs his fingers through his hair and walks around a bit, frustrated.

"Ant, this is the only thing you can do. You have to leave the country. It's the one chance of having anything remotely like a normal life. The only thing waiting for you here is a prison cell."

"What about Jani?"

"She's safe, at the moment. If you leave now, you'll be ensuring she stays safe. Then, once you get set up in Riga, I can tell her how to find you. If that's something you still both want."

"Why wouldn't we want that?"

"I don't know. Because you're 18 and you've been on the run and that's been really exciting, I guess."

"This isn't some summer fling. We love each other."

"Okay. Good. I'm happy for you. If you love her, save her."

Anthony looks on the verge of tears. "What about you and Dad?"

"We're risking everything for you. We'll both be questioned before this day is over. Which is why we need to go now."

As Mara says this, an engine starts. She turns to see an old yellow pick-up connected by jumper cables to a newer black pick-up.

"Looks like our car's ready," she says.

"What do I tell Jani?"

"Tell her to go back to her life. At least for the next few months. Make it clear she has nothing to do with you."

"I can't leave her. Why don't you understand that?"

Mara can see he's yielding. "No contact either. No phones. No emails. You're off the grid in Riga."

They both watch Richard take bits of wood and lengths of rope out of the pick-up's tray, looking like a medieval bandit in that huge coat and hat.

"How do I start a new life without money?"

"I think our father has a solution for that," Mara says. "You need to leave everything behind. No cards. No ID. Nothing that shows who you are. I took that ferry once. I was never asked for my passport."

Anthony nods a little, accepting things. "What about you? Dad's starting to lose it. Now, I'll be gone."

To keep herself from crying, she steps forward and gives her brother a hug. "Two minutes," she says, letting him go.

She walks to the old pick-up, where her father is waiting. She sees now it's a Ford Ranger. The engine is loud, but it gets considerably quieter when Bernd removes the jumper cables and closes the bonnet. It's a two-door cab, meaning Anthony will have to lie on the narrow backseat. She thinks this is good, as it will keep him out of sight.

"I have the horses," her father says. "Where's the outlaw?"

"Coming. I hope. He's going to need money. Who can we rob?"

"It's very convenient the ferry leaves from Travemünde. We can stick up Ma and Pa Steinbach on the way. God, I hope they'll be there."

"When does the ferry leave?"

Her father holds up his hands. "No phone. Bernd, can you check that, please?"

Bernd does some tapping and swiping at his phone with his chunky fingers. "The overnighter heading northeast leaves at 1330."

"We need to get him on that," Mara says.

"For the benefit of those without phones or watches," Bernd says, "you've got about two hours, which is more than enough time to get to Travemünde."

"Thanks," Mara says. "For the car and taking in Anthony and helping out. It's really good of you."

"I told you all along Bernd is one of the good ones," Richard says.

"I'm sorry for what happened here. With the protest and everything. I was running with a bad crowd. Didn't know what I was getting into."

Bernd starts putting the cable into a neat roll, looping it over his hand and elbow. "Your bad actions turned into something good for me. It was after that day that I decided to change things, because otherwise you idiots would have just kept coming and making trouble. Remy told me about hydroponics and this innovation to use the waste from my pigs as a kind of fertiliser, which he'd read about. I wish I'd known about it sooner. Any protesters who try to break in here in the future won't have an eco leg to stand on."

Anthony jogging around the barn makes them all turn to look. He has a small backpack over one shoulder. Janica trails behind him, but she stops once Anthony gets to the pick-up and climbs in. He lies on the rear seat, below the window line.

"Let's go," he says.

Richard doffs his big hat to Bernd and gets in the passenger side.

"I guess that means I'm driving," Mara says, moving around the pick-up. She gets in and shuts the door.

"The last time I drove a car was last century," her father says, clearly proud.

"This car is from last century. You should know it better than I do."

"Drive," Anthony demands.

Mara gets in first gear and hops the car a few cautious metres forward, getting the feel of it. "I haven't driven a manual since I learned to drive."

"Don't stall it," her father says. "It'll need another jump-start if you do. We don't have time for that."

"You're welcome to take over." Mara really works the steering wheel to turn the pick-up fully around and aim it at the gate.

"Put your hood up. Because of the cameras. Stay down, Anthony."

Mara does so and bows her head forward to hide her face. "I need a sun umbrella hat like you've got."

When they're on the road and Mara's finding the gears with increasing ease, she checks the mirror, but can only see her brother's half-bent body on the rear seat, turned slightly away from them, his knees forming a pyramid.

"You all right, Ant?" she asks.

"Leave me alone."

"Stay strong," Richard says. "This is the only thing we can do for you. I'm considering coming along. I don't like the direction this country is heading in. Might be best to escape now. Why don't we all go?"

"What about your house?" Mara asks.

"What about it? It's just a thing. Bernd or Remy could take care of it. Sell it, if need be."

"I can't go to Latvia." Mara turns the Ranger onto the Autobahn on-ramp. "You can't just abandon your house."

"Why not? That's happened all through history. People were often forced to walk away from their homes because of the dangers they faced. Or they left for better lives. When the Wall fell, some people just dropped everything and went west. They literally left potatoes boiling on the stove and laundry drying on the line. Not to mention bank accounts full of money, which turned out to be worthless."

Mara keeps to the slow lane, as the pick-up struggles to go faster than the trucks that occupy it. "If you leave," she says, "they'll know you two are together. They'll find you in order to find Ant. The way you get around the world, you're not exactly inconspicuous."

"I could go undercover."

"You need to stay here and face the questioning. Like I will. We don't say anything about conspiracies or cover-ups. It's up to us to convince the police we have no idea where he is. Ant will be far away. So far away, they'll give up looking for him."

"You're right. That's our challenge. To throw them off the scent.

You just need to hide yourself, Anthony."

"Jani said I should start playing basketball again. Try to make the pro league."

"How does that help you keep a low profile?" Richard asks.

"Why shouldn't he play?" Mara slowly gets past a campervan piloted by an old man leaning way forward over the steering wheel. "As long as he has a new name and his background checks out. Change your look, Ant. I don't see why you should hide. They'll be looking for Anthony Steinbach, not Jordie Whoever, pro basketball player. That might be the best cover of all. Hiding in plain sight."

"Maybe." Richard leans across to look at the instruments. "Didn't they teach you how to drive fast at police school?"

"It doesn't go any faster. If I put my foot down too far, the whole thing starts to shake. Don't worry. We'll make it."

"The first stop is Helldahl. For a daylight robbery."

"To steal a few more candlesticks?"

"We got almost nothing for it," Anthony says. "Gold-plated, and not even pure gold."

"Still, my boy, I don't think I've been prouder of you than when you said you'd lifted that stick. You should've gone for the safe."

"You know where it is?" Mara asks.

"Yes. We're going to empty it."

"I'm pretty sure they're back from holiday. To stick a few more antlers on the walls."

"Another hunting trip? God. Just how did I spring from those loins?"

"Let's hope they're not home."

"They'll be out for lunch," Richard says. "They haven't cooked a meal in years. Whatever the situation, you stay in the car, Anthony. Don't let anyone see you."

"Tell them I'm sorry for taking the candlestick."

Richard laughs. "I'll tell them I took it. In fact, Mara, once we've raided the safe, you take Anthony to the ferry. I think it's time I had a long talk with my parents. This is it. This is the moment."

"Keep me out of it," Mara says. "I can't stand those two."

"They're not crazy about you either. But you'll have to drive back to pick me up."

"Now you're making me want to get on the ferry."

Richard laughs some more. "Oh, I've missed you two. Maybe this is what we should've been all along. A family of outlaws. Rob from the right and give to the left."

***

They reach the house on Helldahl just before 1300. Mara stops in front and keeps the engine running, worried it won't start again if she switches it off.

"They're out," Richard says. "As expected."

"The spare key box is in its usual spot," Mara says. "With the same combination."

"Seriously? Can you imagine what my world was like growing up? It's a miracle I turned out okay."

Mara wonders what her father's definition of okay is. "What about the safe?" she asks. "Do you know that combination?"

"It's always a birthdate. It might take a few tries. Don't sit here idling. Because this car on this street will have the neighbours out in no time."

"Oh, I know. They'll probably be armed this time."

"Drive down to the ferry and buy a ticket. Then swing back up here."

"Will do."

Richard hands Mara some cash from his wallet, then gets out and closes the door. Mara watches him get the key and go to the front door. Once he's inside, she drives to the end of the street, then circles around to head back down Helldahl.

"How you doing, Ant?"

"I got one foot on that boat already."

At the terminal, she's able to buy a ticket from the pick-up, for a single adult, though she has to say several times that she doesn't need a ticket for the vehicle.

Back at the house, there's a silver BMW parked in front of the garage.

"Oh, fuck."

"What?"

"They're back."

The front door is flung open. Richard comes running out, coat billowing behind him and with several bundles of cash clutched to his chest. Mara lowers the window in time for him to drop the

309

bundles in her lap.

"Anthony, I love you, son," he says, out of breath. "Take care of yourself. This is your new beginning. Time for a big adventure." He steps back and slaps the door with a hand. "Go, Mara, go."

Richard walks backwards from the vehicle. Again, Mara has to go to the top of the street to circle around. When she comes back past, she slows down to see her father standing in front of his parents, who are both lean and gaunt, with desert tans and matching scowls, looking more than ever like brother and sister. Her father awaits their wrath, but has his left hand behind him, making wavy motions to keep Mara driving. She heads down the hill at getaway speed.

Anthony leans forward to look at the cash. "How much is there?"

"I don't know. Thousands? You'll have to hide it. You don't want people knowing you're carrying this kind of cash." She starts passing the bundles behind her.

Anthony stuffs the cash into the bottom of his bag.

"It's going to be all right, Ant. You can do this. You've got the gift of a new start, the chance to really make something of yourself."

She turns towards the terminal, where the ferry blows its final boarding call.

"No big goodbye," Anthony says, climbing into the front. "Just stop."

He gives Mara a quick hug and gets out of the car. She watches him go. He doesn't look back. A horn sounds behind her, forcing her to pull away from the terminal.

She drives back to Helldahl, fighting emotions, wondering if that's the last time she'll see her brother. She thinks that image of him getting on the ferry is far better for her memory than any visit to prison would be.

It's not necessary to go all the way to the house, as she sees her father walking down Helldahl. He gets in and closes the door.

"What ...?"

He holds up his left hand. "Did Anthony get the ferry?"

"Yes. But ..."

"Just drive. I need to process."

Mara manoeuvres the pick-up, which she thinks is driving better the longer it runs, through Travemünde, out to the highway and onto the Autobahn. They pass Lübeck and get a good halfway back to Hamburg before Richard finally speaks.

310

"The combination was Anthony's birthdate," he says, taking off the hat and flinging it onto the dashboard.

"You did the right thing. Anthony wasn't safe here."

"I told them the money was for him. For a year abroad. That's how I got out of there alive."

"They'll figure it out soon enough. But it wasn't the moment after all."

"Papa started to take his belt off. Yes, really. Like when I was a boy."

"He hit you with his belt?"

"Whipped is more accurate. Always said it was for my own good. That it hurt him to do it. Spoken like a true lawyer. The punishment was good for me and bad for him."

He falls silent. Mara doesn't push, as her father so rarely talks openly about the past.

"I guess he was trying to shape me like his father shaped him," he continues. "He was in the SS, my grandfather. I've checked the records. The Nazis were meticulous record keepers. He wasn't a fervent believer, but perhaps he was someone worse than that. A careerist, who got involved in order to get ahead. You can bet there were plenty of them. Opportunists seizing the day. Then, when it was all over and they were defeated, they denounced everything, claimed they were only ever following orders. They switched sides and pursued new avenues for their own gain."

"What about your father?"

"Maybe I've been too hard on him all these years," he says, looking out the side window. "I don't agree with his politics, but he's allowed to have an opinion, as dumb as it may be. I never ever considered hitting you or Anthony for one second, so that stopped with me. I'm not like him, but he's a product of his time. Like my mother is. Born during the war. There must be some serious trauma buried deep within them both, from what they experienced in their first few years of life, whether they remember it or not. You can be sure, though, that they never talk about it. If you think I'm closed off about the past, those two take it to a whole other level."

Mara is disappointed to see the first exit sign for Hamburg, as she'd like to keep on driving and have her father keep talking in a way he's never done with her before.

"What I said on the trip up, about families abandoning their

311

houses in desperate times, that happened to my mother. In Linz."

"She's from Linz?"

"You didn't know that? Her family left at the end of the war. Once the city was taken by the Allies, her family couldn't go home. Their house was on the north side of the Danube, in Urfahr, which was occupied by the Russians. The soldiers just took over everything, pilfering every house and capturing women when they could. My mother's family fled with just the clothes on their backs. Imagine that. She was two. The family house became a Russian brothel."

"How do you know all that if they never talk about it?"

"From your mother," he says, turning to look at Mara. "She wanted to know. We took a trip to Linz, years before you were born. Before we were married. She was curious about my family. She was curious about everything, which is why we lost her. Back then, she wanted to know why my parents didn't like her. In Linz, we found the answer."

"Is she Jewish?"

"That's what I thought, but I was wrong. Her real name is Agnieszka. Her parents shortened it to Agnes when she started school, because they wanted to distance themselves from their roots."

"She's Russian."

"On her mother's side. My parents must have done some research and found this out. Agnes wasn't the first girlfriend of mine they checked up on. You know, preserving the purity of the bloodline and all that. They didn't want me marrying a descendant of a Russian. My mother wouldn't even look at Agnes. It was like she didn't exist."

"I had no idea."

"When we were in Linz, we found the old Löwe family house and learned its history. But while things became clear for us, it didn't really change anything. My parents still hated Agnes. We just had a better understanding as to why, and perhaps could even forgive them a little."

"Why couldn't your parents see past the history and accept her for who she is? She had nothing to do with all that."

"I agree. Especially because Germans are often the first to shout it was the previous generations that did the bad stuff and they shouldn't be held responsible for it." Richard points at a sign. "There's the turn-off to Moorfleet. Don't miss it."

312

Mara gets off the Autobahn and arcs around the off-ramp. She would still prefer to keep driving, as she fears the minute she stops, so will her father's revelations.

When they stop at a traffic light, Mara asks, "Is that why she left? Because of your parents?"

Richard puts on his broad hat. "I know you want a big story. You always liked drama. A clear reason that will explain everything, but she simply wanted other things. Things I couldn't give her. Things I didn't want. Different experiences. I loved her so much. It broke my heart when she came to me one day, absolutely out of the blue, and said that she couldn't do it anymore. She said exactly that. 'Richard, I can't do this anymore.' Couldn't be a mother. Couldn't be my wife. Couldn't live in Othmarschen. Couldn't juggle her career and a household. The hardest part was that she said she still loved me, but she hated me because I was holding her back."

A chorus of horns sounds from behind. The light is green. Mara drives forward.

"I'm sure now you can appreciate why I never wanted to talk about it, and why going to work each day, as a lawyer for the family firm, felt like a punishment. More so than any whipping I got from my father's belt."

"She didn't want me. Or Anthony. How do you think that makes me feel?"

"She didn't want me either. This is why I never said anything. I'm not going to be the kind of parent who passes on whatever pain he receives to the next person in line. Agnes destroyed me by leaving, but it stayed with me. I carried it. I didn't pass that incredible hurt onto you."

"You just let us grow up motherless instead, with no idea what happened."

"Now you know. Deal with it." He points to the left. "Down there."

"To your place or Bernd's?"

"The farm."

The cursory way he says this makes Mara think he won't say anything further. She lets him go back into his shell, hiding inside his big coat. But she's grateful for all that he said; the closeness she feels to him as they pull into the farm is something she hasn't felt since she was a little girl. When the Ranger chugs to a halt, she gets out and moves around the vehicle with the intention of giving her father a

313

hug, but he's out before her and already headed for the back path behind Bernd's house.

"Successful?" Bernd asks.

"I think so. Thanks for the car."

"Easy."

"Any news?"

"They made the announcement."

"The hunt begins. But we were never here. Anthony was never here."

"Don't worry. I've had plenty of workers over the years who were never here. My grandfather hid escapees from the Neuengamme concentration camp during the war."

"Is that right?"

"Yep. Remy's grandfather was born in my cellar."

She looks at the house. "So hard to imagine how the world was back then."

"It's not exactly perfect now."

She goes back to the driver's side, to check she has everything. On the floor is one of the bundles of cash, which must have fallen under the seat during the dash from Helldahl. Printed on the white band holding the bundle tightly together is €5,000. She's sure Anthony has at least five of those bundles; it's reassuring to know he has a good amount of cash to get started with.

"Hey, Bernd?" she calls out.

"Yes?"

"How much do you want for this?"

"I should give you money to take it off my hands." Bernd's smile is that of someone who's spent his whole life in the countryside. A smile that makes him squint and cracks lines around his eyes. His face becomes open and unguarded, and he looks ready to help in any way he can.

"I'll give you 500," Mara says. "Cash, right now. If you fill it up from your fuel pump over there."

"Deal."

She shakes the big hand he extends. Given their sudden cordiality, she thinks he may apologise for butting her in the head with his rifle. But he just keeps on smiling.

"I'll get the papers," he says. "They're in the house somewhere."

"Thanks."

314

Mara pockets the key and starts walking around the barn. All the pigs are in the paddock between the two barns. Their squeals and grunts sound almost happy.

She finds Janica sitting on a stack of pallets, her back against the barn. Bernd's sons and the local builder continue working, but Mara guesses Janica's contribution to the project stopped when Anthony left.

"Is he gone?" Janica asks.

"Yeah."

"You think he'll make it?"

Mara sits down on the pallets. "I sure hope so."

"How will we know?"

"Word will be passed along the dragon telegraph line."

"The what?"

"Never mind. I'll know. Then, I'll let you know, when the time is right. But now, I'm taking you home."

Janica nods a few times. "I kind of lost interest," she says, looking at the workers. "Ant's energy, it's just infectious. You know? When he gets into something, he really gets into it."

"I know. That made him easy to handle as a kid, once he found that one thing."

"You raised him, is that right? He doesn't talk about it much."

"The early years, yeah, I was pretty much his mother. I was just a kid myself."

The builder and Bernd's sons get a section of the front wall up. It's made of yellowish plastic and gives a good idea of how the greenhouse will look once completed.

"Was it Ant who got you into Circus?" Mara asks.

"That was my idea. I wanted to make a difference. Look what happened."

"Don't blame yourself."

"Maybe he'll meet someone else," Janica says. "Then what'll I do?"

"He's probably thinking the exact same thing about you."

Mara tries to picture her brother, now Germany's most wanted teenager, sitting on the ferry, crying in a corner, with €25,000 in his bag.

"Poor kid," she says.

"What?"

"Look. When Ant loves something, he goes all in. The only sport

315

he's ever loved is basketball. Never wanted to play anything else, because it meant cheating on his love. He takes the same approach to relationships."

"Really?"

"Guaranteed."

"He's good enough to go pro. Wherever he is."

"Maybe he'll get that chance. The point I'm trying to make is that he loves you and he'll be loyal to you. If you want to join him when the time is right, I'm sure that will be the only thing he wants."

Janica smiles sweetly. "He said you were tougher than this. Harder. Meaner."

"It's been an emotional day, and it's not over yet. The police are going to come knocking. They're probably already at my father's place. That's why we need to get you home."

"What do I tell them?"

"Just answer the questions. Don't give them any more information than you need to. If they ask you where he is, tell them the truth. You don't know."

"Okay. I'm ready. I live in Bahrenfeld. How do we get there?"

Mara holds up her keys. "I'm proud to say I just bought my first car. A Ford Ranger that's almost older than me."

***

It's late afternoon when she reaches Elbe Help. There are plenty of vacant parking spaces, and none of the parked cars look overtly like unmarked police vehicles; no one's sitting in them, and there are no takeaway coffee cups on the dashboards. But the police must be looking for her. In Berlin maybe, because that's the address she has in the system.

She can't wait to show Russell her wheels.

A few vehicles pass. Vans and trucks. Plus an old man on an electric bike. When the road's clear, she puts her hood up, gets out and runs for the stairs. Inside, she goes straight into JJ's office and closes the door.

"Hey, what's going on?"

Mara puts an index finger to her lips.

"I thought I'd seen the last of you for today."

With a notepad and pen, Mara goes to a corner of the office and

316

gestures for JJ to join her. She keeps the notepad close to her chest and writes: Don't take the train.

JJ looks at her quizzically.

Mara writes: That's the blockade. They're going to stop trains reaching S.

Another questioning look.

Mara writes: Info from our dragon friend.

JJ mimes ripping paper in half.

Mara shakes her head and writes: Don't cancel tickets. Too obvious. I have a car. You can come with me.

JJ signals "OK" with her fingers.

Mara writes: Hamburger Berg, 0700. Yellow pick-up. Bring supplies.

Another "OK" signal.

Mara rips the paper off the notepad, scrunches it up and puts it in her pocket.

"The police were here," JJ whispers, "looking for you."

Mara feigns surprise. "Really? What on earth for?"

"It's all over the news."

"Well, if they come back again, tell them I'm at Gus's gym."

"I will."

"That's Gus's gym," Mara repeats, loudly, as if to an audience. "On Grosse Elbstraße."

They smile at each other, though JJ seems distant; a smile of acknowledgement, not appreciation.

Mara leaves the office and goes down the stairs. She waits in the stairwell until the road is clear, then jogs to her car. She trundles further down the street and parks outside the gym. She thinks it's unusual for there to be no other cars parked out the front on a Wednesday evening, when normally every bag would be taking a pounding.

There's no one inside. She finds Gus in his office, sitting at a laptop with reading glasses perched at the tip of his twice-broken nose.

"Mara," he says, rather coldly.

"You all right? Where is everyone? Where are the barefoot boys?"

"Gone. The place has been empty since Saturday."

"What happened?"

"You're asking me what happened? Zina clocked that young guy, that's what happened. Beautifully, I might add. What a talent. But

317

that drove them all away. Those MMA boys all know each other and they've taken their business somewhere else."

"So much for loyalty."

"They were the only thing keeping me afloat. Now, I'll have to close the gym. After 56 years. I can't believe it."

"Gus, listen to me. You're not closing. You're better off without those guys and the others they bring with them. All those stinking feet. This is your chance to reinvent the place. Get more girls in here. Train more refugees. Apply for sponsorships and funding."

Gus smiles. "I love your energy, Mara. That all sounds good. Can we do that? I can't even pay this month's bills."

Mara takes the bundle of cash from her pocket. "Here," she says, removing the white band and keeping €500 for herself. "That's four grand. I have to go away for a few days, but when I'm back, I'll help get things started."

"I'm not taking your money."

"Call it a loan, then. Or me buying in as your partner. Use some of that cash to get this place cleaned up. Make some flyers and stick them up at refugee centres. Ask Tinaya to help you. I know she will."

"She's a good girl. She's got potential. A fighter's heart."

"Tell her that. She'll be so happy to hear it. I'm sure her friends will help out too."

"All right."

"There must be money available for this kind of thing. Social funding. Integration through sport. Something like that."

"I'll ask around."

The loud knock on the front door makes them both look in that direction.

"I'm pretty sure that's for me," Mara says.

She goes to the door, suddenly excited for all that the gym can be. She expects to see Gornau and Callenberg, or clones of those two, when she opens the door. Instead, there's a tall, solid-looking woman filling out every centimetre of her blue pants suit. She's in her 50s. Her blonde hair is loose and long, the fringe that hangs below her eyebrows giving her face a rather severe frame. The black sedan behind her, with all the windows up, screams police car.

"Mara Steinbach?"

"That was fast. I'm impressed."

"What do you mean?"

"Nothing. Are you interested in learning how to box? You've got great hands for it."

"I'm Detective Hannelore Stammer." She holds up her ID. "Have you seen Anthony Steinbach?"

"Not for a few months. Why?"

"When did you last see him?"

"It was, uh, I don't know, maybe sometime around New Year. Yeah, Ant had a basketball game in Berlin. I went and watched. He dominated."

"You haven't seen him since?"

Mara looks past the detective, at the black sedan, certain there are people sitting in there. "He was supposed to stay with me, but he decided to go back on the team bus."

"Hmm." Stammer nods a little, waiting for Mara to talk.

"That's it."

"Can we go inside?"

"Sure. If you want." Mara holds the door open. "There's just old Gus in here with me tonight. No one's training."

Stammer enters and Mara follows her down the hallway to the open area.

"Where is everyone?"

"I guess you could say the gym is going through a southpaw transition."

"I have no idea what that means."

Mara gets in a boxing pose, putting her right fist forward. "A southpaw is a leftie. We're swinging the gym more in that direction."

"Hmm."

Stammer takes out her phone and taps something into it. Mara notices the index finger on the detective's right hand locks at the middle joint; it hints at an injury gained through ball sport, which seems likely as Stammer has the solid middle-aged build of someone who once played serious sport.

"Interesting," Stammer says.

"What is?"

"This place is untouched."

"I have no idea what that means," Mara says, mimicking the detective's matter-of-fact delivery.

Stammer smiles. "It means we can talk freely. Look, I know who you are and I know what you're doing."

"Do you?"

"Yes. Nils is my son. I've known Christoph nearly his whole life, because I used to work in St Pauli. Penelope Perceval was a very good friend of mine."

Mara decides to remain cautious. "Is that right?"

"Nils told me about your theory of how women get ahead in the police force. He was very upset."

"Oh, poor Nils. What other theories did he tell you about? Was he also upset about the police lying to cover up that officer's death?"

"Christoph and I are discussing the options. He surfaced some interesting medical issues, affecting some of the officers who worked the protest where Officer Marten died."

"Medical issues?"

"Christoph is looking into it. Tainted water bottles, for example, is one possibility. The problem, though, is your father. When I spoke to him a few hours ago, he seemed very intent on proving his son's innocence, with the help, he said, of Lersner-Löwe."

"He doesn't work there anymore."

"I know. But Karl Steinbach is still on the board. Your father said his father will help."

"One big happy family," Mara says, trying not to smile.

"You weren't aware of this?"

"I have no control over what my father or grandfather decides to do. That they might work together comes as a complete surprise to me."

"It could get messy."

"I think my father's just trying to scare you. With lawyers. Anyway, sounds like things are messy enough, with tainted water bottles and poisoned police officers."

Stammer brushes stray strands of her fringe from her eyes, in a slightly annoyed fashion, as if she doesn't like her haircut. "I can see why Nils likes you. You're very combative."

Mara folds her arms. "I haven't seen Anthony. You got what you came for."

"Can you account for your whereabouts today?"

"Sure." Mara shouts: "Hey, Gus! Where have I been all day?"

"Here," Gus shouts back.

"Hmm."

"That alibi's rock-solid."

320

"There's footage of you, leaving and returning to a farm in the Moorfleet area, driving that old yellow thing parked outside, with an unidentified person in the passenger seat."

"Oh, that's right. I ducked out there to buy it. Took it for a test drive, then slapped the cash down. Now, I love it, so don't talk badly about my car."

"Who was in the passenger seat?"

"My father. He knows the owner. And he, my father, wears that big hat because he's very paranoid about the surveillance state we live in. Such as the police knowing I'm here, even though you tell me this place is off the grid."

"So, you weren't here all day?"

"I was gone for about an hour, just to get the car."

"Hmm. Be sure to change the registration to your name. You don't want to be caught driving an unregistered vehicle."

"Good point. I'll do that."

"Organise insurance too. Your vehicle might be worthless, but you want to be covered in case you hit something of value."

"You're just full of good tips, detective."

Stammer walks to the hallway, then stops. "By the way, you should know that Hans Spitz shot himself yesterday."

"What?"

"Normally, people offer condolences in such a situation, but in this case, I will simply relay this information."

Mara shakes her head in disgust. "That fucking coward."

"Coward?"

"His whole career, he preyed on women and abused them. But those women got back on their feet and kept going like the incredibly strong women they are. Then, this guy, the second it goes bad for him and he's the victim, he puts a gun to his head. A fucking coward."

"Hmm." Stammer smiles slightly, like she agrees, but isn't willing to say that outright.

"Do you know who's taken over the station in Kollwitzkiez?" Mara asks.

"One moment." More phone tapping with that unbent index finger. "Someone named Lauter."

Rain dinks against the car's roof, like some kid is lobbing small Lego bricks at the car from a window above. The dashboard clock shows it's 0708. Under the clock, there's a cavity the radio once filled.

She doesn't have a map, but she knows it's well over 600 kilometres to Stuttgart. It will take them all day to get there, given the Ranger's tendency to start shuddering when pushed beyond 100 km/h. Which means upwards of seven hours of driving, not accounting for traffic and breaks. They have the time, as the first protest is scheduled for tomorrow, when all the G8 leaders and their entourages arrive. But she still doesn't like it that JJ is late. She wonders if it's tactical; that JJ likes to make people wait for her. More likely is that JJ is just another person who lives on their own time. JJ probably sent a text message, to excuse her tardiness; but Mara's phone is charging in Gus's office. She would rather be helping out at the gym than steeling herself for this road trip.

One thing she's liked since coming back to Hamburg is getting around without a phone. Then, Perceval's description of the smartphone as the ultimate informer reinforced her conviction to live without it. If anyone is tracking her, they will know she's in the vicinity of Gus's gym for the next few days.

Of all the people she's come into contact with in the past few weeks, Detective Hannelore Stammer is the one she wants to have as an ally. Perceval has been useful, but it's Stammer who had serious presence; she's the one who could pull some strings, if needed. JJ hasn't been of any use so far. Mara wonders if she's gone about that relationship all wrong, feeling the need to prove herself to JJ when she should be getting to know her. That starts with opening up about herself.

Everything looks blurry through the windscreen, as the rain trickles down it. Every few seconds, a large drop falls from the tree she's parked under and really splats against the glass, the noise of it shocking her each time.

She's worried about what lies ahead. Based on what's happened at global summits like this in the recent past, the demonstrations will likely descend into rioting and looting. That is, if enough protesters manage to get into the city. Or will this demonstration be nothing like that?

Through the rain rippling on the windscreen she sees JJ coming towards the car beneath a rainbow umbrella and carrying a khaki backpack. She also has a canvas shopping bag hanging from one elbow, while the hand not holding the umbrella balances a cardboard tray containing a pair of coffees.

Mara leans across and opens the passenger door.

"Sorry I'm late," JJ says, passing the coffees to Mara. "Supply run."

"No worries. Thanks for getting all this."

Mara places the holder on the middle seat, then helps JJ put the backpack on the narrow rear seat, next to her own backpack. The canvas shopping bag goes on the floor, a few apples spilling out. JJ gets in. She gives the umbrella a few shakes outside before fixing it closed and shutting the door.

"Woah," she says. "This better not be an omen."

"I bet the sun's shining down south."

JJ gets settled in the seat. "Hamburg just has the wettest rain."

"Isn't all rain wet?"

"I don't know why, but even when it drizzles here, you feel drenched within five minutes."

Mara starts the car. "I've always liked the rain here. It washes everything away."

"Thanks for the ride. We can talk in here, right?"

"I don't have my phone."

"Me neither."

"We're off the grid in this old yellow duck."

JJ smiles. "Will we even make it to Stuttgart?"

"Slow and steady will win this race." Mara backs onto the road. "We would have less chance on the train. We'd go all that way just to get turned back around."

"And there's no way I'd sit on the floor of some van for seven hours with Gomez and his crew."

"Agreed. That sounds hellish."

Mara gets them to the Reeperbahn. They stop at the traffic lights, near the Davidwache police station. People dart across the street, jackets up over their heads.

Both sip coffee.

"Ah, black as night," Mara says. "You remembered. Thanks."

"You don't like milk?"

"Milk is for muesli. I want to taste the coffee. I really like eating coffee beans from shots of Sambuca."

Another smile from JJ. "What's the plan? Are you precious about letting other people drive your car?"

"I've barely had it for 24 hours, and I love this thing. I'm happy to split the driving with you."

The light turns green. Mara drives forward, narrowly missing a guy blindly running across the intersection.

"The rain makes people crazy."

"So does the heat," JJ says. "When it's actually hot."

"Yeah. Sorry there's no music." Mara points to the gap in the dashboard where the radio should be. "The way I see it, we both know things about each other we probably shouldn't. So, why don't we just run with that? We've got the whole day to regale each other with stories from our wild pasts. What do you think? No secrets in this car?"

"That's very forward. But I like the idea of us being honest with each other, especially as things didn't start that way between us."

"That's right. This is our chance to change that."

"But within reason. We shouldn't be forced to talk about anything we don't want to."

"No total confessions. Just interesting stuff to pass the time. I'd really like to get to know you, JJ."

"Then why don't you start."

"Okay. Let me think."

Mara drives past the ferry bridges of Landungsbrücken and the red-brick warehouses of the Speicherstadt. They get across the Elbe River and onto the Autobahn heading south, but she still hasn't said anything. She sticks to the slow lane, behind a convoy of trucks.

"Do you need a prompt?" JJ asks.

"I think I do. There's too much to choose from. Prompt me."

"What happened with Anthony? You don't have to give me every detail, but I'd feel a lot better knowing he's somewhere safe."

"I folded him into a suitcase and snuck him across the border."

"Now you're trying to prompt me."

"Did you use to do that?" Mara asks. "Back in divided Berlin?"

"Hey, we're still on you. Tell me about Anthony and I'll tell you about Charlie."

"As in checkpoint? Interesting. There's been nothing in the news today, no announcement of any arrest. So, I guess he made it. I really

324

hope so. I can't say much, but I will say he's not in Germany and he won't be known as Anthony anymore."

"Good. I felt guilty about that. About what I said yesterday. I have a responsibility to him. I shouldn't have told him to run."

"I think I overreacted too."

"You have me wrong, Mara. I'm not only ever trying to save or protect myself. I'd say I'm the exact opposite."

"In the end, you were right. Anthony's only option was to run. He's done that now. He's gone."

"Do you think you'll see him again?"

"Hard to say. Of course, I want to see him. I don't want to believe that's it."

"But not if it risks him getting caught."

"I'm sorry I laid all the blame on you in the Dragon," Mara says. "It was a heat of the moment thing. I sometimes get very protective of Anthony. We both grew up without a mother, and I tend to mother him a little."

"What happened to your mother?"

"Slow down. It's your turn. Tell me about how you smuggled people out of East Berlin."

"I thought you'd want me to go straight into the details of me being a Stasi informer."

"I assume the two are connected. Aren't they?"

JJ nods. "They are. It was an amazing time. I don't think I ever felt so alive. Everything mattered. Each day, it seemed like everything was on the line. Can you imagine how that was?"

"I can't."

"Berlin was the nucleus of the world then. Every second person was a spy or an informer. You wouldn't believe the lengths people were willing to go to just to escape East Germany."

"But you were in West Berlin. How were you involved?"

"I helped with receiving people as they came over, if they made it across. Plenty of people tried and failed."

"How did you do that if you were also working for the Stasi?"

JJ is quiet for a moment, then says, "I didn't do it willingly. No one did. They had leverage on me. I had no choice."

"Money?"

"The Stasi were far more ruthless than that. Money didn't matter to them. No, they were devious. They went after the people you cared

325

about. Your friends, family, lovers, children. They just had to find your weak point and trap you."

"But you're American. You didn't have any family in Berlin."

"I had Nate."

"Oh, that's awful. They used your child to recruit you?"

"They threatened, at the start. But when I wouldn't cooperate, they took him. He was barely a year old." JJ grimaces at the memory. "Nate's father, Alex, he was a doctor. Still interning when we met. God, I was so young. That was when I was working nights as a nurse. Alex's family was one of those that was split by the Wall. His mother was in East Berlin. His father was in West Berlin. There were lots of families like that."

"What happened?"

"These bastards came in the middle of the day. In broad daylight. They knew my schedule. I was asleep. I had Nate in the room with me. They took him."

"Oh, my God."

"He ended up with Alex's mother, who wasn't a bad woman. But that was where Nate would stay unless I started cooperating. Worth remembering that East Germany wasn't exactly teeming with people of colour back then. Nate would've had a terrible time growing up there. I had to get him back. That meant becoming an informer."

"JJ, I'm so sorry."

"That's how the world was. The Stasi knew everything about me, including the role I played helping the smugglers. They told me to keep doing this, but to help them stop certain people from getting out. Not the ordinary citizens with dead-end jobs who dreamed of the west. The professionals. The doctors and engineers and scientists. They needed to stop them from leaving."

"It's all so hard to believe. A government organisation, manipulating people like that."

"They destroyed lives. Literally. That was another thing kept quiet in East Germany. The suicide rate."

"I remember my father saying something about that, that East Germany had one of the highest rates in the world."

"What a lot of people forget is that no one at the time saw the end coming. Everyone in Berlin, on both sides, fully accepted the Wall and thought it would be there for a long time. It was part of the fabric of everyone's lives. That was why many people on the east side had no hope. I say this because Nate was kidnapped just a few months before the Wall fell. But at the time, I felt like I'd sold my soul to the Stasi in exchange for my son, and that's how my life would be from then on."

They drive for a while in silence. Autobahn 7, three lanes wide and the key artery connecting the north and south in this part of western Germany, is surprisingly bare. There's a smattering of trucks and campervans keeping in the right lane, along with slow vehicles like Mara's. Sports cars and large SUVs speed down the left lane, despite the rain, silver and black blurs sending up mists of spray in their wakes. Even though there's little traffic, some cars trundle along in the middle lane. It makes Mara think of Russell and his space article; Germany's middle class, using their mid-priced cars to metaphorically lay their towels on the Autobahn's middle lane.

"I like to think now," JJ says at last, "that the Stasi using people to manipulate others was one of the things that brought East Germany down. Because nobody likes to be manipulated or exploited. They sowed hatred within their own people, under the banner of security. All those people who started protesting, meeting in churches and marching in Leipzig, a lot of them were wronged by the Stasi. Wronged at a very personal level, like I was. We marched in West Berlin for the same reason. To change the world."

"Then it changed."

"Out of nowhere. It was the most incredible thing. All these people, on both sides, instigating this revolution. No shots were fired. No armies mobilised. It was peaceful and completely people-driven. If anything, it was a massive party. East Germany, Poland, Hungary and Czechoslovakia. Dominoes falling along the Iron Curtain. The protesters completely changed the political landscape of Europe, which had been there since 1945."

"Were you there? At the Wall?"

"Sure. Everyone was. This was history, being made, right there and then. No one was going to miss it. And we all wanted that fucking monstrosity gone. It's hard to imagine anything like that ever happening again."

"So, you don't think we're going to change the world in Stuttgart?" Mara asks.

"There aren't the right circumstances for it, and not enough people want it. I would never say this at a meeting, or even at Elbe

Help. But on this no-secrets road trip, I can speak my mind. It feels good to do so."

"Doesn't it?"

"Back then, we had the Wall. This physical thing we all looked at and could focus on. We knew who the enemy was. We knew what we were fighting for and what was at stake. Can we say the same now?"

"What about Vilem and his war on oppression?"

"I'm not convinced," JJ says, shaking her head. "It presupposes there's someone behind it. Who's doing this oppressing? The government? The police? One specific person? This use of oppression is like Bush and his War on Terror. A kind of universal branding. A justification."

"There's definitely been a police crackdown in the last few weeks. Plus, this conspiracy to frame Anthony."

"True, but do you really think the entire German police force is full of such bad people? Everyone knows there are right-wingers in there, but they're the minority. I can't believe the police would start shooting protesters tomorrow."

"No, but you can be sure there'll be batons and pepper spray."

"What's your take on it? You were in the police. They're mostly good people, right?"

Mara thinks of the Kollwitzkiez police station, her last reference point. With Spitz ousted, and now dead by his own hand, Lauter had somehow parlayed being the snitch into becoming the temporary station leader.

"Same shit, different arsehole," she says to herself.

"What?"

"Nothing."

"Come on. It's your turn. I gave you a lot."

"You did. I'm grateful."

"Repay that. How right-wing is the police?"

"To be honest," Mara says, "I don't know. It can depend on who's running the station, and also on where it is. Definitely a minority in Berlin, but there could still be lots of cops who keep their politics to themselves. Now, you go outside Berlin and into the towns and villages of the old east, things are very different out there."

"That doesn't surprise me. Would you say a minority is ten per cent?"

"If you want to play a numbers game, then, yeah, ten per cent would mean something. Even five per cent would. Because there are about 50,000 police officers in Germany. Five per cent would mean 2,500 potential supporters of the far right."

"I wonder what it's like in the army."

"Just as high, I'd say. Again, depending on who's running things and where. If the head of the unit is a right-winger, he would probably want similar-thinking people under him."

"Or her."

"Sure. There are just as many right-wing women out there. With a police station, the boss wants the kind of people who will support him. Or her. People with extreme views often gravitate towards each other. To form their own little tribe."

"I don't like the word tribe. It makes me think too much of colonialism. Maybe it's more they find a family."

"That's how Zina described. She found her second family in the police. It was more diverse when she joined, before the family became fucked up and a wicked uncle tried to fool around with all the girls."

"Who's Zina again?"

"A very good friend. You'll meet her in Stuttgart. We're going to stay with her."

"Good. That saves us sleeping rough in one of the parks. I'm too old for that."

In the silence that follows, Mara undertakes a car that's camped in the middle lane and crawling along, windscreen wipers at maximum. The middle-aged couple in the car stare stoically straight ahead.

"Why did you leave Berlin?"

JJ looks at Mara. "I'm not really sure I can tell you that."

"You don't have to. No secrets, but no obligations either."

"I haven't thought about it in a long time. It's one of those things you work very hard to bury inside yourself."

Mara really wants to know. "Another east-west story?"

"Yes, but it ran deeper than that."

"Racial?"

JJ nods. "I'd consider a slavery analogy, but that might be too deep and disrespectful to those who suffered real slavery."

"The Stasi made you ... their slave?"

"Just about. The rhetoric was always about cooperation and

329

exchange. More accurate was ownership. They owned me."

"Horrid."

"You know, my grandmother, bless her, had 'coloured' written on her birth certificate. I still have it. Can you believe that? 'Coloured'. Her grandmother didn't have a birth certificate at all. What she had was a certificate of ownership. I know I shouldn't have thought about it in this way, but there I was in West Berlin, feeling like my great-great-grandmother. Owned by a white man."

"But all that was over once the Wall fell, wasn't it? You could've packed up and gone back to the States."

"I thought about it. Alex and I were no longer together, but I still wanted him around, as Nate's father. West Berlin, and then Berlin, was a far more open and tolerant society than I'd ever experienced in the States, even on the west coast. I didn't want Nate growing up over there. One of the reasons I left Tacoma in the first place was because I didn't want to be seen as black first and a person second. It wasn't perfect here, but it was a lot better. For the most part, I was a person. I lost that for a while, because of the Stasi. Then I got it back."

"How?" Mara asks. "You don't have to answer. If it's too hard, or maybe incriminating, you can hold back."

"It's definitely incriminating. I killed my handler."

"What?"

"Slashed his wrists in the bath. Made it look like the kind of suicide the East Germans had always tried to cover up."

"JJ, really, you don't have to tell me this."

"I want to. Because I'm in it now. I'm there. I'm standing in his office. I'm holding Nate's hand. He's not making a sound, like he's as scared as I am. It's the foreign office in Berlin, where this guy works now. I need to renew my residency permit. I thought all the Stasi stuff was behind me, but here he is, right in front of me, still a bureaucrat, deciding whether I get to stay here or not. It's three years after unification, and I'm back to having this white devil owning me all over again. The guy who stole my baby while I slept after working a twelve-hour night shift in a hospital. Now it's me he wants. He wants possession of my body."

"That's awful, JJ."

"That's life. There are some people, they just want to own others. They want to hold your fate in their hands. Play God. They control you and it's just devastating how often they try to use it to their own advantage. You have to fight to get it back from them. To get back control. Because I am nobody's slave."

"JJ, I think this is going too far."

"I killed that motherfucker. It was easy. He wanted me, so I went to him. The deal was to have dinner at his place, and he would give me my new permit at the end of the evening. A trade. Sex for a piece of paper." JJ takes a deep breath. "I stole a syringe full of tranquiliser and some plastic gloves from the hospital. I dressed up real nice and went to his place and smiled like I was going along with things. When he had his back to me, I jammed that needle in his neck. The look on his face when he turned around, I'll never forget that. I owned him, and he knew it. Oh, that felt good. It felt like I was doing it for every woman in my family who came before me, and that was all the motivation I needed to finish the job."

Mara glances at JJ, whose face is firm and proud, free of any hint of regret.

"I dragged him into the bathroom," JJ continues. "He was so heavy. Like he weighed far more than he should. He had this huge apartment, in Friedrichshain. No doubt a benefit from being in the Stasi that carried over to the new Germany. He'd told me he was divorced and lived there alone, but he had a couple of rooms set up for when his kids visited. I couldn't look in those rooms. I just did what I had to do. Got him in the bathtub and helped him slash his wrists with a razor. He bled like a pig. I stood there until he was dead. There was so much blood in the tub, it looked like he was taking a bath in it. I grabbed my permit, got out of there and never looked back. Left for Hamburg the next day, with Nate."

"You got away with it."

"That man would've owned me forever if I hadn't done something."

"Wasn't there an investigation?"

"Are you planning to rat on me?"

No. Why should I? It was over three decades ago."

"As far as I'm concerned, he killed himself. Trying to own me again was suicide. That's what I've told myself all these years. Back then, ex-Stasi were jumping off buildings all over the city. What was one more?" JJ sighs. "I'm so glad I told you this. I can't believe I carried it for so long. I feel … unburdened."

"Maybe we should stop this. I was wrong even to suggest it. No secrets? Stupid idea. Sorry."

"No. This is good. This is really good. Better than any kind of therapy. It's so liberating to talk."

"I think we'll have to stop anyway."

"Why?"

"Because there is no way I can top that."

JJ absolutely roars with laughter, letting it out like she's been holding it in for more than half her life. Mara laughs as well, and it feels so good to laugh with someone like this. As they undertake yet another slow middle-lane vehicle, Mara sees the two people turn to look at her and JJ laughing so hard.

Mara lowers the window and shouts, "Get out of the middle lane, idiots." She winds the window back up. "Oh, thank you, JJ. For sharing that story with me. I feel honoured."

"That was all for me. Now you. Let's get something big off your shoulders. You owe me something now. That way, we'll both get to Stuttgart feeling emotionally lighter than before."

"And somehow bound to each other."

"Yeah."

Mara wonders if this was actually JJ's intention, with her big reveal. "I never killed anyone, that's for sure."

"Not even as a police officer?"

"No."

"You're pretty lethal with your fists," JJ says. "You never got close?"

Mara chews her bottom lip. "Sort of. In juvie."

"You were in juvie?"

"A couple of stints, yeah. Looking back, it was all just a big cry for help. Trying to get attention."

"Whose?"

"My father. Zina. Maybe even my mother. She left us when I was eight. She worked in the BND. Probably still does."

"Foreign intelligence?"

"I thought maybe if I got my name in a system, it would throw up a flag or two, and she'd come in from the cold and rescue me."

"Did that happen?"

"No. But juvie was good, in some ways. The structure. The discipline. I kind of needed it, at the time. Maybe in another life, I

332

would've gone into the army to get that."

"Or the police. Which you did."

"Eventually. Juvie was an important part of the journey. I met Susie there."

"Our Susie? She was there?"

"Getting pulverised. Juvie's not like prison. They don't have resources for, like, guards or security or whatever. You might have 50 girls in a block and one person watching over them. A lot can go unnoticed. Most of it was bullying, and Susie was an immediate target."

"Because she's small?"

"Not that. You don't know about her family?"

"I just know she's Susie and she wants to save every living creature. And she's a talker. I told her about not taking the trains, to spread the word."

"Good move."

"So, what about her family?" JJ asks.

"They own a big chunk of the harbour. Really old Hamburg family, well-established."

"Ah, she's just another little rich kid raising hell with a safety net. Did she pay you to be her bodyguard?"

"Back then, I didn't know who she was. Some girls were beating up on her, taking her stuff, and I stepped in. She seemed so helpless. So, I got involved. I only found out later about the harbour connection."

"Still, you fought for Susie when she couldn't. Or were you trying to establish yourself as queen of the joint? You have that air about you. That you want to take charge."

"Don't worry. I'm not gunning for your position. But that was definitely part of it. Not being the queen. Just to be left alone. Establishing yourself as someone not to be fucked with in a place like that means people will stay away from you. Anyway, there was this one girl who wouldn't leave Susie alone. Even after I knocked her out, she kept coming back. Each time I decked her, she would go off and recover. Then she'd be back, and it would start all over again. It reached the point where I thought she was enjoying it. Like it filled some gap inside her. Or dulled something, made her forget stuff she wanted to forget. Sorry. I'm rambling. There were some pretty fucked up girls in juvie.

333

"I can believe it."

"I was one of them. I was working through my own shit in there. This girl just added to it. I thought the only way to break the cycle was to hurt her so bad she'd have to go to hospital."

"And? Did you?"

Mara pictures the scene. The damp bathroom that reeked of bleach. The circle of girls, who were so bored that watching a fight was tantamount to entertainment. The girls in the same white clothes so it looked like they were all test subjects in some secret lab experiment. Susie moving around, taking bets. Mara with a ripped-up bra to protect her knuckles. Her opponent, big and bulky and strangely pretty, smiling to reveal her chipped teeth as she shuffled forward.

"When you box," Mara says, "like in a proper fight with referees and judges, and you're winning, there's sometimes a moment when you know you've got your opponent and they're just somehow staying on their feet. The ref should stop the fight, or a trainer should throw in a towel, but that doesn't happen. In that moment, and it's a really brief moment that stretches in time, you know that any further punches could cause some serious damage. Honourable boxers, those who have been taught well and taught right and who respect their opponents, will hold back. They'll wait for the boxer to go down, or they'll step forward and hit them just hard enough so they go down. Don't believe the movies, where people can supposedly take blow after blow to the head. It only takes one decent punch in the right place to knock someone out. That said, proper boxers shouldn't go into the ring trying to hurt someone. If they're trying to do that, they're boxing for the wrong reasons and they should go do the cage stuff, which might explain why MMA has grown in popularity. Because it strikes me that in MMA, the fighters are all trying to hurt each other and it's an underground fight club where ruthlessness and violence are celebrated."

"I've never heard someone talk about boxing like that. It's fascinating. If I understand correctly, you're saying you held back on this girl."

"No, I crossed the line. I got her to that point, swaying and just about out on her feet, and I hit her as hard as I could. Even before I did it, I knew it was wrong. I felt like I'd broken a sacred code. Within the sport, but more importantly, within myself. I'd used these special

334

skills that I'd trained and honed since I was eight years old to really hurt someone. As all the girls cheered in the bathroom and made me feel like some kind of champion, I felt like a monster. I knew right then I'd never box again. Not officially or competitively. That was it. I was done."

"I think you were too hard on yourself. They were extraordinary circumstances."

Mara wonders if JJ is referring to herself, outwardly justifying that ex-Stasi murder.

"Maybe. But I lost my integrity. A person is nothing without their integrity. I didn't box after that because I'd gone against the gods. Zina always said, 'Don't fuck with the boxing gods, because they will fuck with you.' Even if I'd tried to get back into it and fight my way up, I was sure the gods wouldn't have allowed it. I'd have ended up being pummelled by an opponent who would show me no mercy, as I had shown no mercy in the juvie bathroom."

"What happened to the girl?"

"She needed her jaw wired and was in hospital for a month, so I heard. I was out by then."

"They let you out? After you put a girl in hospital?"

"Officially, she fell. Slipped on bleach in the bathroom. The one thing you don't want to be in juvie is a snitch, and the absolute last thing you'd do is snitch on the girl who could break your jaw."

"They probably thought they'd be next."

"That whole thing was well in place before I did my first stint. It's a terrible rule, because it encourages people to look the other way. Sometimes the truth needs to be told. It takes a brave person to stand up, buck the trend and do what's right. Someone should've snitched on me. I deserved it."

"Do you think anyone will try to tell the truth, with the cover-up of Marten?"

"Doubt it." Mara considers telling JJ what Detective Stammer had said, about other officers having medical problems that day, potentially from tainted water, but decides to hold this back, for now. "It's too big anyway. It's the kind of thing the police should confront themselves."

"That's not how it happened with the sexual abuse scandal. That came from the media."

"The media was the conduit, but it came from the police. From my

335

friend Zina and a few others. They took the story public to force the police to respond. And it worked."

They pass the first exit signs for Hannover.

"I'm really looking forward to meeting your friend Zina," JJ says.

"She's dynamite."

"Are you all right driving?"

"Let's swap at the first bathroom break."

"Deal." JJ reaches for the canvas bag. "Hungry?"

"What are you offering? A road trip like this calls for junk food, doesn't it?"

"Only healthy stuff. An apple?"

Mara reaches out a hand and JJ puts an apple in it.

"I'm really glad we're doing this," Mara says. "Driving together and talking."

"Yeah."

They bite into their apples at the same time.

**

The sun is setting when they reach the outskirts of Stuttgart, the trip having been extended by two hours as JJ wanted to visit the Cathedral of Saint Salvator and Fulda's other churches. This resulted in them wandering the old town and having a long lunch on the square opposite the wood-framed city hall. They'd left the rain in the north and Fulda was awash with sunshine, making it ridiculously pleasant to sit on the square and consume coffee and cake like the locals.

Mara, at the wheel again, is surprised to see a police checkpoint set up just after the turn-off towards the Unterer Schloßgarten. JJ is asleep, her neck cradled in the seatbelt and her head on a folded pullover pressed against the window.

There's no avoiding it. They get stuck in the line of traffic, edging towards the checkpoint. She lowers the window and sticks her head out, as other drivers do, and sees that the police are checking IDs. There are two female police officers, in yellow vests, each working a lane of traffic on the driver's side of the cars. They don't take much time with each vehicle, giving the IDs a cursory glance at most.

As they draw nearer, Mara gets things ready: her ID card, driver's license and vehicle registration, which is still in Bernd's name. She also considers what to say, how to justify being in Stuttgart, in someone else's car. She reaches across to wake JJ, then decides to let her sleep; to let that be part of their story, that they're two friends on a road trip to visit another.

No cars have been pulled aside, and no one has been asked to leave a vehicle. It's all happening rather swiftly, like it's just for show.

The car in front is sent on and Mara is waved forward.

"Evening," the police officer says with a toothy smile. She has BAER on her uniform. "Can I see your ID, please?"

"Sure." Mara passes it through the window.

"A Berlin address and a vehicle with Hamburg plates, all the way down here with us. Can you explain that?"

"I recently moved back to Hamburg, and just bought this car yesterday. I've got all the documents, if you want to see them."

"Why haven't your registered in Hamburg?"

"There wasn't time to do the car, and with my address, I've just been lazy. I need to do this when I get back. Not easy finding an apartment in Hamburg."

"Same here. Rents are skyrocketing. Any apartment viewing gets hundreds of people."

"Sounds like you're looking for one."

"I am. Just split up with my boyfriend. Need to get out of that toxic environment."

"Don't let men define your life. Take control."

"Yeah." Baer clears her throat. "So, what's your business in the city?"

"Visiting a friend. Zina Koranteng. She's also in the police."

"Zina?" Baer leans down on the window. "We were at the Ostheim station together. About five years ago."

"She was my boxing coach growing up. We've stayed close ever since."

"Love Zina." With a look inside the car, Baer says, "And you brought her mum with you."

Mara smiles, but doesn't reply.

"She's beautiful, like Zina," Baer says, almost in a whisper. "I don't want to wake her."

Mara keeps on smiling.

Baer hands Mara her ID card. "You get going. Say hi to Zina for me."

"Thanks. I will."

Baer steps back and gets in position to beckon the next vehicle.

"Hey, uh, what's going on?"

"The G8 summit. There are checkpoints like this all over the city. Just as a precaution. Get moving now. We don't want to hold these people up too long."

"Of course. Stay safe."

Mara drives forward. But she's too quick releasing the clutch and the car jolts, waking JJ. She's slow to get her eyes open and rubs them a few times.

"Are we here?"

"You were out for nearly two hours. I have to say it really dragged. I missed all the revelations."

"It was that big lunch."

"Zina's place is nearby. I just got to figure out where to park this beast."

They both look out the window. There are no outward signs of preparation in this part of the city. But when they skirt the south side of the central station, they see barriers set up along the roads and police vans parked in rows.

JJ sits up. "It's going to be on tomorrow. Look at how easily we got into the city."

"There aren't many people around the station. I guess a lot of trains really were stopped."

"But we just drove straight in. Others will too."

"It might be different tomorrow, if they try to stop all the protesters coming here for the day."

Mara turns the car up the hill towards Diemershalde. Once again, she's making an educated guess of where Gaisburgstraße is, and then happens on it. Parking is easy, the street relatively free of cars.

"They've all escaped," JJ says. "Left the city for the weekend."

Mara parks the car and turns the engine off. "Or they moved their cars somewhere else. Out of danger. I hope mine's safe."

They take their backpacks from the rear seat and get out, groaning in unison after spending almost the whole day in the cab, then walk close together, in step along the footpath.

***

338

"I'm going to bed," Mara says.

"So early?" JJ asks.

"Lame," Zina says. "You barely made it to the end of round one."

They're sitting in the kitchen, crammed around the little table that's littered with empty plates and glasses that still hold the dregs of red wine.

Mara stands and pushes the new chair up to the table. "I did a lot of driving today, while others just slept."

"Your old truck is surprisingly comfortable," JJ says.

"Truck?" Zina asks.

"My Ford Ranger. Lemon yellow and bought yesterday. It's parked outside. You can't miss it."

"I saw that thing. That's yours?"

"Yes, and you can't have it."

"I'm so proud of you, M. You finally own something."

"I do. I'm growing. Now, goodnight, you two."

Zina and JJ chorus "Goodnight" in return. As she leaves the kitchen, Mara stops at the doorway to see Zina refilling JJ's wine glass, JJ signalling that she only wants half a glass.

In the small living room, Mara decides to take the camping mat on the floor, leaving the sofa for JJ. She didn't have the foresight to bring a sleeping bag, but Zina has given her one for the night. She pulls it out of its sack and flattens it, breathing in the mustiness of sleeps from years ago.

"Bad girl," she says, as she lies down and gets settled, admonishing herself for going to bed without brushing her teeth. This makes her feel, along with the hard surface she's lying on, like she's camping. She closes her eyes and imagines such a scene, roughing it with Zina and JJ. Somewhere south, Italy or Croatia, on the coast. It's a warm night and they've been out in the sun all day. She's the first into the tent, while her surrogate parents stay up late, drink wine and talk.

"How long have you lived here?" she hears JJ ask.

"Over ten years," Zina says. "I was transferred. From Hamburg."

"You never wanted to go back?"

"Every day. Just never got the chance."

"Did you grow up there?"

"I was born in Bremen. We moved to Chemnitz later on."

"How was that?"

"How do you think? Very difficult. Every single day was like something you had to get through rather than enjoy. But it was motivating. It's the kind of place you find yourself fighting really hard to get out of. It pushed me to reach a point where I could leave on my own, like I'd beaten the city."

"I know that feeling. What about your parents?"

"Mum moved straight back to Bremen after my dad died. She couldn't get out of there fast enough either."

Mara, her eyes still closed and very snug in the sleeping bag, is finding it comforting to listen to JJ and Zina. She fights her fatigue, to stay awake and privy to their conversation.

"How did Mara come into your life?" JJ asks.

"She was eight years old. A puny little thing."

JJ laughs.

"She was feisty, even then. But scrawny, like she was underfed. I was worried that her parents weren't taking proper care of her."

"Did you meet her mother?"

"I saw her, but I only ever spoke with her once, when she first brought Mara to the gym."

"Gus's gym?"

"You know it?"

"It's down the road from Elbe Help. That's a charity I run."

"Nice. I'm not sure why she brought Mara there. She didn't seem to have any interest in boxing. I mean, it's not like little Mara was begging her parents to box. It felt more like Agnes was dumping Mara on us, thinking we would be some kind of fitness-focused babysitter."

"I bet a lot of parents would think of the gym like that."

"Or they think their kids are hyper and boxing will help them get rid of their energy and aggression."

"What about Mara's father?" JJ asks.

"I met him later, after Agnes was gone. At the start, it was only Agnes who brought Mara to the gym."

"Maybe she was having an affair, with someone living near the gym?"

This makes Mara open her eyes.

"That had crossed my mind. Some kind of ulterior motive. Even though it was none of my business. Agnes struck me as a planner. Someone smart and organised. But she didn't strike me as a cheater.

You know, with some people, regardless of how they look or act, you can just sense they like to fool around, that they'll do the dirty on you."

"Oh, I know."

"But she seemed loyal to me. Honest and genuine. But distant."

"Distant? How so?"

"Like she wanted to be somewhere else. They had money. Mara's father was a lawyer. They lived in Othmarschen. It all seemed pretty perfect, from the outside looking in."

"It always does, and it never is. She left."

"She did."

"Do you know why? Mara isn't exactly open when talking about it."

"I respect that," Zina says, her tone a little less conversational. "If she doesn't want to say anything, then I won't either. But I will say Agnes just stopped bringing Mara, from one day to the next. Richard, her father, did it for a while. Then, Mara was riding to the gym on her own. She often ran there, to improve her fitness. She had so much potential. She had the drive, back then. The engine inside that you need to have to get really good at something."

"Was she? Good?"

"Oh yeah. I made it to the Olympics, which was huge, but driven mainly by me wanting to get out of Chemnitz. Without doubt, 15-year-old Mara would've taken the 15-year-old me out in the first round. She could've won medals. Maybe even gold. Who knows what she could've been as a pro? She needed a new coach, when she was 14, because the level of coaching has to match the level the boxer's aspiring to. I'd taken Mara as far as I could. We were so close though. I didn't want her out of my life. A new coach would've meant a new gym, and I was really scared I'd lose her."

Mara fights the urge to cry.

"But you did lose her."

"I did. I fucked it all up."

"You mean this Spitz guy fucked it all up."

"Okay. Mara told you about that. Yeah, it's me in that article. But I don't blame Spitz. He's not the master of my destiny. What happened to me is on me. I did the right thing at the time by speaking up and calling Spitz out for what he did to me, but I know now I should've done it differently. I should've trapped him. Got the leverage I needed

341

to ensure my position would be safe and only he would suffer. My mistake was believing there would be people in the police who would want guys like Spitz to be caught and punished. Instead, they just wanted to cover it all up."

"Not anymore. You exposed him."

"Too late, really. All the damage was done. My exile down here. My stalled career. My reputation. All the other women he got to after me. I could've stopped it."

"I read last night that he shot himself."

"That's no shock. Guys like him, they're weak, and they hate themselves for being so weak. That's why they abuse women, to make themselves feel strong. But no matter how many women they abuse, that weakness, that frailty, it remains, and it eats them up inside. They have a hole created by their cowardice and insecurity they can't fill."

"That's really well said."

"I bet it was a relief for him that it was all over. He was exposed and he could go off somewhere and end it."

"You sound like you regret speaking out."

"I regret not doing it sooner. But yeah, I also regret doing it now. They're going to come after me. Someone just has to dig into the records, go looking for women who worked with Spitz. Women, like me, who filed official complaints. The police try desperately to hide these things, but someone will find it, probably before Spitz is even buried. And when they do, that'll be the end of my career. It's just a matter of time."

"Meaning you will come out on the losing end of all this."

"Isn't that how it always goes? A woman just takes it and she's a victim, then she stands up and she's a bitch."

"Also well said."

"To be honest, what happened in Hamburg took me totally by surprise. I was shocked by what he did and how he did it. That he even tried. I thought we were way past this sort of thing."

"The human male is a creature evolving very, very slowly."

"Some are going backwards. Anyway, I'm ready for it. I know I'm done. If I get named as one of the article's sources and that ends my career, then so be it."

"What will you do then?"

"Move back to Hamburg. Ten years here and I still feel like a visitor. Never made any close friends. Hardly ever go on dates. They talk so much about the difference in Germany being east and west. But I think there's a much bigger difference between north and south."

"Maybe."

"I never settled here. These aren't my people. I never got along with them. That's not because of my skin colour. It's a character thing. I've got a northern character."

"I like that. A northern character. But I think the east-west divide is still pretty big."

"I have no plans to move back to Chemnitz, that's for sure."

They laugh together, like old friends. In the lull that follows, Mara closes her eyes again. She can feel sleep coming, like a weight settling on her.

"Thanks for letting me stay here," JJ says.

"No problem at all. Any friend of Mara's is a friend of mine. Except that guy she brought here last week who ruined my kitchen chair."

"What guy?"

The sound of the door closing wakes her. The first thing that registers is that she's alone in the apartment. The second is the stiffness she feels down her left side, especially at the hip and shoulder, from sleeping on a thin camping mat that barely provided any semblance of cushioning. She rolls onto her stomach and rests her chin on the pillow, her arms underneath. The sofa is neat. JJ's sleeping bag is gone, as is her backpack. Zina would've been first out the door, with all of Stuttgart's police on duty today from dawn, meaning JJ has probably just left, to get to the protest meeting point early.

While she loves Zina, and feels a certain closeness to JJ after the revelatory road trip, she's glad to be alone. The silence is good. It's tempting to skip the demonstration, crawl up onto the sofa and go back to sleep. But she needs to be there, to bear witness, be present. So, she heaves herself up and does a dozen quick push-ups to get her heart going. Barefooted, she pads to the bathroom, looking into Zina's bedroom on the way; the covers look kicked off, Zina having got up in a hurry.

She showers and brushes her teeth, then inspects her various wounds in the mirror. Her forehead is scarred, and there's bruising around her shoulder still, from being hit by the baton two weeks ago. Her knuckles have thin, yellowish scabs. In the kitchen, wrapped in a towel, she sees that everything from last night has been cleared up and put away. It's spotless. The oven's red digital clock shows 0756.

There's a note on the table that reads: Duty calls. Take the spare key and stay safe out there. Z.

Underneath that: Same here. JJ

She wonders why JJ didn't wake her.

She puts the kettle on and spoons instant coffee into a cup.

Back in the living room, the outfit she packed for the protest comes on piece by piece: blue jeans, white t-shirt and black St Pauli hoodie. There had been no mention at Monday's meeting in the Otzenstraße bunker of wearing yellow shirts. But what she does have is a yellow balaclava, with plastic eye covers, that Tinaya made for her on Tuesday. Looking at it, she thinks it is the same lemony colour as her pick-up.

She's not hungry, her unsettled stomach betraying the

344

nervousness and trepidation she thinks it's right to feel. The way she felt pre-fight, when she would turn that nervous energy into humour; crack jokes to make it seem she was calm and relaxed. But there's no one to banter with now.

In the kitchen, she makes and quickly drinks a coffee, then places an apple in the front pocket of her hoodie. The balaclava, neatly folded, goes into that pocket too. She considers what else to take, not wanting to enter the fray with too much stuff on her. A €20 note goes into the front pocket of her jeans.

"I need Gus to hire me at the gym," she says to herself. That would solve the money situation, and she'd much rather be coaching girls than policing the streets. She rinses the cup out and steels herself to face the day. She's on the protester side; her days in police uniform are over. There's no going back, certainly not to a Kollwitzkiez station run by Lauter.

But she definitely misses Russell. She thinks getting him to move to Hamburg would be ideal.

The gym. Becoming a boxing coach. Never wearing the uniform again. Moving Russ to Hamburg. All these plans she's making for the future when today is supposed to be the first day in the war on oppression. Vilem is scheduled to give a speech at 0900 in the Stadtgarten at the university to kick off the protest march towards Schloßplatz, via the central station. She needs to get down there. The last thing she takes is a disposable camera from her backpack. This goes in the hoodie's front pocket as well, which bulges in obvious and unsightly fashion, like that of a careless shoplifter.

The spare set of keys is hanging by the door. She takes it, pulls the door closed and double locks it.

Outside, the morning is grey and foggy. Her car has a layer of moisture on it, but not nearly enough to clean it. She runs a finger down the left side, cutting a line through the moisture that leaves the tip of her index finger wet and brown.

It's quiet. There's no one on Gaisburgstraße. The first store she passes is closed. The further she walks, down towards the city centre, she sees everything is closed. The locals have either left the city or are staying indoors for the day.

It's strange to walk through Diemershalde on a Friday morning with no people or cars on the streets. The narrow roads usually clogged with cars parked bumper to bumper now seem like broad avenues.

It feels like lockdown all over again.

Her progress is impeded at Charlottenplatz, which is blocked off by police. She detours southwest, then cuts through the deserted central shopping area, void even of homeless people. She bites into the apple. Many of the stores are shuttered, their roller doors pulled down. A few places have their windows barricaded with wooden boards.

Another police blockade, this one on Theodor-Heuss-Straße, forces another detour, northwest, where she joins up with protesters heading towards the university. She takes some photos, only looking out of place for the camera she's using; everyone else, young and old, is taking photos of themselves and documenting their attendance with their phones. Social media posts don't interest her, but she would like to talk to people, to get their stories and have them explain why they are here and why it matters to them.

She thinks these people don't look anything like the soldiers Vilem would need to fight his war.

The Stadtgarten is awash with the new Modra flags she had a hand in designing. Vilem has succeeded in having these mass-produced and distributed for today. Those with nothing to raise their flags aloft wrap them around their shoulders, while others hold the flags in the air, their hands gripping the corners and letting them catch what little wind there is.

To Mara, it all looks makeshift and unconvincing, like a company handing out merchandise and people taking it because it's free. She wonders how many protesters understand the significance of the flags they are holding. One thing is for sure: it's visually unifying. All these disparate people, some who tote backpacks and have the weary eyes of people who travelled all night, look like a singular group, thanks to the Modra flags.

It's hard to pick out people in the crowd on the Stadtgarten's broad lawn. It's already full and people are still flooding in. Someone is speaking, at the front, his voice distorted and badly amplified by a megaphone. It sounds like Vilem, but she can't see him. Whoever is talking is standing at crowd level.

She moves towards the side, to skirt the crowd and get closer to the front. A hand grabs her arm, and she turns. It takes a moment for her to recognise him in street clothes.

346

"Callenberg?"

"Hey."

He's good-looking and more relaxed out of uniform as he stands, with a closeness that assumes protection, with a gaggle of teenage girls; all four of them are gathered under one flag and taking selfies.

"What are you doing here?"

"Kimberley, my daughter, she wanted to come. Wouldn't take no for an answer."

"She would've gone anyway, with or without your permission."

"Yeah, better they go with me and Thomas than on their own." Callenberg gestures towards a chunky man in his 40s, looking ridiculous with a Modra flag tied around his neck like a cape.

"Were you stopped?" she asks.

"By what? We drove straight into the city."

Mara looks at the girls. "How old are they?"

"13 and 14. Don't look so worried. They've been part of Fridays for Future for years."

"Just keep them safe."

"Everything's set up really well." Callenberg scans the crowd. "I don't see any negative elements in here."

"Be careful. We don't know what's coming."

Callenberg looks confused, like he's not getting what Mara's saying, or he doesn't believe her. Mara starts to move away; she can't help him today. She needs to find JJ.

"Wait," Callenberg says. "I told Kimberley about your boxing centre. She wants to come and try it. Would that be okay?"

"Absolutely. She'd be really welcome. Her friends too."

"Great. I like the idea of her being able to defend herself."

"It's boxing. Not self-defence."

"We'll come by next week."

"Yeah. Sure. Stay safe."

She moves around the side of the crowd, forced to drift outwards, as the crowd continues to swell, predominantly with young people; there are plenty of high schoolers, like the four girls with Callenberg, under the watch of parents. She's suddenly much more aware of the crowd's demographic, and watches many of them, wanting a flag, converge on a blue van parked in front of the library. Mara follows them. The double doors at the van's rear are splayed open. Two people inside, in white t-shirts emblazoned with the Modra flag, are

347

handing out flags from cardboard boxes to the throng of people in front, who all have their arms outstretched. Two other people, in the same white t-shirts, are picking up the plastic sheaths being dropped on the ground once the flags are unwrapped.

She takes photos of the scene with the disposable camera, then joins the crowd at the back of the van, to get a flag to take home to Tinaya. Once the boxes at the doorway are empty and have been cast aside, the two guys in the van jump down and close the doors on the remaining unopened boxes inside the van. Those who missed out pull at the shirts of the two guys as they move around either side of the van to get in the cab. Some people then bang at the sides of the van as it drives off. Disappointed, they slowly disperse back into the crowd, where the distorted and unintelligible voice continues to crackle through the megaphone. Among them is Susie, who is excited enough to see Mara that she steps forward and hugs her. Mara feels like she's being hugged by a distant cousin who once stole her boyfriend.

"You made it," Susie says, pulling back and behaving like they haven't seen each other for months.

"So did you. How was the trip?"

"Kind of fun. Kind of awful. We drove all night, in vans. We had sleeping bags and mats, but it was still pretty uncomfortable."

Mara steps back to put some distance between them. "The same vans we took to the protest?"

"You could feel every bump. Some people were sick, because there were no windows. But I slept through most of it."

Mara's very glad she drove down with JJ.

"I'm pissed I missed out on a flag," Susie continues. "Did you get one?"

"I'm sure you'll be able to pick one up before the day is over."

"I don't want a used one."

"They'll send a box to Elbe Help. That's where the flag came from anyway."

"Yeah, from you and girls in the curry-curry corner."

"The what? Don't talk like that."

Susie is offended. "Hey, I didn't come up with that name. That's what the student volunteers call them."

"They shouldn't. I'll let them know that when I'm back."

"That's one of the tamer things they say. Out of the office, they call

348

them the Burqa Bitches."

"Who the fuck do they think they are? That kind of talk is absolutely not on."

"Listen to you. Sound like a convert."

"This has nothing to do with religion, Susie. This is about respect."

"Then the Burqa Bitches should be more respectful of the country they're in and dress more like we do."

Mara turns around and walks away, to keep herself from punching Susie.

"Where's your brother?" Susie asks, hurrying to catch up.

"Not here."

They get into the crowd. Mara wants Susie gone.

"Gomez is looking for him."

"The whole country is looking for him, because Gomez ratted him out."

"No way. He didn't do that."

The crowd is too tightly packed to get closer to the front. Climbing up onto a nearby bench helps Mara get a better view. She confirms it's Vilem talking into the megaphone, but still can't understand what he's saying. JJ is a few metres away, to his right. Gomez and Jesper are also there, among the people who are mostly white men in their 20s, gathered around Vilem. She recognises a few faces from last week's meeting in Berlin.

Looking over the crowd, she wonders if they are all just waiting for the signal to start the protest properly. Plenty of people are chatting amongst themselves. While there is no coordination to how they're all dressed, the numerous flags are providing a certain uniformity.

Vilem stops talking and makes a sweeping motion with his right arm. This gets the crowd moving, though Mara notices Vilem, JJ, Gomez, Jesper and others at the front just stand there while the crowd goes past.

"Hey," Susie says. "Let's go."

Mara ignores her. She watches the protesters shuffle slowly forward, flags held up or draped over shoulders. It all looks very relaxed and calm. If there are any troublemakers in this crowd, they're doing well to hide themselves. Callenberg and his girls pass not far from her vantage point. He gives her a wave and beckons her to walk with him in an overtly friendly way, which she thinks greatly

349

increases the probability of him being a single dad. Thomas is no longer wearing the flag as a cape, perhaps having been called out for looking stupid in it by one of the girls.

Despite having taken little care with the plastic covers from the distribution van, the crowd has left almost no garbage in the Stadtgarten. What trash there is seems accidental: mandarin peel, sweets wrappers, the odd tissue. She jumps down from the bench and goes to where the leaders were standing, hoping to find JJ and walk with her, and lose Susie in the process.

But they're all gone.

The crowd thins as it moves forward. She weaves between the clumps of people towards the front. No one is carrying a banner, which has the curious effect of making this demonstration seem like it lacks a cause. The media, if they're here, will report this G8 demo as a group of mostly young people marching under the new flag of a water charity, whatever that means.

The route takes the crowd onto Kriegsbergstraße, walking towards the central train station. The police have blocked this broad street, on both sides, but as there's no traffic today in the locked-down city centre, the police presence and the barricades down both sides of the street create an overwhelming sense of confinement. Mara sees that the protesters could easily be trapped here, if the police moved to block the corner up ahead, but she doesn't think any of these protesters are here for a fight. Those who are must be somewhere else in the city. Because when she gets to the front of the crowd, there's no sign of JJ, Vilem or Gomez. She lets herself be carried forward, up towards the huge intersection at Arnulf-Klett-Platz, where the road bends towards the central station. From there, the plan is to walk down Königstraße to Schloßplatz.

Those at the front slow down and stop as riot police move into position to block off the street. It's hard to count the white helmets, as there are so many and they're all very close, strung together like pearls on a necklace. A water cannon moves between the crowd and the riot police, but is facing away from the crowd, as if ready to deal with something else. People around her start to shout, questioning why they've been stopped and wanting to know what is going on. There's pushing from behind as the march staggers to a halt. A handful of riot police come over and form a line to hold the crowd back.

Mara looks to her left. Coming down Heilbronnerstraße is what looks like several hundred protesters, all dressed in black, replete with black balaclavas. Some wave Modra flags. They pour like motor oil down the road. They move in close formation, with the wide-legged walk of men, weapons in hand: baseball bats, sledgehammers, lengths of metal, even the odd hockey stick.

Pitchforks against machine guns, she thinks. Her first reaction is to get the hell out of there, but the crowd, many of them kids, hems in behind her, to see what's going on. She's stuck, barely a metre from the police line in front.

The riot police hurriedly make a line of their own, moving forward to intercept the wave coming down Heilbronnerstraße, the water cannon manoeuvring into position ahead of them.

She says a silent prayer that there is only water in that cannon, and another prayer that all these kids will get scared and run back the way they came.

There's no pause or stand-off. No attempt at de-escalation. The protesters plough into the police. There's grunting and shouts of pain as baseball bats and metal rods thump against police shields. The water cannon sends the first streams straight down the middle of the protesters, attempting to split them and disperse those at the rear. The people around Mara begin to flee, calmly at first, then in a panic as the first volley of tear gas canisters is lobbed onto Heilbronnerstraße, into the space created by the water cannon. The riot police have gas masks and are ready for this. The protesters, in simple balaclavas, are not. As the gas hits their eyes, people let out screams that sound far different from those caused by a baton. Higher-pitched and angrier. Mara stays where she is, along with the few others who stand strong. The police swiftly move in and start arresting the protesters in black who haven't fled, looping plastic cuffs around wrists, pulling them tight, and hitting the protesters with batons for good measure. It's efficient, brutal and scary to watch. As these protesters take serious beatings, those around Mara gasp and raise hands to their mouths in disbelief. Some point phones at the scene, filming and photographing. When the police don't bother to stop this, Mara takes photos with her disposable camera, until the film is full.

Those who managed to escape arrest run towards the central station. She follows them with her eyes, looking further ahead to see

351

that a similar battle is taking place on the other side of the station. Water cannons, the green-grey smoke of tear gas, and balaclava-wearing protesters fighting with police or running for safety.

She looks around at the people standing near her, glad to see all of the kids have fled. Those remaining could get the police fighting on both sides, if they all choose to fight alongside her. The brutality she sees impels her to do something. She can't just stand here and watch, and she thinks those around her are feeling the same thing.

But they have to act now.

With a flourish, she takes the yellow balaclava from her hoodie pocket and pulls it on. She moves a step forward, getting closer to the police line, hands loose at her sides, letting the adrenalin build.

"Who's with me?" She turns around and shouts again, "Who's with me?"

The chorus of support is enough to get the police talking into their radios. Mara watches this group of people, who now feel like a battalion under her command, don balaclavas and fold flags into triangles to tie around their faces like bandit masks.

"Stay away from the water cannon and the gas," she says. "Don't get hit in the head."

Then she turns to the line of police, imagining that each of these guys is a clone of Lauter, and attacks the one in front of her. Punching, ducking, weaving, knowing full well how hard it is to move in all that gear and that she has the advantage of quickness. She gets one cop down, then another, and all around her, this group of strangers is into it as well. The police are forced to commit more officers to fight on this new front. The protesters in black take this opening to reform outside the central station and start running back. Mara is past the first line and joins the battle with those in black, jumping onto the back of a cop and yanking his helmet and gas mask off. Then, she helps a protester on the ground who's being hit by a cop. She uses the helmet as a weapon, swinging it hard into the cop's side and knocking him off the protester. She helps him to his feet and their eyes meet. Brown eyes, sharp features, Slavic, she's sure of it. He nods at her and she nods back. She grabs the fallen cop's baton and whacks him in the leg with it.

Really into it now, her body pulsing with adrenalin, she goes from one fight to another, focusing the baton on legs and kidneys, and taking a few blows to the body herself, while keeping the mantra going: don't get hit in the head.

Something explodes in the distance, sending a mushroom of black smoke above the city.

The water cannon veers back around to take aim at Heilbronnerstraße, where the police are now losing and are being driven back towards the central station. As the protesters in black make progress, they pick up batons and other weapons, and use knives to cut free their cuffed comrades.

Mara joins them, blending in with her black hoodie, but conscious of the conspicuousness of her yellow balaclava. At the far end of Heilbronnerstraße, a convoy of police vehicles is blue-lighting towards the intersection; reinforcements who will trap the protesters at this corner. She has to get out of there.

Another explosion. And another, closer by, causing those around her to instinctively duck down. Cars, she thinks. Set on fire and left to burn, until the fuel tanks explode.

She forces her way to the fringe of the fighting, sidestepping a couple of cops. There's vacant street to the right and she runs for it. A group of protesters follows her, police in pursuit. Further down the street, more cops have gathered and are walking ominously towards them.

All the shops and restaurants she passes are boarded up or shuttered. A helicopter chug-a-chug-a-chug-a-chugs overhead.

Mara and the other protesters are forced to scramble down the first street to the left. They reach the barricade at Königstraße and flood over it. A handful of protesters bringing up the rear are dragged back and cuffed by cops. There's no attempt to pursue those protesters that made it over the barricade, which leads Mara to think they're trapped here now, on the pedestrian mall between Schloßplatz and the train station. Once at the centre of the mall, she sees a street-wide line of police at the Schloßplatz end, while in front of the station, two water cannons are tail to tail, spraying protesters.

The group of protesters she's with, which includes a few who marched from the Stadtgarten, are unsure what to do. Their heads turn in every direction trying to make sense of what's going on, trying to find an escape.

"We're trapped," someone shouts.

She thinks the only chance is Schloßplatz and getting through that line.

"We need to fight through," she says, pointing towards Schloßplatz, "at that end."

She signals for those around her to form a group and follow her. Those in black speak a language she doesn't understand. But they follow her instruction and together they start moving down Königstraße.

Numbers look about even, but the police up ahead are wearing heavy and cumbersome riot gear. She turns her walk into a run, and the others match her, somehow understanding that they need the advantage of momentum and speed.

An explosion nearby makes them duck, but they don't break stride. Mara hears glass breaking and people cheering, the looting possibly already starting. There's no time to consider that, because the group collides with the police, who try to hold firm against this charge. The fights happen in close spaces, like an ultra-violent mosh pit. Mara takes down one cop with a running stiff arm to the chest, then gets in a one-on-one with a guy who looks very young under his helmet. He's holding his shield and baton like he doesn't quite know what to do with them. She moves to her left, to avoid the baton, then punches him a few times in the ribs. Lower, around the kidneys, there's less padding, and this is a good switch to aim for. She lands a solid punch on his left side and the familiar yelping "aah" that results from direct contact with a kidney is satisfying to hear. He goes down onto his knees and drops his baton to clutch his hand at his side. She steps back, ready for her next opponent, but the police are retreating. The young cop is lifted and dragged back into their ranks by a pair of colleagues, his baton swept up off the ground by a third. Then they're hustling back towards Schloßplatz, some of them limping. Those around Mara cheer and hold their weapons aloft. They start moving forward, thinking they've broken the line, but the police move barricades to completely seal this end of the street, then regroup behind them. More police arrive to fortify the position.

Now we really are trapped, Mara thinks.

The protesters in black respond to this by pulling boards off shop windows and gathering anything that will burn into two bonfire-sized piles about 20 metres from the barricade. One bonfire is set up at the base of a tree; the other around a metal bench. She sees protesters with canisters of lighter fluid and boxes of matches. As the fires begin to roar, a voice comes over a speaker, ordering the

354

protesters to put down their weapons and turn themselves in. The protesters ignore this and throw wood and anything else combustible they can find onto the fire. They smash the windows of shops and emerge with chairs, tables and boxes. The burning piles grow bigger and bigger as the protesters try to merge the two bonfires into one.

Mara keeps her distance from the fire, which produces a lot of smoke. She doesn't agree with this, but she's certainly not going to try to stop it. She looks through the flames and smoke to see if more police are gathering behind the barricade. There don't appear to be, but there are some officious-looking people in suits with ID badges dangling from their necks. They have their hands on their hips or agitatedly talk on radios and point. She looks for Perceval, but doesn't see him. Then her view is blocked by a pair of water cannons rolling ominously into position directly behind the barricade. She steps further back, expecting the cannons to douse the fire. But nothing happens.

As chaos reigns around her, she wonders if the police strategy is now to corral the various groups of protesters into this one area, this pedestrian mall, to contain the situation and prevent clashes from happening around the city. She jogs away from the fire and towards the train station end. There are hundreds of protesters running around. Some are looting shops, for food and drinks. The water cannons in front of the train station are driving the protesters from that end onto the mall. The police move in with barricades to seal that end as well, the water cannons positioned behind them. A handful of protesters leap the railing to take the stairs under the street to the station, but they're driven back, clutching their faces and eyes, by cops brandishing pepper spray.

A bonfire has also been lit at the base of a tree at this end of the mall. Anything that can burn is hurled onto it. A pile of chairs, strung together by wire outside a café, is hauled towards the fire.

Mara moves back from this fire, to position herself in the middle of the mall.

It's like a war zone. They are all trapped here.

The police have blocked both ends, plus the side road where she entered from. She wonders about the explosions and where all the other protesters are. She soon has an answer as streams of people spill out of the passageways between the shops on the mall. The dusty smoke of tear gas comes with them.

One guy running past in a balaclava has the build of Jesper. She grabs his arm and makes him stop. His clothes are soaked.

"Jesper?"

"Mara? That you?"

In this mayhem, it's a relief to find someone she knows. "What's going on?"

Jesper folds his balaclava up to his nose and really sucks in air. "We fought the cops at Charlottenplatz. But they had three water cannons and they gassed us."

"Anyone hurt?"

"Lots of people. There was a massive crowd. Thousands. That was the key meeting point from the south side."

"The cops had a big force there. I saw it this morning."

"Yeah, like they were waiting for us. They were absolutely ready for a fight."

They move to the middle of the pedestrian mall. The fires at both ends burn higher. The looting continues around them, with a steady flow of protesters emerging from a smashed-up drugstore with bottles of water to wash their faces and eyes.

"There was this moment," Jesper says, breathing more calmly, "before the fight began, when it felt like we were an army. A unified force, with people from different countries. We just didn't have any weapons. Armed, we could've tried to take the city."

"Is that what you want? To start shooting cops?"

"To level the playing field, at least."

"The cops don't have firearms when they go into battle with protesters."

"Then we need water cannons and tear gas of our own. It's not fair that we're always so outmatched. We torched a few cars, but the cannons drove us here. A lot of people just ran for it."

"What about JJ?" Mara asks. "Was she with you?"

"At the start, yeah. I don't know what happened to her. It was crazy. People were pushing each other out of the way to get to safety. The cops were beating people. Like nothing I'd ever seen before. They weren't even making arrests. They just left people bleeding on the ground."

In his agitation, he starts to pull the balaclava fully off.

"Don't," Mara says. "There are cameras everywhere here."

356

"Like that fucking matters now. We'll be lucky to get out of here alive. We're trapped here, right?"

"Come on. You need some dry clothes."

Someone's managed to break the glass door to the Galeria Kaufhof department store. Inside, protesters grab books and pads of paper to burn, while looters fill their pockets with anything valuable. That no alarms have sounded since the looting began and the lights are off inside the department store makes her wonder if the power has been cut to this area. In the dull light, they go up the frozen escalators to the clothing section. Jesper changes out of his wet clothes, leaving them in a pile on the floor. Mara swaps her St Pauli hoodie, flecked with blood, for a padded hiking jacket.

"Are you really going to leave your clothes here?" she asks.

"What use are they? I don't want to carry them."

"Then don't leave anything in the pockets."

As Jesper makes that final check, Mara puts her hoodie in a bin, just to be safe. She keeps her back turned to him as she breaks open the disposable camera, taking the film out and throwing the remains away.

"What do we do now?" he asks.

Mara turns to see Jesper looking far more conservative in his grey slacks and blue pullover.

"We can't go back out on the street," she says.

"I don't want to go back out there."

"It's just a matter of time before the cops move in and start arresting everyone. Those fires are probably stopping them. They'll wait."

"Why don't they use the water cannons to put the fires out?"

"They might've put something in them, something potentially flammable."

"Are you serious?" Jesper asks. "They can't do that. That's inhumane."

"It is."

"We need to get out of here."

"And leave everyone on the street?"

"It's over. I'm done with all this."

"But JJ could be down there. And others from Circus. Don't you want to warn them?"

Jesper points towards the mall and says, "Those guys out there, I

357

don't know who they are or where they're from. But it looks to me like they've come here specifically to light fires and loot shops. They're right-wingers. Or anarchists. I don't know. They're not my people."

"What about your unified army?"

"Hardcore right-wingers are not people I want to fight alongside."

"You're hardcore left and setting cars on fire. How are you any different?"

Jesper goes to the windows, to look down on Königstraße. Mara follows him. From this vantage point on the second floor, they see that the fires at both ends have grown. The initial fire at the Schloßplatz end is now burning far up the tree. Those not feeding the fires are going in and out of shops. She sees one protester come out of an ice cream shop with a huge silver container cradled under one arm; his balaclava is folded up to his nose and he's digging out ice cream with a scoop.

"Why are they stealing?" Mara asks. "Where are they planning to take it all? There's nowhere to go."

"It's not about stealing. It's about destroying. The next thing they'll do is start setting all these shops on fire. We need to get out of here."

Jesper pulls at Mara's arm, but she shakes him off.

"We can't just abandon them all," she says.

"Like I said, those guys aren't my people. I'm not responsible for them."

Jesper starts walking away.

"Where are you going?"

"To the roof," he says. "Get up there and find a way off this block."

Mara isn't convinced, about the plan or teaming up with Jesper. She also feels an obligation to the people on the street below, but then decides they've all put themselves in this predicament. There's nothing she can do. She can't stop them, and she can't stop the police. The trap on Königstraße is too neatly set. But she can try to save herself and make sure Russell gets the photos.

She follows Jesper up the stationary escalators to the top floor and the glass doors leading to an outdoor eating area. Mara expects to see police on the roof, but it's empty. Jesper takes a chair and tosses it at the glass. It bounces back, the doors unmarked. They take the chair together and start ramming its metal legs against the glass

358

until it cracks and splits, and they make a hole large enough to get through.

Mara walks to the edge. The air is thick with smoke from the fires. Through it, she sees a helicopter hovering above Schloßplatz, but she can't tell if it's a police helicopter or one from a media outlet. A volley of tear gas canisters flies through the air from the train station end of the mall. Down below, the dark clouds from the fires combine with the noxious haze of the gas. Protesters start running into shops to take cover. The clouds waft up to the roof.

"Run," she shouts. "They're gassing the street."

They go to the far end of the building and cross an empty parking lot. At the edge, they look down on the street Mara took when escaping the battle at Heilbronnerstraße. The street is strangely void of police and protesters.

"How do we get down from here?" Jesper asks.

Mara moves to get a different view and sees that police are stationed behind the barricades where this street meets Königstraße. All the cops have gas masks on. The protesters fleeing from the tear gas try to climb over the barricade, which topples over under their collective weight, sending them all sprawling. The police step forward and start hitting the protesters.

"Oh, my God," she says.

As the smoke clears a little, she sees protesters lying on the ground down on Königstraße.

"Mara," Jesper shouts. "Come on. Down here."

He's at the entrance to a staircase, leading down from the carpark, having smashed the door open with a fire extinguisher he now drops. Mara runs to the stairs and they both descend to street level, where they listen at the door for anything outside. Jesper reaches for the door handle, then looks at Mara, who nods. He grips it and the handle turns. The street is clear. Mara takes off her balaclava and dumps it in a garbage bin. Jesper does the same with his.

"What now?" Jesper turns around, looking in all directions. "The centre's crawling with cops."

"But not here. We go back to the university. We can blend in with the crowd there."

"If there's anyone left."

They run down Kronenstraße, away from the smoke drifting

down from Königstraße. When they reach Kriegsbergstraße, the broad street is bare, save for a few flag-totting stragglers heading back to the demonstration's starting point.

Mara sees a flag caught at the base of a barricade. "Help me with this."

They get the flag free, then Jesper gives Mara a leg up over the barricade. Once Jesper is over, she hands him the flag.

"Get us both under this," she says. "And try really hard to look like an innocent, peace-loving student."

Jesper extends the flag like a small blanket and gets one side around Mara's shoulders. They start walking down Kriegsbergstraße, in-step, like survivors who are lucky to be alive.

Up ahead, two police officers are ushering people back towards the Stadtgarten. As she walks, head bowed, hiding under the flag she helped design, she thinks tears are required. She zeroes in on the conversation last night between Zina and JJ; how Zina left her in Hamburg, how sad and helpless she felt, and how it meant she never got the chance to reach her boxing potential. Zina abandoned her, just like her mother did, without saying anything and without any attempt to make things right. The one constant she had and the one person she could rely on were gone. She focuses on the 15-year-old version of herself, tough but insecure, both hating that person and wishing she could go back to being that person again, to do things differently. Respond better to adversity, rather than blame others. And it's that regret that causes the tears to flow.

When they reach the police officers, she's crying softly, the pain and regret welling up inside her.

"Are you hurt?" one officer asks with genuine concern.

"We just wanted to march," she says. "What's going on?"

The officers wave them through.

In the Stadtgarten, there's only a scattering of people; they lie on the grass like exhausted audience members of a music festival that finished hours ago.

"That was impressive," Jesper says.

"What?"

"That you cried on cue like that."

"Don't they teach you that at acting school?"

Mara looks around for Callenberg and his troop of girls, but they're not there. She hopes they made it out unscathed.

360

"Can I have the flag?" she asks.

He gives it to her. She folds it and jams it into one of the jacket's pockets.

Jesper puts his hands on his hips. "What the hell just happened?"

Mara starts walking away.

"Hey? Where are you going?"

"I need to walk."

"Can I come with you?"

She ignores him and walks quickly, across the Stadtgarten and past the library. Avoiding the city centre to get back to Diemershalde will take hours. She doesn't care. She's happy to walk; to leave all the violence and chaos behind her.

She hopes Zina and JJ are all right.

Past the Congress Centre. Then Berliner Platz. There are people on the streets here, and most of the stores are open. Locals are going through their routine daily activities while the centre burns a few kilometres away. She can't hear the helicopter, but she can see it, hovering like a dragonfly between the plumes of smoke.

She keeps walking, down Breitscheidstraße. The footpath is crowded, and there's the typical urban soundtrack of engines, horns and voices. She finds it reassuring, the sounds of normality, and it's relaxing enough to make her slow her stride to a stroll. The fight's well over, for her. People even smile at her, like she's one of them.

A clock shows it's 1024.

She thinks: all that happened in an hour?

As the adrenalin has abated, it's been replaced by hunger. She breaks the €20 note in a bakery, getting a roll filled with cheese and lettuce and a bottle of water. She downs half the bottle in one go, trying to wash away the tang of tear gas. The food helps, as does the act of eating and drinking. She feels more like herself again, back in her own skin; she's not sure she likes the version of herself who donned a balaclava and fought with police.

The guy working in the hole-in-the-wall photography shop says he has nothing to do and can develop her photos while she waits. She sits outside, in the sun, and finishes the roll and water. There's nothing here to suggest that anything remotely bad is happening in another part of the city, not even any residual smoke. She wonders if the locals even know what's going on. Or do they know and don't care?

361

She buys an ice cream and thinks about those protesters pilfering silver tubs from the ice cream shop on Königstraße; they're probably now sitting in the back of police vans or have been left bruised and bleeding on the ground. This makes her wonder if that was the police strategy all along, like it was at the last Fridays for Future march in Hamburg; to send the very clear message that protesting will not be tolerated, that people are more likely to end up in hospital than in prison.

The photo assistant comes outside and hands her a stiff envelope with her prints.

"Are you a journalist?" he asks.

"Why do ask that?"

"They're good shots, but I would've thought a pro wouldn't be using film anymore."

"I'm old school."

"Looks like you were right in the thick of it. Was it as bad as looked on TV?"

She thinks of that mercenary mass of guys in black, coming down Heilbronnerstraße. No banners, no chants, no mandate, and probably no idea what the G8 even is.

"That all depends on what they showed. I didn't see any media where I was."

"So, you were like, undercover, with the protesters?"

As she realises the assistant has looked closely at all her photos, she starts to see something sleazy in him; like he might be the kind of guy to put hidden cameras in an apartment he rents out to tourists.

"Isn't there some kind of privacy rule for developing photos?" she asks. "You shouldn't be spying on personal stuff like this."

"Hey, I was complimenting your work."

She puts the envelope in the left pocket of the stolen jacket, where it sticks halfway out, and continues walking. At Schwabstraße, a street map there shows that she can follow this street to Marienplatz, then skirt the centre to Diemershalde. It looks like a long walk, even on the condensed map.

Zina's apartment is where she wants to be, safe inside and quiet. But she doesn't dare take the U-Bahn or a bus. It's better to be on the street, moving among the people, like a local.

As she walks, she does a body check. A few things hurt – left shoulder, right ribs, lower back – but nothing feels broken, nor is it

362

painful enough to prevent her from walking. She was so caught up in the fights, she doesn't remember taking the hits, but the bruises will provide their own proof.

It feels like a win to have made it out. A victory on points.

This area of Stuttgart, like so much of the city, is affluently middle class. Neat apartment buildings that never climb beyond five floors high. The cars are clean and well-maintained. The shops are doing a brisk trade. Everyone seems to have enough. There's little diversity. No one here will get out and march against economic or social inequality. No one looks oppressed.

The walk starts to get hard.

She gets onto Olgastraße knowing she can take it all the way to the bottom of Zina's street.

The whole trek takes nearly three hours. She's exhausted when she enters the apartment. The flag and envelope of photos are dropped on the kitchen table, and the padded jacket gets hung on the back of a chair. She puts the kettle on and washes her hands and face at the kitchen sink, too tired to walk another five metres to the bathroom. Her dripping hands grip the counter as the kettle reaches its crescendo. It turns off, but she doesn't move.

She has the overwhelming feeling that she missed something important today; that she ran with Jesper when she should have stayed on Königstraße. Now, she doesn't know what to do. The options present themselves – drive to Hamburg, drive to Berlin, drive south and away from everything – but they all seem too selfish. The car gives her freedom, but that doesn't mean she'll be able to get out of the city. There will be checkpoints in place, as an easy way for the police to bump up the arrest stats.

She boils the water again and makes an instant coffee, using the same cup from this morning. It's a relief to sit down. Her calves and thighs throb. She looks at the photos the slimy developer left greasy thumbprints on. The shots of the gathering in the Stadtgarten aren't that interesting, but do provide context. They're also proof that plenty of people, including lots of kids, were there to march peacefully. The ones of Heilbronnerstraße are stunning. It seems so much more physical in these photos than it was in real life, which she finds strange. Maybe it's because when she was in the moment, she was looking at everything, and also missing lots of things; these photos allow her to see everything captured in the shot. She's struck by how big the protesters in black are: brawny guys, athletic, powerful. Guys who pump weights seven days a week, who are maybe former soldiers with no wars to fight but who keep themselves battle-ready.

The coffee helps soothe her. She wants another one, but can't get up.

Holding these photos in her hands is having the peculiar effect of pushing the events further into the past. Like there was a two-week delay between taking the photos and getting them developed. She also thinks there's something about this that feels like the prelude to something else. Not day one in the war on oppression, as Vilem had wanted. But a glimpse of the future, where the police clamp down on protests using extreme force. Now, it's a question of how the protesters will respond. Vilem's next move could well be to utilise these brutal police strategies as a way to build the army he wants; get ex-soldiers and hooligans and right-wingers and left-wingers and Fridays for Future teens turned militant and anyone else who thinks the world has short-changed them all fighting under one flag.

On the table is the notepad from this morning, with Zina and JJ's scribbled messages. She tears that page off, picks up the pen and starts writing:

Hey Russ,

Greetings from Stuttgart. I guess I could be clever and say Greetings from Baghdad, given everything that happened this morning, but that would be a stretch. I'm not sure what to call this, but despite all the big talk, I'm not calling it war. I was at the protest, right in the middle of it, but I got out just as things started to go bad. That was hours ago. I write this from Zina's apartment. Truth is, I'm scared to go outside...

***

The knock on the door wakes her. She lifts her head from the padded jacket that's folded into a pillow and straightens in the kitchen chair.

She's really sore.

The knock comes again, harder, demanding, a fist pounding on the door.

That's JJ, she thinks.

She goes to the door and opens it on Perceval, looking exhausted.

364

He's in a dark blue suit, no tie, and has an important-looking ID badge hanging from his neck. He smells of smoke.

His face is grim as he says, "Get your things."

"What? Why?"

Hands in his pockets, he edges into the apartment. "You have to go. Now."

"Go where? Who's after me?"

"Not you."

Mara closes the door. "JJ? Is she all right?"

"I'm not privy to the whereabouts of Julietta. Please, start packing."

"Not until you tell me what's going on."

"You are behaving in a fashion that conveys ignorance," Perceval says, looking around the apartment, taking it in. "Are you unaware of what has transpired today?"

"I was there for the start of it. I was in the peaceful protest."

"Were you at any point on Königstraße?"

"That depends."

"Yellow balaclava. Correct? The way you moved was very familiar."

Mara goes back into the kitchen and sits down, groaning as she does so. "Look, what's this about?"

"We don't have the benefit of time. Pack your belongings. Leave no sign that you were here."

"Has something happened to Zina?"

"Your vehicle is out front. I will wait for you there. If you aren't outside in two minutes, I will leave. After that, I will not be able to help you."

"How do you know about my car?"

"Please open the door for me," Perceval says, still with his hands in his pockets.

Mara stands up and does so.

"Two minutes," he adds. "I will also update you on the travelling dragon, if you need further motivation."

"Can I leave a note?"

"No. That would be a sign you were here."

After Perceval exits, Mara leaves the door open. The mention of Anthony gets her moving, even if her body is stiff and sore. In the living room, she stuffs things into her backpack, deciding to take

Zina's sleeping bag and camping mat, just in case. She dumps all this by the front door. In the kitchen, she quickly washes the coffee mug she used and puts it back in the cupboard. The note from Zina and JJ goes into her pocket, while the photos and letter to Russell go into a padded envelope she's lucky to find in a drawer. With the address written on it, she seals it, pocketing that slither of excess paper and the pen.

Jacket on, she gathers everything and closes the door, double-locking it. Outside, she finds Perceval leaning against her car.

"There better be a good explanation for all this," she says, unlocking the driver's door and putting her stuff on the rear seat. The envelope for Russell goes into the slot where the radio should be.

Perceval stands next to her, holding out his right hand. "Allow me to drive."

"No. It's my car."

"This will be our only chance to leave the city."

"I feel like I'm being kidnapped."

"Think of it as being escorted."

"Sounds like I need it."

She drops the key in his palm, then moves around to the passenger side. Perceval gets in and starts the car.

"I do love old cars," he says, as Mara gets in.

"I still want to know how you even know I have a car."

"These old vehicles have such character. Such history."

Perceval puts the car in gear and edges onto the street.

"Stammer," Mara says. "You were at the gym. In her car."

"You have wonderful instincts. You should consider becoming a detective. I'm certain Hannelore would agree to be your mentor."

"Why didn't you come in with her? She knew everything."

"I wasn't alone."

With effort, Perceval turns the big car around, then drives slowly to the end of Zina's street.

"Who else was in the car?"

"What do your instincts tell you?"

Mara is thoughtful for a moment, considering who might have the strongest interest in seeing Anthony caught. "Jawinski," she says.

"Very good. His plus-one was your friend, Ms Lersner."

"Not my friend."

"They were most disappointed when Anthony wasn't

apprehended."

Perceval reaches the intersection and stops. There's no traffic, in either direction, but he lets the car idle, looking all the while in the rear-view mirror.

"What's up with Ant? Did he make it? How's he doing?"

"I had a lovely chat with my aunt this morning. She informed me that Jordie is getting settled and, with the right training, he will act as her chauffeur."

Mara lets out a long breath. "That's really good to hear."

"You did very well."

"Thanks." She leans forward and looks at the vacant road. "What are you waiting for? It's clear."

"One moment." He continues looking in the mirror, at Gaisburgstraße.

Mara turns to look through the cab's narrow rear window that's freckled with dirt. Three police cars drive onto Zina's street and stop in front of her building.

"There they are," Perceval says. He drives forward and makes a left, moving away from the city centre.

"Are they looking for JJ?"

Perceval turns off the main road and starts taking back streets through Stuttgart's southeast suburbs.

"Talk to me. Please."

"I shall," Perceval says. "Once we're out of the city. One thing at a time."

"Why not now?"

"Be patient. We have checkpoints to circumvent, which is why I'm driving. Having a hysterical passenger will draw unwanted attention. Refrain from asking questions. Try to relax."

"How do you expect me to relax? It's obviously bad news."

"You will be best served right now to maintain your professionalism. You have done fine work thus far. Don't undo all of that with an undue outburst."

"That's a bizarre way to give a compliment," she says. "At least tell me where we're going."

"The airport, if we make it through."

"I'm staying with my car. I'm not flying anywhere."

"Correct. I'm departing by plane."

"To Hamburg?"

367

"Berlin," Perceval says, sounding like that's the last place he wants to be.

"Why?"

"Because ..." He trails off as they approach a checkpoint set up at the Dobelstraße tram station. There is one police car, plus two prisoner transport vans.

"What do we do?" Mara asks.

"Tell the truth."

A stout police officer, who looks a year or two from retirement, steps in front of the vehicle and holds up his hands; he's got one of those old white paddles, with a red circle and light on one side. Perceval stops. The police officer waddles around to the driver's side.

Off the street, Mara sees half a dozen vehicles pulled over to the side, all of them with foreign license plates; the initials show their countries of origin, with two from Poland, two from the Czech Republic, one from Slovakia and one from Serbia. She assumes the occupants of those vehicles are now sitting in the transport vans.

Perceval lowers the window and holds up his ID badge. The officer squints at it. Then he steps back to look at the license plates.

"Going the wrong way, aren't you?" The officer points back the way they came, and adds, "Hamburg's that way."

"If you would be so kind as to let us through."

"Slow down. Where are you going in this old pile of junk?"

Perceval subtly raises his right hand, to prevent Mara from saying anything. He then uses that same hand to take his police ID from his jacket's inside pocket. He hands it to the officer, who this time takes glasses from his shirt pocket and puts them on.

"Christoph Perceval?"

"I'm based in Hamburg, as you can see. My daily driver is in the shop and my colleague Ms Steinbach here was kind enough to offer her vehicle."

"I still need to know where you're going."

"We are headed to the airport. I'm urgently needed in Berlin. I can show you my orders, if you like."

"No need for that."

"I'm afraid I don't have all day to sit in this, as you called it, old pile of junk, to drive there. I need to catch my flight."

"Understood." The officer hands the ID card back to Perceval and

368

takes off his glasses. "If you have the power to do so, then do something about these protesters. They're out of control."

"Noted."

The officer lingers, leaning down to look through the window at Mara.

"You're doing a great job here," Perceval says with full sincerity. "Keep yourself and your colleagues safe, and keep arresting the troublemakers."

"We're up against it. We need to tighten our grip on our country. Especially after what's happened today, and what happened up in your city."

Mara watches Perceval working hard to keep his mouth closed. He appears to grind down and swallow the sentence that formed there.

The officer finally steps back, flips the handheld sign around, to show the green circle for go, and waves them on.

Perceval drives forward and winds up the window, working the old winder so hard he nearly rips it off.

"Be careful with that," Mara says.

Perceval glares at the road ahead and drives fast. "Did you hear him? What the devil is that about?"

"Forget him. We're through and you can tell me what's going on. Why were the cops all over Zina's place? Why are you going to Berlin?"

"We can't talk freely while we're driving. I will pull over once we're out near the airport." Perceval exhales loudly. "Tighten our grip. He is everything that's wrong with the police right now."

They drive the rest of the way in silence, following the signs to the airport. When they're close, Perceval pulls off the Autobahn and stops in the massive, empty parking lot of the trade fair centre. He turns the engine off.

"You don't want to go to the terminal?" Mara asks.

"I'm certain there will be police present. You can't risk it. I can walk from here."

"So? Spill it. All of it."

Perceval removes the ID badge from around his neck, like someone gladly relinquishing command. "This is not easy for me to say, so I will simply state the facts. Zina is dead."

"No, she isn't. This is some kind of joke."

369

"I'm not attempting humour. This wounds me to my core."

"You met her once."

"I know how important she is to you. Was."

"No. It's not true. I can't believe it." Mara fights back her tears. "What happened?"

Perceval takes out his phone and turns it off. "There will be stories told about this, but I wanted to ensure you got the truth from me."

"Just tell me what the fuck happened."

"I was behind the barricade. At Schloßplatz. I saw you, black top and yellow balaclava. But then I lost sight of you."

"I got out of there, just before they gassed the street."

"How? It was all blocked."

"The roof of a department store. There was a parking area up there and I got down the stairs from it. I was lucky."

"Did you stay hidden?"

"I think so. I took the balaclava off when I got down to the street. No one saw me. Then I walked back to the university. In different clothes."

Perceval smiles. "It's like you were born to do this."

"I feel like I failed every step of the way. Failed my friends. I mean, Zina ..."

"There was nothing you could do about Königstraße. You were correct to abandon that scene. How did you get back to the apartment?"

"I walked. Took a massive detour, to avoid the city centre. Out in those parts of the city, it was just a normal day."

"They weren't aware of what was happening."

"Or they didn't care."

"You acted precisely and at the right time." Perceval takes a deep breath and lets it out. "You would not be sitting here otherwise."

"The water cannons," Mara says, struggling to breathe. "At Schloßplatz. They were there, but they weren't being used to put out the fires. Oh, my fucking God."

"The rumour regarding the cannons turned out to be true. Unfortunately. Zina was there, part of the Schloßplatz detail."

"In riot gear? That's not normally her thing?"

"In uniform. As extra security. She wasn't there to engage."

"But she did. She knew what was going to happen."

"Or she followed her instincts," Perceval says. "She observed the cannons weren't dousing the fires and deduced that they were potentially tainted. Things were getting out of control at the train station end, where protesters started setting fire to everything."

"That's when the gas came."

"The cannons were activated not long after that. But I heard no order for their activation." Perceval takes another deep breath. "It wasn't immediately clear that the cannons were chemicalised. It was only when the streams hit the fires that things went wrong. Very wrong. It was like a flamethrower. Zina went over the barricade to assist. To halt the cannons and help those who were burning. But it was too late. She was hit before the cannons were shut down."

"She burned to death?"

Perceval nods slightly. "Along with a few protesters. It was horrific. The ... smell of it. I still have it on my clothes. I'm so sorry, Mara. Really. I can't believe what I witnessed today."

Mara starts crying. She bangs her fists against the dashboard.

"Easy, easy," Perceval says.

Mara gets out and slams the door. She kicks the fender, then grabs the tray's railing with both hands and starts shaking it. Perceval gets out and jogs around the car. He grabs Mara from behind, pinning her arms to her sides. She struggles against him, but he continues to hold her. He's surprisingly strong.

"This isn't fair."

"I know, I know," Perceval says, his mouth close to her ear. "You need to choose your moment to grieve. Not now, not here. Just breathe, Mara. Breathe."

"Let me go."

"Breathe."

"I said let me go."

Perceval releases her. She walks away from him, wiping the tears away with her palms. Behind the terminal, a plane roars into the sky.

"That's the story, right? They'll put it all on her. That's why the cops are at her apartment. To plant evidence and all that. Say she put chemicals in the cannons."

"That is my assumption, yes."

"Well, that's already full of holes," Mara says. "Why would she jump the barricade then?"

"They may get creative and make vicious connections to her

371

relationship with Spitz, to claim this as a suicidal action."

"That's outrageous."

"I came to the apartment specifically to get you out of there and prevent you from being arrested."

"Oh, I'm supposed to be grateful? You stood by and watched while my friend was torched, and now you want my gratitude?"

"That's not how it is."

"How did you even know I was there?"

"At the apartment? I guessed. And, I hoped."

Mara leans a hand against the railing and takes a few breaths.

"You will get every chance to mourn her," Perceval says.

"When? She'll be cast as the villain in all of this."

"At first, but maybe there will be the chance to change that. There is the possibility that what happened today is connected to what happened in Hamburg."

"Chemicals in water? Stammer said you're looking into that. Who's behind it then?"

"Someone who knows a lot about chemicals and water."

"Milan Kollar? Why would he kill a police officer in Hamburg, then kill protesters in Stuttgart?"

"To instigate conflict. To accelerate it. Officer Marten's death enabled the police to implement emergency security measures. This made the protesters angry and motivated them to unify."

"With help from Vilem."

"Now, we have dead protesters, killed by police. He may be trying to establish two clear sides here and set them on the path to a larger conflict."

"Except a police officer tried to stop it. There has to be footage of Zina doing that."

"If there is, I haven't seen it. Then there is the problem of her association with you, the sister of the suspect wanted for Marten's murder. You were both arrested a week ago, together, establishing a trend of disobedience. Your roommate wrote the exposé about sexual harassment in the police, which led to the suicide of Hans Spitz. That story could lose much of its significance if Zina is discredited and made into a scapegoat."

"They'll probably twist it to say that Zina shot him."

"She's gone. She can't fight back against any of this. And there is no one to fight for her." Perceval holds up a hand. "That's not your

372

task, Mara. Everything can be attributed to Zina. Don't think they won't do it."

"It's all just wrong. It's the police who are the bad guys."

"Not all of them. This is coming from high up. That's where things need to be changed."

"Is that why you're going to Berlin?"

Perceval doesn't reply.

"Well, I guess you should go then. Thanks. For getting me out of the apartment in time."

"You're welcome."

Something in the way Perceval's shoulders slump makes Mara feel sympathy for him.

"I mean it," she says. "Thank you. It must've been hard, after what you saw, to keep yourself together long enough to get me out of there."

"I feel guilty for what has happened to Anthony, and now to Zina. Very guilty. Ashamed."

"Then let's fix it all. We'll go to Milan's place and arrest him. Drive there right now."

"On what charge? There is no evidence. I only have theories. And I am required in Berlin."

"You keep saying this, but you don't say why."

Perceval folds his arms, appearing defensive. "To prevent this conflict from escalating."

"You think you can do that? Wars have started over much less than this. The First World War started because some idiot shot an Austrian duke no one really cared about."

"You know your history. Do you also know Gavrilo Princip was a Bosnian Serb?"

"I just remember in school being shocked that this massive war that killed millions began in such a small and insignificant way. Was he the assassin?"

"He was the catalyst. The trigger, if you'll pardon the pun. All the seeds for conflict were already sown. You do recall it was your father who posited that Milan Kollar is a Bosnian Serb?"

"That's all a bit too neat, isn't it? Can you make some historical connection to Kollar living in Linz?"

Perceval points a finger at Mara, then keeps whatever he wanted to say to himself. "Better not."

"I'll figure it out."

"Ask Nils. He's brilliant at making connections. Very methodical, like his mother."

"I don't want any more connections. I want truth."

"We would just be animals wandering aimlessly through time and space if there weren't things to connect us."

Mara sniffs and looks at the ground. She can't believe she will never see Zina again.

"I will try to make a case for Zina," Perceval says.

"You can't let them paint her as evil. She was good. Pure good. After everything she went through, you can't allow the police to turn on her like this. She was loyal, through it all."

"A confession from Milan Kollar would absolve her and Anthony. Do you think you could get this?"

"No. But watch me try. What's his address? You said in Hamburg that you have it."

"Do you have a pen?"

Mara looks in the cab for the pen she took from Zina's apartment. She finds a scrap of paper, and also grabs the envelope for Russell.

"Here."

He writes down the address.

"I need you to do something." She holds up Zina's keys. "Maybe it's a waste of time, but there's a police officer in Stuttgart, about my age, named Baer. She could really use an apartment."

"Do you know her?"

"Not exactly. But my instincts tell me she's in an abusive relationship. Maybe the apartment will help her get out of it."

"Do you have any more information about her?"

"She worked a traffic checkpoint, last night, near the Unterer Schloßgarten."

He takes the keys. "I'll see what I can do."

"Please. Then at the very least, we can both remember Zina for this final act of goodness."

As he hands her the scrap of paper, she hands him the envelope.

"What's this?" he asks.

"Can you send this to Russell? Or hand-deliver it when you're in Berlin?"

"Since when did I become your courier?"

"He's a lovely guy. Have a cup of tea with him."

"I will ensure he gets this. But I will keep my distance. I need to be watchful of who I associate with."

"Now it sounds like you're going to Berlin to take on the top brass."

"This is all political. The police are just a tool, which is central to the problem. I'm aware Jawinski is already travelling to Berlin. This may terminate my career, but I can no longer stand by while the truth is twisted to suit any given purpose. That goes against every principle I have."

"If it all goes south, you'll still have the Pink Dragon."

Perceval gives her a sideways glance. "Nervous, are you?"

"Why do you say that?"

"You're using humour to cover it."

"I've just lost one of the most important people in the world to me, and now I'm about to storm some bad guy's lair, without so much as a tyre iron for a weapon, to try and get a confession out of him. So, yeah, pretty nervous, and messed up."

"Go there to talk. Don't attack. Focus on the task. Under no circumstances try to be funny."

"You should've seen me before a bout. I was like a stand-up comedian, warming up the crowd."

"You should choose your moments for humour."

"Just like for grieving?" she asks, mocking him.

"Yes. Whatever feelings you have now, you need to put them aside and do your job. It may well get worse before it gets better."

"Why do you say that? What do you know?"

"I know my flight leaves in half an hour. Take care of yourself, Mara."

"Why will things get worse?"

Perceval starts walking away. "When you get to that address," he says over his shoulder, "It may not be Milan you want to speak to."

Mara watches him jog across the car park. It takes a while for the words to sink in.

"Hey? Hey! What the fuck does that mean?"

But he's already out of earshot and crossing the street to the Departures terminal.

The misted-up windows dull the morning light, but it's still glary enough to make her squint and grimace. She lies on the cab's narrow rear seat, Zina's sleeping bag up to her chin, feeling like garbage and trying to hide from everyone. It's a new day, but it's a Zina-less world, and that's not a place she wants to live in.

As she sits up, the half-bottle of Sambuca hits the floor. Foolish, she thinks, to have finished that bottle, to have even wasted money on it; as if alcohol could take any pain away or make her forget. All it did was amplify everything, stirring up memories of Gus's gym and the beautiful woman with the almond-coloured skin who taught her right and taught her well; who was in her corner until she was 15. Then she wasn't, leaving a massive gap that couldn't be filled.

Now, she was gone for good. The gap is permanent. She's going to have to find a way, somehow, to work around it.

She rubs a sleeve at the book-sized window, creating a porthole view of the miserable car park. On the Autobahn, about 30 metres away, vehicles zip past, driving away from Munich. The rest area is dismal. The one picnic bench is in two pieces, looking like it was split with an axe or chainsaw, while the blue and white portable toilet smells beyond bad. She had to hold her breath last night when she used it.

Perceval told her to choose her moment to grieve. This is what she chose: an utterly awful stop-off point outside of Munich, crying into a drink that she usually consumes for health, happiness and prosperity.

She wants to start crying all over again. Remorseful, bitter tears that will sting. She tries to swallow it all down.

The pain feels black. The blackest black, whatever that's called.

She needs to get it together. To get grounded, be present.

It's Saturday morning. A week ago, she and Zina were on the train to Hamburg, all excited about teaching Tinaya and her friends how to box.

Just memories now. Like all of it.

She gets out of the sleeping bag and climbs into the driver's seat. She needs to use the bathroom, but she's not setting foot in that portable toilet again.

The Ranger rumbles to life, its sound familiar and comforting. She lowers the window and blasts the fan at the windscreen. The mist clears, slowly, from the bottom up, with warm air that smells faintly of exhaust. She uses water from a bottle to rinse her mouth, and spits out the open window.

The windscreen clearer, she eases the car forward, letting it warm up, but the old pick-up seems just as keen to leave the ratty rest area.

The Autobahn's right lane is vacant, but a lot of cars are speeding down the middle and left lanes. The cab shudders a little as each car overtakes, their high speeds causing streams of wind that feel insulting. The mocking laughter of someone standing too close.

The windscreen fully demisted, she turns off the fan and winds up the window, wondering what the state of this Zina-less world is this morning. The final Königstraße body count. The media fallout. The response. The attribution of blame.

It takes 20 minutes to reach the first petrol station. She drives almost with her legs crossed. The bathrooms are pricey, with €1 to use a stall and €5 to have a shower. She chooses the latter, because of the glimpse she catches of herself in the mirror at the bathroom's entrance; looking like a mad-cat lady abandoned even by her cats.

She spends so long under the shower, the attendant knocks on the door to see if she's all right.

Once cleaned up and feeling slightly better in fresh jeans and a t-shirt, she sits in the restaurant, drinking black coffee. There's a television behind the counter, on a news channel. It shows a video of Königstraße, yesterday, but it's shot from too far away; the images are blurry and it's hard to discern whether the charred remains shown on the ground are people or the remnants from the bonfires. Then it cuts to footage of G8 leaders, shaking hands and waving to cameras, getting on planes and into cars, all of them leaving Stuttgart. The next report is from Berlin, where white men in suits clutch dossiers and enter meeting rooms with purposeful strides. Jawinski comes on screen, walking up to an array of so many microphones not all of them fit in the frame.

She goes to the counter and asks the waitress, "Can you turn that up?"

The waitress takes the remote and points it at the screen.

"… holding an emergency meeting in Hamburg on Monday," Jawinski says. "All state leaders will be in attendance. We've

377

extended invitations to ministers for the interior in neighbouring countries as well. The crisis we're dealing with in Germany extends beyond our borders. In recent weeks, we have seen protests get completely out of control in France, Austria and Denmark. This is a problem many European countries are facing, and we would do well to face it together, to implement solutions that help make our streets, towns and cities safer."

"Does that involve tighter controls on the population?" a journalist asks.

Jawinski's face is stern and serious, the face of a politician looking to score political points. "The safety of everyone is my prime concern. I want people to feel they can go shopping on a Friday morning in the centre of Stuttgart without any fear of being caught up in flagrant acts of hooliganism. What I don't want is our children growing up in a society where the only way they think they can instigate change is through violence. I don't want our children in balaclavas, setting cars on fire, looting shops and destroying public property."

"Do you want to give the police more power?"

"This would be a last resort. We need to fix the problem at its source. We are talking about the foundation on which our fair and just society is based. Currently, we are dealing with a small minority of the population intent on breaking the law, undermining our peaceful way of life and ruining our communities. These people need to be stopped. If making our streets and schools and workplaces and homes safer requires a firmer hand from our law enforcement services, then I'm sure you will agree that would be the best solution in the short term. We are at the point of losing control. We need to get back control, to ensure the safety of everyone. I repeat, this is not just a problem in Germany. Europe needs to unite to swiftly bring about the return to normality we all want."

"How many people died yesterday?"

"We are all saddened by the events in Stuttgart. Our thoughts and prayers go out to the families of those involved. An investigation is underway to determine what happened with the water cannons. Specifically, that the contents were tampered with. The latest information I have is that it was a rogue local police officer, who has connections to protest groups, acting alone. We are looking into her motivations and monitoring communications and social media

378

networks to see how much further this goes. In the same way, we are also monitoring the online activity of the hundreds of protesters who were arrested yesterday, who comprise many different nations, proving further that this is a European problem. Hamburg residents shall rest assured that there will be a comprehensive police presence during the security conference, with officers from all over Germany attending to keep the city safe and prevent any protests from descending into violence. Thank you."

He backs away from the microphones and walks out of the frame. Nicola trails behind him.

The waitress turns the sound back down. "Is it just me, or did he just admit that they're watching us?"

"It's all in the wording. Not watching. Monitoring."

"They're watching. Like the Stasi. How can they get away with that?"

"Sounds like it's going to get worse before it gets better," Mara says, thinking of Perceval trying to talk sense into rooms full of politicians who only care about protecting their positions.

"Makes me want to throw my phone in a river."

"Why not do that?"

The waitress's grin causes lines to appear on her face, betraying her age and that she's certainly old enough to remember a world without the internet.

"I can't do that. Everything's on there."

"Yeah, in one convenient place where they can look at all of it."

"What does that mean?"

"Forget it." Mara pays for her coffee and leaves.

Back on the road, the Ranger slowly eats up the kilometres. Braunau am Inn comes and goes, as a collection of buildings seen from a distance. She ignores history, passes over the Inn river and into Austria. Her focus is on getting to Marchtrenk, to Milan Kollar's house, which may also be the home of Agnes Kollar, who may once have been Agnes Steinbach. That's why she's not grieving properly today. Perceval was right. This is not the moment for that. Because seeing her mother will be more than enough to process. It's the only thing she can think about. What to say and how to say it. She's trying to surface memories from years ago that might be relevant. The potential of Milan scheming to lead Germany and Europe towards revolution is taking a backseat to the more immediate and personal issue of confronting her mother, who she hasn't seen in 18 years.

When she reaches Marchtrenk, she double-parks outside the tourist information centre, like a farmer come into town for the day, to get a map and directions. These take her down narrow roads towards the Traun River.

She thinks it makes sense that Milan would have his estate near water.

There's only one place on the street that Perceval wrote down. No number out the front. No name on the letterbox. There's a steel gate, a lighter grey than the wall, with a camera pointed to the driver's side of arriving vehicles. No intercom. No buzzer. She lowers the window and stares up at the camera.

A few minutes pass.

She turns the engine off, opens the door and climbs up onto the cab's roof. She expects to see a large house on a rise, the driveway from the gate leading up to it. But the track is gravel and curves to the left, disappearing down between a thick line of trees. No house. No cars. No dog running around. No signs of life.

She climbs down and sits in the cab again. Something flashes on the camera and catches her eye. They know she's here, she's certain of that.

A few more minutes pass. She uses the time to tidy up the cab, stuffing the sleeping bag away and putting all the trash into a bag. Finding the rainbow umbrella under the passenger seat makes her think of JJ and hope she's all right.

There's a loud clunk and the gate opens slowly, sliding to the right, into the wall. She starts the engine and follows the track. The Ranger's big wheels rip at the gravel, sending it pinging into the underside. Past the trees, the track arcs around to lead to the front door. The house seems modest, set on this large piece of land and behind a wall; it's relatively small and blandly suburban, lacking the usual ostentatious trimmings of someone showing off their wealth.

She parks next to the grey SUV that took her to Wels station and gets out. A few things still hurt from yesterday, but that pain is at the back of her mind, colourless. Under a covered garage is an electric roadster, shiny black and plugged in.

As she walks to the front door, it's opened. There she is: her mother.

"Hello, Mara."

She looks much older than Mara expects, more filled out and weary. Her loose, shoulder-length blonde hair isn't as shiny, and has the stringy, separated look of coloured hair. But she's still pretty; still has a glimmer in her eyes, that her father called curiosity. Mara likens it more to a selfish inclination to look beyond the person standing in front of her and towards the things only she wants. Shorter and stockier than Mara remembers, and unapologetic, with feet firmly planted and looking like she can handle herself.

"Hey."

Her mother offers a careful smile. "It is so good to see you. I'm sure you're full of questions."

"Yeah, I had a long list. But now, only one. Did you put something flammable in the water cannons?"

"What are you talking about?"

"You heard me."

"Are you referring to Stuttgart?"

"What else?"

"I saw that on the news. Shocking. But why would you think I'd have anything to do with that?"

"Milan then. The chemicals expert."

Her mother folds her arms. "Is that why you've come here? You finally make the effort to track me down after all these years, only to make baseless accusations about something that happened yesterday?"

"Zina." Mara can barely get the words out. "She died, trying to stop it. They're saying it was her."

"Zina? Your old boxing coach?"

"How many Zinas do you know? They're going to put all this on her."

"You'd rather I take the blame? Or Milan perhaps?"

"Are you to blame?"

With a shake of her head, her mother says, "That would go against everything we believe in. We would never poison water. We've spent years trying to purify it and make it available for everyone."

"Modra."

"We've done amazing work all over the world. Life-changing work. We've given everything to preserve life, not end it."

"Did you quit the BND to work for Modra?"

Her mother's stare is hard. "So, Richard told you something."

381

"He did. But only very recently. Right after he stole a pile of cash from his parents and we got Anthony out of Germany."

This makes her laugh.

"That's not funny," Mara says.

"Oh, yes it is. Stealing from those old cretins definitely fills me with joy."

"The money was for Ant. For a new start. Because they're looking all over the country for him. For a crime you probably committed."

"More chemicals in water? You've come here with a serious agenda, Mara, which is an utter shame, because I'm very happy to see you. You've grown into such a beautiful woman."

"I'm not here to arrest you. I just want answers. I'm not in the police anymore."

"I know." Her mother closes the door and takes a few steps forward. "How's Anthony doing? Have you heard from him? Is he enjoying Riga?"

This renders Mara speechless.

"You need to work on your poker face. You're giving so much away. It's always interesting to see how people respond when they get information only they think they know. It's times like these that people show their true character, I like to think. When all the veils are dropped."

"And? What am I showing?"

"You're thoughtful and combative. Protective. Just like your father. But also questioning and suspicious. You've come here, searching for answers."

"I'm not getting any. You've dodged every question I've asked so far. They teach you how to do that in the BND?"

"Among other useful life skills, yes."

The way her mother smiles disarmingly makes Mara wonder if this was also part of her BND training.

"Have you had breakfast? Why don't we go around to the terrace? After all this time, we deserve better surroundings than the driveway."

Her mother starts walking and Mara follows, a few steps behind. When they're around the side of the house, the river comes into view, as a darker green seen through the gaps between the trees. There are small, low-roofed, clear-walled structures that house various hydroponics and aeroponics projects. Up on the slate terrace, which

382

feels cold and sterile, a table surrounded by six chairs is set up for breakfast, with a lush spread of fresh bread rolls, a board of cheeses, a bowl of green apples, a large pitcher of pulpy orange juice and a pot of coffee. Milan is swimming in a narrow pool next to the terrace. It's barely wide enough for one person, but is one of those counter-current pools, allowing endless swimming without ever moving forward. Mara watches him ploughing against the current. It looks like torture.

"He does an hour every morning," Agnes says, watching Milan swim. "It's hypnotic. Try not to look at him."

Mara continues to anyway, catching Milan's eyes through his foggy goggles each time he breathes on his right side. That eye contact is the only acknowledgement she gets from him. He strokes on, in mind-numbing fashion, the pool humming.

Agnes sits down at the table. "Coffee?"

Mara takes a chair at the far end of the table, happy to put some distance between them. "Yes. Please."

"How do you take it?"

"You tell me. You seem to know everything else." When her mother shrugs, Mara adds, "Black, thanks."

"Simple. Help yourself to anything."

Mara sits forward a little to grab the mug of coffee poured for her, but takes nothing else.

"Some eggs?"

The male voice makes her turn. It's the goon who knocked her out, who later gave her €100 at the Wels station. He's jammed his bulky frame into another short-sleeved shirt, which shows off his hirsute, muscled upper arms. He tips a frying pan towards Mara, showing her the scrambled eggs inside.

"You're not going to whack me on the head with that, are you?"

He smiles, making his round face rather cherubic and weirdly cute. "Only if I'm told to."

"Let's hope it doesn't come to that. Hit me with breakfast instead."

He sets a place for Mara, then serves her. She notices his knuckles are red and raw.

"What were you?" she asks. "Light heavyweight?"

"You know your divisions. Cruiserweight. Just. Always took plenty of time in the sauna to get there. But not now."

Mara gestures towards the pool. "You could work off the excess flab in there."

"The pool is only for Milan. The sauna here is for me."

"You're still boxing though. I can see it on your hands."

"Speedbag," he says. "It's good for the reflexes. Speedbag plus crosswords, at intervals, to keep my brain sharp. Many of my old friends, they're not so sharp anymore. I don't want that to happen to me."

"Were you any good?" Mara asks.

"As a junior, yes. I was selected to go to Sarajevo, to a special sports academy. But then the war came." He serves eggs to Agnes, then holds the empty frying pan at his side, gripping it like he could indeed hit someone with it. "Everything else seemed less important then. The war was the only thing."

"What about after? Did you get back into it?"

"I tried, but I didn't have the fire."

"Fucked with the gods, did you? During the war?"

He gives her a curious look. She sees no pride in his eyes.

"I missed too many development years," he says, "and I wasn't right in the head."

"I get it. You have to box for the right reasons." Mara looks at her mother. "You don't want to be in the ring trying to work your own shit out."

The goon nods, then turns to head inside. As he walks behind Agnes, he gives her right shoulder a rather intimate squeeze.

"Veselin is from Mostar," she says, once he's gone.

"The place with that bridge?"

"There's far more to it than that, but yes, the place with that bridge."

As Mara eats the eggs, which are garnished with chives she assumes were grown in one of the greenhouses and taste good, she thinks it was easier chatting with Veselin than it is with Agnes. She should be letting loose all the anger pent up over 18 years, but she's feeling nothing. In any quiet moment, all she can think about is Zina.

The droning noise of the counter-current pool is really annoying, like a swarm of angry bees.

"A lot of what you see on the table is grown here," Agnes says. "We barter for the cheese with our produce."

"What about these eggs?"

"There's a chicken coop down near the river. It used to be closer

384

to the house, but we moved it further away because of the noise and smell. The chickens would peck holes in the greenhouses as well."

Mara finishes and puts her fork down. She sips her coffee, which is also very good. It feels unreal, to be sitting here, with her mother, in Austria.

"I'm really glad you're here," Agnes says.

"Why didn't you make an appearance the first time? When Veselin kidnapped me."

"I'm sorry about that. I wasn't here. Milan thought you were going after Anthony."

"Does Anthony know you're here? Is that why he went to Linz?"

Agnes shakes her head. "He must've been sent there by someone in Circus who knows Vilem."

"Or Milan."

"Doubtful. Vilem is the face and voice of Modra. Milan prefers to stay in the background, away from the limelight and any distractions."

Mara thumbs towards the pool. "Underwater is a good place for that. Do you consider Vilem your son?"

"I didn't expect you to be this direct."

"I didn't expect you to dodge every question."

"His mother is Ornela, Milan's first wife."

"How long have you two been married?"

"We're not married."

"But you have his name. Modra is registered in Switzerland under Agnes Kollar."

Her mother smiles a little, seeming to be impressed that Mara knows this. "Your little helper find that out? Well, I'm her. I'm also Agnes Steinbach."

"What about Agnieszka?"

"Richard told you about that too. Probably to explain why his parents hated me."

"He also told me you just left," Mara says, trying to resist her mother's attempt to gain her sympathy. "From one day to the next. 'I can't do this anymore,' and boom, you were gone. With Ant just a baby."

"Is that how he told that story?" Agnes sips her coffee and looks in the cup. "There's a lot more to it, but it's understandable that the story he told himself is the one he would tell you. To make things

385

easier. To make me the villain."

"Is he wrong?"

"He's protecting himself. And protecting you."

"But it's true? You couldn't do it anymore?"

Her mother looks up. "It wasn't just one thing. There were many things. It was Othmarschen, where I didn't know anybody. The family routine. Coping with his diabolical parents. Trying to balance all that with a very demanding job in a BND dominated by men. Don't ask me about the gender split there. If you're a woman working in foreign intelligence, all these men think the only thing you're good for is honey-trapping and making coffee. I fought gender bias every day in that place, while fending off various advances, blatant and subtle. It was exhausting."

"Come back to the BND later. Tell me your side of the story, about leaving us."

"They're connected. I was transferred. To Tallinn. It was too good not to take. An opportunity I would never get again, and it was just after I'd come back from maternity leave. I figured I'd have to start from the bottom all over again, as I did after I had you. Then they offered me my own branch in Estonia. Richard and I argued about it for weeks. I wanted us all to go, but Richard thought it was too risky. For you and Anthony, he said, but I think he was the one who was scared. I kept trying to convince him it was his chance to cut ties with his parents, get out of the family law firm and live his life. It would've been an adventure, for all of us. That's what I wanted. Richard said no. And he said he would never let me take you and Anthony. He left me no choice."

"You had a choice. You chose to take the transfer. You abandoned us for your career."

"You're 26 now," Agnes says. "Have you been in any long-term relationships?"

"I've been too busy overcoming early traumas and trying to get my own life sorted. Haven't had the chance to factor anyone else in yet."

"You'll learn this on your own. The fact that Richard and I didn't agree on this one thing, admittedly a big thing, we both knew we could never go back to the way it was. We had this between us and always would. If I had stayed and tried to play happy families while working basically as a secretary for the BND boys, your father and I would've drifted apart anyway. I wanted Tallinn and he didn't. Once that was clear, and you know how stubborn he can be, he was never going to change his mind. I knew we were done, if not now, then further down the road. So, I chose now and took the position in Tallinn. I'm really sorry I left you and Anthony behind and that I couldn't nurture you both through childhood. But I don't regret it. Tallinn was the best time of my life."

"Why?"

"I ran a special branch of the BND during the tech boom that saw Estonia morph from an old Soviet outpost into one of the world's leading countries for innovation."

"What does the tech industry have to do with foreign intelligence?"

"That's a good question," Agnes says. "The BND back then had a futures department. It wasn't all cloak-and-dagger spying. Estonia was targeted as a country with high potential for recruiting, but it was a society at the time that was further ahead compared to Germany in terms of gender equality. A lot of the great ideas were coming from women, and the BND wanted a woman running the show there."

"So, you recruited them. As what? Spies?"

"Sort of, but not really. Look, Germany became economically powerful through innovation and ideas. It has very limited natural resources, but what it's always had is smart people making high-quality things. Engineering, mechanics, pharmaceuticals. But sometimes, the ideas need to be imported. That means importing people."

"You found people in Tallinn with great ideas and brought them to Germany?"

Agnes nods. "It was certainly more complicated and challenging than that, but in essence, yes. It's important to say that Germany has always had the means to bring innovations to fruition, which couldn't necessarily be done in places like Estonia or other countries. It's one thing to have a great idea, and another thing to make it happen."

"This isn't new," Milan says. He's still in the pool, his elbows on the edge, goggles up on his swim cap. It's only now that Mara recognises the current has been turned off and the hum from the pool is gone. "America did the same thing during the Second World

387

War, and for years after that. They brought Nazi scientists over to build the bomb, then those same scientists went on to set up the space program. It was those stolen Germans who got the Americans first to the moon."

"All through the history," Agnes says, "countries have stolen ideas from each other. That meant relocating people in order to get ahead, kidnapping them if necessary. It was about war and weapons, but then it became about power and money. The BND's futures department had branches all over the globe."

"Had? Not anymore?"

"There was a shift in the innovation trade. It became harder to lure people away from their homelands."

"Probably my fault," Milan says.

"Yes, it was," Agnes says, but without sounding like she blames Milan. She sits forward and pours herself more coffee. She holds up the pot for Mara, who declines.

Milan gets out of the pool. "There now exists an open marketplace of ideas."

"The dark web made it possible to sell anything to anyone," Agnes says. "If someone has a good idea, they can sell it to the highest bidder. Get rich, live anywhere they want. The innovators have the power now. The only allegiance they need to have is to the bank that holds all their money."

Veselin comes out of the house. He hands Milan a towel. Milan is lean and muscular in that way that looks creepy on older men. He's too fit for his age, making it look questionable, perhaps aided by supplements and surgery.

Mara thinks Milan looks vain.

"Tell her about the tap filter," he says, looking at his body as he towels down. "That brilliant teenager you sent to Hamburg. What was her name? Marla?"

"Marleen. She …"

"Wait," Mara says, jumping in. "Tallinn is just up the road from Riga. Did you have anything to do with Anthony getting into Latvia? You know he's there."

Milan walks to the table, towel around his trim waist. "Watch out, Agnes. You have a clever girl here."

"Poisoning the water cannons wasn't clever," Mara says.

"You think that was me?" He pours a glass of pulpy juice. "Why

388

would I do that? I would never do anything to harm protesters. I respect them too much, even when they're tearing the city up. I'm not fond of the police, and they're starting to take things too far in Germany, but I have no reason to get involved in any of that."

"Your son is involved. He was there, at the demonstration."

Milan calmly sips juice. "He's planting seeds. Like a good farmer's son."

"For what?"

"A career in politics. He's ambitious, no doubt about that."

Mara tries to remember the presentation Vilem gave in Berlin. "Are you saying Modra is going to become a political party?"

Milan smiles. "It has a great flag. Don't you think?" He finishes the juice and heads inside. "I'm going to take a shower. Wash this salt off me. Tell her about Marleen's filter."

"Fuck the filter," Mara says to her mother. "Tell me how you got Ant into Latvia. How did you even know he was going there?"

"You don't run a successful branch of foreign intelligence without getting to know a lot of people and forging important alliances. I've got a ton of contacts in Tallinn and the Baltic states."

"That's the second step, leaning on someone who's in your pocket. First, you needed to know he was headed that way."

"Yes. Correct."

The two of them stare at each other. As Mara see-saws between whether it might have been Richard and Perceval, she wonders again why she's not feeling anything. It's like her whole body is numb. She's certain her stubborn father would never have asked Agnes for help. Perceval, on the other hand, knew about Agnes Kollar, about this house in Marchtrenk, and was the one who suggested Riga.

"A friend of yours reached out to me," her mother says. "It was all rather cryptic. He said he had an important package for Cleopatra, being shipped to Riga by boat, and could I help him get it past customs."

"He probably thought someone was listening, but he always talks in a strange way."

"He didn't give his name. Don't use it now. I don't want to know. For me, that call never happened. But, I do know people in Riga who can help get a package past customs, and I contacted them."

"That's ... good of you."

"Don't look so surprised. That's not the first time I've helped your

389

brother."

"What?"

"Or you. If you take the time to think about your life and how you got to be where you are, you might identify points along the way where you got some valuable assistance. Such as someone who went several times to juvenile detention, and who was arrested as an adult, being so easily accepted into the German police academy."

"I aced all the tests. Zina put in a word for me."

"I'm sure she did. A good recommendation from a beat cop from Hamburg."

"Stuttgart."

"Wherever. You can be sure that my words had more weight."

Mara wants to leave. She slumps in the chair a little, feeling eight years old again, and wondering how else her mother meddled in her and Anthony's lives from afar.

"What happened to Zina was tragic," her mother continues. "But you need to know that I had nothing to do with it. Same with Milan. He rarely leaves the property. I can't speak for Vilem, though. He's on his own path, but I seriously doubt he would do something like this."

Mara thinks of Vilem, the gifted orator, charting a course into politics. All the rhetoric about protesting and the war on oppression now seems like a way to rally his base.

"Would you like to stay a few days with us? I admit I was shocked to see your face on the monitor, but I'm glad you came here, Mara. All along, I wanted you to find me."

Mara sits up. "Find you? That's the dumbest thing I've ever heard. Why should I try to find you? You left me. I was a kid. I couldn't understand that stuff going on between you and Dad, and I don't really understand it now."

"I ..."

"You were selfish. You wanted your career. You forgot all about us. Like we didn't even exist."

"Mara, calm ..."

"Don't you fucking say that." Mara stands up quickly, knocking the chair backwards. "Don't you tell me to calm down. I may never see my brother again. And I lost the most important person in my life yesterday."

"Who also left you."

"She did, but not for selfish reasons. Not to go off on some mission

390

to steal smart people and ship them back to Germany. Zina was forced out of Hamburg. Exiled. Punished for fighting back against a broken system."

"Just sit back down. Let's talk about this."

"I'm your daughter. Anthony's your son. Didn't that mean anything to you? You just turned your back on us."

"You think it didn't hurt me to do that? It was the hardest decision I ever made."

"To go and have the best time of your life. You said yourself you don't regret it. You probably met Milan at some futures conference. Was he just another asset you picked up along the way?"

"Hardly. Milan practically wrote the book on the privatisation of innovation. The way he went about selling his ideas, it ended what I was doing, because others just copied him. All the branches were shut down, one by one. Tallinn was one of the last."

"I'm so sorry for you."

"Don't take that tone with me. I didn't know what to do then. I was lucky that Milan recruited me, to run Modra."

"The water charity or the political party?"

"Clean water is a mandate plenty of people can get behind. Wouldn't you vote for that? To hell with the BND and its futures department. Water is the future. Milan made me understand that."

"Until someone poisons the well and people die."

Agnes holds up her hands. "Not us. Not Modra. Stop accusing me of that."

"Thanks for breakfast, but I think I'll disrespectfully decline staying here a few days." Mara starts to walk off the terrace. "Enjoy your second life. Or your third, or whatever reinvention you're up to."

"Mara, wait."

She doesn't look back. She goes around the house and gets in the Ranger. She feels a sense of massive injustice that she lost Zina and gained Agnes, within the last 24 hours. As she drives forward, she sees Veselin standing at the open front door. He waves, and this makes her stop. As he lumbers over, she lowers the window.

"I hope you're out here to give me more money," she says.

"Do you need it?"

"I wouldn't say no."

"I like your car," he says.

"I think I've got just enough cash to get back to Hamburg. It really drinks the petrol, even when I sit behind trucks. Feel very free to donate to my petrol fund."

He taps at his pockets, like an uncle looking for a present he might have brought for his niece. "It's all I have," he says, handing her a €50 note.

"Thanks. That'll save me from conking out somewhere near Hannover."

He leans his big, hairy forearms on the open window. "I like your mother. Very much."

"Which version? Agnes Kollar or Agnes Steinbach?"

"Everything in this house, it's very open."

"Are you saying you're a happily connected threesome? An unholy trinity? I'd rather not think about that. In fact, I'm going to forget that I came here at all."

"Stop judging. We live how we want. It's taken me a long time to be happy. The chickens run around. We have the big terrace. The clean air. There's lots of space."

"Good for you. All three of you."

"Your mother," he says, speaking with pride, "she travels all over the world. Water projects in many countries. She's a good person doing good work."

"She sure is. She's so good, she's trying really hard to make me stay. I guess those water projects are more important. Maybe you go back and tell her I'm thirsty."

He smiles and chuckles. "Agnes is also very funny."

"I'm not trying to be."

"You're not a child anymore. Don't carry that pain, because it won't change anything. Don't be a judge. Be the one who fights."

"You're ... yeah, you're right. Be in the moment."

"Control what you can control. Look forward, not back. If you're thinking about the last round, you'll get knocked out the next one."

Mara nods. "You know, you're pretty wise for a goon."

He chuckles, his face turning cherubic again. "Come back one day. When you're ready."

"That big security gate's always open. Right?"

"For you, yes."

Veselin steps back, then makes his right hand into a fist the size of a shank of ham. Mara makes a fist with her left hand.

392

"Keep working that speedbag," she says, as they bump fists.

"Drive safely. Get ready for the next round."

"I will."

"Look for Vilem in Hamburg. He'll be there for this summit that's being organised."

Mara hears something in Veselin's tone that makes her think Vilem is not to be trusted.

"I'll open the gate for you," he says, walking backwards to the house.

"Thanks, V."

He nods. "I like that. M."

Mara puts the car in gear and drives up towards the trees. Once through the gate and back on the road, she finds the Autobahn and points the car north.

The bed still smells faintly of Zina, the sheets unchanged, and this brings the hurt back.

Focus on now, she thinks. This day. This moment. This round.

She gets ups and pulls the sheets from the bed, yanking so hard the bottom sheet rips at one corner. She bundles it all in a pile that goes onto the floor, next to her abandoned police uniform. Then, still in the clothes she spent ten hours driving in yesterday and was too tired to change out of, she starts cleaning out her closet. Anything deemed worth keeping goes on the bed. Everything cast off is dropped to the floor.

"Good morning," Russell says from the doorway.

She sticks her head out of the closet. "Hey, Russ. Morning. Do we have any big garbage bags?"

"The blue ones? Under the sink."

She starts to move, but Russell blocks the way.

"Are you moving out?"

"No. Of course not. Maybe."

"I'll get the bags. I'll make some coffee while I'm in there."

"Thanks. Don't put anything in it."

"I know how you like it, Mara."

"You are now, officially, the person who knows the most about me."

"What an honour." He backs out of the doorway and pivots. The wheels squeak on the floor as he rolls to the kitchen.

The pile on the floor is much larger than the pile on the bed, making it seem there's little from her Berlin life worth keeping. She wants to leave it all behind, this Berlin version of herself, and keep only Russell. She's not losing him.

Cleaning out her closet is providing clarity; the last three weeks have changed her.

She redresses, in jeans and a t-shirt, chosen from the to-keep pile.

Russell comes back, a blue roll of bags in his lap. The coffee machine gurgles in the kitchen. He unfurls a bag from the roll and tears it off.

"Is this all going to charity?" he asks, shaking the bag open.

"The stuff on the floor, yes."

"The uniform as well?"

"Yeah."

"I think that's a mistake," Russell says. "It's part of you. Even if you never wear it again, I think you should keep it."

She bends down and extracts the uniform from the bottom of the pile. "I'm in a bad way right now, so I'm going to trust you on this."

She folds the pants and shirt, placing them on the bed.

"The memory of Zina is tied into it too," Russell says.

"It is. But I'm not taking the boots. I hated wearing those fucking boots. They made me feel like a soldier."

"So, this is it then? You're leaving for good? That's why you're here?"

Mara takes a bag from the roll and starts filling it. "The prime objective is to move us both to Hamburg."

"I'm not doing that. Berlin's in my blood. Even if I am scared I'll run into some Union Ultras at some point."

"You can always tase them."

"Ha. I can. But I can't leave this city."

"Then visit me. Regularly. I'll get Perceval to install some chair-lift thing, to get you up to my penthouse suite."

"Was that him who delivered your envelope yesterday?"

"He didn't come in? I told him to say hello. To meet you."

Russell shakes his head. "It would've been good to talk to him. For the article. But now you're here, I can talk to you. You're the missing piece. What I've got right now is a bunch of small stories, but nothing holding it all together. Your story can be that glue."

"I don't think so. There's something bigger here."

"Stuttgart could end up being an isolated incident. A tragedy, without doubt, but not something that will happen again. The police have already been exonerated." Russell ties the first bag shut and flings it over his shoulder, into the hallway. "Mara, I'm really sorry about Zina."

"She deserves way better than this."

"The police are saying she did it. On her own. The media's running with that, mostly."

"The police are a pack of fucking liars."

"I haven't checked this morning, but last night, Zina was trending as a martyr. Protest groups were claiming her as their hero, saying that the police framed her. There is video of her trying to pull people to safety before she gets hit by the cannon."

She wonders if Perceval had something to do with that. Did he turn to social media when the politicians wouldn't listen to him?

"I don't like it that they're making her a martyr."

"Every revolution needs a Che-like figure," Russell says. "Someone who dies for the cause."

"Zina never supported any protest groups."

"It doesn't matter. There's a good chance she will become a symbol for the protest, whether she stood for it or not."

"A lie that everyone believes, so it becomes the truth."

"That's good," Russell says. "Can I use that?"

"Go for it, but don't quote me. I'm not the missing piece of your story. But I know what is."

"What?"

Mara closes one bag and starts filling another. "Modra. The planet-saving water charity is about to become a political party. That's what all of this is about. Politics."

"Do you know this for sure?"

"Got it from the mare's mouth. Vilem Kollar's out there, not trying to unite protest groups. He's trying to raise his profile and gain voters."

"That is the missing piece," Russell says. "The end game."

"The whole war on oppression thing was like a campaign strategy."

"This move into politics, is this just in Germany?"

"I don't know. That meeting he held here had plenty of people from other countries. Vilem said he'd been travelling all over the continent, meeting people. Maybe he was establishing the Modra political party in each country."

Russell ties another bag shut. "This could be what's revolutionary. A Europe-wide party specifically targeting young voters and those who want to save the planet. The Greens are too centre these days, and old, and not really standing for anything. But a clear mandate for clean water, universal income and whatnot, these are things lots of people support. I wrote a story a couple of years ago about how young voters have no interest in politics, because it's basically dominated by middle-aged men. They don't see any representation for themselves. So they don't vote."

Mara looks at Russell. "Are you saying that you think Modra can win?"

"They could definitely gain some traction. I don't know about winning. If you take Germany as an example, there's a massive section of the population that doesn't vote. They might step up and vote for Modra, particularly if they have a young, charismatic leader who speaks for them."

"Young. Diverse. Climate-focused."

"All the photos you sent me," Russell continues, "one key thing they show is how multicultural the youth of Germany is. This is a big change from 20 years ago. It's like that in quite a few European countries now. You have to appreciate that these young generations coming through, with many of them having marched in Fridays for Future demos in their teens, they don't identify with politicians who are predominantly white men who grew up with rotary-dial telephones. Plenty of these leaders don't even think climate change is real. No wonder young people think they're not being listened to."

"They don't have a voice."

"I think you're wrong about that. They have a voice, but no one's listening. That's the problem. The police try to clamp them down and shut them up, and the government's full of grumpy old men. Now, here comes Vilem Kollar, and he's young and he's going to stand up and be the change that all these young people want. He's one of them. If he manages to lead a revolution, it could simply be a generational shift, without any shots being fired."

"Out with the old, in with the young?"

"More good stuff. I'm using that too. I need an exclusive with Vilem, before anything is made public."

"He's going to be in Hamburg for this security summit tomorrow."

"Take me with you."

"I was hoping to stay here a few days. Get my bearings again."

"You pulled your sheets off the bed, and now you're packing, like you're evacuating. You have one foot out the door."

Mara sits down on the bed. "I want to avoid this meeting, in case it turns into something like Stuttgart, with protest groups battling the police. Have you seen any footage of that? Or are they just showing Königstraße, over and over again?"

"Any excuse to show that footage. I've seen some bits of the fights. It looked brutal."

"The guys that were there for the fight, they weren't part of your generation of young voters. They were just thugs. Hooligans."

"Do you think Vilem organised that? He got these groups to come and fight the police?"

"I don't know. Maybe they have nothing to do with Modra. They were just there for the fight."

"However it happened, it got the whole world's attention. The launch of the Modra political party can now be shaped as a response, to make it sound like the young people have spoken."

"I don't really know Vilem. I don't know how to get in contact with him."

"You'll find a way. I can't send my article until I've spoken with him." Russell spins the wheelchair around. "I'm packing a bag. We leave in an hour."

The prospect of more driving makes Mara's shoulders drop. But at least she can help Russell with his story and take her stuff to Hamburg.

She goes into the kitchen and pours herself a coffee. There are some flattened moving boxes in the storeroom where they keep cleaning supplies; they're the same boxes she used when moving in. She folds them into shape and takes them into her room. As she fills them, mostly with books and clothes, she's surprised by how little she has. The bike can go in the Ranger's tray, but the punching bag will have to stay. She wonders if Russell will leave it there, as some kind of monument to their time as roommates. There's no point taking the bed or furniture. Leaving the room furnished like this will make it easier for Russell to rent it out if he wants to.

She starts taking boxes and bags out to her car. The bike is the last thing, and she places this on top of the plastic bags, to keep them from blowing open. There's space for Russell's chair and an old length of rope she can use to fasten everything down. The last thing she wants is to get pulled over by the cops on the way to Hamburg for driving with an unsecured load.

Back in the apartment, Russell's bags are by the door. She finds him in the kitchen, making cheese sandwiches for the trip. He finishes one and is about to wrap it, when Mara takes it from him.

"I need to tell you something," she says, biting into the sandwich.

"This isn't goodbye. Let's not go down that road."

"No, but you can rent out the room. Better than that, fall in love and get that new love to move in. Turn my room into an office. You can punch the bag whenever you get frustrated or blocked. Punch the bag and think of me."

"Actually, I am seeing someone. I've been dying to tell you, but all this other stuff has been coming up."

"That's awesome, Russ. Who is he?"

"You know him. Marcello."

"Schomberg? From Kollwitzkiez?"

"We met when I did that story. Just hit it off right away. Magical. Lauter actually was the one who introduced us. You have every right to hate him, but Lauter turned out to be extremely helpful in a number of ways."

"Because he guessed he had something to gain. He's running that station now."

"I know. But he doesn't have it easy. Things have changed there. The closets are open, you could say. That piece of garbage Spitz unwittingly brought in many gay men. Before, they were discrete. But they're open now. Marcello says Lauter's been surprisingly good about it."

"Again, because there's something for him to gain. He can go all in on diversity, the way Spitz went all in on sustainability."

"That's better, don't you think?"

"Marcello's a great guy. He was always good to do a shift with. I'm happy for you, Russ."

"He only has positive things to say about you. Though I would expect nothing less. Lauter remains a prick, but he did tell me he was sorry for what happened. He said he was in a bad place, at the time. Mentally."

"Fuck that," Mara says through a mouthful of sandwich. "There is nothing that will let me forgive him."

"He thinks you two are even, because of how much you hurt him."

"He deserved it. When you see him next time, tell him to stick his apology up his arse."

"I probably will see him again. He's made it clear that all partners can be plus-ones at Kollwitzkiez station social events. To me, that's significant progress."

"We'll see how long it sticks. That was a great story, by the way. About Spitz."

"So good he blew his brains out. It's just a matter of time before someone figures out that Zina was the source."

"Perceval knows, but he won't tell anyone. If it does come out, the police will spin it to suit whatever narrative they want."

"You've become very cynical in the last three weeks."

"A lot's happened."

"What about Anthony? Germany's most wanted teenager."

"I found him and helped him escape. He's safe."

"Isn't there someone in the police who can expose all these lies? They're not all bad people."

"It's a top-down problem."

"Maybe I should take a shot at it. The article on Spitz brought about change."

"He was replaced by Lauter, practically a clone."

"I think you're wrong. Lauter won't dare lay his hands on anyone. The balance of power has shifted. Any predators in the police force, or maybe even anywhere, they're the targets now. They know it. Everyone's watching. They'll creep back into their dirty little holes and keep their hands to themselves."

"Or pick up a gun and blow their brains out."

"Win-win."

This makes Mara smile. She finishes the sandwich, smiling as she chews.

"So, Anthony's somewhere safe," Russell says, putting the sandwiches in a bag. "You don't have to say where. What else do you need to tell me?"

"This is the big one. I found my mother."

"Wow. Really?"

"She's up to her eyeballs in this. Brace yourself. Her name is Agnes Kollar."

"No! She's the one behind Modra?"

"The water charity part. The political party is all Vilem, so she says."

"How did you find her? There are no pictures or videos of her anywhere. It's like she doesn't exist. Anything with Modra and their projects is always with young volunteers and children."

"It's her."

"How do you feel about that?"

"Ah, classic, Russ. I knew you would ask exactly that question. On that incredibly long drive here, I knew you would ask me about my feelings."

"Am I so predictable?"

400

"You're reliable."

"And? Share your feelings."

"I feel nothing," Mara says. "It was Perceval who guided me there. He knew."

"More."

Mara explains how her mother worked for the BND, including in Tallinn, and how Perceval contacted her to help Anthony get out of Germany.

"She's in this weird relationship with Milan Kollar and his right-hand man, Veselin."

"People can live however they want. There's no blueprint for how a relationship should be."

"You're right. Sorry. She kept saying that she and Milan had nothing to do with the protests and what happened in Stuttgart."

"How did you get to Modra putting something in the water cannons? Why would they have anything to do with that?"

"Perceval again. That's his theory, and he's connecting it to the murder in Hamburg as well. But he can't prove anything. I thought I could confront Milan Kollar with it and he would confess."

"As if it would be that easy. They would just deny everything."

"Yeah. I'm starting to think they had nothing to do with it. But it was hard to figure out when Agnes was telling the truth."

"BND tricks, I bet. Still, you found her. That's good, isn't it?"

"I'm not sure yet," Mara says. "I need to process it. Weirdly, I like Veselin the goon the most. I'd be happy to see him again. My mother, I don't know."

"I know it's hard, but you should try to forgive her, no matter how it all happened. She wanted to live her life."

"It's such a long time ago. She left to pursue her career. That was it. It wasn't like she met someone else. She just wanted to work. That was more important than me and Ant."

"You're looking at it from your own point of view, which is understandable."

"You mean I'm being selfish."

"I'm trying to get you to see all the sides. Maybe you were better off. If she'd stayed and been miserable or unbearable, that could've led to a whole other kind of childhood trauma and hurt. You'd be talking to a therapist now about how your mother was there but always distant and nasty. Or something like that. Instead of a mother

401

who just wasn't there at all."

"Good point."

"Every family is fucked up, in some way. When I came out to my parents, my father was so supportive, but my mother didn't talk to me for years afterwards. Like, ten years. That really hurt me."

"I'm sorry, Russ."

"No child reaches adulthood without issues of some kind."

Mara watches Russell wash two apples and put them in the bag. "I'm going to miss you, Russell Wex."

"Not just yet. We've got a road trip ahead of us. A final fling."

"I'm ready."

"But I'll miss you too, Mara."

They hug.

"Having said that," Russell says, "I'm already sold on the idea of Marcello moving in and turning your room into my new office."

"Do it."

He places the bag of food in his lap and wheels out of the kitchen.

"We need to figure out how we can stay in contact," Mara says. "I'm kind of anti-phone these days."

"The old-fashioned post worked well during our clandestine operation. How about we continue on as pen-pals?"

"I'd like that very much."

**

She drops Russell at a hotel just around the corner from Hamburger Berg, agreeing to meet him back there in an hour.

At her building, it's an effort to haul all of her stuff upstairs, but the boxes and bike make it feel like she's properly moved in now, and not just holing up here like a criminal on the run. She hopes Perceval will let her continue to live in his apartment, even as the status of her undercover mission becomes increasingly tenuous. Part of her would be glad to be done with Circus and the protest scene, to focus instead on working at Gus's gym and building that into something.

With her single-speed bike now here, there's no need for her to use Ant's old bike, which she left out at the house in Moorfleet. It's too big for Tinaya, but she could sell it and use the money to buy Tinaya a bike that's the right size. Reminded, she takes the Modra flag from her backpack, folds it into a taut square and slides it into her back pocket.

After all the driving, and the trips up and down the rickety stairs, it's hard to get going again. But she's due at the hotel and not willing to let Russell down. She sends a text to Perceval, requesting an emergency meeting at the Pink Dragon, then heads down the stairs.

At the hotel, she waits in the lobby for Russell. It's busy with people who look like media types, here to cover the Security Summit, as Jawinski has branded it. She wonders if Nicola came up with that name. Jawinski doesn't come across as particularly creative or clever; he's more a bludgeoning tool than a fine instrument.

People on phones speak different languages – Danish, French, Dutch and others – suggesting this summit is being attended by ministers from neighbouring countries, as Jawinski wanted. Or they're here in preparation to cover another potentially violent protest, to turn a body count into clickbait.

Russell comes out of the elevator. He rolls towards Mara.

"Looks like you've got some competition," she says.

"They don't scare me."

Outside, Mara points towards the Reeperbahn, and that's the direction they go.

"All the hacks are here for the press conference," Russell says. "But hopefully only you and I know about Vilem Kollar. That's the big story here. Any ideas how to get to him? Today, ideally."

"The only person I can think of is JJ. But I don't even know if she's back from Stuttgart, or if she got out of there unscathed. She could've been arrested, still sitting in a jail cell down there."

"How do you plan to find her, phone-less Mara?"

"Perceval. He'll know where JJ is. We're going to meet him now. Hopefully."

"At the Pink Dragon? Suddenly, I'm very excited."

"That's where we're headed. Better turn your phone off."

"Is that one of the rules?"

"Perceval assures me the Dragon is off grid."

Russell stops pushing his chair for a moment to turn off his phone. "I can't wait to see this place, and to meet Perceval. He's already a fully formed person in my mind."

"Let's hope the man in the flesh lives up to that." Mara moves around to push Russell's chair. "I'm only guessing he's already back from Berlin, to be here for the summit."

They pass a kiosk that has racks of newspapers out front, with Stuttgart dominating all the headlines.

"You know, Mara," Russell says, "I'm sorry to say this, but if Zina hadn't been blamed for Stuttgart, Germany would've been crucified by the media abroad, with every headline linked to our history. 'German Police Cremate Protesters', or something like that. You could bet the UK press would've put 'Nazi' in every single headline."

"They can use the other go-to winner instead. Terrorism. Zina's story will quickly evolve to make it sound like she was always a terrorist."

"Which means she will become a hero for some. I caught up on this at the hotel. On social media, some people are saying the police poisoned their own well and Zina was the only one to jump the barricade to save people."

"That's the truth."

"Is it? We don't know if the police poisoned the cannons. What's awful is that Zina's life and legacy are being manipulated to suit different interests. Hero, terrorist, protester, extremist, martyr. Who she actually was is getting lost."

"I can't even believe we're talking about her in this way. That she's even gone."

They turn onto Große Freiheit, busy and full of men on this Sunday afternoon, and head into the Pink Dragon.

"Mara," Maurice says brightly. "So nice to see you."

"Hi, Maurice. This is Russell."

Maurice comes around the bar. "Yes, indeed. Russell Wex."

They shake hands.

"You know him?" Mara asks.

"It is an honour to meet you," Maurice says. "I very much enjoy your work."

"Thanks. That's nice to hear. I get a lot more hate mail than fan mail."

"They're wrong. All of them. I especially liked that recent piece on space. Humorous and pertinent."

"I got a lot of negative feedback on that one," Russell says. "People said I was making a mockery of our cultural values."

"I know. I read the letters to the editor. Some comments were brutal."

"Since when does reserving a sun chair with your towel count as

404

a cultural value?" Mara asks.

"It was more about insulting the middle class," Russell says.

"The backbone of Germany." Maurice returns to his elevated place behind the bar.

"My editor said the exact same thing. I reminded her that the backbone goes down the middle of the body and doesn't do very much thinking."

Maurice laughs. "That's good. Now. What brings you in here? Because there's nothing in here that will tickle your fancy, Mr Wex."

"Careful with your assumptions there, Maurice," Mara says.

"My dear, you don't work in a place like this for as long as I have without developing a very keen radar."

"It's no secret," Russell says. "Plenty of the hate in my hate mail takes aim at my sexuality."

Mara looks around the club, which is empty save for two guys asleep near the stage and a tall girl dancing languidly in front of them.

"I'm meeting Perceval," she says. "I sent him a message, but I'm not sure he's in Hamburg. Can you contact him?"

Maurice cocks an ear towards the door. "I think I hear the humble rumble of Penelope's car." He then looks upwards and adds, "God rest her beautiful soul."

Perceval strides in, wearing his blue table tennis tracksuit.

"Thanks for coming on short notice," Mara says.

"This better be very good."

"Where's Nils?"

"He's got his own big game today." Perceval looks at Russell and adds, "You can't be present. Please leave."

"No. If he goes, I go. You really want to hear what I found out in Austria."

"You got that confession?" Perceval asks, sounding doubtful this is the case.

He moves towards a booth in one of the corners. Mara and Russell follow him.

"No confessions, sorry," Mara says.

"What a surprise." Perceval slides into the booth. "This is all off the record. No phones or devices. By all means, Russell, let the girl distract you," he says, gesturing towards the stage.

"No chance of that," Mara says, pushing the wheelchair to the

405

front of the booth.

"Proceed and make it quick," Perceval says. "I'm already late for warm-ups."

"How can you think about fucking ping pong at a time like this?"

"The A-squad is competing in the Hamburg semi-finals. I am currently ranked A3, to play third singles and second doubles. My presence is crucial to securing victory."

"Ping pong?" Russell asks.

"Table tennis. You can participate. The club competes in the wheelchair division."

Russell smiles. "I am so disappointed you didn't knock on my door yesterday. I wouldn't have let you leave."

"There wasn't time for chit-chat. Berlin was all activity. One meeting after the other, and nothing was achieved."

"What happened?" Mara asks. "Did you tell them the truth?"

"I never had the chance to speak. Jawinski dominated. He is clearly shaping to make a power move."

"To force an election?"

"Possibly."

"What about Zina?"

"There is nothing I can influence there, I'm very sorry to say."

"The protest groups are using her for their own promotion," Russell says.

"Are they now?" Perceval starts rotating his left hand, loosening up his wrist. "Yet more contriving for political gain. Of course, you didn't hear me say that."

"And JJ?" Mara asks.

"She made it back to Hamburg."

"She wasn't arrested?"

"The arrest statistics were greatly inflated. But I didn't say that either."

Perceval now uses his right hand to flex his left hand forwards and backwards.

"How can I find her?"

"You are unaware of her place of residence? You never followed her home?"

"Never had the chance. But I'm certain you know where she lives."

"Indeed I do. Hafenstraße 112."

406

"The old squats?" Russell asks.

"A perk of Circus leadership, I presume." Perceval goes back to rotating his left hand. "Now, what about your sojourn to Austria, Mara? What information can you share?"

"Why didn't you me tell who Agnes Kollar really is?"

"I felt it was something you should learn for yourself."

"Fuck that. You should've told me."

"I thought it best for you to focus on one thing at a time."

"Who are you to make those decisions for me?"

"Perhaps I was wrong. Your mother had quite a reputation in the BND."

"I don't give a shit about her standing in the BND," Mara says.

"But you found her. What did she say?"

"She and Milan denied everything, but they did say Vilem is launching Modra as a political party."

Perceval's hand stops in mid-rotation. "Pardon?"

"Vilem has political aspirations. I'd say all his trips around Germany have been to establish local leaders for Modra, to be ready once they launch the party. I'm sure you could research all that, show where he's been and maybe even who he met with. I'm guessing this will happen in the next few days. He's in Hamburg, or on his way here."

"Analysis of social media and comms networks picked up chatter about some kind of announcement in Hamburg. We assumed it was for another protest, with all the groups coming here, to demonstrate against what happened in Stuttgart."

"That has to be a false lead," Russell says. "Mara, you said they usually mobilise from word of mouth. They stay off anything digital, so it can't be followed. Why would they now be doing the opposite?"

"Perhaps the time is too short," Perceval says. "They need to get the people together quickly. This might require extending the blockade around Hamburg."

"That didn't exactly work in Stuttgart," Mara says. "Thousands of people got through."

"This will be far more comprehensive. Our officers are moving into position to block every access point to the city. No protesters will get in."

"That will require a huge number of police," Russell says.

"Many are already here. More are coming."

"To turn Hamburg into a fortress."

"Just what Jawinski's always wanted," Mara says. "His own little police island. Whatever you do, don't tell anyone about Modra becoming a political party. If that comes out too early, Vilem will know it was me. I don't trust him."

Perceval slides out of the booth. "Oh, are you still undercover and working for me?"

"I don't know. Am I?"

Perceval and Mara stare at each other.

"I'd say she's given you something very good," Russell says, "with the information about Modra's political move."

"Well said. Perhaps you shall also consider a move into politics."

"Not my team. I prefer objectivity."

Perceval, standing now, extends a hand to Russell. They shake.

"A pleasure to meet you. But from my side, you were never here, and we never met."

"Shame. I was just starting to like you."

"Likewise."

"Well, if you're ever in Berlin, you know where I live."

Perceval smiles and walks out.

"Good luck," Maurice says, as Perceval passes the bar.

Russell looks at Mara. "What a piece of work he is. Are all your meetings with him like that?"

"He's normally good to work with, deep into it and committed. I've felt all along like he's on my side."

"Maybe you should consider learning how to play table tennis, so you can become a mixed doubles team."

"His priorities are clearly off today. How can he go and play when all this shit's about to go down?"

"Steady on. People are allowed to have lives."

"And I'm allowed to have an opinion."

"That you are."

"I get the feeling something happened in Berlin. They'll make him take the fall for not finding Marten's killer. That was the task that set all this in motion."

"No disrespect for this Marten guy, but there are bigger things in play now. Way bigger. I need to talk to Vilem."

"Let's go to JJ's place. She should know how to get in contact with him."

"Do you think she'll even help? Where are you guys at with each other?"

"I drove her to Stuttgart. She owes me for that, at least."

Russell backs away from the booth. "Good. Just get me out of here."

"You don't like this place? Now who's judging."

"I've written a few too many stories about human trafficking and modern slavery not to feel uncomfortable in places like this. The bartender's probably read them all."

"If he has, he doesn't appear to be holding any grudges towards you. He's pulling to be your number one fan."

"That could be because this is one of the few strip clubs that actually operates in a fully legal manner, with Perceval being the owner."

"Could be."

"I still don't want to be in here though."

As Russell rolls towards the door, he waves to Maurice. Mara grips the handles and pushes the wheelchair. Outside, they take the grimy back streets away from the Reeperbahn and head to Hafenstraße. At the Onkel Otto bar, where drug sellers are loitering, they have to make a long detour to avoid the steps.

"How do you stand it?" Russell asks, pointing towards the harbour. "All this industry and noise, right in the middle of the city."

"I've always loved the harbour. Hamburg, the gateway to the world."

"Now it's Hamburg the fortress."

"If the city's crawling with cops, I haven't seen any yet. They must all be in the centre, guarding the Rathaus."

"All I can think about is what might happen in Berlin if there aren't enough police there to keep law and order. If a whole lot of them are ordered to come here, there could be a crime spree in Berlin. They should've got the army to come here instead."

"I'm guessing Jawinksi doesn't trust the army, after that Day X fiasco. Remember that? All those army right-wingers gearing up to take over Germany?"

"I was undercover at Union then. The Ultras thought it was all a joke. Some kind of prank. But I recall there were some police officers involved as well."

"There were. There might even be more cops leaning to the right

409

these days, just keeping their opinions and their prepping to themselves."

"Here it is," Russell says. "112."

Mara looks at the old building. "I seriously doubt there's an elevator in there."

"Get her to come down. Push her buzzer."

Mara looks at the buzzers. Only half of them are labelled, in pen, and Jabali isn't among them. The door looks flimsy, like it doesn't close properly. She gives it a shove with her shoulder and it opens.

"Are you planning to bang on every door in there until you find her?" Russell asks.

"Isn't that what a journalist would do?"

"It's what a cop would do. A journalist would wait patiently for someone to come out and ask politely if they've seen her."

"I'm done being polite." Mara looks past Russell. "It doesn't matter. Here she comes."

JJ is talking animatedly on the phone as she walks, head down, along the street towards them. But when she looks up and sees Mara, she ends the call and starts jogging towards her. They hug.

"You're all right," JJ says, arms around Mara. "I had no idea what happened to you. I was so worried."

"Same here."

JJ lets Mara go and steps back. "When I heard the news about Zina ..."

"What happened to you? I saw you at the university, during Vilem's speech, but then you were gone."

"Where were you? All the Circus members were at Charlottenplatz. But then the police moved in and everyone ran for it. That's how bad it was. The police were out of control."

"How did you get back here?"

"Hitchhiked to Frankfurt, then took the train from there."

"You didn't get stopped anywhere? I hit a roadblock south of the city."

"What were you doing going south?" JJ asks. "There weren't any roadblocks to the north. I think they were glad everyone was leaving the city."

"No one from Circus was arrested? No one died?"

JJ shakes her head. "Thank God. But the police in those water cannons are the ones who should be arrested. That was murder."

"According to the police," Russell says, "that was Zina."

JJ looks at Russell. "Who are you?"

"Russell Wex."

"Why do I know that name?"

"I'm a journalist."

"He did the story on sexual harassment in the police," Mara says.

"Right." JJ turns to Mara. "I'm so sorry about Zina."

"Really? Looks like she's going to play a major role for you and Vilem and protest movements everywhere. Your first revolutionary hero."

"I don't agree with any of that," JJ says. "But I prefer her being honoured that way than butchered by the police and the media."

"Vilem's all about PR. Maybe this is his doing. He got this story going."

"He's too busy for that," JJ says.

"I'm sure he is. Where is he now? Here?"

"Why?"

"I'd like to interview him," Russell says.

"We know what's coming," Mara says. "We know about Vilem's announcement."

"Then I think you know more than I do. What is it?"

JJ possibly not knowing about the plan for Modra catches Mara by surprise. "I can't say, just yet."

"That doesn't seem fair. All I know is that Vilem's on his way here from Schwerin. He asked me to gather the Circus members I trust the most for a meeting tomorrow morning at ten. I want you there, Mara."

"Where?"

"Otzenstraße."

"The police are ready for it," Mara says. "It'd be crazy to try to protest."

"Vilem didn't say anything about a demo. He just wants this meeting."

"Can I join?" Russell asks.

"Are you planning to tell our side of the story? If yes, I can ask Vilem and clear it with him. But right now, I need to get moving, to organise everything for tomorrow. I have a lot of ground to cover."

"Because you're doing it all in person," Russell says.

"Yes. No phones. Remember that tomorrow too."

"Sure," Russell says, his tone suddenly a little cold.

"Mara, if you see Tinaya, I want her there as well. All of the girls who helped you design the flag. They deserve to be part of this. Vilem wants to meet them."

"I know where they are," Mara says.

"Good." JJ goes to the door and shoves it open, like Mara did. "I'll see you tomorrow."

Russell and Mara look at each other.

"Do you think she's lying?" Russell asks, moving away from the entrance. "About not being aware of Modra's political move."

"I think she's telling the truth, but it was weird how she didn't press me about it."

"That was clever not to tell her. It's always good to keep some important information in reserve."

"That has to be what the meeting's for. A kind of press conference in the bunker. If that's the case, Vilem will definitely want you there."

"Let's hope so. This could be a huge story. Where are you going now? I need to get back to the hotel and do some work."

"Gus's gym. To find Tinaya. I'm pretty sure she's there."

"Not a very German-sounding name."

"She's from Afghanistan," Mara says. "A refugee, along with her friends."

"And they designed the Modra flag? That fits."

"Hey, I helped too."

"I bet you were really good at judging it."

"Very funny."

"Can you help me up this hill? I'll be able to make it to the hotel from there."

"Sure." Mara starts pushing the wheelchair. "But if my hands just happen to slip halfway up and you roll back down out of control, I can't be held responsible for that."

"That's just mean." Russell helps the wheels along.

"You want to grab dinner later?"

"Yes. Get me from the hotel at seven."

"Maybe Marcello's on the way here. If many police have been brought in, he could be one of them."

"Good thinking. I'll ask him. If he's here, he can come along."

"Absolutely."

They reach the top of the hill and separate at the roundabout near

Park Fiction. Russell heads back towards the Reeperbahn while Mara goes down the hill's other side, towards Fischmarkt. Life seems exceedingly ordinary on this Sunday afternoon. Park Fiction is crowded with people, sitting on the grass and drinking. There's a scrappy basketball game in progress on the short court, with a mix of guys in basketball clothes and guys in street clothes. It makes her think of Anthony and hope he's okay; she wonders if there's anything more she can do to help him.

On Pinnasberg, a family spills out of an apartment building, the father pushing a double-pram and the mother holding hands with her son; he comes up to her hip and has to reach his little arm up in order to hold his mother's hand.

The sun is out. People are gravitating towards the river. They sip coffees, eat ice cream and chat amongst each other. Nothing seems terribly important today, other than enjoying simple pleasures.

Down at Fischmarkt, people sit against the fence between the cobblestones and the river, their feet dangling over the edge. They gather in groups of two, three or four, with barely any separation between the groups as they jostle for any available space in the sun. Five metres from the fence is a line of campervans, parked close together in a car park, front wheels up on little ramps to keep the vehicles level, their owners positioned in camping chairs nearby.

There's an event happening at the Fischauktionshalle. Outside the entrance, well-dressed people are gathered around circular tables that have white sheets over them, hanging all the way to the ground. They sip champagne from skinny flutes. Mara picks out Nicola, wearing a tight-fitting, dark red dress. Their eyes meet. Nicola excuses herself from the people she's standing with and walks towards Mara.

"Hey, stranger," Nicola says. "I thought I might see you on Friday, for another lunch."

"I was out of town."

"Anywhere nice?"

"I went to Berlin, to pick up some stuff."

"So, back for good?"

"Looks like it. What's going on?"

"Just a meet and greet." Nicola gives Mara a long look, then adds, "I'm sorry to hear about your brother."

"Why? He didn't do it."

413

"A witness says otherwise."

"That's all there is," Mara says. "A witness statement. I've seen the footage. The protester is unrecognisable."

"Is he?"

"You get that witness to withdraw the statement, then the police will have no reason to arrest Anthony."

"They'll still keep searching for him."

"Maybe. But not with the same enthusiasm."

"It sounds like you're asking me to manage this." Nicola sips her champagne. "Couldn't your father do something? He's good at making this kind of noise."

"As I understand it, Lersner-Löwe represents Circus."

"You've done some research, I see."

This makes Mara think Nicola knows about her breaking into the Lersner-Löwe office. "The head of Circus told me. I'm back in the protest scene."

"You sure are. Quite the star, apparently."

With Nicola building a wall and being coy, Mara decides to take a different approach, softening her tone. "Come on, Nic. It's Anthony. He used to worship you."

"If you tell me where he is, I could try to help him. I could represent him."

"I don't know where he is. But I know who the witness is. I'm sure if I give him the right motivation, I could get him to withdraw his statement."

"You should leave that to me. I wouldn't want you getting in any trouble."

"I suggest you tell your witness that there are some people in Circus who don't like rats."

"It's not a secret, is it? About this particular rat? Look, I'd like to help, but there's not much I can do on a Sunday."

"Tomorrow then?" Mara asks.

"I'll look into it. Perhaps there'll come a time when you can do something for me in return."

"Yeah. Okay. I'll owe you."

Nicola smiles and has another sip of champagne. "You know, you're the second person to ask me to do this."

"Who was first?"

"Karl. Your grandfather."

414

Nicola walks back to the tables and starts mingling again.

Annoyed, Mara skirts around the auction hall, then passes De-Voß-Straße, where Zina once lived in a tiny studio flat, which was all she could afford as she gave half of her salary away each month to support her extended family.

Mara thinks again how wrong it seems to have her mother back in her life and Zina gone from it. Now, Nicola's in her life as well, and she will want something at some point.

At the gym, the door is held open by an old medicine ball, its laces frayed and guts threatening to spill out. As she enters, the first thing she notices is that all the photos have been removed from the hallway. Instead, there's a large white noticeboard, currently empty. A shoe shelf fashioned out of a single long plank and pairs of bricks at intervals extends the length of the hallway. Five pairs sit on top of the plank, all small and well-worn, plus one pair of men's shoes underneath. She kicks her own off and puts them next to Gus's.

At the end of the hallway, Tinaya sees her, lets out a little yelp of delight and comes running towards her. This is a hug that Mara wants. She throws her arms out and gets involved, lifting Tinaya up so her socked feet kick in the air.

"I'm so happy to see you," Tinaya says.

"Same here."

They let each other go, then Tinaya hugs Mara again, like a little sister would: arms around Mara's waist and an ear to her chest.

"You're good? You're okay?"

"Better now," Mara says. "I feel like I've come home."

Tinaya lets Mara go. "I can't wait to show you what we've done."

"Getting Gus to take his shoes off is already an achievement."

"I thought you were arrested. Or worse. It was just horrific what happened down there. Zina ..."

"None of what the police said about her is true. Trust me on that. But I don't want to talk about it right now."

"I respect that."

"I brought you a souvenir."

She reaches into her back pocket and produces the Modra flag. She hands it to Tinaya, who unfurls it and holds it up.

"I saw it on TV, but it's way more beautiful in real life. Thank you, Mara."

Another hug, the flag between them. Then, Tinaya loops the flag

415

around her neck, like a scarf, and takes Mara by the hand to lead her down the hallway.

"Come on. You have to see this."

"Where are all the photos?"

"We moved them into Gus's office. They're on the wall in there."

"That's good. We can make our own history."

"While not forgetting the past. Because you're in those photos."

Mara wants to say that Zina's in them as well, but holds this back, to avoid the loss collapsing on her all over again.

In the gym's main area, Mara is glad to focus on the changes that have been made, to get her mind off Zina. There are four other girls, around Tinaya's age, doing cleaning jobs around the gym. The first thing she notices is that it smells different. All the old equipment is still there, but the place is cleaner than it's ever been. The smells of stale sweat and MMA feet have been replaced by pine and lavender. All the old posters have been removed and the walls painted, making the place feel fresher and less of a male domain. She thinks the gym now feels like it's aboveground, when before it had an almost cavern-like atmosphere. It's then she notices how clean the windows are, letting in far more natural light than before.

In the office, Mara can see Gus asleep at his desk; the office windows are also clean, probably for the first time since they were installed.

"What do you think?" Tinaya asks. "Do you like it?"

The only structural change is that the stretching area has been moved from near the locker room entrance to the opposite corner, next to the ring. In its place is a cordoned-off area containing child-sized chairs, a low table and what looks like a chest of toys.

"Is that a daycare centre?" she asks.

"We took some things from Elbe Help," Tinaya says. "The chairs and toys. That's all right, isn't it? Do you think JJ will mind? A lot of that stuff just sits around in the storeroom."

"I'm sure JJ will be fine it's here."

"Good. I was worried we'd be accused of stealing."

"It's great what you've done in here. The place looks fantastic. It's a new place."

"Gus wrote letters for all of us, so we can work here as volunteers. He's such a good man."

"He's gold, old Gus," Mara says. "That's for sure."

"He told us about the money. That you put in."

"It wasn't exactly my money, but I'm happy to see you've put it to good use. What we need to aim for is getting you all employed here. That daycare area will need supervisors."

"The idea is for mothers to come here, with their children," Tinaya says brightly, as if this is something she herself might do one day.

"And fathers," Mara says, thinking of Callenberg. "Everyone's welcome here, as long as they welcome everyone else. Any sign of prejudice and we'll show them the door."

As the girls nod their collective agreement, Mara is amazed at how invested they are in the gym. Not only because they want to learn to box, but because they have the chance to be part of building something of value. Something that adds to the community, that might also help to establish their own places within it. The gym has the potential to give Tinaya and her friends a future they want; away from the sewing machines and the snide comments of Elbe Help's student volunteers, and out of the refuge accommodation centre in Rothenburgsort.

"We'll help with taking care of the children," Tinaya says.

"Maybe we can set up some kind of donation system," Mara says. "A tip jar or piggy bank people can drop coins into. Then we can share that among you all."

"We're not here for the money. We're here because we believe in it. This is the kind of place none of us ever dreamed of having, growing up in Afghanistan."

Mara feels the tears welling up. "Zina ... she ... I know she'd be so proud of you. Proud of this place."

Tinaya steps forward and hugs Mara. Hugs her really hard. The other girls join in and they wrap their arms around Mara, who now chooses this moment to grieve. She lets go; lets herself be hugged by these girls who carry more than their fair share of grief and pain. As she cries, the girls hug her harder.

It feels really good to be at the centre of this.

A camera flash makes her open her eyes.

Gus, standing a few metres away, lowers the camera and says, "That's the first one for the new wall."

Day 22

She walks from Hamburger Berg to the hotel, almost dragging her feet.

The slight hangover is worth it, feels earned. All those shots of Sambuca with Russell last night, toasting their health, happiness and prosperity, with Marcello watching on, smiling, needing to stay sober. After an emotional afternoon, spent mostly reminiscing about Zina with Gus, that dinner lifted her spirits. She was so happy to see Russell and Marcello in full couple mode; so happy for them. It was a Zina-less world, but she would find ways to keep going. She would find things worth doing, people worth knowing, relationships worth building. Yes, Russell and Marcello should adopt a child. Yes, Mara would be that child's godmother. And no, it's not too early to talk about families, because people should enter relationships knowing where they stand on this and talk about it openly. And that's rubbish that the world today is no place to have a child. Life goes on, no matter what.

It was very reassuring for Mara to hear Marcello say he believed Zina was innocent. Because, he said, if she had done it, that meant she had access to the storage facilities where the cannons were serviced and filled several days earlier; there was no way she could have done it on the day. This made Mara angry with herself, as she hadn't considered this. But then she had another shot of Sambuca and said they should focus on the next round, not worry about the last one.

At the hotel, there's no sign of Russell in the packed breakfast area. She doesn't want to wait with all the hacks, so walks over to Heiligengeistfeld. The sprawling expanse is today crammed with police vehicles. Vans mostly, but there are also squad cars. She checks the license plates of the vehicles that drive off, heading for the shift changes at the blockade points around the city. Marcello said last night that it was police officers from many of the eastern parts of Germany who had the night shift, while the officers from Berlin and western Germany had the day shift. The plates show the vehicles have come from all over the country, including the M of Munich, DO of Dortmund and F of Frankfurt. There's a veritable army of police, and that's just on Heiligengeistfeld. She thinks there must be other mustering points like this one, to the east, north and south of the city centre. They can't all be here.

One thing she doesn't see is a water cannon.

Back at the hotel, she finds Russell sitting in the now-empty breakfast area. He has his laptop open and glasses on.

"Hey, Russ," she says, lowering herself slowly into a chair.

"Morning, Auntie Mara."

"Not sure I'm ready for that just yet. Makes me sound like I'm old and living alone in a house full of pets."

"I think the name sounds very good."

"Where is everyone? I was here earlier and it was packed."

"They're swinging from the chandeliers. There's not an empty room in the place. But Jawinski called a 9am press conference. They've all gone there."

"Not you?"

"That's not the story."

"He's probably just going to brag about the police jamboree happening in Hamburg. Have you seen all the cars parked near the football stadium?"

"Marcello sent me a photo. The press conference is a warning, I'm sure, to stop protesters from coming here. Coffee?"

"Yes. Coffee is good." She takes the silver jug, lines up the circles on its lid, and pours. "New glasses?"

"Something I'm road-testing. Making the ruse real."

She sips the bitter, lukewarm coffee.

Russell turns his laptop around; Mara sees herself on the screen, from Russell's eye-view.

"I look like I swam 50 laps in a pool of Sambuca."

"I think you look fabulous. Like a member of the resistance who's been roughing it in the trenches."

"Thanks."

Russell swivels the laptop back to him. "That night in Berlin, it got me thinking this is something I really should have. My editor organised it. She got an assistant to bring these up the hill to me this morning. I'm just trying to figure them out."

"JJ said nothing trackable."

"I'm a journalist working in a visual era. The story will be nothing without video and images. Okay. I'm connected to the server. Editor's online. Let's see if this works."

"Don't send her any pictures of me. Please don't."

419

"Say something."

"What?"

"Anything. It's just a video and audio test. Mara Steinbach, anything you say can and will be used against you in a court of law."

"Russell Wex is the best journalist in Germany," she says. "He's coming to you live from the Hanseatic Police State of Hamburg."

"Keeping everyone safe." Russell checks his laptop. "Leonie says she got it."

"You're taking a big risk here, Russ."

"It's just a pair of glasses. No one will notice." He taps the right side once. "That turns them off. Oh, this is exciting. We'll get all of it."

"All of what?"

"The interview with Vilem. Whatever he announces. An exclusive."

"But then they'll know it was you. Afterwards, once everything's published."

"If they let me in, the story would be all words, coming from me anyway. There's no real danger. If anything, I'm helping them. The whole point is they're about to go public. They need me."

"I'll protect you, no matter what happens."

"I know you will." Russell snaps his laptop shut. "The whole no phones thing is just to save themselves. So they can't be caught. It's self-preservation, like wearing balaclavas at protests so they don't get recognised. I wrote about that yesterday."

"What's interesting is Perceval saying there's digital chatter about a demo taking place here."

"Yeah, because yesterday, JJ got her most trusted Circus crew together through word of mouth. Something's up with that."

"You think the demo is a fake?" Mara asks.

"Isn't it? Going digital now doesn't seem like the usual method, that's all. Anyway, I think we've reached the day you talked about. What everything's been building towards."

"Yeah, by the end of today, you can vote for Modra. Clean water for all. Woo-hoo."

"You don't think big enough, Mara. You need to see beyond the ring you're boxing in."

"Hey, you don't get to make those kinds of analogies."

"All these police," Russell says. "This Security Summit, abbreviated as SS, if you don't mind. It's a stage set up for something

420

big to play out on. I have no doubt Vilem understands this."

"Let's do one thing at a time. Let's get your interview with him and go from there."

Russell points at his glasses, loving his new toy. "The world will see it and hear it. Are you ready?"

"I haven't eaten anything, but this putrid coffee killed what little appetite I had."

Russell slides the laptop into its bag. He rolls back from the table and places the bag in his lap.

"Are you taking your computer?" Mara asks.

"No choice. This news is happening today. Part one of my story is set to go live this morning. Part two I need to complete after talking with Vilem. I'll have to do it on the move. The chair comes in really handy for that. I can type while you push."

"But no phone, right?"

"It's in my room. Feels weird getting around without it. I keep subconsciously reaching for it."

"You get used to not having it. And it feels good."

They head out of the hotel.

"Where are we going?" Russell asks. "To one of the bunkers?"

"Otzenstraße. But I want to stop at home first." Mara pushes the wheelchair. "You need to get a motor for this thing."

"That would mean giving up. I'm not ready to do that. Marcello's renewed my motivation. I'm going to fully commit to physical therapy when I get back to Berlin."

"Good. That's really good."

"I'll walk again."

Everything is open. It feels like a normal Monday morning. It's a reminder that the locals here are a bit more stoic in the face of hardship and trouble, she thinks, than the conservative, well-off Stuttgarters; Zina's north-south divide showing itself again.

At her building, she leaves Russell waiting outside and goes up the stairs to her apartment. There, she rummages through the boxes and pulls out her unwashed police uniform. She puts it in a canvas bag, then places that bag inside a backpack, along with a bottle of water and an apple.

Back with Russell, he asks, "What's with the backpack? Are you secretly carrying a phone now?"

"Just some supplies, and a disguise, in case we need to make a

421

getaway."

"Let's hope it doesn't come to that."

As they get moving again, a car door closes nearby. "Mara."

She turns to see Nils jogging up to them.

"What are you doing here?" Mara asks.

He absolutely towers over Russell, who leans back and cranes his neck to look up at him. "Christoph told me to keep an eye on you today."

"You're nice and early for that," Russell says.

"Nils, this is my good friend Russell."

"Hey. Sorry. I overslept. The game went long in Halstenbek. Double overtime."

"Did you win?" Mara asks.

"No. It took me ages to get to sleep. I kept reliving all my mistakes. Over and over."

"Sports can be a real bitch like that. All the coaches say to let it go, but that's a lot easier said than done."

Mara starts pushing the wheelchair, to get them all moving. She doesn't want Nils there, as he's just one more thing to worry about, but the way he sticks to her side makes her think there will be no getting rid of him.

"Where are we going?" he asks.

"To get Russell a story. He'll be your cover. If anyone asks, you can say you're his assistant."

"I like this development," Russell says.

Nils takes out his phone. "Let me just update Christoph that I'm with you."

"Do that, then put your phone in your car. You can't take that phone where we're going."

"Okay. Got it."

Nils jogs back to his car.

Russell smiles. "Who needs a motor when you can have an assistant?"

"He can do all the pushing," Mara says, moving around in front of Russell.

As Nils jogs towards them again, Russell says, "You never said he was such a pretty boy. You like?"

"Too tall and angular for me. All those corners look dangerous."

When Nils joins them, Mara gestures to the wheelchair's handles.

"Yeah, sure," Nils says. "I can do that."

The three of them head down Hamburger Berg.

"So, what's the big story?" Nils asks.

"An exclusive interview with Vilem Kollar," Russell says.

"Is he really here?"

"Yes, and he's got something to announce," Mara says. "By the way, I had the pleasure of meeting your mother last week. Tough woman."

"She has to be, to do the job she has, for as long as she has."

"I like her. It's impressive, the way she is."

"To be honest, she wasn't that taken with you."

Russell laughs a little. "Still struggling with first impressions, Mara?"

"We were in the gym," Mara says. "I can't help it if I'm intimidating in there."

"She wasn't intimidated. She said she didn't like it that you held things back. You didn't tell her the truth."

"I admit I was selective in what I said. But I didn't lie."

"She expected more of you."

"I didn't realise I was supposed to win her over, while she was grilling me about my brother."

"Who's still at large."

"Yes, he is."

They pass a supermarket busy with shoppers, then go up the hill towards the red church at Otzenstraße. Mara expects to see Circus members gathered there, but the square is empty. There are no police, and no vehicles that look like unmarked police cars.

"Why aren't the cops watching the bunkers?" Mara asks.

"All resources are being focused on the blockade and keeping the city centre secure."

Russell turns and looks up at Nils. "How's that going?"

"Last I heard, the blockade's working. Some protesters trying to get to Hamburg were stopped and turned away."

"That doesn't exactly sound like that big of a deal. How many were there?"

Nils shrugs. "I don't know the exact numbers."

"Maybe you were right, Russ," Mara says. "All that chatter was fake."

Across the square, Mara sees Jesper, Gomez and a few others go

423

down a side street towards the bunker.

"Wollenknecht," Nils says.

"AKA Gomez," Mara says to Russell. "His real name is David Wollenknecht."

"Now you say that, his whole upper-middle-class story unfolds before my very eyes."

Mara turns to Nils. "When he was arrested, did he at any point get eyes on you?"

"I don't think so."

"Okay. Good. Hopefully, you're covered. JJ knows you from the Dragon, but she'll keep that to herself. Let's go inside. You might get some curious looks. If anyone asks, just tell them you're with me."

There are two big guys at the entrance, with the broad stance of soldiers at ease, guarding the door. One of them recognises Mara and smiles.

"Video girl." He turns to his partner. "She's the cop basher."

"Yeah? That was awesome."

"Is everyone already here?" Mara asks.

The first guy shrugs. "I don't know how many people were invited. But it's pretty packed in there."

"Well, we are. So, can you step aside and let us in?"

They part to allow the three of them to enter. The door closes behind them with a metallic clang.

"Sounds like a prison cell closing," Russell says.

"I suggest you lurk at the back and speak only when spoken to," Mara says over her shoulder.

"How will I get the interview that way?"

"I was talking to Nils."

The bunker's open area is almost full, the people gathering in tight groups. Among them, Mara sees Tinaya and the girls who helped design the flag, Gomez and Jesper with their hangers-on, Susie with Rab and Matze, and JJ at the front with Vilem and a few faces Mara recognises from the meeting in Berlin. There's a palpable air of excitement, everyone's attention focused on Vilem, like he's a rockstar about to take the stage.

Mara thinks no one here, apart from Vilem and his inner circle, knows what the plan is.

Russell gently grabs her arm and pulls her close to him. "It seems JJ trusts a lot of people. There's got to be a hundred in here."

"I don't trust some of the people she trusts," Mara says, looking across at Gomez and wondering if Nicola will get his statement withdrawn.

Russell taps the side of his glasses as Vilem goes up onto the stage. Everyone stops talking, almost immediately. Jesper starts clapping enthusiastically, but stops when no one else joins in.

"No need for applause," Vilem says, with a broad smile. "I haven't done anything yet."

Some people laugh.

"Welcome, everyone. I'm honoured to have you all here on a day I hope will go down in history. There will be an announcement made later today, regarding the future of Modra. A future that includes all of you. I wanted to do this at the Hamburg Rathaus, but the police have basically set up a wall around the city centre. Don't worry. This is a good thing, because it means we can go to the Altona Rathaus instead. We will walk there, from here. It's important we don't arouse any suspicion. We can't look anything like a protest group. So, we will leave here in staggered formation, in small groups. I also suggest you take different routes, maybe get a coffee along the way. Make it look like you're regular people out on a regular Monday morning. But be sure, this will not be a regular day. Please be in front of the Altona Rathaus in an hour from now."

"What then?" someone shouts out.

"We take the building," Vilem says.

A strange silence follows.

Nils breaks it: "What does that mean, take the building?"

Vilem scans the crowd with narrow eyes, like a performer trying to locate a heckler. "What do you think it means? We take action by occupying the building. Look, you can spend the rest of your lives walking the streets, carrying banners and being beaten up by police. Or you can do something about it. This is your chance to be the people who change the world. This is your chance to make history."

"How do we do that?" Jesper asks.

"Stop thinking this is something you're not able to do. We can do this. Together. We go in, secure the exits, and remove any people from the building. We make it ours and fly our flag from it. Once everyone is out, we lock it down and let no one in. We occupy."

"With what?" This from Gomez, standing near the stage now, as if wanting to be one of the leaders, or thinking himself one. "How do we take control of a government building without any weapons?"

"We already scoped the building. There is no security there. Weapons will just bring negative attention and cause panic. We can simply walk in and use our force and will to take control of it. We are more than enough people to do this. If anyone makes trouble, be brutal with them. Remember, the police have been brutal with us, so why can't we be brutal with people who try to stop us?"

"Vilem," JJ says, trying to be the voice of reason, "you're asking too much. We're not your foot soldiers, to be called into action whenever you want."

"I never said you were. We're all in this together. Am I wrong? There were plenty of you in Berlin shouting your support for our war on oppression."

"That was before Stuttgart. How do you expect the police to respond to this?"

"The police are waiting for protesters in the Schanzenviertel and the city centre. They're also busy blockading the city. They're not expecting us to go after Altona. We won't face any resistance. We can just walk in and take it."

"Let's do it," a woman shouts.

"Yeah," a voice from the back cries out, the crowd starting to get behind Vilem.

"This is our chance to make a statement," he says, louder, "bigger and bolder than any demonstration or protest march. This is us taking control of our future. A peaceful occupation to make the leaders of this country know that we are here and we want to have a say in our future."

Shouts of agreement.

JJ raises her hands. "No one is forced to go. The choice is yours."

But she's drowned out by a rising chant of "Modra, Modra, Modra." Vilem raises his right fist in the air and the chant gets louder. He swings his fist towards the door, and everyone starts flooding out. Mara ducks behind Nils as Gomez and Jesper pass, wanting to avoid their attention.

With just about everyone gone, Russell moves towards the stage, where Vilem and JJ are engaged in a heated discussion. Tinaya comes up to Mara.

"Is this really happening?" Tinaya asks.

"Not for you. Don't get involved in this. None of you girls should."

"But it's a peaceful occupation, like Vilem said. A visual statement."

"You can't risk getting arrested," Mara says.

"Vilem specifically asked me to help him raise the flag. Our flag, Mara. The one we created. I have to be there for that. I can't let him down."

"Tinaya, please. There's no way any of this can end well. Walk away now, while you have the chance."

"I've spent my whole life walking away. You're the one who told me to stop doing that. You told me to get my feet on the ground and put up my fists to fight. I'm doing that today."

Tinaya joins her group as they head for the exit.

"Fuck," Mara says to herself.

"They're refugees," Nils says. "Right? They'll be deported if they get arrested."

"I know that. They know it too. But it's like Vilem's got them brainwashed."

"Can't you stop them?"

"Not right now. I'll fight that round when I get to it."

"Is this it?" Nils looks non-plussed by it all. "Is this the revolution?"

"Occupying a local government building in Hamburg isn't quite the same as chopping off the chancellor's head in Berlin, is it?"

Mara watches as Russell, glasses on, talks with Vilem. She hopes the direct feed to Russell's editor might sound an early warning, enabling police to respond and prevent a siege from happening.

"There's no reception in here," she says.

"What?"

"Nothing. Hey, Nils, what's the deal with public buildings today? Are they even open?"

"Not in the centre. The Altona Rathaus, I don't know. Probably yes."

They are among the last to leave. Outside, JJ locks the bunker's door.

As they head up Otzenstraße, Nils pushes Russell alongside Vilem, so their talk can continue. The two guards are up in front, while Vilem's close supporters trail behind him. Mara and JJ are about ten metres further back.

"What's he doing here?" JJ asks.

"Don't worry. He's just helping Russell for the day. I asked him to, so I don't have to do it."

"If Vilem finds out he's with the police, that could ruin everything."

"Technically, he's just an intern. He's trustworthy. No phone on him."

"We can't send him away now, anyway. He knows what's going on."

"What is actually going on, JJ? What's the point of all this?"

JJ walks a few metres, seeming to consider her response. "I think it's a stunt. Vilem told me earlier about his plan for Modra. This is what you were talking about yesterday. Right? You know about the political move."

"I do."

"How?"

"That's a story for another time."

"I definitely want to hear it."

"So, you think this is all just PR?" Mara asks. "A dramatic way to announce the Modra political party?"

"What else? If you hadn't brought Russell along, we would've documented it ourselves. Nothing will happen, Mara. Everyone's chosen to be part of this. Including you. This could be a big moment."

"So all that resistance you put up in the bunker was just for show?" When JJ doesn't reply, Mara adds, "We're about to forcefully take a building, just to hold a press conference and fly a flag?"

"Vilem's about to become a prominent politician, potentially the spokesperson for a generation. He already has a huge amount of support. He needs to think of his own security."

"I don't want to see anyone getting hurt," Mara says.

"People have already got hurt. Protesters have died."

"But why take the building? Come on, JJ. There has to be another way."

"I tried to talk him out of it, but now I think he's right. We need to do something that gets attention."

"We'll all be in jail before lunchtime. Tinaya and her friends will get shipped home."

"Mara, you need to lower your voice and calm down. We're just going to use this building as a location for this announcement. If we end up occupying it, then that's fine with me. This is the kind of

428

protest move that's happened many times in the past. If you don't want to be part of it, now is your chance to run."

"I'm not leaving my friends."

"That's good of you." JJ keeps her voice even and conversational, making it hard for Mara to read her true thoughts. "I think you should stay, because of Russell. He's exactly what Vilem wanted. Someone on our side, telling our story."

"Russell's not on your side. He's not on anyone's side."

"I guess we'll see about that." JJ walks ahead, leaving Mara on her own.

As the stragglers of the group, they take the most direct route, getting onto Königstraße and going up the hill to Altona.

Another Königstraße, Mara thinks, though this one is a busy thoroughfare connecting St Pauli and Altona, and not a bottleneck pedestrian mall. There are people out walking, many of them with dogs. Children are entwined in the various fixtures of a playground near the S-Bahn station. Blue sky is poking through the clouds, hinting at another sunny afternoon during which locals will battle for space by the river. Late starters are hustling to work, on foot and on bikes. A bus passes, going in the direction of the city, heads in every window and a string of bodies down the aisle. The odd jogger huffs past.

It all seems mundane and routine; all these people with no idea what's about to happen.

She's tempted to be done with it. Take one of the side streets to the left and go down to Große Elbstraße, to Gus's gym. Because that's something to focus on. That has a future. She thinks Russell will be all right. It's Tinaya she's worried about.

So she keeps walking, up to the big intersection and across to the Platz der Republik. Vilem's followers are waiting at the statue of Kaiser Wilhelm I, portly and on horseback, high on a plinth. The Kaiser is looking to the north, but the horse's head is turned to the northwest, ears up. She wonders if this has any significance.

Mara thinks they look like a big university class on a field trip, JJ their professor.

An elderly woman comes out of the Rathaus Altona. It's a stately, vaguely Greek-looking building all in white. Above the entrance are four sets of twin columns, and above those columns is a large engraving of people rowing a boat in a stormy sea. Like the statue, if

429

this engraving means something, Mara has no idea what. When she looks back at the crowd, Tinaya is standing next to her.

"What happened? Where are the others?"

"They left," Tinaya says. "Cowards. They just want to save themselves."

"That's not cowardly. That's smart. Where did they go?"

"To the gym."

"You should do that too."

"I'm not leaving. I want to raise my flag."

"It's not your flag, Tinaya. We just designed it. It's going to stand for something else pretty soon, and I'm not sure what that is."

Mara watches the two guards from the bunker go to a van parked to the side of the Rathaus. They each take a black bag, close the double doors, and carry the bags into the building.

"Last chance," Mara says. "This could go badly."

"I'm not running away."

"Okay. But stay with me. Stay close."

Tinaya nods.

Vilem sweeps a hand forward and everyone starts going inside at the same time, shuffling forward like an over-enthusiastic tour group.

"Get everyone out of there," he says. "Use force if necessary."

"The whole building?" Gomez asks.

"Yes. Shut any windows and secure all the exits. Move furniture in front of any doors that lead outside."

Gomez nods and runs off, his followers in tow.

In the lobby, Mara sees a distraught man sitting behind a glass partition, waving a clipboard in the air and shouting that all visitors must sign in. Vilem signals for his two bag-carrying guards to get the receptionist outside. They kick down the door to his cubicle and drag him out. Vilem holds the main door open, as staff and visitors are forced outside. Some flee with fear; others move with the subdued annoyance of people doing a fire drill.

Mara sees Russell has used the wheelchair lift to get to the top of the stairs, where he's watching over the proceedings below.

A man dressed all in white is hauled out of the cafeteria by Rab and Matze. When he sees Tinaya, he shakes himself free and goes up to her.

"You fucking refugees. We never should've let you in."

430

He lurches towards Tinaya, but Nils steps in and pushes the man down the short steps to the main door, where he's ushered outside by Vilem. Nils and Tinaya's eyes meet. They share a moment, before Tinaya looks away.

Through the glass doors, Mara sees the people already outside are milling about, unsure what is going on. Nearly all of them are on the phone. The last of the people are herded towards the lobby; they have the greyish pallor and self-importance of career civil servants. Mara is surprised by how few people there are in this big building and how little they protest their forced eviction.

Gomez comes running back. Jesper is with him.

"Is that everyone?" Vilem asks.

"Yeah. I think so."

"Good work." Vilem turns to his guards. "Shut the doors."

One guard opens his bag and takes out industrial-sized cable ties. Three are looped around the door handles and pulled tight. Furniture is also moved in front of the doors, filling the lobby from the entrance to the stairs.

"Make sure any other exits are secured like this," Vilem says. "Split up. The police will be here soon."

Mara sees Vilem take a gun from one of the bags and hook it in his belt, behind his back. The guards head off to do as ordered, with one going left and the other going right. Vilem then goes up to Tinaya. From inside his jacket, he produces a flag in a plastic wrapper and holds it up.

"Can you help me with this?" he asks Tinaya, who nods eagerly.

"You too, Mara. You had a hand in this."

"Why should I help?"

"Because you designed it."

Tinaya, JJ and Vilem go up the stairs, and Mara follows, so she can keep an eye on the now-armed Vilem. At the top, Vilem points at Russell, signalling for him to come as well, and together with Nils, they go out onto the first-floor balcony, where two flagpoles extend outwards above the ground, to hang flags in drop-down fashion. Vilem gives the new flag to Tinaya and she takes it from its wrapping, her hands shaking a little.

"We're making history," Vilem says. "There's no need to be nervous. This is the transition of power Germany's been moving towards for decades now."

431

Tinaya unfurls the large flag.

Vilem points at Mara and JJ. "You two, get that other flag off the pole."

"The Hamburg flag?" Mara asks. "Why? There's another flagpole that's empty. Use that."

"We're not flying both of them. That's not what this is about. Take it down. Now."

JJ is the first to move, pulling the levered rope that brings the flag closer to the balcony. The Hamburg flag is unhooked, replaced by the Modra flag. Once that's done, Vilem ushers Mara and JJ away, so that he and Tinaya can wind out the flag. Nils takes the Hamburg flag from Mara, folds it neatly and puts it in a corner of the balcony. They all move to the edge and look down at the Modra flag swaying in the breeze.

"Beautiful," Tinaya says.

Many of the people on the square below, cast out of this building, and others who have joined to watch, point their phones up at the flag.

Vilem checks his watch. "We need to find a TV," he says moving back inside. "Follow me, all of you."

They do so, but Mara is the last to move. Before passing through the door, she sees the blue lights of police cars speeding down Max-Brauer-Allee and hears sirens coming from the other side of the building. She needs to get Tinaya out, somehow, before the police come in. They've done this business with the flag. Now's the time to get out, if they can, because this is no longer a peaceful occupation.

Everyone is in the cafeteria, taking advantage of what's available; eating rolls and pieces of cake, and drinking bottles of juice lifted from shelves and fridges. There's the pop of sparkling wine, which is passed around, drunk straight from the bottle in celebration. Susie's annoying machine-gun laugh rings out.

Mara looks for the two guys with the bags, but can't see them anywhere. She wonders where they are in the building.

Vilem gets the television on and raises a hand for quiet. The set is small, one of those boxy cubes from another era, and secured to the wall in a frame that looks like it could drop at any moment. They all look up as Vilem flips through the channels, finally landing on a news broadcast.

"Everyone be quiet," he orders, turning the sound up as loud as it

432

will go.

The screen shows live footage from cities around Germany, with various shots of police surrounding officious-looking buildings. The newsreader explains that there have been attacks all over the country, with attempts to occupy city halls and government buildings, in big cities and small towns. Some of the footage shows the Modra flag flying outside the buildings.

"That's it," Vilem shouts. "Look at that. We did it. The flag is everywhere."

Everyone watches, excited about this development and that they're part of it. But there are gasps when footage from Dresden is shown. Bodies lie on the ground, under black covers, lined up on the square in front of Dresden's Neues Rathaus.

"Oh no," Vilem says, moving closer to the television and craning to look up. "No. It wasn't supposed to be violent. You fucking Nazi morons."

The screen then shows footage of violent clashes between protesters and police, in Rostock, then shaky video of a shootout on the streets of Nuremberg.

Vilem's hands are on his head. "They're ruining everything."

The screen moves to Altona; close-up footage of Tinaya and Vilem taking the Modra flag and unfurling it on the balcony, plus shots of Vilem's speech in the bunker.

"What the fuck?" Jesper says. "That's us."

"Is he filming everything?" Gomez asks, pointing at Russell.

"Of course, he is," Vilem says, his eyes still on the screen, which now shows protesters looting shops in Duisburg and Leipzig. "Haven't you seen a set of smart glasses before?"

Gomez and Jesper move in on Russell. Nils tries to stop them, but they push him out of the way. Russell tries to fend off Gomez's hands as he grabs at the glasses. Once Gomez has them, he throws them to the floor and steps on them.

"Thanks a lot," Russell says.

"Let him be," Vilem says. "He's part of the process."

"He filmed all of us," Gomez shouts. "We're fucked."

"Wrong. We're headline news, for good and bad reasons, but all publicity is good. We'll spin it our way."

Gomez steps forward to punch Russell, but Mara grabs his extended arm and pulls him back.

"So now you pick on someone in a wheelchair," she says. "You fucking rat."

"I'll take you now, bitch."

Mara tosses her backpack to Tinaya as Gomez squares off in front of her. No one moves to stop them. Out of the corner of one eye, Mara sees Vilem still watching television.

"I'm so sick of fighting you," she says, raising her fists.

"You're the reason I got arrested."

"You got yourself arrested. Then you told them everything to save yourself."

"What was that?" Vilem asks, lowering the volume.

Mara stands still and lowers her fists. "You know what? I'm done fighting you. You want to hit me? Go ahead. Maybe then you'll feel better about yourself."

"Why are you two fighting at all?" Vilem glances over his shoulder. "We're changing the world."

"She's a spy," Gomez says. "She's been spying on us all along."

Vilem turns around, pulls the gun out and points it at Gomez. "What did you say?"

A few people gasp in shock.

"Vilem, I'm on your side," Gomez says, raising his hands. "She's the one you can't trust."

"This was supposed to be peaceful, Vilem," JJ says. "You said no weapons."

Vilem ignores this. "I trust her. She set all of this in motion, by taking a stand against the police. You never did anything like that."

"I got the water cannon."

"Once Mara told you where it would be parked." Vilem gestures with the gun towards the television. "All of these people who have successfully occupied buildings across Germany were inspired by her. She showed what's possible. But you, you haven't inspired anyone."

"That's not …"

"Trouble follows you like a plague. And you're weak. You were arrested and told them whatever they wanted to hear to save yourself."

"In doing so, he snitched on my brother," Mara says.

"He did what?" Vilem points the gun back at Gomez. "You fucking rat. I hate rats."

434

Vilem shoots Gomez in the chest.

The sound is incredibly loud in the cafeteria. Gomez collapses to the floor, hands on his chest, blood seeping between his fingers. He coughs a little, spittles of blood forming on his lips.

"How dare you name my brother like that," Vilem says. "You filthy traitor."

"I … got … my statement …"

Jesper and JJ bend down to attend to Gomez. Someone brings over a stack of napkins. JJ takes it and tries to stop the bleeding. Gomez screams in pain, the horrific sound echoing. The napkins quickly turn red. Blood also starts to pool out from underneath his body, spreading across the floor. Jesper steps back, careful not to get blood on his shoes.

"Vilem," JJ says. "He needs an ambulance. He's dying."

Vilem is looking at the screen again. "Yeah, that'll happen. He's been shot."

"What are you doing? This is nothing like what you talked about."

"Every revolution has its casualties. Just look at this. People have died in Dresden and Nuremberg and elsewhere. They won't let us take the country without a fight."

"I thought we were just trying to make a statement," JJ says, her voice shaking. "Gomez is one of us."

"He was never one of us."

JJ, her hands red, kneels over Gomez as he lets out his last breath. He expires with a whimper, looking young and helpless, lying on the floor. People hold their hands to their mouths and look away.

"He was one of these idiots," Vilem continues, gesturing to the screen that's again showing footage of bodies on the ground. "An extremist who thinks that violence is the only option, but they squeal like a pig when put up against the wall. And bleed like one. It was all supposed to be peaceful. We don't have to bend the people to our will, or force them to follow us. We just have to take control and show them the new way. The better way. Modra can make Germany better for everyone."

Mara steps towards Vilem, determined to diffuse the situation. "It can," she says softly. "But not like this. Not this way. We all support you, but that will mean nothing if you start shooting us."

"Not you. Just him."

"I understand that. You don't want to shoot anyone else. That's good. Maybe you give me the gun, as a way of showing everyone in here is safe."

"No."

"All right. You keep it, but put it away. You're scaring us. Let's not see anyone else get hurt."

Vilem puts the gun behind his back, hooked into the belt of his pants.

"Thank you," Mara says.

"How could you just shoot him like that?" Jesper asks.

"He was a liability," Vilem says. "Working with the police. A traitor who could no longer be trusted. Are you also a liability?"

"No, of course not."

"Good."

On the screen, Vilem can be seen, the Modra flag behind him, speaking to the camera.

"Finally," he says, raising the volume again.

"Hello," Vilem's prerecorded message begins. "My name is Vilem Kollar. I'm excited to launch the Modra Party and to offer citizens a new alternative in a political climate where the current parties in power only serve the interests of the very few. Modra is the party that will speak for everyone, and especially for the interests of those who matter the most: the young people who are the future of Germany, whose voices are so seldom heard. Modra is your future. Modra is Germany's future. Modra is the planet's future. We want to ensure that everyone has clean water and ..."

The screen goes blank and all the lights go off. The fridges in the cafeteria stop humming.

Vilem presses buttons on the remote. "What the fuck?"

"They've cut the power," Mara says.

Vilem reaches up and slaps the side of the TV, making it fall to the floor, where it smashes.

"Calm down," Mara says. "Cutting the power is standard procedure in a hostage situation."

"This isn't a hostage situation."

"The police are probably handling it as one. Because they probably heard the gunshot."

"What'll happen next?"

"They'll call, to ask about your demands. Do you have any demands, Vilem?"

436

"Everybody stays here." Vilem grabs Mara's arm. "You come with me."

Mara looks quickly at Nils, trying to communicate that this is the chance to get people out of the building. Nils shrugs slightly, too scared to move.

Vilem, still holding Mara's arm, leads her down the stairs to the entrance. The two guards flank the doors, where they stand either side, guns in hand. Vilem crouches down to look through the windows, taking Mara with him. She sees police cars on the Platz der Republik, beyond the statue of the Kaiser. That's where the officers stand, behind their cars, in a long line.

"I didn't expect this many," Vilem says.

"In a city currently full of the whole country's police force, just about?"

"Where's the media? Do you see any vans?"

"I'm sure they're coming. You don't need the journalist anymore. He's not able to broadcast anything without his glasses."

"That's right."

"He's useless to you now."

Behind the line of uniformed cops, Mara picks out Perceval in a grey suit, standing next to Hannelore Stammer, in a suit of slightly darker grey. Stammer has a phone to her ear.

The ringing comes from the reception cubicle. Vilem gestures for Mara to answer the phone.

"What do I say?" she asks.

"Tell them to move back so the media vans can get closer."

"Why don't you tell them that. You're the voice of the Modra Party, not me."

"Answer it," Vilem orders.

Mara goes into the cubicle, scanning it quickly for anything that might be used as a weapon. The most dangerous item is the bulky phone itself. Vilem stands in the doorway. She picks up the receiver.

"This is Detective Stammer. Who am I speaking with?"

"Someone from Circus."

There's a pause, with the line crackling, then Stammer asks, "What are you all doing in there?"

"Hiding in the dark. Why did you cut the power? No one's being held in here against their will. We're ... occupying."

Vilem smiles and nods, liking what Mara said.

"Please put Vilem Kollar on the line. We know he's in there."

Mara holds the receiver towards Vilem, fighting the temptation to beat him with it. "They want to talk to you."

"I'm not negotiating with the police. We like it here. We're staying. The flag out the front shows that this building now belongs to Modra."

Mara puts the receiver back to her ear. "Did you get all that?"

"He's greatly overestimating the power of a flag."

"Agreed."

"How many hostages are being held in there?"

"Zero. The building was evacuated. Everyone is here by choice. Ask the people outside. We … uh … we left no one behind."

Vilem laughs really loudly at this. "Oh, nice."

"That noise from before," Stammer says. "Was that a gun?"

"The television in the cafeteria fell from the wall."

"It sounded like a gunshot."

"Well, there was also a disagreement." Mara looks a Vilem, who smiles, liking the terminology. "Resolved by a bullet."

"An internal party problem," Vilem says. "No, a family problem."

"Why won't he talk to me?" Stammer asks. "What does he want?"

"He requests that the police move back to allow the media to get closer to the building."

"He's doing all this for publicity? He doesn't have any real demands? He should, because otherwise we will storm the building. If there are only hostiles present, we will have no choice but to come in by force."

Mara takes the receiver from her ear and cups a hand over the bottom part. "They want your demands. Without them, they'll come in, guns blazing. Give them something, to hold them back."

"Okay. I know what to say."

Mara takes her hand off the receiver and holds it up to Vilem, like it's a microphone.

"The government of Germany shall be dissolved," he says grandly. "Modra now controls numerous buildings across the country. We won't relinquish control until the current government stands down and new elections are held. In the meantime, Modra takes interim control of Germany."

Mara, trying to hide her disbelief, puts the receiver to her ear. "Got that?"

438

"He's not serious, is he?"

"He sounds sincere to me."

"Tell them to turn the power back on," Vilem says.

"They won't do that."

Vilem stands there, a disappointed look on his face, seeming to consider his options. Mara thinks there's something improvisational about him, that maybe he doubted he would ever get this far and now doesn't quite know what to do.

"We'll survive without it," he says. "We want elections and full control of the country until those elections happen, when Modra will win the majority anyway. We just need a fair vote and compulsory voting."

"Why's that?"

"Everyone should have a say."

"That I actually agree with," Mara says.

This seems to appease Vilem. He moves out of the cubicle's doorway and up the stairs towards the cafeteria.

"Can you please put Kollar on?" Stammer asks.

"He's gone."

"Mara, what are you doing in there?"

"I just got caught up in it all. I didn't wake up this morning with the intention of being part of a revolution. If you can call it that. Can you tell me what's happening elsewhere in Germany?"

"It's an ongoing situation. There are standoffs, like this one, but most of them have been resolved."

"It looked bad in some places," Mara says. "More streets littered with the bodies of dead protesters."

"Police officers have also died today. And innocent people. The group in Dresden had automatic weapons and fired them at will."

"I guess if you team up with right-wing extremists, something's bound to go wrong."

"Who do you have in there?"

"Lefties, mostly. Not very extreme. Plus a journalist." Mara pauses, considering whether to mention Nils or not. She decides Stammer deserves to know. She lowers her voice and adds, "There's a young guy in here as well. Really tall. Must be a basketball player."

"Get him out of there."

"I will. And the journalist, who's in a wheelchair. Do not, under any circumstances, fire at the protesters or try to take over the

439

building. A couple of guys in here are very well-armed, including Vilem."

"Now it seems there are two hostages."

"Both of them came along by choice. It's not their fault they ended up in here, but I'm going to get them out."

"I'll give the order to fire at Vilem when there's a clear shot."

"Don't do that. Don't make him a hero. You need to arrest him and put him on trial. Be patient. Wait for an opening. They can't stay in here forever."

One of the guards starts to move towards her, so she hangs up the phone. From a drawer, she takes out a metal stapler and pair of scissors. She pockets them, thinking they're useless in the face of guns, but better than nothing.

Back in the cafeteria, Gomez's body has been dragged out of the seating area and behind a counter, leaving a smeared red trail that already has a few shoeprints in it.

Mara scans the crowd and sees that Susie, Rab and Matze are missing. If they did manage to get to an exit, clear it of any furniture and go outside, that could then provide an entry point for the police.

She doesn't have much time. She needs to get Nils and Russell out, then somehow escape with Tinaya. The only way to do that is to get Vilem on her side. He's away from everyone else, near the door, pacing and shaking his head. They are all looking at him, except for JJ, who is moving between people, checking on them, trying to calm them down. The group is splintered. Jesper is huddled with Gomez's followers and some others, who all look like they want to go home. Those in need of comfort and support gravitate towards JJ. Dividing these two groups is the broad smear of Gomez's blood. Tinaya, Russell and Nils form their own small group. In a corner, Vilem's close supporters all have their heads bowed over phones, possibly in damage control mode.

It appears everyone is too scared to talk.

Mara goes up to Vilem and whispers, "Calling for an election is smart."

"I know. Modra will win. Compulsory voting will ensure that."

"Yes, everyone with a voice. You have their attention now. You've established a platform on what's been an important day."

"It's not over yet. This is just the beginning."

Mara wonders whether Vilem has noticed the absent three. "I

440

suggest you don't allow things to escalate any further. Keep it political. It's an act of political protest completed to bring about positive change."

"I think I should hire you as my speech writer."

"I'm just trying to present to you the situation as I see it. You saw on the news that violence doesn't help. It undermines the party and turns Modra into a radical group. I'm sure you don't want that."

"I don't. I made the wrong allegiances, in some parts of the country. I'll learn from that. We will distance ourselves from what they did. My team is already doing that."

"They had the Modra flag."

"I can say they used it without our consent. A splinter cell looking to make gains of their own with an agenda that's nothing like ours."

"Let's focus on the situation here," Mara says. "You're making a meaningful political stand. But right now, it all looks negative. Like you're a child screaming that the world isn't fair. You need to show good faith."

"How do you suggest I do that?"

"The media is here. They will cover this story. Your announcement was on the news. There's no reason to keep the journalist and his assistant in here. Let them go."

"Why should I do that?"

"You just want representation, for everyone. You want to give a voice to all the young people, by offering Modra as a voting alternative. That's good. That has value. Don't wreck that. Come on, Vilem. Clean water is something everyone wants."

"You sound like Agnes. She's also a wonderful speaker." He smiles. "Fine. Let them go. We don't need them anymore."

"Thank you, Vilem."

"I'm really glad to have you on my side, sister."

That word lands like a punch to her gut. She works hard to control her reaction, like the punch was nothing. "I'll take care of it."

Mara goes to the door and leans down to Russell, whose face is expressionless.

"What were you two talking about?" he asks in a whisper.

"I'm getting you out of here. You and Nils."

"He agreed to that? He's insane."

"Just stay calm." She looks at Tinaya and Nils, who are standing close together. "Tinaya, you come as well, and bring my backpack.

441

We'll say we're helping with the wheelchair."

"Ah good," Russell says. "My disability comes in handy once again."

Nils and Tinaya each get a handle and push Russell to the door, which Mara opens.

"Hey," Jesper calls out. "Where are you going?"

"The journalist and his assistant can leave," Vilem says. "We don't need them."

"Yeah, all right. But Mara and the refugee should stay."

"We're just going to help get the wheelchair down the stairs," Mara says.

"There's a lift for that," Jesper counters.

"And no power for it, genius," Tinaya says.

"Keep an eye on them," Vilem says to Jesper. "This is your chance to step up. I suggest you take it. Prove your loyalty. Maybe do the right thing and help them as well."

They all go out of the cafeteria.

"You better not try anything, Jesper," Mara says. "You don't want to end up like Gomez."

"I can't believe he fucking shot him."

"You heard him. Vilem considers Gomez a traitor."

All four of them get their hands on the wheelchair and carry it down the stairs.

"In different circumstances," Russell says, "I might feel like Cleopatra."

Once at the bottom of the stairs, Mara gets close to Tinaya and whispers, "Bathroom" in her ear.

Nils pushes Russell to the door. The two guards look at Jesper, who nods.

"Vilem gave the all-clear for this," Mara says.

One guard produces a large knife and cuts through the cable ties. Tinaya goes back up the stairs.

"Where are you going?" Jesper asks, who seems emboldened by his new responsibility.

"To the bathroom. That's allowed, isn't it?"

"Make it fast."

The guards hold the doors open. Nils pushes Russell through. Both look straight ahead. The doors are closed and secured again, with fresh cable ties. Through the glass, Mara watches a handful of police officers scuttle forward, guns drawn. They let the wheelchair pass, then move backwards with it, until they're behind the line of vehicles.

Mara goes up the stairs. "I need a bathroom too," she says to Jesper, who blocks her way.

"One at a time," he says.

She pushes him aside. "Try to stop me, tough guy."

He follows her up the stairs.

"You're in way over your head here, Jesper. I'm the one Vilem considers family. You're a failed actor from Denmark."

"Yeah? I'm the one Vilem chose to keep an eye on you."

She closes the bathroom door on him. Inside, Tinaya is vigorously washing her hands at the sink. The backpack is on the floor. Tinaya is about to speak, but Mara holds up her hand to keep her quiet.

"We're getting out of here," Mara whispers. "I need you to do exactly as I say."

"What about the others? We can't leave JJ. We can't leave any of them."

"I'm going to save you. You're the most important person in here."

Mara opens the backpack and takes out the police uniform. She quickly changes, taking the stapler and scissors from the pockets before stuffing her clothes in the backpack. She hands the apple to Tinaya, who looks at it, wondering what to do with it. Mara also gives Tinaya the backpack.

"Carry this. Now, stand here and wait."

Tinaya shoulders the backpack as Mara positions herself behind the door.

"Be patient, young warrior," Mara whispers.

There's a knock on the door. "Hurry up," Jesper shouts.

"When he comes in," Mara says as quietly as she can, "throw him the apple."

Tinaya takes a step towards the door, but Mara motions for her to move further back.

The door is opened and Jesper enters, just as Tinaya moves backwards.

"What is taking you so long?"

Tinaya tosses the apple towards Jesper. He instinctively catches it. Mara uses that diversion to step out from behind the door and punch him in the kidney. He tilts to his right, absorbing the blow and

443

turning his head, opening up his chin perfectly to side-on contact. Mara punches him on the point of the chin, flicking the switch that rolls his eyes back into his head. He's out before he hits the floor. As she stands over him, she wonders how he managed to survive so many protests and get himself in deep with hardcore hooligans without ever being found out as soft. To his credit, he did manage to catch the apple, which still lies in his open palm.

"Come on," Mara says to Tinaya.

Mara edges the bathroom door open and sticks her head out. The hallway is clear. She turns behind her and puts an index finger to her lips. Tinaya nods. They go to the left, away from the stairs, and duck down to get below the glass line of the cafeteria door. Mara assumes this is the direction Susie, Rab and Matze went, to avoid being seen by the guards at the entrance.

They run down the hallway and turn right, heading for the far end of this square building. The sounds of gunshots nearby stop them in their tracks.

Tinaya turns, like the shots have come from behind.

"That was outside," Mara says.

"Warning shots?"

"I don't know. I hope so. We need to keep moving."

They pass a pile of furniture that has been dragged aside from an exit. A slither of daylight is visible through the still-ajar door. Tinaya runs towards it, but Mara gets a grip on the backpack and stops her.

"Not that way," she says, pulling Tinaya back into the hallway.

When they reach a set of stairs, Mara stops.

"Up here," she says, and Tinaya follows her.

Mara knows this building, especially this side of it, as she passed it so often as a child and teenager, on the way to the gym. There's a balcony at the back of the Rathaus, as at the front, which couples emerge onto after getting married in the registry office. She needs to get onto the balcony, for the police to see her in uniform, so they don't just shoot at her like they seem to have shot at Susie, Rab and Matze when they went out the downstairs exit.

On the first floor, they have to drag a heavy wooden table across the floor to get to the glass balcony door. Mara saws slowly through the thick cable ties with her office scissors, only to find the door is locked.

"Fuck me," Mara says.

444

"Mara!" Vilem shouts from the floor below. "What are you doing up there? I can't let you leave."

She takes a few steps back, then throws the stapler as hard as she can at the glass door. It shatters. Tinaya wants to go through first, but Mara stops her. She gets out onto the small balcony and raises her hands.

"Don't shoot. Don't shoot."

At seeing one of their own, the cluster of police surrounding the back of the building lower their weapons. Mara turns back to help Tinaya through and sees Vilem as he reaches the top of the stairs. He raises his gun and shoots at Tinaya. Mara just manages to get her through the door as the bullet plugs into the wall, the sound of the shot and Tinaya's scream ringing in her ears.

It's too high to jump. Mara climbs over the balcony's railing and edges towards a large ladder-type structure, the rungs of which are far apart. Once she's on it, Tinaya follows, just getting onto the ladder as Vilem shoots again; she nearly falls, but manages to hang on with one hand. Mara helps steady Tinaya long enough to get both hands on the rung, and together they climb down, jumping the last section and falling to the ground. Mara looks up to see Vilem at the balcony, gun pointed at Tinaya, but he's shot in the shoulder before he can fire again. He goes down behind the railing.

Mara turns and helps Tinaya up from where she's fallen to the ground; but she needs more support, some problem with one of her legs. Mara pulls Tinaya's right arm over her own shoulder, to support more of her weight. Two police officers come towards them and help them both get behind the line of police cars.

"Now's your chance to get inside," Mara says to the officers. "I'll take care of this one. I found her hiding in the building."

Once behind the cars, Mara, still supporting Tinaya, turns to see Susie, Rab and Matze lying on the ground at the building's far corner. Susie is writhing on the ground, clutching at a wound in her side. Rab and Matze aren't moving.

A group of police are gearing up to take the building, moving towards Susie and to the still-ajar exit. More officers follow them.

Mara lets Tinaya stand alone, on one foot; she can see blood running down onto Tinaya's shoe.

"I'll take the backpack," Mara says.

Tinaya hands it over, grimacing with each movement.

Mara shoulders the backpack. "Can you walk?"

Tinaya nods.

"We need to get to the steps across the road over there and down to Gus's gym. Now."

"Okay."

There are no offers of assistance; no medics running to help. The police on this side of the Rathaus are fully focused on the building.

Mara puts Tinaya's right arm back over her shoulder and together they start moving.

Police tape has been set up on the street. The onlookers behind it applaud as Mara, the heroic police officer, helps Tinaya, the innocent bystander, to safety. Someone even lifts the tape for them. The sound of gunfire makes Mara turn. She sees two officers go down at the doorway, before being dragged to safety by colleagues.

"Come on," Mara says. "Keep going. We have to get away from here before someone stops us."

Tinaya struggles, barely able to put any weight on her right leg. They reach the steps and go down slowly. More shots ring out from the Altona Rathaus, but Mara decides that's not her problem anymore.

They reach the bottom and Tinaya sits down on the last step.

"No," Mara says, pulling her up. "Just a bit further."

"I can't. It hurts too much."

"Come on. Warriors don't give up. This is just the first round of this fight."

"Vilem shot me."

"I know. But you're still fighting. Stay on your feet. Don't let him win."

They inch down the hill of Elbberg and get onto Grosse Elbstraße. The gym is only a couple of hundred metres ahead, but seems much further away with the slow progress they're making.

There are people around and cars on the streets, but no one stops to help.

Tinaya's face has turned pale. Her right foot is leaving a thin trail of blood on the footpath.

"Stay with me," Mara says. "What colour is your pain?"

"What?"

"Tell me the colour you see."

"Red. Blood red."

"No, that's too obvious."

They walk a few more steps, edging towards the gym.

"Pain can be good," Mara says. "It can remind you of things. It can make you stronger. Give me a colour that means something to you."

"A rose." Tinaya smiles a little. "A red rose. Like the one my mother gave me before I left. I don't know where she got it from, but it was beautiful."

"That's nice. Focus on that colour. Remember her."

"I miss her so much."

"You'll see her again. If you make it to the gym, I know you'll see her again."

Tinaya's eyes are almost closed, but she keeps moving. When they finally reach the gym door, Mara bangs on it. After a moment, it's opened by two of the girls. They get either side of Tinaya and help her inside, where they lay her down on a mat.

Mara is impressed that through it all, Tinaya hasn't cried; she just grits her teeth and faces the pain.

The girls huddle around Tinaya, trying to make her comfortable.

"A red rose," she says softly, on the verge of passing out.

Gus comes out of the office with a first aid kit. "What happened?"

"She was shot in the leg," Mara says.

"Let's take a look," Gus says, bending down to Tinaya.

"You're in good hands, Tinaya. Gus is a fantastic cut man."

Tinaya sits up. "He's going to cut me?"

"He'll fix you."

Tinaya drops back down.

"Mara, get me a towel." Gus lifts the layers of clothing to inspect the wound. "In my desk drawer is a small bottle in a blue and white box. Get that too."

"I don't drink," Tinaya says. "I can't have alcohol."

"You can when you've been shot."

Changed back into her hoody and jeans, Mara stuffs the police uniform into her backpack, then goes into the office. She grabs a towel, finds the bottle and runs back to the mat. Gus has cut Tinaya's pants from the bottom upwards. As the fabric parts, the gash, which looks like a nasty knife wound, is exposed but none of the girls look away.

Mara places the towel under Tinaya's leg, elevating it. The blood quickly covers the blue towel, staining it black.

447

"Give me that bottle," Gus says, reaching out. Mara hands it to him.

"I'm not drinking that," Tinaya says, turning her head away as Gus brings the bottle close.

"Drink," Mara orders.

"This is Klosterfrau Melissengeist," Gus says. "You don't have anything to worry about. Nuns make it. Have done for hundreds of years."

"Think of it like medicine," Mara says. "Made by nuns."

"No. I can take the pain."

"Tough girl," Gus says, having a swig of it himself. "I still need to use it as a disinfectant. Is that all right?"

Tinaya nods.

"Good girl. Now lie back and think happy thoughts. Hold her steady, girls. Here we go."

He pours the alcohol onto the wound. Tinaya screams, her leg lashing out and almost hitting him.

"It'll be over soon," Mara says. "Gus is really good at this."

"Such a fighter." Gus puts the bottle aside and poises over the wound, bent needle in his fingers. His old hand shakes a little. "Now, I need you to stay very still. Hold her, girls. Don't be shy. Use force."

Tinaya screams again as the needle goes in and the first thread pulls one end of the wound shut. Then, she passes out.

"Finally," Gus says. "This girl could go far. What a pain threshold she has."

Mara can't watch. She heads to the bathroom and washes her hands, then goes outside. There's an old bench next to the wall, where she and Zina used to sit after workouts, facing the afternoon sun and protected from the wind. She sits down and tries to process the day. It's too much, so she just thinks of Zina and how much she misses her.

"Just memories now, Z."

Grosse Elbstraße is busy with traffic. Out of the steady stream of cars, one emerges, pulling over and parking in front of the gym. Stammer gets out.

"I can't get a moment alone," Mara says to herself.

Stammer stands there for a few seconds, staring at Mara. "Can I join you?"

Mara looks past the detective at the car, its dark windows

448

ominously up. "Anyone in there?"

"Not this time."

"What about Nils?"

"He's being questioned, along with Russell."

"By who? Why aren't you doing it?"

"My son is involved. I'm compromised."

"So, Perceval then."

"Hmm. He's involved."

Stammer lowers herself onto the bench. She seems taller sitting down, her height more in her torso than in her legs. They sit for a few moments, enjoying the sun.

"Thank you. For getting Nils out safely."

"Is it over?"

"The building is secure," Stammer says. "But not without casualties."

"What about elsewhere in Germany?"

"All the situations have been contained."

"Is Vilem dead?"

"No, but two police officers are. Two protesters who were shot outside are also dead. One is wounded, but she'll survive. In the building, there was a body in the cafeteria."

"That's David Wollenknecht. What about the two guards? They had bags full of weapons."

"Those two men are also dead. Vilem has been taken into custody."

Mara nods. "What will happen to him?"

"A lot will depend on the testimony of the witnesses. We're already getting conflicting stories. Some are saying Vilem shot Wollenknecht. Others say it was one of the guards. What do you say?"

"Let's assume Vilem didn't shoot anyone. What will happen to him then?"

"He'll likely go to prison, but not for very long. Maybe a few years."

"Time enough to write a book while he's in there."

"Hmm."

"The Modra manifesto."

Mara can't decide if those who are lying about Vilem are doing so because they support him or because they're scared of his retribution. But surely Nils and Russell told the truth?

"If convicted of murder, he will be in prison for much longer."

"What about everything else that happened today?" Mara asks. "Will that be put on Vilem?"

"Not unless he openly claims it."

"Maybe you should ask him if he poisoned the water cannons in Stuttgart."

"That's out of my jurisdiction," Stammer says. "I can't comment, except to inform you that the case is closed."

"Convicted before she's even buried. Zina had nothing to do with that. The police should be ashamed they made a criminal out of one of their own."

"Hmm."

A few more moments pass. Mara hopes that Tinaya is still passed out on the mat. Any screams coming from inside the gym will surely pique Stammer's interest.

"So? What now?" Mara asks.

Stammer reaches into her jacket pocket and pulls out a card. "Here. I'd like us to stay in contact."

"Dinner and a show perhaps?" Mara takes the card. "I'm glad we know each other, but I'm not in the police anymore."

"Strange. Witnesses reported a police officer with Steinbach on her uniform rescuing a young woman from the Altona Rathaus today. There's video of it as well."

"What a hero."

"I wouldn't go that far."

"I'm done with the police. You can tell Perceval I'm done with him too. I'm out of this."

"Christoph might be done as well," Stammer says, "pending an internal investigation."

"Then he can focus all his attention on the Pink Dragon, or turn pro as a ping pong player."

Stammer smiles. "He got close. When he was a teenager. He stopped playing for a few years in order to take care of his mother, when she was near the end."

"I really wish I'd met her."

"Take comfort in the thought that she probably would've liked you. She was funny. Tough and generous. She helped so many girls in St Pauli. You also seem to enjoy playing saviour."

"I wouldn't go that far," Mara says, copying Stammer's monotone.

delivery.

The detective thumbs behind her. "Gus knew Penelope. I remember seeing him at the funeral."

"St Pauli can be such a small world."

"This world isn't kind to people who fall into bad situations. You should choose your next moves carefully."

"There's no choice to make," Mara says. "I'm planning to become a boxing coach. Gus and I are going to turn this gym around. Make it something special again."

"That's good." Stammer stands up. "Even if you don't contact me, I'll know where to find you."

"Hmm."

Smiling, Stammer says, "Or I'll find you at Hamburger Berg. It would be smart to make that official, with the apartment. Sign a contract with Christoph. Get registered. Sort out your car. Make yourself look like a proper citizen. Being out in the open is always the best cover."

"I'll keep that in mind."

"That applies to living in Hamburg, and in other places. Like Riga, for example."

"Good advice. Say hi to Nils for me."

"I will."

Stammer goes to her car, opens the door and lowers herself into the driver's seat. Her torso height requires her to sit down, then swivel her legs under the steering wheel. Mara waits until the car is out of sight before standing up and going back into the gym. The girls are on their hands and knees, cleaning up the stretching area, with sponges and a bucket. Tinaya is lying on another section, asleep, a blanket over her.

"How's the patient?" Mara asks Gus.

"She'll live to fight another day. She's got spirit, that one."

"Thanks, Gus. For sewing her up."

"I'm getting too old for this."

"Maybe, but tell me. In your long, distinguished career, did you ever cross paths with Penelope Perceval?"

Gus takes the bottle from the blue and white box, has a long drink, and just smiles at Mara.

***

451

The blocked roads in the city centre force her to detour through the Hafen City and take the long, back way to Moorfleet. Tinaya, still woozy and suffering from shock, drops in and out of sleep in the passenger seat.

She stops at a special bakery and buys three vegan Franzbrötchen. In the adjacent supermarket, she gets a bottle of Sambuca and a bag of coffee beans. Asking her father for help requires arriving with gifts. If he doesn't agree, she can still take the responsibility herself and apply to become Tinaya's guardian. But she thinks this is something her father should do, because having Tinaya around will be good for him; it might also help Mara build a bridge to her father, as they attempt to create a new little family.

She misses Anthony, but resolves to say a prayer for his prosperity when eating that Sambuca-flavoured coffee bean. There may still be the chance of him coming home, with Gomez's statement having been withdrawn. Tinaya will get the prayer for health, and the hope for happiness will go to her father.

The narrow driveway is barely wide enough for the pick-up. Tree branches scratch at the windows, loudly, waking Tinaya.

"Where are we?" she asks.

"Home. Hopefully."

Travel Page (cont.)